CHEERLEADERS CAN'T AFFORD TO BE NICE

CHEERLEADERS
CAN'T AFFORD
TO BE NICE

A NOVEL BY SUSAN
SULLIVAN
SAITER

DONALD I. FINE, INC.
New York

Copyright © 1990 by Susan Sullivan Saiter

Library of Congress Cataloging-in-Publication Data
Saiter, Susan Sullivan.
   Cheerleaders can't afford to be nice : a novel / by Susan Sullivan Saiter
     p. cm.
   ISBN 1–55611–181–9
   I. Title.
PS3569.A4545C47   1991
813'.54—dc20   90–55091
                                               CIP

Manufactured in the United States of America
10 9 8 7 6 5 4 3 2 1

To Sonny, Laura, and Samantha
and
for Danny

Saturday, August 19, and Sunday, August 20, 1989

~~~

ONE

I AWOKE in the middle of the night with the sickening feeling that Ben was dead.

The letter with its worked-over folds lay white, ghostlike on the table next to my bed. I thought of the last time I saw him, the Thanksgiving of the year I was divorced.

I had just moved to Milwaukee and started a teaching job. Mom and Dad were supposed to come up from Chicago for dinner. Ben, who was staying at some hippie commune in Minnesota, had even spoken of showing up.

This was the first time I'd invited them all for a holiday, so I did it up big. I went out and bought a sixteen-pound turkey. I made stuffing and mashed potatoes and the whole thing. I even had little red tassels to put on the turkey legs.

Mom had said vaguely mid to late afternoon. At four the turkey was done and by five I was becoming a little anxious. I waited and waited. I took the turkey out. By seven it was starting to shrivel. Scooping out the dressing, I began to worry that they'd been in an accident. I put the dressing in a bowl, stuck the salad and cranberries in the refrigerator, and called the highway patrol. No accidents involving anyone by the name of Rawson. I cut off a slice of white meat, took a bite, chewed and chewed, but I couldn't swallow it.

I called home. Mom answered.

"Mom, I was expecting you for dinner," I said.

"Oh well," she said matter-of-factly. "We decided it was too far to drive just to eat. Happy Thanksgiving, anyway."

I started to tell her about the big dinner I'd made, but I didn't want to sound like a fool, which is what I would have sounded like to her. So I acted like it was no big deal, and said, "That's okay. It's only Thanksgiving."

"We'll see you on Christmas," Dad said on the extension phone.

"Of course," Mom said.

After I hung up, I looked at the foolishly dressed-up turkey, and I tried to convince myself that somehow this was my fault, that I'd expected too much. And then the doorbell rang. It was my other guest, one I'd forgotten about—Ben. That was about the only time I could recall ever being really glad to see him.

"Boy, am I hungry. And cold. I hitchhiked all the way from Duluth. Here," he said, his red, raw hand giving me a paper bag.

It was a grocery store pie in a cardboard box with a little cellophane window.

"Thanks, Ben, it looks good. Mmmm, cherry."

Ben took off his coat and let it slump to the floor. The lining was shredded, cotton insulation clung by threads. He smelled so sharply of tobacco that I had to stand back. "I decided I was going to force myself to eat cherry pie again. Remember that time when the cherry pie dripped all over the floor, when we thought it was blood? That was in Columbus. I never ate the stuff again because I felt like I was eating our family blood."

"Gee, thanks for reminding me, I'd almost forgotten," I said, giving him a playful poke with my elbow.

"How can you forget something like that?"

"I make myself forget."

"I can't forget anything."

"Maybe you're not trying hard enough."

He sat down in the armchair. Even when he was sitting and

relaxing, he was stiff. His arms hung straight down outside the arms of the chair, except when one of them was holding a cigarette. He held cigarettes like people hold a marijuana joint. His legs were too long for most chairs and yet he planted his feet straight in front and below. They angled up and then shot straight down from the knees as if his legs were made of Tinker Toys. Same with his back. He looked uncomfortable, but if he was, he didn't seem to know it.

"Remember Mom's lipstick, Croz? Cherries in the Snow?"

"That I haven't forgotten," I said, putting silverware back on the table and hiding the wine.

"You and me are the cherries, remember?"

"What's that?"

"Remember? I came into your room one night. You were trying on some of Mom's lipstick. I said it was a dumb name for a lipstick because how could there be such a thing as cherries in the snow, wouldn't they freeze and die or something."

"Uh huh," I said vaguely, not really remembering.

"It's true, isn't it, Crosby, what you said?"

I surveyed the table, tapping my foot. There was a lot of food, but then I had a feeling Ben was hungry. "What did I say?"

He came and sat at the table and lit a cigarette. I began carving the cooled turkey. My appetite was coming back, in fact I was ravenous. "You said that it wasn't a dumb name, because look at me and you—we were cherries in the snow."

I laughed. "I said a lot of brilliant things, didn't I?"

Suddenly his face lost its childish look and went tough like a street punk's. That look flashed away so fast I wasn't sure I'd seen it.

"Oh Ben, it was true then, I guess. Jesus, we had to believe something, live by some kind of a little kid philosophy, didn't we?"

"Yeah," he said, taking a long drag from his cigarette, letting an ash fall onto his plate, and smiling off at nothing.

When I opened the letter saying he had disappeared from a homeless shelter in New York, suddenly nothing was more important than Ben. I'd rushed to the phone and tried to get hold of the woman who sent it. I was told that the shelter she ran was closed on weekends. If I hadn't had an unlisted phone number, she probably would have called me, I reasoned, and minutes, seconds counted. I tried to locate her home number in the confusion of all those New York boroughs and suburbs and finally had to give up.

Sitting down to think, I reread the letter, the demanding handwriting pressing its urgency deep into the paper.

Cathedral of St. John the Divine
Amsterdam Avenue and 112th Street
New York, New York
August 16, 1989

Dear Ms. Rawson:

I am writing to you in regards to your brother, Benjamin J. Rawson.

Ben was a regular guest at our ten-bed shelter for homeless men since last winter. Two weeks ago, he stopped showing up. As many of our guests live on irregular schedules, I didn't make much of it. However, last evening, another occasional guest, Tyrone Davis, related news that concerned me.

According to Tyrone, the two of them were attacked and beaten when they sought shelter from a thunderstorm in the lobby of a brownstone. The attacker, a resident of the building, then pushed Ben into the street. He was bleeding and appeared to be unconscious when Tyrone, fearing for his own safety, ran off.

I called the police, but they had no information on your brother. You may wish to contact them again. Or you might want to come to New York to continue the search by getting in touch with the social service agencies Ben used.

I contacted you instead of your parents because he spoke of you often and had kept your former address, from which I traced you.

If I can be of help, please let me know.

In God's Name,

Antonia P. Williams
Shelter Director

I tried to picture Antonia P. Williams, and I tried to picture a homeless shelter in New York. Both images faded into one of Ben bleeding to death on a dark street.

I poured myself a glass of mineral water and went out and squeezed into the chair on my tiny balcony and stared at the mountain, my mountain, in the distance.

The more I thought, the more unlikely it seemed that people, the police, would let anyone bleed to death in the street, even in New York City. If he'd been hurt badly enough, he would have been taken to a hospital. And even if he had bled to death in the street, we would have heard, wouldn't we?

I leaned back and closed my eyes. The timing of all this couldn't have been worse—the letter had arrived one week before I was at long last to start law school at the University of Southern California. And to further complicate the situation, I couldn't even afford to quit working and go unless a condo sale I was about to clinch in my last act as a California real estate agent went through that week.

On Sunday, the day after I got the letter, I puttered around, making bread and casseroles from various items I'd bought bulk at the food co-op, freezing them for when I became an impoverished law student.

The urgency I had felt was giving way to resentment by now; my family, my brother, were not going to disrupt my life again, especially at this important time.

Gnawing at me also was the fact that I did have an alternative to USC: the Theodore Grundy School of Law. Grundy admitted anyone and, unlike the prestige schools, allowed you to attend part time while you worked. A degree from Grundy limited you—you could only practice in California with it, and it didn't exactly strike awe in the hearts of potential clients. But then it *was* a law school.

But I didn't like that alternative. I played the radio loud to get Ben out of my head.

But Ben was my little brother. He'd always idolized me.

What I needed was a workout. I got in my car and drove to the health club. Taking a big breath of sunshiny air, I thought of how much I liked my life. I had my own condo, I had a boyfriend, a good, solid, decent guy, and I had a good, solid, decent chance of becoming a lawyer, my dream since my undergraduate days when I'd studied education instead.

Oh, my life was hard at times, but it was mine and I was running it the best I could. And it was my life to run, just as everyone else's was his or hers to run and no one was responsible for anyone else's, not even a brother's.

On my way home, I drove past the condo I was about to sell, feeling protective, proprietary, important.

When I got home I pulled out a big box of old letters from the back of my closet and stuck this latest one in. While I had the box out, I leafed through my collection. I paused over some from Ben, most of them ten or fifteen years old:

Dear Crosby,
    I went back to Detroit to look for our old house. The street and sidewalk got older, but the house didn't. Remember Ronny Northberger down the street? I think I saw him. He still had his hair combed like a Dairy Queen cone on top.
    I'm staying at a mission here in Akron. I get by panhandling plus Dad's trying to get me supplemental security income. Your brother Benjamin John Rawson

And another, from Pittsburgh:

Croz:
    I got a room here. I stay with a pal named Rook I met while I was in the hospital. We like sloe gin. We eat good because he gets SSI. Last night we had five Almond Joys apiece for dessert. He got TB once and coughs still. He has epileptic fits. He kept getting robbed while he had fits. He's got medication now and isn't so bad. Make love not war, Ben.

And another:

Crosby:
    Sometimes I can't think about something in particular like you're supposed to. I get depressed and feel like the world doesn't like me. But most of the time I know it's just my imagination.
    I think I was happiest in Des Moines. It scares the hell out of me that it won't be like that again. Maybe I'll visit you but I don't have any cash. Maybe you could spare some. Dad says he won't give me any more because I just blow it. Ben.

My last letter from Ben. No date, no return address.

Croz,

Things are okay for me except I'm broke. I went to a carnival last night after cashing my SSI check and got suckered into a ring toss game to win free cigarettes. I didn't give up until every penny was gone and then I didn't have enough to even buy a pack of cigarettes. Talk about bad luck!

Mom and Dad don't want me to come near the house any more. Sometimes I wake up from a dream where they're dead and I'm sweating all over. Hey, I just remembered that time you joked and told me Mom was dead.

Wishing you good luck,

Benjamin Rawson

I leaned back against the wall. The time I told Ben Mom was dead. How old was I? Eight, nine?

I'd come home from school to find a note taped to the door. It said that Mom was playing bridge until six. I'd folded up the note and waited for Ben. When he came home I said, "Ben, I hate to have to tell you this, but Mom's dead. She had a heart attack and they took her to the hospital."

He looked at me like I was God or something. And a cruel thrill went through me. I could feel it again. I shivered to get rid of it.

Ben's expression didn't change. He just stared and said, "What are we gonna do?" in a hoarse voice.

"Go to the funeral, I guess," I said.

He put his lunch box down on the floor and sat on the davenport. He was very still. I had another idea. I got my friend, Pam, on the phone and asked her to call Ben and say she worked at the hospital.

When the phone rang and Ben answered it, I picked up the extension in the bedroom.

"Hello, Ben?" Pam said in a disguised voice.

"Yeah," Ben said, his voice still raspy.

"This is Mrs. Jones at the hospital where your Mom just died. I called to tell you you have to pay the bill here or you're going to jail."

I started to giggle so I had to hang up. I stayed in Mom's

bedroom for a while. I heard Ben go into his room. I went in. He was lying on his bed, sucking his thumb. He wasn't crying, just staring with his face in crying position. You couldn't make him cry no matter what you did.

At six thirty, when Mom's car wheels came grinding onto the driveway, I went into Ben's room and tickled his ribs. "Just kidding," I said. "Mom was playing bridge."

The car door made a quick Mom-click as it closed, and Ben ran out to greet her. When they came in, his face was a big sun. He took a handful of Mom's navy blue and white polka-dot skirt and tried to hug her leg.

"Careful," she said when he pulled too hard and the skirt came up to reveal a flurry of crinolines and a garter snapped to the top of her hose.

"Why?" Ben said. "Afraid I'll pop your polka dots?"

"Afraid you'll pop me," she said. "Ben, why are you being so clingy?"

"I thought you were dead."

Mom patted his head and laughed. "Now wherever did you get such a silly idea?" She flopped down on the davenport and Ben climbed on next to her with his thumb in his mouth. They lay there together and I played jacks on the kitchen floor while Mom recounted the bridge game gossip.

I got up and made some vegetarian chili to store in the freezer. Well, it wasn't me that made him go crazy. I was just an ordinary bratty little girl. Maybe a bit brattier than ordinary, but maybe I had to be. Was it my fault if Ben couldn't handle it? Couldn't handle much of anything?

Whose fault was it? Anyone's? Would the question never go away? Grown a little angry at myself, I dug the letter back out and reread it. I folded and refolded it, thinking, wondering what I could possibly do. No one had yet been able to help him. Not much, anyway, and from what I understood he had gotten worse over the years.

Besides, what would I do with him, even if he were okay? Bring him here? Help him out there? How? I didn't know the first thing about New York, except that on TV and in movies it looked to be crammed with rich people and their predators, with some forgotten people fallen into the cracks.

I put the letter in my pocket and went back to the kitchen. I blanched some herbs and put them in little freezer bags, recalling how New York had been the city of my dreams as a child. I used to tell Ben that when I grew up I'd live in New York City and wear negligees and sweep around my pent-house balcony like Eva Gabor in the opening scenes of "Green Acres." And when I was in a generous mood, I said I'd let Benny come and live with me.

I pulled the letter out again, the looping, aggressive hand-writing becoming as familiar to me now as the map of a town I was getting to know.

So this Antonia P. Williams thought it was up to me to go perusing the streets of the biggest city in America looking for my brother. Well, I wasn't so sure she was wrong. He needed help before, he needs it now. I should assume he's alive but in need of help, and I should drop everything and go find him.

"Let's face it, Crosby," I said out loud. "Guilt is pumping through every vein in your body."

I hurled a handful of coriander into the sink and got on the phone and made plane reservations leaving for New York the following morning.

Next I called my best friend at work, Sarah, for whom I had once filled in during a family emergency. "Sick elderly aunt," I said.

She told me she'd be glad to take over my sale to help out.

"Don't worry, this is a piece of cake," I assured her. "Senior citizens, lovely people. And both sides are pretty close."

Then I remembered that she was from New York and asked if she knew of a safe but inexpensive hotel. She recommended one with the dubious name of the Royale Payne, located, as she recalled, somewhere in the vicinity of the Fifty-ninth Street Bridge.

I called and made a reservation. I felt a little better, but this letter really had jolted me back to the reality of my family situation. We had let Ben go for so long that half the time we pretended he didn't exist. In fact, this letter telling me that he had been lost only reminded me that I wasn't aware that he'd been found.

I needed to talk to someone. My boyfriend, Dean, was in Washington on business, but I wouldn't have discussed it with him had he been there—I didn't want him to know about Ben. I didn't want my other friends to know either.

I knew better than to call Mom and Dad for any kind of comfort or advice, but there was no one else to discuss Ben with.

After I read them the letter, there was a long pause, then Dad said, "Sounds like Ben, all right."

"Sure does," Mom said on the extension. More silence, then, "Crosby, what's new? How's your job?"

It made perfect sense for them to ask about my work. That's all I ever talked about. "I'm on the brink of a big sale. And I'm finally doing it—I'm going to law school. Registration is Friday, classes start Monday."

There was another pause, and Dad said, "Good, Crosby, good. Better late than never, I always say. And who knows, it could work out, right, Vera?"

I heard hear Mom blowing out smoke from a cigarette. "I wondered how long before you'd decide to go or get off the pot."

"Mom, Dad, don't you think Ben's condition sounds serious this time?"

"Oh Christ, it's always serious," Dad said.

"That kid's got a head made of rock," Mom said, then her voice softened a little. "I just don't know what we can do with him."

"If you want to go help him, that's very nice of you," Dad said. "But I've got a business to run."

After retiring, Dad had opened up a small tire store.

"Be careful," Mom said, "And when you see Ben, tell him we'll send him a few bucks. He probably needs a haircut. Remember you, Crosby, always bitching about his hair?" Mom couldn't stand to have things be serious and depressing for very long, and this was supposed to make me laugh. Well, she could sit there and laugh all she wanted, but it was me who had gotten the letter.

"And keep us posted," Dad said, falsely enthusiastic.

1957

No one told Ben and me that we were moving this time. The movers just showed up one day and started packing and hauling things out of the house.

Ben went into his usual hermit act and hid in the cabinet under the bathroom sink, but I joined right in and helped carry stuff. After a while, I went to get Ben. "Come on, this is exciting," I said. He reminded me of a raccoon or something you'd see hiding in the back of its cage on Marlin Perkins' "Zoo Parade," his eyes glistening in the dark, his scared little face wondering what's going to happen to him.

Last thing I did was take down my wall map of the USA. We'd already lived in three of the forty-eight states. I could see how you could get hooked on moving the way you did on a hobby or collection; our family was making a state collection.

After we got to our new house in Westlake Hills, a suburb of Kansas City, I tried to ignore the nervousness in my stomach and to think positively, like Dad.

"A brand new life, a brand new chance," Dad said to Mom as we stood looking at boxes to unpack. "Any mistakes, any failures in Crestwood Valley Cliffs are forgotten."

"Forgotten and forgiven by that big corporation in the sky, huh?" Mom said.

You had to put your hand over your eyes a lot of the time in this house. The sun blazed in from all directions because there were no trees to block it. All that light made the furniture look bad. Mom and Dad's dresser had several nicks and cigarette burns and nail polish spills. It looked like a victim of a war. When they brought in the davenport and sat it down, it slumped, like it was tired. I couldn't figure out if this last move had gouged and scarred the furniture more, or if it had been like that before and I just hadn't noticed.

The carpet in my room smelled of pee. The curtains had the characters from "Hey Diddle Diddle" all over them. It must have been a baby's room before. I went to look for Mom to ask if I was going to get new curtains. She was out in the backyard.

"I'm going to put cosmos here, moss roses there," she was pointing and telling Ben.

"Can I get new curtains?" I asked.

"You'll get them eventually, don't worry."

"When's eventually?" A couple of times in the past, we moved before eventually came.

"When we get settled and have enough money."

It was dark by the time they brought my bed in. The torn part of the box springs trailed it like a ghost from our last move.

After the movers left, Dad cleared an area in the kitchen while Mom went to find a food store. We had sandwiches made with fresh soft Tip Top bread, fragrant baloney, lots of mayonnaise. Then we had Neapolitan ice cream and watched "Highway Patrol" and "Date with the Angels" until the "Friday Night Fights," live from Madison Square Garden came on. Madison Square Garden was in New York City. A lot of shows on television were about people in New York City, including my favorite, "My Little Margie." From what I saw on that TV screen, there was a big difference between the places we lived and New York, and I wondered if I'd ever get to see it.

Ben and I went upstairs and made forts out of the boxes. It was comforting to hear the Pabst Blue Ribbon and Gillette songs downstairs on the TV. We tried to knock down each other's forts. As soon as one of us got through and wrestled the other to the ground, we'd rebuild. We took the shades off the lamps and moved them around so they'd cast big round shadows on the walls. Ben said they looked like planets on "Space Patrol." We pretended we were Vena and Rocky Jones, and that space men from the living room would come upstairs to kill us. When we stopped being space rangers, we put the lamps on top of the boxes and sat feeling the atmosphere in the house to see if it was starting to be comfortable. The lamps on top of the boxes cast scary, long shadows; we looked around in silence for a while.

Mom took us for our first day at the new school. She gave everyone that red lipstick smile of hers, and I wondered how anyone could stand to have another mother. Kids who didn't move to new houses wouldn't know how much having the same Mom and Dad all the time can mean to you. Or even how much having the same brother can mean to you. It's like having a traveling, portable best friend.

This school was a lot like my last one, Jefferson Elementary, a one-story yellow brick building that smelled like crayons and construction paper, with blond wood desks and a brand new floor that made your shoes sound important.

We found the principal's office and Mom filled out papers while Ben and I sat still and quiet.

The principal said, "You're lucky you're coming in right at the beginning of the year so you'll be able to make friends right away."

We took Ben to his class. When he turned to watch us leave, his face looked all confused.

Mom remembered what Dad told her to say to my teacher, whose name was Miss Barnes. "Crosby was in the high reading group at her last school. Maybe she should go into the most advanced group here, too."

"Sometimes children drop back when they transfer to other schools," she said. "But don't worry, we'll put her in the right group."

The principal was wrong—everyone had made friends last year in first grade or maybe even kindergarten and didn't act like they needed any new friends. It was hard sitting there with no one to talk to while everyone else horsed around. So I pretended I didn't want to talk to anyone and just stared straight ahead at the alphabet letters over the blackboard. I imagined there was a great big yellow light above me, a twinkling one that would always be there to make me happy whenever I wanted it to be.

Miss Barnes asked what everyone did during summer vacation. When it was my turn, the air got hot and I thought about that light over my head.

"Mostly I played checkers with my brother and cards with my mom." From the look on everyone's face, I had to tell more. "My mom's a very competent bridge player. We play honeymoon bridge. You can play even if you're not married."

One girl, a blonde that everyone had wanted to sit next to, put her hand over her mouth and said something to a girl with shiny black hair that looked like a paintbrush. They turned and looked at me, and then started to giggle.

"A *competent* bridge player," Miss Barnes said, closing her mouth and trying not to smile but looking more like she was tasting the word. "Where did you learn that big word?"

I knew you shouldn't say big words around most people. Instead, you should tell them things you'd read, like the fact that monkeys and apes are not the same thing, that monkeys usually have tails, that apes are smarter. That chimpanzees and gorillas are apes while gibbons are monkeys. People found information like that fascinating. But you couldn't use big words or they'd think you were a weirdo egghead and they wouldn't be friends with you and you'd end up playing honeymoon bridge with your mother for the rest of your life.

I said quietly, "I guess I saw the word in a book," wishing I hadn't.

"Did you do anything else on your vacation?" Miss Barnes asked.

I also knew you were supposed to say you did what other people did. I scanned my brain for something, then remembered that after Dad once talked of taking us someday to see Mammoth Cave, I'd gone and looked it up in the *World Book Encyclopedia.*

"We went to Mammoth Cave in Kentucky. We saw—" I

started to say "stalagmites and stalactites," but caught myself. "Those big icicle things hanging from the cave ceiling and growing on the ground."

No one laughed, so I knew I had hit on the right thing.

At recess no one played with me, so I went in a side door and found the school library. I looked up *horses* in the *World Book Encyclopedia* and reread some. When the bell rang, I went back to the room and I didn't feel quite as lonely.

Things got better for me when we read for the teacher. The book was easy and would have been boring if it hadn't been about Dick, Jane, and Sally. I loved those kids. When I read about them, I got so carried away I felt for a while that I was them and had a perfect family like theirs.

Everyone was really still when I finished reading. So still that I thought maybe I'd read a little too well. But I sneaked a look around and there was admiration in the air.

At lunchtime Karen, who had glossy braids and a nylon blouse with a fancy slip showing through walked with me. We slowed down for Martha, the girl that everyone had wanted to sit next to. They asked if I brought a lunch or went home. Thank God I didn't have a mother who worked or anything embarrassing like that. "I go home," I said.

"Maybe we can walk with you. Where do you live?" Karen said.

They had me there. I knew I was supposed to go three blocks to the right, then left a block, then straight again for another half-block. I already knew our phone and house numbers, but I wasn't positive about the name of the street. It was something like Sonesta Way or Sonata Way. The family had been joking about it; Ben called it Sinatra Way, because the day after we moved in Dad went out and bought a mahogany hi-fi set and a Frank Sinatra album. Then when Mom said the neighbors acted stuck up, Ben joked that our street was Snotty Way. (Though Dad said the new neighbors weren't snotty, just higher class than we were used to.)

I pointed in the direction of my house.

"We live that way too," Martha said. "We can walk with you."

I said that would be fine but that I had to wait for my brother who was in kindergarten.

"Oooh, how cute," Karen said. "We'll wait, won't we, Martha?"

We stood there for an eternity and Ben finally came out with his sweater hanging half off his arm. I wished he didn't have to look so scared and lost, but no one else seemed to notice and they made a big fuss over him because he was such a baby.

Dad arrived home wearing the civilized and polite look he always brought from work, which lasted until he took off his suit. He broke into a big smile when I told him about reading group. "Gonna take after the old man, huh," he said, adding more pepper to the pan of hamburger and onions Mom was frying.

"That's enough," Mom said. "What do you think we are, a bunch of Greeks?"

Dad worked in the public relations department of U.S. Tires and thought being bright was important. "Gonna go to college. University of Missouri. Or, hell, maybe Vassar. Want to go to Vassar, Crosby?"

"And who's going to pay for that?" Mom said. "Santa Claus?"

"And Ben will go to Harvard," Dad said. Maybe it was because he was busy tasting the chili, but he said that in a lower voice with less enthusiasm.

"It's too bad our boy got the looks, our girl the brains," Mom said loud enough for me to hear. She and Dad playfully wrestled over the pepper.

What she said was so true it didn't even bother me. You couldn't imagine how good-looking Ben was—like Mom, when she got fixed up. Mom had to use Lady Clairol to keep her hair as light as it used to be, but Ben had a great big head full of blond hair that looked almost silver in the summer sun and turned gold in winter. Grandma said his skin was like marzipan. His eyes were the color of magazine pictures of the ocean in Florida.

At dinner I said, "I still don't think school is going to be too easy here. Especially arithmetic. They're doing long division and it's really hard."

"You can do it," Dad said. "Ben, how's kindergarten?"

"It's really hard."

Everyone laughed except Ben. But we kept it up and finally he laughed, too.

Then it seemed like we'd used up all the free moves life has to offer, the ones that don't cause you problems with the outside world or within your family. After Kansas City, fighting and moving seemed to take up most of Mom and Dad's time. The worst fights seemed to come about a month or two before the moves. We didn't always relocate just because Dad got fired or transferred. I think we moved sometimes just to move, just to get away from the last disappointment that had caused the last fight, like moving would make us happy and normal and all the things other families seemed to be.

The next summer, one night they had a huge fight about moving again when Mom screamed, "I'm going to divorce you!"

I heard Ben rustling around in his bed. I lay there praying to God to please not let us get divorced. No one would talk to us, and Mom would go around to bars wearing pointy bras and tight sweaters and those high-heeled bedroom slippers with the toes cut out.

There was no divorce. There was an uneasy calm for a while, then a few good days, then another fight. At last they made up and we headed for Upper Sterling Meadows, Minnesota.

1958

THREE

L IKE THE OTHER towns we'd lived in, Upper Sterling Meadows itself was pretty new. Our subdivision had just
opened, and the concrete on our street was still goosebumpy
and dark gray. Everyone had a baby maple tree out in front
supported by rope. Four styles of house hugged the street's
lawns—ranch, colonial, split-level, and mediterranean. We
had a split-level. Dad told Mom we'd get a split-level with two
full baths as soon as he got promoted.

Mom and Dad got invited to parties thrown by people he
worked with. On the way out the door, Mom would be beautiful in perfume and a swirly skirt that danced around her legs
as she walked, Dad lickety split in a suit. When they came
home, they'd talk about all the people and Dad would put on
his Frank Sinatra albums and they'd fox-trot around the living room. The sound of "Chi-ca-go, Chi-caaaah-go, that tod-
dlin' town," or, "Do do that voo-doo that you do so well"
would let Ben and me know that all was well, and we'd fall
off to sleep feeling like Dick and Jane.

But Ben couldn't stand too much happiness. Just about every
time we had a family outing, he screwed it up. Maybe he

wanted to make a public spectacle of himself so that someone, anyone, would come and straighten out the chaos inside
his head.

One Saturday morning we sat at breakfast, all of us a little
glum because the TV was on the blink and some important
shows were being missed. The horizontal hold on the old
Motorola had been screwed up for a long time, and the movers had knocked off a knob so you had to use a screwdriver
to turn the volume up or down, and then half the time you
got a shock. There wasn't a lot of money yet, so Dad was
always saying we couldn't get a new set until he got promoted.

Dad and I were eating Wheaties with sliced bananas. Ben
hated serious cereal so he fixed a pimento loaf sandwich with
the heels of the bread that were left. Mom was having black
coffee and the remains of a Jane Parker raisin pie from the
night before, complaining that whenever Dad got groceries,
he'd pick "a goddamned raisin pie" from all the hundreds of
"goody possibilities" at the store.

"At least there's a little nutrition in the raisins, Vera."

Mom made a face at him while she chewed.

"Anyway, our Monkey Wards charge-a-plate came in the
mail this morning," Dad said. "Maybe we ought to try it out
on a new TV set."

"Can we get a color TV?" Ben said.

"Color?" Dad said. You could tell he was about to launch
into a speech about how expensive color was, but then he
made a big exaggerated smile at Ben. "Come to think of it, I'm
left out of a lot of conversations at work because we don't
have a color TV. I can't even discuss what shade Captain
Kangaroo's eyes are. Maybe it's worth the expense."

Ben took a bite from his sandwich and thought as he
chewed. "Maybe his eyes are gray. Then we'd be wasting our
money."

Dad laughed and said only a few TV shows came in in
color, anyway, and we'd wait until it made financial sense to
get one. Anyway, Dad said, black and white was good enough
for Benny to see Jim Bowie and Wyatt Earp. "So you won't
grow up to be like those sissy dancers you like to watch on
'Arthur Murray' and the 'Hit Parade.'"

"While we're charging things, we ought to get a new fridge," Mom said. "The one we have is so old that I'm not sure whether you plug it in or stick a chunk of ice in it."

"Okay. A new TV and a new Frigidaire," Dad said. You could just feel it—happiness and enthusiasm jumping through the air. Things were going to be great, we were going to have money and a nice clean home with modern appliances.

We trooped out to the car, a Pontiac which Ben hated because he thought the grille looked like it was mad. Dad drove, of course, his crewcut looking so alert and optimistic, Mom smoking and turning the knobs on the radio, her babushka with a pattern of triangles and circles all over it making her look both stylish and modest, and Ben and I in the back, bouncing on the seat and burping to fight off car sickness from Mom's cigarettes.

Because Dad was in such a good mood we joked with him not to get turnpike trance, and he hunched over and twisted the steering wheel back and forth like he was going to crash and Mom screamed and yelled at him and almost but not quite broke the spell.

The shopping center was crowded with families and it made you feel a part of something. Fall was early in this part of the country, Dad said, and you could feel it, like the sky was getting higher and less interested in what was going on down on earth.

"First let me fix my face," Mom said, getting out her compact and Cherries in the Snow lipstick. She made a wide frown-smile—like a clown's—when she put it on. Then she rubbed her lips together, blotted it on some important-looking papers from the glove compartment. Dad had already gotten out of the car and couldn't see to yell about it. She held the compact back and checked her teeth for lipstick. The blue-red of the lipstick made her eyes go darker blue, almost violet and startling, and brightened her skin so it seemed like someone had just turned the lights on.

When she saw me watching, she stuck her tongue out at her image and laughed. I don't think Mom ever really knew how pretty she was—she thought people's compliments were only politeness.

While Mom and Dad looked at refrigerators, Ben and I chased each other around between the stoves. They were so bright and new, it was like playing cowboys-and-Indians in a modern American dreamland.

When it looked like we were going to get thrown out of the store, we joined Mom and Dad. I said I wished we could go crazy and get one of those giant refrigerators with the magic-touch icecube trays or at least one with revolving shelves, but Dad said we had to stick to basics. He looked at Mom, "Only someone like Lardner"—his new boss—"needs one of those."

Mom laughed. "Old Lardass . . ."

Dad shook his head and nodded at us.

"Oh, lay off, John," Mom said.

"Do you have to talk that way in public?"

I started feeling sweaty because I thought they'd start a fight here. There were times when I felt like Herbert Philbrick—he had to spend nine frightening years saving the entire nation from the A-bomb, and here I was almost nine years old and still trying to save my family from its own world war. I jumped in with, "The other refrigerators are nicer than anything we've had before." Dad patted me and he and Mom looked around some more.

One that caught my eye was a pink one. It wasn't as big as the one Lardass needed. I asked Mom if we could get it.

"That refrigerator is for left-handed people especially," a salesman said. "See, the handle is on the right." He opened it awkwardly.

"Hey, Ben's left-handed," I said as Ben approached, his left thumb in his mouth.

The pink refrigerator was bigger and prettier than the other ones in our price range; the salesman told Mom and Dad that it was marked down because it was last year's model, was painted an unusual color, and had the left-handed door.

Dad wasn't interested, and looked at some boring white ones, all the way to examining the rubber door-liner, so I thought that was going to be it.

Ben said, "Hey, since I'm left-handed, you guys can just call me whenever you want it opened."

Mom put her arms around me and Ben. "Yes, John, let's get the left-handed pink one."

"Left-handed? Pink?" he said, winking. "Sounds vaguely unpatriotic."

"If it weren't for the pink color, that refrigerator would have been long gone," the salesman said, putting his hands behind his back and rocking ever-so-slightly from foot to foot.

"Knock another twenty-five off the price and I'll take it," Dad said, smiling at me.

"Sold American," the salesman said.

I tap-danced all the way up the escalator to the TV department.

Dad wanted to get a twenty-one-inch console, but Mom insisted a seventeen-inch would do fine. "We're saving, remember?" And then she said something she'd been mentioning lately. "Now that the kids are in school, I want to go into nurse's training."

"I don't see why you can't do that anyway, hon," Dad said. "Things are going well for us now."

Ben and I talked Mom into the big TV. I was so happy I twirled around. Ben twirled around too, and then started jumping and spinning and whistling. Mom told him he'd get dizzy and to stop. He kept doing it and slammed into a portable TV set. "Heckle and Jeckle" was on. Ben lost his balance and the TV went over and crashed to the floor and there was a lot of electricity and screaming and then Heckle and Jeckle shrank to a little dot of light and disappeared. Mom ran and picked Ben up and hugged him and then shook him. Then Dad grabbed and spanked him in the store. Ben's face showed nothing—it was the same face as when he was walking down the street or sitting eating his pimento loaf breakfast.

A bunch of salesmen ran over to stop the TV from sparking.

"Let's get out of here," Mom said.

"I think we ought to stay and—" Dad started to say, but Mom had Benny and me by the arm and was jerking us to the stairway. Dad followed us with his long strides. When we got downstairs, we ran out of the store before anyone could do anything about it.

Unfortunately, Dad's inspiration to get a new TV crashed with the one in the store. Dad said we couldn't really afford it yet anyway, that he'd send to the factory for a new knob for the old TV. In the meanwhile, we'd have to put on tennis shoes and stand on a rubber bathtub mat when we wanted to adjust the volume.

Monday, August 21

$$\approx$$

FOUR

I LUGGED MY BAGS onto the plane, hardly believing I was doing this.

There had been no way around the rush of it all. Classes started the next Monday and it looked like the condo sale would be clinched by the end of the week. So I had to do this immediately or else live with my conscience until the end of the semester. And that might be too late. Whatever "too late" might mean I didn't want to think about right that minute.

I set up a little aerial nest—my own special pillow behind my head, mineral water and Chinese party mix in the pouch, the USC law school course catalogue on my lap.

I lay my head back and closed my eyes. I couldn't shake the worry I had about Ben. I wouldn't put any crazy act past him. In fact, it would be out of character for him not to do something crazy. And that wasn't going to make him any easier to track down.

What if Ben was psychotic? Could he help himself if he had been seriously injured? From what I understood, he'd gotten worse since I last saw him, eight or nine years ago. But then they'd tried various medications and had some temporary successes, so who knew?

Trying to ignore my nervous stomach, I leafed through the catalogue. First-semester required courses—"Law, language, ethics." What a luxury nowadays to study ethics, much less to use them. More classes, some with practical titles, such as "Procedure," "Contracts," and some with esoteric titles like "Torts."

Was I really going to go? In some ways, I felt as if I already had, putting a husband through law school, typing and re-writing his papers. After he left me for his ex-wife and kids, I took a Law School Admissions Test preparation class my-self and did okay. I took the LSAT twice, and three years ago finally got a forty-two, one point shy of UCLA's minimum but enough to squeak into USC. Three-year-old LSATs were the limit—then you had to take them again. So I had to go this year or never, it seemed, especially if I wanted to work in a baby if all went well with Dean, my boyfriend.

As we began the jumbly ride down the runway, it meant I was really doing this. I looked out at my latest adopted home. I felt homesick already as it pinwheeled away.

How could I get anything done for Ben in the time I had? Well, I'd just have to work fast. And hard. A call to the police that morning had gotten me nowhere; if I showed up in person, I was told, I might have a little more luck.

My attempts to reach Antonia had been unsuccessful as well. They expected her at the cathedral later, so I'd left a message that I'd arrive in New York in the afternoon. Then I'd called Bellevue Hospital. He wasn't a patient currently. The clerk said that confidentiality regulations forbade her revealing his history as a mental patient. When I went into my saleswoman-of-the-year mode, telling her it was my brother that I was looking for, she said that if I came in person and talked to the supervisor that afternoon, I might persuade her to give me more information.

I'd planned to come home—mission accomplished or not— on Wednesday. I had to be overly cautious, because if any-thing happened, it was good-bye USC, hello Grundy.

The plane dipped, or was it my stomach? Good old Grundy, which opened its arms to people who couldn't make an A or B or even C law school, which let you work part time, which began its term later than the other schools and accepted applications even after classes had started.

But why was I being so pessimistic? I was going to USC, was going to improve myself intellectually, financially, and yes, even "ethically"—not that lawyers were paragons of morality, but compared to real estate agents, they came off pretty well.

And not that it was going to be a lot of fun—I knew that. Dean was a lawyer, too. He told me law school was like his mother said her facelift was—something you're reasonably glad you did but which you'd absolutely never go through again.

Dean really was happy that I wanted to be a lawyer. When I worried that I couldn't make the payments on my condo while I was in school, he assured me I could rent it out and come live with him before they threw me out on the streets.

Before they threw me out on the streets. We'd laughed at that.

He'd also offered to lend or give me money, but Dean-O, being a public defender, didn't have a lot to spare.

I picked up the catalogue and read about torts. The queen of hearts, she made some torts . . . I couldn't concentrate. I laid it down and tried to put together the chronology of Benny's life since he left home. Two years younger than I, he would have graduated from high school that many years later than I did. No wait, three, because he flunked. No, four—he failed two years. He finally did it, hit the only milestone of his life since his birth—graduating from high school—the year I finished college.

All I knew about the subsequent years was that he drifted in and out of psychiatric hospitals. Yes, there were chunks of his life I knew nothing about, years when I was too threatened by him and his problems, times when I tried to know as little as possible about what he was doing.

But way back in the past we really did try, didn't we? Mom and Dad always tried their best to bail Ben out of things. Well, maybe their second best. But then that's the kind of family we were, a second-best kind of family. Maybe we figured we didn't deserve better. We ate hamburger and Kroger brand canned tomatoes even in times when we could afford steak and salad. In Mom's mind, there was something wrong with wanting better, and there was something wrong with wanting to excel—getting a B or a C was perfectly acceptable, an A meant you were a troublemaker, a showoff. She was none too happy about my deciding to go to Northwestern rather than the local public university, even though I got a full scholarship. No ma'am, second best, and don't think you deserve any better. I laid my head back. With Ben around, though, I had to admit, that wasn't such a bad rule.

But when I left home, left my parents, my brother, I met people who thought they deserved more out of life. I'd never settle for second best again, I had vowed. That must have been why I headed at ninety miles an hour with my eyes closed into that last marriage with a glamor boy who insisted on going first class all the way. Once he got into a Rodeo Drive show-business practice, his ex-wife came back into his life. Coincidentally, Ben came back into mine at about the same time with a surprise visit. I never let myself think that Ben was the last straw in that marriage, but I don't think he helped matters.

After the divorce, I decided it was time to leave teaching and go out and make some money. So I got a real estate lisence. I didn't get rich, but I made enough for a down payment on my condo, a car, and a law school savings account. I'd taken care of myself. Problem is, people get hurt when you're only trying to take care of yourself. I must say, however, that Ben didn't even know he was getting hurt half the time. Or was it that he had enough pride to pretend things didn't hurt?

Like that time he visited me in college. I had just pledged Beta Alpha, which, incredibly enough, I'd been invited to join even though I'd once worn loafers with nylons to a loafers-with-knee-socks rush party.

The housemother hadn't believed he was my brother. He'd drifted in and asked in his loud, cracking voice if his sister Crosby Rawson lived there. I had been on my way down the stairs to the lobby at the time, and I froze, just out of sight. The housemother, using the same voice she used on the non-English-speaking cleaning lady, said, "Miss Rawson has no brother. I think you have the wrong sorority house."

I'd spun around and hurried up to my room. A few minutes

later, the housemother called and asked me to come to the lobby. I went downstairs all ready to say yes he was my brother and so what. But I took a good look at him. His hair hung in clumps like half-cooked spaghetti. His jeans were extreme bell-bottoms, flaring out like lampshades, and they were bright orange, swiped with dirt and God knows what, and one of the bell's seams had ripped. (My sorority sisters, who judged a man's worth by whether he wore Weejuns and straight-leg Levis, might in the wildest of imaginable dreams have been capable of overlooking the dirty and the torn, but the bell-bottomed and the orange, never).

He exuded an odor of cheap cologne on rotten meat. Out of the side of my vision, I saw a couple of my hard-won Beta Alpha sisters move away, whispering and snickering. Another looked shocked, and a couple of others just plain disgusted. I raised my eyebrows and said, "Obviously he's a lunatic if he says he's related to me."

Ben didn't look surprised or even very disturbed by this. He just gave me a smile and one of his half-waves and said, "Okay, Croz, see ya later."

I was up most of the night trying to study for a history test, but all my usual tricks for memorizing dates weren't working. At three A.M. I was interrupted by a call that sent me sailing for the phone so my roommate wouldn't wake up—I knew it would be from him. He was in the Evanston jail—vagrancy, for sleeping on a picnic table, and for disturbing the peace—cheering and yelling while listening to a baseball game on his radio.

The next morning, I went down and bailed him out. I put him on a Greyhound bus back to my parents' house, handing him a ten-dollar bill. "Get a haircut," I said.

"Hey, man, you must be puttin' me on," he said. Lately, he'd been talking as if he were wearing headphones and someone were feeding him lines. And then you'd say something and he wouldn't react for a minute, five minutes, an hour. He'd come back with an answer as if you'd just brought it up two seconds ago.

"Hey, I'm a cool head. I thought all you college types were hip, you know, make hair, not warfare. You always wanted to be "in," Croz."

Now he was trying to act cool, and he didn't know how. Trying to act cool, but he kept looking at me for approval, waiting for me to give him some cue as to whether he was saying the right things. But he was hopeless.

"Aren't you against the war, the draft, Crosby?"

"I suppose I am. But I make an exception in your case. They ought to draft you."

I shrank down in my seat, remembering that. Ben's number came up, all right. He went to boot camp in some hot sweaty place in Virginia. Then he went to Vietnam and got through several months before they saw that they had made a major tactical error in drafting my brother. What was funny was that before they decided he was not U.S. Army material, he got through the hell of Vietnam without so much as stubbing a toe. That was Ben all over, going through war as if it were a meadow full of daisies, going through life as if it were a mine field.

I was amazed that the army kept him for as long as they did. Mom said they just thought he was like nine-tenths of the other soldiers, stoned on pot to keep fear from driving them crazy.

He got out on some sort of mental discharge. That seemed to be the turning point; he got really crazy then.

He joined the Krishnas and shaved his head, then decided it wasn't for him and came home. Dad said he could live at home if he let his hair grow. So he let it grow, all right. He went away for a while and returned with it down to his shoulders and dyed an uneven brown. As he told it, he'd picked up a case of lice and didn't know where to get free medical services. Someone had told him the dye would kill the lice.

For weeks he never went out, living in a bathrobe. I remembered seeing him walk around the house in that robe. From the back he looked like Jesus.

Dad told him he'd have to get a job, so he found a gas station to hang around. He washed cars, cleaned the bathroom, did other odd jobs until he decided to drive off in someone's newly tuned-up car one day. The police found it abandoned that night, out of gas.

He didn't work after that. He let his hair grow out again, really long. Instead of wearing it in a single ponytail at his neck like some of those guys did, he put it up in two ponytails, like a little girl, for a while.

And as far as we knew, he wasn't gay or anything. Just Ben, that's all he was.

I wondered what I was going to tell my Dean-O. I didn't want to lose him. I was in love. This time it was no handsome smoothie of a show-biz lawyer, but an assistant public defender with a slow way of talking, a way that made you think that instead of grabbing for the easiest words, he was always looking for the truth, and if he had a tragic flaw, it was that he had too much faith in people.

If only I were stepping into his big hug right now instead of the big empty sky that led to New York. Looking up into that wide pumpkin smile of his, with the spaces between his real teeth and the too-perfect stuck-togetherness of his false ones.

Along with his lumbering jock's walk, it was the obvious dental work of Dean O'Neill that attracted me to him. That fake-looking bridge had football player written all over it. A football player to make me a cheerleader until I was eighty.

I was cold. I got a blanket from the overhead compartment. Dean's he-man looks may have attracted me to him, but it was his neatness that made me see him as marriage material. There he was, a hulk of a guy you'd think would be clumsy and messy, but no, he was the neatest person you'd ever meet. I knew it the first time I saw that car, confirmed it when looking through the glove compartment. It smelled of air conditioning and leather. In it was the order and security I'd been looking for all my life—insurance car papers in a polished leather binder, maps that looked like they'd never been touched, a Swiss army knife, a neatly folded, clean cloth for wiping off dust, a flashlight that actually worked (never in their lives had Mom and Dad had a flashlight that had operating batteries in it. Ever.) There were also: a Hershey bar, in case he was stranded in the mountains; a bottle of Evian water, in case he was stranded in the desert; a roll of quarters for the most hellish case of being stranded, he joked, on a

Southern California freeway. That glove compartment said order and security to me in a calm, easygoing voice. When you tried to close the glove compartments that I grew up with, you got a big bite of a rat's nest of crumpled maps of the Midwest and all other kinds of junk.

Yes, I had to admit, it was that glove compartment of Dean's that made me fall in love with him.

I still had my doubts as to whether someone with a glove compartment like that could love me after getting a load of Ben. I mean, could he or anyone else adjust to a brother-in-law who had set the house on fire twice? Who had broken into a pet store in the middle of the night to steal a bird to eat the cockroaches that had gotten out of hand in his latest flophouse?

Serious doubts.

Dean wasn't the least bit stuffy. But he was thinking of running for public defender in the next election, when his boss was to retire. And he was well-liked by the liberal congressman he worked for and was even thinking maybe someday he'd like to go to Washington for good. I was nervous at the idea of an election, which would open him up to dissection by the press. After all, once the press starts looking into family closets these days, they don't stop until they find someone like Ben, and boy oh boy would they ever hit the jackpot. No, I didn't want to screw up Dean's chances. This world needed people like him in office. Also, I didn't want my brother's name dragged around publicly, even if he'd never even know it was happening.

I had a lot of faith in Dean, in his ability to overlook differences, family shortcomings. And yet, what would happen if he saw beneath my California freckly tan, my state-of-the-art Nautilus body, my whole gourmet-health-food sun-dried-tomato exterior? I wasn't sure what would happen, and I wasn't sure what should happen. I knew you didn't have to love someone family and all; but I wasn't sure that you didn't owe them a listing of family skeletons, at the least the ones that might fall out of closets every time you walked by them.

I managed to nap but I woke up right away. I took out the brochure. Torts again. I could use the word *torts* without blinking someday, let someone else guess at what it meant.

I put the brochure down. The next time I saw Benny after the sorority incident was in 1972, the year I graduated from college.

He showed up at the graduation ceremony uninvited. Standing there at the fence, he could almost have passed for a hippie in his plaid flannel shirt and jeans. But then you saw that there was something else going on with him, something not quite—his shirt was buttoned wrong and he stood oddly, his stomach out, his arms just hanging.

I was glad for the procession, the formality. As I approached him, I noticed that he looked clean-shaven and washed. He put his hands in his pockets and got that sort of proud smile he'd had as a kid when he saw me coming down the street.

But you never knew what he'd do next next. I thought of the time he climbed up on the scoreboard when I was trying out for cheerleaders, and I ignored him as I went by.

After the ceremony, the family was gathering for pictures. Ben stood off, fifteen feet or so away from the rest of us, and no one spoke to him or invited him to come over. We tried to make him invisible. But I couldn't help but see him as he squinted into the noonday sun, his feet not knowing what to do, and I thought of going over and saying something to him. Mom and Dad hadn't seen him since he'd graduated a couple of weeks before, when he'd gone off to some rock festival. Mom glanced over at him and told me a couple of weeks wasn't enough. You couldn't tell if she was joking or not. Maybe she didn't know if she was joking or not.

But then one of the Beta Alphs came over and hugged me and said, "What a nice-looking family. Can I meet them?"

And my boyfriend, Paul, put his arm around me and we were a pretty graduation picture. We joked about Paul's delaying graduation to avoid the draft, and even Dad-the-Vietnam-hawk admitted it was a smart move.

I knew how good we looked, our gowns billowing in the coltish wind. But Ben had made his presence felt, and no matter how much we pretended everything was great, this day was like our whole lives, and the sun never quite got to shining completely.

We walked together, my family and my sorority sister and my boyfriend, over to the Beta Alph house, where there was to be a tea for the graduates. I turned and looked at Ben. He was already walking away in the other direction, his arms loose and his hands cupped like empty hooks, his shirt hanging unevenly in the back. And then I noticed something else— his hair looked freshly cut. He'd had that ragged mess made to look respectable, maybe for my sake, to pass sorority-girl inspection.

≈≈≈
F I V E

To keep the aqua shag carpet clean when showing the house, the sellers had laid strips of plastic all over it. "Let's leave them right where they are," Dad suggested. "Then this carpet won't get dirty like all the others."

"What do you think this is, a department store?" Mom said.

"Your problem is you want to go back to the Depression, when everything was so wonderful."

Mom put her hands on her hips and stared out the sliding door window at the backyard, where a lonely little evergreen bush surrounded by a tiny fence was trying to make things cheerful. "You may have a point. Living with you makes the Depression look good."

Dad may have won the battle on the plastic issue, but he lost the war because of his temper. His biggest problem, in fact, was that he was like a tinderbox ready to go off. You almost felt that if Mom lit one of her matches too close to him, the explosion would take the house and maybe the whole Midwest with it.

He came home one evening and said hello to us in a nice way. He saw without really seeing that Ben was in the living room drinking chocolate milk on a part of the carpet that the plastic didn't cover. He went to the bedroom to change his clothes. When he came downstairs in his chinos and at-home shirt, he shouted, "Benjamin, haven't I told you not to drink chocolate milk, or *anything,* in the living room?"

Of course all that startled Ben, and he spilled the chocolate milk. Mom came running out of the kitchen to see what all the commotion was, and by then the chocolate was on the carpet and Ben had his heel in it. Dad grabbed Ben by the arm and flung him over to the davenport, and Mom screamed, "You leave him alone."

I took Ben by the hand to the kitchen. We found the Spic and Span and some rags. While Mom and Dad were having it out, we scrubbed the chocolate.

"Those kids destroy everything," Dad said. "Everything."

"You think objects are more important than people," she said. "You want all the things around you to be perfect and clean and nice, and you don't care what happens to the people."

By now, Ben and I were coming to the conclusion that the chocolate was in there to stay. The rug was cotton, and it was like a thirsty desert.

"Dummy, why'd you let him catch you?" I whispered, and then pinched him. "You got chewed out for that a hundred times in the old house."

"I didn't know it wasn't okay in *this* house," he said.

"You should have been watching him," Dad shouted, and he grabbed the plastic that was left on the hallway and up the stairs, ripped it up, opened the door that led to the garage, and flung it into the air. There was a flat, crisscrossing path on the carpet where it used to be, like a trail in the snow for playing Fox and Geese. "There. Now you and the kids can make a total mess in here and I won't interfere."

Mom went up to her bedroom. Dad turned on the TV and opened the paper. Looking at Dad's face out the side of my eyes, I thought maybe he yelled when what he felt like doing was crying.

I don't know which would have been worse, the plastic or the way the carpet ended up looking. Instead of a desert, it became a big aqua sea with dirty oil slicks floating all around in it. At any rate, Dad had been right—without the plastic, it didn't stay clean long. But soon, Mom and Dad seemed to stop noticing, as though they sensed that we were going to up and move anyway into a house with a brand-new, clean carpet, and the next people here would have to deal with this one.

"I saw some cute wallpaper with early American kitchen scenes on it at Penney's," Mom said one morning a few days later.

"Wait and see if we're going to stay here, otherwise wallpaper would be a waste of time and money," Dad said.

"But I just measured the kitchen. I just planted daffodil bulbs," Mom said, more like she was summing up her experiences here for her own purposes than really protesting.

One evening that winter Dad came home and said to Mom, "This job's not leading to assistant PR director. I've had it with U.S. Tires. I've had an offer from Mid-America Rubber that's sure to lead to director. But we'll have to move to Des Moines."

The carpeting now was filthy, so I guess the move was right on time. And somehow, like our house, our lives seemed to be in need of new carpeting.

Ben and I went to the bedroom. He got out the checkerboard.

Mom said in a flat voice, "Miss Cutsinger said Benny's off in another world. What do you think another move will do to him?"

I looked at Ben to see what he thought it would do, but he just puckered his mouth like he was thinking and pushed his checker to another square.

"It'll be good for him," Dad said. "This is dead-end here. We'll never have enough money unless we go. Hey, hon, time to dust off that nurse's chapeau and that hypodermic needle and bedpan, because you're going to become one of the angels of mercy."

"Looks like Des Moines is going to be home," I said to Ben, getting myself in the mood to move. " 'I-oway, I-oway, that's where the tall corn grows,' " I sang. "Hey, Benny, we can have corn on the cob every night."

Ben broke into a huge, trusting smile. "Yeah," he cried out. "Des Moines—home, sweet home."

Monday, August 21

~~~

S I X

A s THE PLANE SKATED down the runway at LaGuardia Airport, Frank Sinatra tot-tot-totta-totted into "New York, New York" on my airline headphones.

I couldn't hear Frank without thinking of my father, how he bought into the myths, both the uppers—the American success stories, the you can do it if I can—and the downers—going for it and losing, but what the heck, sipping your cocktail, letting your broken dreams create a velvet melancholy. Poor Dad spent his life longing for the sophisticated, Frank Sinatra-high, the kind his life never was able to seduce into our messy little living rooms.

I got my pillow and untouched snacks together. Oh, I supposed Dad managed to hand down some of those unfulfilled reveries of sophistication, too, only I did them one dream better; he pictured riding lawnmowers and spotless prefab houses, and I imagined doormen and antiques. Those childhood fantasies of New York were my pretty dream of escaping what Dad had wanted; miraculously I was going to turn rich and not have to deal with Chemlawn and sod rollers and suburban peer pressure. And yet the joke seemed to be on me—I was probably going to live my parents' dream for

38

them, and not my own. What had I been thinking way back then, that I could escape the American way of life? I, too, would be forever a prisoner of the suburban developments, which wasn't so terrible, I knew now; it was something I dealt with the same way I dealt with the knowledge that someday I was going to die. The only one who had escaped, I realized, looking out at the August haze over New York, was Ben.

Ben escaped? I thought, entering the dingy airport. Banished was more like it. He couldn't make it in Middle America, not even on the fringes like the rest of his family. He didn't work out, so he was thrown away, by my parents, by me, by our throwaway society, junked like a car that had turned out to be a lemon.

As I stood in line for a cab, I swore that even from this far I could smell both the city's garbage and its excitement. What had Ben come here for? What was it that he'd wanted? Probably just a place that he could blend into.

I had to admit that the New York, New York skyline razzle-dazzled me, and I let myself absorb the city as I rode into town. It was the epitome of everything in this country, and yet my impression had always been that it was unlike the rest of it, New York being so extreme, so intense.

And then there was me, unextreme me, trying to pull this off. Oh God, but I'd turned out boring, flipping around in my little working-girl Belle France dresses, bouncing across condo development sidewalks in my Avias, flying the freeways of Los Angeles in my plastic Japanese car.

And trying to pull off this law school thing. I hadn't been reasonably sure I could afford USC until a month ago when I sold a house and then had this condo on the line. Last winter when I applied I was pretty sure of having the money because houses were selling then faster than you could say genuine-Italian-marble-floors-with-his-and-her-Jacuzzi-baths. But the housing market died sometime between spring and summer, and I'd all but resigned myself to forgetting the whole idea or else saying the hell with it and going to Grundy.

I thought of a Grundy diploma and I heard my mother's voice repeating her favorite line: "Just who do you think you are, Missy, that you should turn your nose up at—" fill in the blank. The Theodore Grundy College of Law fit perfectly.

I kept a close eye on the taxi meter. I had gotten traveler's checks to cover a hotel room at $64.29 including tax per night for two, three at the most, and Sarah swore I could eat on fifteen a day, using the delis for breakfast and lunch, having a little fun at dinner, spaghetti or Chinese or something. I had an electric heater for tea water and soup, a box of peppermint tea bags, a bottle of Glen-Ellen Chardonnay, and a six-pack of mineral water in my luggage. I allowed myself ten a day for cabs—after that, I had to walk or take the subways, which Sarah swore with somewhat less assurance were safe during the day. I had an extra forty for a gift for Ben, assuming he turned up, and then there was my contingency fund. If I found Ben, I'd take him out for dinner, a really nice one. I could spend up to sixty on that. Then I had two hundred from my savings to buy him whatever he needed immediately. I also had a vague idea of trying to hook him up to some social service agency, and I assumed he was still picking up supplemental security income checks. However, I suspected that they didn't sustain him; he used to fritter away every cent— on himself, on anyone around him—the minute he got a check. I had another three hundred for emergency. And there were always my credit cards, though I didn't want to run up my bills if I was going to be living for the next three years on garbanzo-bean casseroles.

We went over a bridge and zipped along a highway, then got into traffic that was like a wild cattle stampede. I gave up on bracing and sat back limply, trying to look somewhere between bored and annoyed like the rest of the cowboys in the traffic.

But already I was fascinated—so many people from so many social classes and nationalities. New York, even more than California, attracted people from all over.

All kinds of people, including people like Benjamin John Rawson. And boy oh boy, was he—were we—from all over.

I wondered what it would be like to live here, idle rich or ghetto mother or just average Joe (if there was any such thing in this city)—to actually have lived here all your life. To have lived in any city all your life, for that matter, but for God's sake in this one.

I knew I had missed something by not being "from" anywhere in particular, and yet there were some advantages to all the moving. I was flexible, I could meet new people easily. I could recall details about past years that most people had forgotten. In fact that talent got me a thousand dollars toward my law school savings when our head office was coming up with an ad campaign based on fifties and sixties nostalgia. They hired me as a freelance consultant. My secret was that I could vividly recall any year by remembering where we lived, because I associated the grade I was in with the city. The ad people thought I was some kind of a genius. I could give them songs, clothing fads, hairstyles, TV shows, World Series teams, Miss Americas, slang words—all that for any given year. The only things I got stuck on, embarrassingly enough, were presidents.

Often I went back to towns in which I once lived and searched for my old houses. The most striking change, of course, was in the size of trees—one big maple tree growing in the front yard. Or sometimes the tree would be inexplicably gone.

Pulling over to the curb, I'd take in the house. I'd wait for something to happen to me, for the time machine to be turned on, for magic. The magic happened to me every now and then; as during a visit to the Smithsonian, when I saw doll furniture like I'd once had.

But the houses didn't have that effect; I'd not be jolted with that "There's home!" feeling, even though the place usually looked the same. It was surprising, in fact, how much the houses hadn't changed, deteriorated. Those houses must last forever, like the non-biodegradable stuff they worry about in landfills.

I'd drive by the schools, and often they'd be closed or put to another use, as senior citizen or day-care centers, underscoring the baby boom's impact on society through all its ages.

Sometimes I'd be unable to find the school or house. I'd drive around and come to one that I might have lived in, but I couldn't be sure.

I'd be afraid to look up old schoolmates, worrying that I wasn't remembered, or that I was—for something Ben had done. Or I'd be afraid that to those who had not forgotten me,

I'd be such a faint image of something passing through that the person, having plenty of real old friends, wouldn't be interested in seeing me.

We zoomed up to a curb and the driver roped his cab to a stop. The neighborhood was okay, and the Royale Payne looked rather nice from the outside. As I headed toward the entrance, I passed a huddled group of people whom I at first took to be members of some religious cult. In spite of the heat, many wore blankets and stocking caps. But when they held out cups and bags asking for money, I realized they were some of New York's famous homeless people. A little frightened, I gave them what coins I had and then handed out a few dollar bills. I told myself not to be so shocked; after all, there was a sizable number in Los Angeles. It was just that I didn't get downtown very often. Most of my time was spent in my little town of La Querencia, a middle-middle-class community of mostly retirees and singles.

It didn't hit me until I was opening the hotel door that my brother was one of these people. I simply hadn't put the two together. Surely he wasn't as bad off as they, I said to myself, turning to look again. Was he?

The image of him in the middle of a dark street, blood trickling from his head, flashed into my consciousness. I felt dizzy and closed my eyes, still seeing drops of blood splattered on brilliant white concrete.

The hotel desk was surrounded by a wire mesh cage with a bulletproof screen. I looked around at the rest of the lobby. I had to appreciate the fact that it was, as Sarah had said, almost charming in a musty, thirties sort of way.

I told the bellhop I'd carry my own bag. I got a big New York sneer at that, but I'd given his tip and then some away to the people outside the door. Loneliness tugged at me as I waited for the elevator, which took ten minutes to arrive. When the door opened, a big, tough New York spider marched out.

The room was decorated in faded maroon and brown. A buckling Modigliani print hung over the head of the bed. If they had wanted to put another single bed in there, it wouldn't have fit. The telephone was on the floor, the TV suspended over the bed as in hospitals. Any fears I'd had of seeing more spiders were quickly allayed by a peppery insecticide odor.

I squeezed around the bed to take in the view. It was mostly the black tops of other buildings and water tanks, but in distant view were some smashing modern high-rises and the scallop shapes of a bridge.

I called the shelter. Antonia wouldn't arrive until seven, when it opened. I guessed I'd have to just show up—I didn't even know if she'd gotten the message that I was coming. I figured I had an hour before I should leave.

I went into the bathroom. The faucet dripped, counting the seconds I'd have to be here. My face in the mirror looked strained. I dug through my suitcase for my bottles and jars. I massaged on face cream, wiped it off, swiped on astringent, then moisturizer. I took two aspirin and went to lie down.

The room must have had about twenty coats of paint. A big crack branched across the ceiling. The more I looked at it, the more it looked like a map. Maybe it was New York, I thought, trying to find some humor in all this. I rolled over and got out my street guide to Manhattan from my suitcase and unfolded it. I rolled back and compared them. Yes, it was Manhattan.

Where was the Cathedral of St. John the Divine on that map? Somewhere toward the northwest. Hopefully I'd have an itinerary for the rest of the stops after tonight.

How many stops had there been on the map of my life? I still had the one I'd made up when I was a child, the one with stars on every city we'd lived in. It hung in my bedroom. When I needed to sleep sometimes I tried counting the houses and cities we'd lived in. That was difficult because I couldn't remember the ones we'd lived in when I was a baby. That counting exercise was as hard as my other sleep-inducing game—adding up the number of men I'd slept with. All I knew for sure was that the latter number was smaller than the former.

I fell asleep and had that uncanny experience of waking up exactly when I wanted to, at six o'clock. I was furiously hungry, but there was no time to eat. I had to get to the shelter by seven.

I kept what I had on, a beige skirt and polo shirt, slipped

into some flats, and hurried out to get a cab.

When I told the driver where I was going, he slammed down the little red flag. "Fuckin-A pain in the ass. You know how hard it is to pick up a fare in that neighborhood?" and my neck snapped as we took off, lurching and stomping and snorting, into the traffic.

We got to a swanky section and the cab stopped lurching and began to glide smoothly, as if it wanted to fit in. Park Avenue. I stared at sleek people out for a snooty stroll in their dark, tailored clothes, at the tourists in pastel outfits, their heads tilted back to take in the heights. There's nothing, I noted, more elegant than a New Yorker, nothing fresher and cleaner than a New York tourist.

We rode on. And nothing dirtier than a New York homeless person, I observed. When we reached Central Park, they were everywhere, pushing shopping carts hung with swaying plastic bags and covered with rags flapping like pennants. They pushed their carts into the park with determination, as if they were on a mission somewhere. As we screeched to a stop at a light, I saw a man asleep on the sidewalk, a garbage bag his blanket, a pizza box his pillow.

This fresh-looking tourist suddenly noticed the meter. Well, the driver would be spared from having to make a trip to that neighborhood, because if I wanted to take a cab back to the hotel later, I'd reached my daily cab expense limit.

"Let me out here, please," I said.

"With pleasure."

As the cab leaped across the street for another, more promising-looking fare, I nervously shook out my subway map to see where the nearest number 1, 2 or 3 train station was.

1959

S E V E N

W<small>E GOT A RANCH HOUSE</small> in Heather Wood Villa, just out-side of Des Moines. The house was smaller than the last, but it had a two-car garage with a monogram on the door— WFM—in big black and gold letters. They stood for William Frederick Miller, the father of the previous family. Dad said it would be an ordeal to get rid of them, and anyway, we'd probably buy a bigger house once he was promoted. It was a little weird to have someone else's initials on our garage, but it didn't matter too much because the letters were in such fancy script you could hardly figure them out.

The garage situation was unusual because Dad was a per-fectionist about everything else, and the more often we moved, the neater he became. Mom, though, grew to be more and more the opposite of Dad. She acted almost as if getting dressed and doing housework were a waste of time. Sitting in front of the TV, smoking and drinking coffee filled her days when she wasn't playing honeymoon bridge with me. Sometimes it was even solo honeymoon bridge, sitting on the floor with her long legs out at angles like a little kid's, four bridge hands fanning out in between them. When she got up, she'd leave the cards and they'd end up in a big mess. I'd

45

count them as I picked them up to make sure I got them all, and half the time there'd only be forty-nine or fifty.

The house was full of coffee cups on saucers popping with red-ringed cigarette butts. And you never knew where you'd find a wad of chewing gum stuck for later. Newspapers fluttered all over the floor, dishes sat expectantly in the sink and on the dinette, swirls of sheets and unwashed clothes lay on the beds. I made my bed because I'd lose things in the covers if I didn't, and Ben made his because he was a copycat, so if there was a mess in the house, Mom was the usual suspect.

The bathroom was the worst. Half the time there'd be Mom's girdle on the floor, upside down and inside out, with the two leg holes staring up at you. Every few days, her double-edged razor was left out, the blade only half rolled in, so you'd about slit your wrists trying to wash your hands. In the morning, the blobs of toothpaste all over the sink would end up on your sweater's elbows, and swirls of Maybelline Sable Brown mascara swept the lower part of the mirror so you had to stand on the toilet to comb your hair.

Mom read a lot of articles in magazines about depressed housewives, and she thought that sounded like her. But I didn't think she fit into any kind of category you'd ever see in a magazine. Whatever it was that got her down sometimes or put her into a state, we all kind of excused Mom because we thought of her as an intellectual who would someday become a college-educated registered nurse.

Also for that reason, we excused her cooking. Except for holidays and other rare occasions, she made only one main course for dinner—a mixture of hamburger, tomato juice, and onions. With spaghetti, it was Italian spaghetti; with macaroni, Hungarian goulash; with rice, Spanish rice; with kidney beans, Mexican chili. Every now and then, she'd throw in some barley and then it was something with no name, just dinner. And then sometimes she'd surprise you and for variety's sake use those same ingredients to make meat loaf, stuffed peppers, or hamburgers, but not very often. For dessert, the possibilities opened up, but the usual was burnt pudding—Jello chocolate or butterscotch. I never could figure out whether she burned it on purpose or not— you'd come in and smell it scorching and run and tell her, and she'd hurry to turn it off, like she'd made a mistake. But when we were eating it, she'd remark how she liked it with a little bit of a burnt taste, because that gave it character. Dad did a lot of traveling and came home with ideas about gourmet eating and he actually tried out a couple of recipes himself and said that Mom should learn them. Mom would go and plop down on couch, cross her legs and arms and accuse him of trying to show off, a crime in her book that was worse than murder.

Dad walked in one night with a paper bag full of clanking bottles. "I got the promotion," he announced with a broad grin.

Dad had a smile worth a million bucks, but I have to say that without it he was the kind of guy a lot of people don't notice at first. He was tall, but he had sort of beigy-colored skin and hair, and kind of narrow shoulders and an inoffensive (when other people were around) manner.

I think Dad's best feature was his hands—good, squarish hands that always seem to know where they were going and what they were supposed to do, unlike Mom's, which when they didn't contain a cigarette were long and tapered and hung like parentheses around herself, moving slightly, wondering what she was going to make them do next.

"A promotion," Mom repeated sourly. "Whose job are you taking away?" Mom had been mad all day, ever since a couple of ladies from the Welcome Wagon made a surprise visit and joked about the ironing board having hair curlers and bobby pins and makeup on it and no ironing. They left without inviting her to join anything. I never knew if Mom wanted to be like other people and couldn't, or could but chose not to. "Bill Westle's job? I suppose we have to move now," Mom said.

Dad stacked a couple of his LPs on the hi-fi. "You'd be so nice to come home to," Frank crooned.

Ben and I followed Dad to the kitchen. We leaned against the wall by the door so we could make an easy getaway if necessary. There was something in the air. Mom came in and stood like a snake ready to strike, her cigarette hand arched back so she almost singed her hair.

"Not Westle's job, not yet. Zigling's, almost as big. And we can move over to Park Manor Estates now," Dad said.

"Thank you very much, but I don't want to move again," Mom said.

"Fine," he said. "Then we'll just get some new furniture."

Mom surveyed the room, considering the idea of a truce and no fight. "How about if we start by wallpapering this kitchen?"

"The pink refrigerator looks lonely and embarrassed," Ben whispered to me.

That made me feel sorry for Ben. It was like he was speaking from experience.

Dad pulled things out one by one. "You go tomorrow and get that wallpaper. Now—to celebrate—bourbon, vermouth. A pitcher, a shot glass—without any jokes or girlie pictures on it, you will notice, ha-ha—two 'up' glasses, two 'rocks' glasses. And for the pièce de résistance—a jar of cherries, maraschino style."

Dad handed Mom her drink and raised his glass in a toast. Mom took the cherry out and ate it, then walked over to the sink and dumped the Manhattan into it. Then she went to the pink refrigerator and took out a bottle of RC Cola, opened it awkwardly, and poured it into the Manhattan glass. It ran all over and spilled into the sink. Dad's face reddened. When that happened, the traces of his acne scars showed more. He went over and grabbed the little glass from her, spilling the RC all over her. "These are my goddamn glasses and if you don't want to use them for their proper use, then go to hell. No one in the house touches them."

Mom got that look where she smiled out of only one side of her face and walked slowly back into the living room and then we heard her bedroom door slam. Dad drank the two Manhattans and then glowered at the TV for the rest of the night.

At that time, I began wondering whether Ben was seriously screwy in the head, or just plain mean. In other words, honestly screwed up, or dishonestly rotten. Like with the Claudia Cauliflower incident.

Claudia McCaulliffster and I became best friends on the

first day of class. Big-boned and always dressed in fancy circle skirts and pastel cardigans, Claudia was the most noticeable girl in the class. Her two front teeth were large and white and jagged like a saw, and her bright yellow hair was cut in a Dutch boy style. Being small and getting stuck with curly dark hair that refused to be styled no matter what Mom and I did with permanents or Spoolies or plain old pincurls, I absolutely loved someone like Claudia, who radiated light and good luck.

Claudia didn't need any new friends, but after I showed her a couple of jump rope chants that they'd never heard of there, she let me hold one end of a rope while she jumped with her friends.

When they got tired, they talked about the ballet class they all had together and started doing the splits, sideways and front and back. They looked at me like they expected me to show them some fancy moves, so I said I never took ballet because I was always busy riding the Arabian palamino I used to own.

They froze in their different ballet positions, all five. "Of course, I rode English-style, even though the ordinary people there rode Western," I said, and then I explained the differences between English and Western saddles and bridles and bits. I'd learned all this from the *World Book Encyclopedia*.

Claudia's mother called Mom and asked if I could come over for dinner the next week. Mom got on her sing-songy good manners voice and said that would be nice. Then Mom mentioned that I had a little brother, and Mrs. McCaulliffster said Claudia had one, too, and invited Ben.

I knew right away when I saw Claudia's house that she was about the richest person in town. It made me feel real comfortable. Comfortable like I'd never been before.

We still hadn't gotten our wallpaper, and the old wallpaper had food spills on it from the former people's meals. Mom had even tried to scrub it off, saying, "Disorder is one thing, dirt is another. If I'm going to have dirt on the walls, it's going to be my own dirt."

However hard we scrubbed, though, our house would never be this nice—all beige and wood and soft voices from her parents. Dinner cooking smelled like Christmas. In her room, Claudia had her own record player and a million books.

I leafed through *Black Beauty* and said, "I wonder what it's like not to have to get all your books from the bookmobile."

Claudia was the kind of person who would lend you books, and she offered to, but I knew better than that. Around our household, they'd get lost or they'd get spilled on or Ben would draw pictures of people going to the bathroom all over the inside of the covers, or we'd move away before I got the chance to return them.

In the den (a word I'd only heard on TV and seen in books; to us it was "family room" or "rec room") they had the entire set of *Encyclopedia Britannica.* I immediately looked for H and opened it up to *horse.* It was a lot harder than the *World Book,* but still interesting. I told her parents about the Eohippus, primitive horse, and how a Welsh and Shetland pony were different. That you measured a horse by "hands," and that a horse was unlike most other hoofed animals because it had a single, not a cleft, toe. I explained the difference between a snaffle and a curb bit, and demonstrated how to mount a horse, even though I'd never even been near one in my life.

Her parents listened with interest, and were really polite to us, like we were grownups. Her mother said, "You used to live in—where was it, Texas?—Claudia tells me." She wore a powder blue sheath and high heels, even though she was just hanging around the house. Her hair and face were so clean and protected-looking she could have posed for one of those Beautiful Hair Breck ads. The father had something that looked like a suit jacket, only looser and in a silky fabric.

"Idaho," I said. I was afraid they might know more than I did about Idaho, so I changed the subject to snakes, which they didn't look like they knew anything about. I told how the nonpoisonous northern water snake is sometimes mistaken for the poisonous water moccasin. I added that it still wasn't a great snake to have bite you because it has something in its venom that makes you bleed a lot more than ordinary. Mr. McCaulliffster asked if there were any northern water snakes in Iowa, and when I said there were, he said he'd watch out for them from now on.

Ben didn't say a word. Every time they asked him something, he'd just look at me with those glow-in-the-dark eyes. I'd answer everything, like how he liked Heather Wood Villa, and who his teacher was. Claudia's brother went off and played with his train set. I felt there was something different about my family and I got nervous because I knew they'd eventually find that out.

But, I told myself, Claudia likes you, so just relax.

Her mother complimented my name. "Crosby—so important-sounding for such a little girl," she said.

"It's my middle name, my Mom's maiden name," I told her. "My real name is September."

"That's a lovely month for a birthday. Mr. McCaulliffster's is the twenty-eighth. When is yours?"

"Well, mine is June fifteenth."

She looked confused, but she said, "I see."

"But my Mom liked the name September and not June." I explained that, but I couldn't explain any more, like the fact that it was simply the kind of thing Mom did—this lady in her Beautiful Hair Breck expression wouldn't in a century understand.

For dinner we had roast beef and green beans cut on the slant. I remarked about how pretty they were, and Claudia's mother said, "Oh, thank you. They're French-style." I told her I loved French things.

I was acting polite and putting stuff on Ben's plate and telling him how good it was. Ben refused to eat anything until I ate it first and told him it was okay.

The dinner went off without any major disasters until Mrs. McCaulliffster passed the cauliflower, which was covered with cheese and a sprinkle of paprika.

Ben agreed to have some, but when it was put on his plate he stared for a while and then said to me, "Is that why her name is Claudia Cauliflower, because it looks like Claudia's face? See, Croz, all white, and a clump sticking out here like her big teeth. And then cheese like her hair, and then sprinkles of red pepper like freckles. See, Croz?"

There was a silence that made it hard to breathe. Looking at the cauliflower, I could see what he meant. One teacher had said that Ben was the artist type, because he noticed things like that. I had always tried to make that part of me go away, for fear the results would be the same. So I sure as hell wasn't going to admit that it looked like her face. I thought of killing him, but instead I tried to laugh broadly, like, "Isn't that dumb and cute?" But my face felt bright red-hot, and I had to hold my breath to keep from putting a dent in his shin with my heavy new saddle shoes.

Finally, her little brother laughed and said, "He's crazy," and everyone was kind of silent again. Then Mrs. McCaulliffster passed around a bowl of fruit, and the next thing I know, goddamn Ben says, "Does she have a bottom like yours, with no weenie but just a sliced pear instead?"

Now I really wanted to murder him—after all, he was six years old going on seven, and he knew better. He'd dragged the newspapers and the coffee cups and the aqua shag rug and the swearing into this house that smelled like it had just been vacuumed. And there was something else he dragged in here that I couldn't quite name.

You could hear nothing but forks clinking. I wished they kept the TV on during dinner like we did at home. "Ben's always saying weird stuff like that," I explained, trying to imitate Mrs. McCaulliffster's smile. They all smiled back and everyone started conversing again, but you could tell they just wanted to get it over with fast.

As it turned out, it wasn't such a horrible disaster, because Claudia's family moved shortly after that. Her dad was transferred to Switzerland.

I never wanted to forget her. I felt like I wasn't so weird if there were other people who liked a quiet peaceful house and books like I did. And, in fact, I hoped we got transferred to Switzerland some time, because I'd read that Swiss people were very orderly and that there were mountains. I just hoped we wouldn't end up in the same town as Claudia Cauliflower.

Her moving away helped me forgive Ben. Sometimes you thought he did things just to make people hate him. But if you had to live with him, you tried to convince yourself that it wasn't like that, or you'd be miserable for the next ten years until you grew up. So I told myself that all little kids do things like that, and Ben was just acting like anyone else's bratty little brother. Anyway, I *couldn't* stay mad at Ben forever. He was the only permanent friend I had; a traveling, portable best friend.

Mom seemed to be trying to fit in here, but I have to say she was starting to seem confused a lot of the time. "I have to keep household gadgets out in the open, or I can't find them," she told her new lady friends who came over. They all laughed and joked with her, because she was so pretty and funny and with Dad's promotion we were fairly important.

She'd act like they'd just caught her at a bad moment, but in fact the ironing board was *always* up, and always balanced on top of it were things that she might need that day, or that week, or some time. Like the medical encyclopedia, and the scissors, and bobby pins, and a box of envelopes, and the phone or electric bill, a pen or two, a tube of mascara, nail polish and remover, aspirin, the tape measure, a screwdriver, her lipstick.

Lipstick was a real problem for Mom. As far back as I can remember, she used the same shade, Cherries in the Snow, and kept a tube of it stashed in every imaginable place around the house. She said it was the only color they made that was just right for her, and she was afraid they'd stop making it. Just about every time she passed a cosmetic counter at the drug store or department store, she bought a tube of it. There was a tube—Lustrous or Lanolite, Futurama or refill case—in half the drawers in the living room and bedrooms, in the linen closet, under the sink, on top of the refrigerator, on the knickknack shelf.

But it wasn't just the fear of not being able to buy it some-day that made her hoard tubes of it. "I keep losing it," she told me, and laughed. "I can't seem to find a place for my lipstick to call home."

Mom laughed at herself about the lipsticks. "I'm a lipstick fanatic," she said one time. "It's too bad I'm not a Ubangi to use all of it up." She'd learned about Ubangis in the *World Book Encyclopedia* from when I'd been allowed special permission to check out a couple of volumes from the school library. They showed pictures of the different races, including people in Africa. I'd never seen anybody but a Caucasian in real life, and I found it fascinating, and showed it to Mom and Ben.

"If you moved to Africa, maybe you'd be a Ubangi, because everyone else there is," Ben said.

Mom and I cracked up. Ben always told jokes, but never got them.

"It wouldn't surprise me if I did. Move to Africa, that is," Mom said.

Then we all had a good laugh picturing Dad and his Manhattans in Africa.

EIGHT

"**D**ETROIT," ' DAD SAID, shaking his Manhattan pitcher. "We're going to Detroit."

Frank was singing, "Put your dreams away for another day. And I will take their place in your heart."

"Goin' to the big city, kids." He took a few sips.

Ben got that vacant look and sat down next to Mom. I jumped up and said hey I wonder what Detroit's like. Dad got in a good mood and gave me a cherry from his Manhattan.

"The Motor City. Gotta move on to move up, right, kids? Goin' to the head office. Hey, Vera, regional manager." Dad looked toward but not at Mom. "What do you say to that, Vera?"

Mom stared at the wallpaper and blew out a huge puff of smoke. Then she said, "Tell them to shove Detroit up their ass."

We moved to Detroit, of course, like we of course moved everywhere else, and Mom went out and joined the usual stuff.

Actually, we didn't move to Detroit, but to Harvard Hills Manor, a suburb so far out of Detroit it would have taken Dad

an hour and a half to get to work if he worked downtown—
which he didn't and nobody else I'd ever heard of did. So
much for our big city life.

I didn't care, though, because it would happen eventually
when I grew up and lived in a penthouse with pink walls and
curtains and pink mirrors and a bathtub with a telephone
next to it. As for Benny, I had my worries about him, like
everyone else did, because he was so "fragile," as one of his
teachers put it.

I tried to make Ben feel better, and the night before the
move after Mom and Dad went out for White Castle hamburgers, I mixed up some Orange Crush and Vernor's ginger
ale in Dad's shaker and said, "Cheer up, Benny Bear, it won't
be that much different."

We moved into a colonial house with green wall-to-wall. I
admitted to Ben that I'd lied—it was somewhat different from
Heather Wood Villa, but then he pointed out that the layout
was almost exactly the same as that of the house in Green-
brier Lawns, and we felt as if we could walk around this place
blindfolded.

But of course it had the little things that made it unique.
Like the kitchen wallpaper with little baskets of chicks
against a background of red and white stripes. I had to agree
with Ben, that against the bright red and yellow, the pink
refrigerator looked "like it got the flu."

"He's right," Mom said, blowing smoke and staring like she
hadn't noticed until Ben pointed it out.

"Tomorrow, tomorrow we get someone out here to show
us wallpaper," Dad said, his voice crisp with recent optimism.
Mom brightened a little.

I fixed my room up nice. I put my big map of the United
States of America on the wall and added a star. "We must
really be moving up in the world," I said to Ben, "because
we've already moved eight times, more than anyone I've ever
met who's still a kid."

The stars on the different cities made me feel important,
and I thought maybe the fact that Michigan now had two
stars—one for Ann Arbor, because I was born there—was a
good omen.

We'd moved just in time, because we had to start school two days later. The night before, I was nervous and restless and excited. I needed some candy to take the edge off and I had two dimes. If I could locate my bike, I'd go to a shopping center and get a Forever Yours bar and a pack of Good & Plenty's.

Dad turned on a cowboy show and settled into his chair, the old gray one with the permanent imprint of his head and shoulders, and Mom lay down on her side on the couch hugging a pack of orange Circus Peanut candies. I went out to the garage to search for my bike. It took a while to get through, but I found it, a trusty mount waiting for me behind a bunch of still-unpacked boxes, protected by an army of gardening tools.

As I was climbing on, I heard Ben. "Wait, Crosby, I'm going too."

I didn't see any harm in that, so I told him to get his sweater.

"No, Dad'll see me and say we can't go."

He was right and I figured it was his sore throat and not mine, so I said okay, if he could find his bike he could come along. It was getting dark, but we had good front lights and back reflectors. I heard him rattling around over on the other side of the garage, and then he whisper-shouted, "I got it."

Ben's front light was smashed—from the moving van, I guess—but he could follow me.

We glided down the driveway, a silent pair, passing the front window, where I saw Dad drinking his Manhattan and Mom biting into a Circus Peanut, her legs scissoring over the edge of the couch. From the street you couldn't see them anymore, just the jumping light of the TV. We rolled down the road. There was a white TV light in almost every living room.

We followed the winding streets past houses that were just like ours except for some minor detail, and some that were practically mirror images. On and on we rode, until we came to an almost-ritzy neighborhood. There were rows and rows of ranch houses and colonials, big ones where people would talk in low voices and be polite, like Claudia Cauliflower's family. For a moment, I felt a twinge of envy, but then, who could relax around people like that?

Then there were slightly smaller, older houses with dirt driveways full of old cars and motorcycles. People in there would be the type who yelled at and slapped their kids in public. I was glad I didn't live in the other houses. I was glad I had my parents, even if they were hard to live with. Who else would ever understand me like they did?

By now I was getting worried and thought we might as well give up on the candy and go back home.

It was uphill back to where the nice ranch houses were, and it took a long time, but we got there. There weren't any streetlights here, but there was a big moon you could wrap your arms around. I turned, and there was Ben in its light, following me like a little duckling. I loved him more in that instant than I ever knew I could love anyone.

But this wasn't the way we came. There were things I didn't recognize—a snarling dog, a camping trailer plastered with stickers. We rode some more and ended up at the edge of a woods. We turned around, and went on until we bumped over some railroad tracks and got into an area of average houses, like ours, and I thought we must be near home. But for the life of me, I couldn't find our street and I was getting just a little scared myself. Not of being lost, but of getting home so late Dad would know we'd been up to something. "We'd better stop and ask," I said.

So we went up to a house. An old lady and old man came to the door. I asked where East Tamarack Circle Way was.

"What?" the man said, opening the screen door.

I repeated it.

"I never heard of it," the woman said.

They got out a map of the metropolitan area. It wasn't on there.

"Maybe we'd better call your parents," the lady said.

"No," I said.

"Why not?"

Simple—Dad would have a conniption. "They're not home," I said.

Ben looked at me, confused. "Where'd they go?"

God, he was dumb. "Out for the evening. To a movie."

Ben shone his headlamp eyes on them and said, "She's lying."

His eyes glowed so wickedly I wanted to knock them out. Ben was trying to feel important. And he knew that in front of these people I wouldn't do anything to him. On the other hand, he knew I could beat the shit out of him the minute we got out of the place. I was beginning to think that Ben liked to live on the edge of excitement. No, *I* liked to live on the edge of excitement. Ben liked to go to the edge, then fall off. I didn't know for sure what had made him that way, but I knew we weren't exactly like American dream families so maybe Ben couldn't be an American dream kid. But then why was I trying so darned hard to be?

The man made a nervous laugh and headed for the phone, saying, "We'd better call the police."

"I just remembered the way," I said.

"Are you sure you children aren't lost?" the man said. They seemed sort of scared of us, the way people who don't have kids often are, like we might break or poop on the floor or something. So I easily bullshitted our way out of the house and hightailed it away on my faithful little bike. I didn't care if Ben got lost and was never heard from again. A couple of blocks down the street, I stopped and he was right behind me. He came to a halt and I went over and jerked him off his bike, which fell into the mud.

"That's the last thing we need, the police bringing us home," I whispered. "What'd you say I was lying for?"

"I'm scared."

"I don't think you're scared at all. I think you're just trying to cause trouble like you always do. Can't you be normal?" I shook him until his teeth chattered and he bit his tongue. I stopped and fished around in my pocket and found a piece of Fleer bubble gum. I gave him half of the piece but I kept the comic for myself and laughed like a maniac over it and refused to let him read it, then tore it into pieces and threw them into the dark.

As we went on, I started getting chilly. I realized I didn't know our house number, so even if I found East Tamarack

Circle Way, we still weren't home free. I hit the brakes and waited for Ben. "What color car do we have now?" I asked him. "Red and white, isn't it?"

Ben shook his head while he caught his breath, and then said, "No, that was in Des Moines, the two-tone Edsel Corsair he got a deal on." We looked around at the scene. It felt like we would be okay, as long as there were houses with their lights on. If someone came along and stabbed one of us, the other could scream for help.

"He's got a free company car, a Chrysler, and the lights in front look like it's saying 'Hi,' and in back it looks like sea gulls taking off."

"That sounds like what you said about the Edsel."

"No, it looked like it had something caught in its teeth. This one's green and white, a two-door. It's got whitewall rayon soundless year-round snow tires and a dent in the door from when Dad kicked it the time he locked the keys in it."

If nothing else, Ben was good at details. Maybe too good for his own good. I guessed it was his way of surviving; his eye for those things was like when you're on a ride at the carnival—you feel sick, so you stare at some little thing, a bolt on the gate holding you in or a dirt spot on your shoe, and you keep staring to shut out the swirling dizziness so you won't puke.

"Just look for the damn car, will you?"

"But it's in the garage, so we won't be able to see it."

My heart sank as I realized he was right. We followed the street, a quiet blacktopped one that made smacking noises as we rode over it. I saw a hill that looked familiar. We got off and walked our bikes. At the top of the hill, I turned and looked—there he was, his blond head glowing in the moonlight, his body all business pushing that little bike with all its dents from going in and out of moving vans, the chipped red reflector winking and doing its humble best to keep Ben safe. I felt like I wanted to take care of him; I felt a stronger-than-ever protective instinct stirring in me. I thought of the weird things he did, and I panicked. Was he going to end up like Eddie Snyder in Minneapolis—in reform school? Everyone had thought Eddie was crazy before he became just an ordinary juvenile delinquent.

I sweated and huffed and puffed from worry. Then, sure enough, the houses started looking right and it felt like we'd been here before, like we'd sweated here and breathed here, left our scent, the way wild animals in the woods do to find their way around.

We turned, then turned again and again, sometimes going around the same block and ending up in circles. The street names were nightmarishly confusing: West Tamarack Circle Way, then North Tamarack, then East Tamarack Way but not Circle Way, and a million other combinations that weren't ours.

We passed the house about four times without knowing it was ours. It was Ben who finally figured it out. "Look, Crosby," he cried out. "It's got those two flower boxes under the upstairs windows that make it look like the house has bags under its eyes. And dark bricks under the porch light, like a mustache."

I'll tell you, looking in that picture window at Mom and Dad, who hadn't budged since we left, I was so happy to be home that I almost didn't care about not getting the Forever Yours bar or the Good & Plentys.

Quietly, we made our way back to the garage. We tiptoed in through the side door and listened from the hallway. All we heard was the sound of Indians hooting and horses galloping.

"Let's get a drink of water," I whispered. "Then we'll walk through the living room to our rooms. Act like we never left and were just fooling around in the kitchen the whole time."

As we passed by, Dad turned and said, "You kids got any homework?"

Mom and I laughed and I said, "We haven't started school yet."

Dad looked like he really had forgotten that. He grinned. "When I was a kid, we got it all summer long, by God."

"And you had to walk ten miles to turn it in, through snowstorms," I said.

"Twenty," Dad said, "Through blizzards."

"In summer?" Mom said.

"Damn right. It got colder back then."

"Maybe it was the ice age," Ben said.

Mom and Dad about fell out of their chairs laughing. I was so relieved they hadn't noticed we were gone that I felt like jumping around and shooting a gun in the air like the cowboys on the TV were doing.

But then that other side of Ben emerged, the Ben who never could leave a moment alone, let it unfurl itself and lie there for everyone to enjoy. He got that look on his face, his eyes glowing like they did when he was trying to get attention, good or bad. "We got lost and people were going to call the police."

"What?" Dad said, turning quickly. He was furious. Maybe a little scared, too, if I wasn't mistaken. "The police?"

Dad had been nervous about the police ever since a neighbor called to report shouting and fighting at our last house.

"It was Crosby's idea," Ben said, looking scared now, too.

Dad jumped up. He seemed about ten feet tall and his hair stuck up on both sides like horns. His face was red and saggy. "Don't go out at night in a strange neighborhood."

"We never didn't have a strange neighborhood," Ben said quietly, like he wasn't sure whether he wanted Dad to hear it or not.

Dad did hear. The cowboys started punching each other and falling over saloon tables. I wished one of them would reach out of the TV set and punch Ben.

"Don't smart-off to me, and don't go out without telling us."

I ran to my room. Sometimes I felt sorry for Dad, but right now I hated him. And I hated Mom for sitting there and blowing smoke rings. I hated Ben for being weird and screwing things up all the time, and most of all I hated myself for not being able to figure out a way for all of us to be happy.

I lay there trying to shut out the noise of the TV set. Soon old Ben came in, his mouth plugged up with that thumb.

We lay on the bed, staring up at the dark ceiling. Finally, Ben said, "That was fun getting lost."

"Shut up."

"Want to play checkers?"

"No," I said. I got up and turned on the light and took out my *Mrs. Piggle Wiggle* book. It still had the little card with the due date stamped on it because we'd moved before I had a chance to return it to the Des Moines Public Library. It made me a little nervous to have it around. I'd never be able to return it, unless we moved back to Des Moines, and even then the fine would be so high it'd probably break Dad. Sometimes in the middle of the night I lay wondering if the police or FBI would show up on our doorstep one day.

Ben lay staring at my map as I read. Finally he said, "You glad we moved here, Croz?"

Guilt about the library book had blotted up my anger and I felt like I needed a traveling, portable best friend, so I decided to stop ignoring him. "I guess so. Are you?"

"I guess so."

"Move on to move up, right?"

"Yeah. Maybe you gotta get lost to make your new house feel like it's home, Croz."

He might have something there, I thought. Maybe we'd both gone out and gotten lost as a way of breaking in the new house.

Monday, August 21

≋

NINE

I ASKED A DOORMAN at one of the elegant hotels facing Central Park for directions to Columbus Circle, and went to take my first subway ride.

I sat across from a skinny young black woman sleeping on the bench in a pink jogging suit. The loose flesh of her abdomen was slumped in front of her, a belly that had once held and nourished a fetus, suffered labor pains to give it life. Where was her baby?

Why doesn't someone do something? Why don't you do something, Crosby Rawson? I do. I pay taxes. The only people who do anything more than that are the ones like this Antonia Williams. Saints. Not, I quickly reminded myself, that I was not grateful for the saints of the world, or Ben might not be alive.

If he was alive.

Ben. How did he stand this city? How did he survive? You forget, Crosby, maybe he didn't. The thought that maybe a person *could* bleed to death on the street came to me. And again, I saw blood spattered across a light background. I closed my eyes and saw red drops, perfect, round, shining

64

drops leading me on a trail to Ben. A Ben lying on a sidewalk, out of his misery. The distortion inside his head put to rest forever, slain like an ugly, gigantic dragon.

But it was only the memory of the cherry pie, the blood of the cherries that winter morning that I was seeing in my mind. Everything would be okay. I had to believe Ben was okay.

The train was fast and we were at Cathedral Parkway in no time. I emerged from the subway into a colorful neighborhood with ethnic restaurants along the music-filled streets and laundry flapping on high-rise lines. You could see the former elegance in the old prewar buildings, which stood high all in a row. I began to feel confident and more optimistic.

The cathedral was as big and as grand as a castle. It seemed almost a shame that this work of art should be wearing scaffolding all over; it was like catching a queen in her hair curlers. Yet all the same, it was a magnificent relic of the past, sky-high spires like hopes raised in a city of tombstone-shaped modern high-rises.

I walked around back and found a guard. I asked if there was a shelter for the homeless.

"Over there," he said, pointing to a little annex building with bars over the windows. "But it's for men."

I thanked him, and found that last statement slightly insulting, rather amusing, oddly touching. Walking over to the shelter, I thought of my little flamingo-colored condo, of my tiny balcony. I should feel grateful for it, but I wasn't, not grateful enough. Why wasn't I? Maybe because having a home seemed one of the givens in life.

Inhaling deeply, I knocked. All along, I had secretly hoped that Ben would have turned up by the time I got here, that everything would be fine and we could all go on our merry ways.

The door was answered by a black man wearing two enormous unmatched sneakers, both of them the left shoe. He mumbled something, then walked away. I stepped in and waited next to a clattering fan.

I checked to make sure Ben wasn't among the men, ten in

all, who were unpacking their bundles. No, no Ben, no one who resembled my beautiful, lost brother with his canary yellow hair and scared blue eyes.

Though they were not as wretched as some I'd just seen on the streets and in the subways, they certainly were examples of varying stages of decline; the fatigue on their faces was underlined by grim mouths and scraggly beards. Who were they? Where did they come from? How did they get this way? Had they been like Ben, gradually deteriorating? Were they crazy? Drug-addicted? Retarded? No good? Temporarily down on their luck? With their heads bowed and their backs hunched, they looked like big question marks as they moved about the room.

I stepped in further and leaned against a table, feeling conspicuous. Up close, I could see that some were young, in their twenties and thirties. My self-consciousness certainly was uncalled for; no one paid the slightest bit of attention to me. So I went over to the woman, whom I took to be Antonia, and said hello.

Unlike the men, she looked older up close, my age at least or maybe she even had a few years on me. A few twisting gray hairs in her eyebrows fit with her general appearance of neatness minus. A deep widow's peak framed a face drawn by cynicism and bitterness, but when she looked up at me, I could see a nearly erased trace of hope in the expression as well.

"New volunteer? Are you filling in for Barbara? Well, you can tell her if she misses again I simply can't schedule her any more," she said, and without waiting for my answer, "Go ahead and get something to serve for dinner out of the pantry over there." She handed me a ring of keys.

"No, I'm Ben's sister. Crosby Rawson."

"Ben's sister?" She paused, looking at me now as if following the path of a tiny insect crawling around on my face.

"I came from California to find him. I tried to reach you from home this morning."

She picked up a clipboard. "Come back tomorrow."

"Tomorrow? I just spent six hundred dollars to get here. And I have to sell a house and start law school by Friday." To answer her look, I added, "Not mine . . . I sell real estate."

"I see." She made a token smile and then went into an area set off as the kitchen. She began to heft boxes onto a table.

I went over and watched, not knowing whether to help, how to help. "You said Ben was hurt. I don't know what to do."

She paused and gave me a more sympathetic look. "I don't either. I suggest you contact the police, the hospitals. Go in person, they'll do more for you."

And she was off, helping the men pull cots around the room.

I stood with my arms crossed. I had been expecting Sister Theresa with the classy manners of Audrey Hepburn in *The Nun's Story*. Instead, here was someone who asks, orders me, in a moral sense, to risk my future in law school, then to risk my life as well in this lunatic asylum of a city, and she brushes me off and tells me to come back tomorrow.

But after a few minutes, I felt the fatigue of a long day and decided that I could easily talk myself into going to bed early.

"What time tomorrow?" I said.

"Eight, sharp." And she gave me the address of an office she used for counseling.

As I opened the door, she said, "Of course, I can always use an extra volunteer. I might find some time after lights out to help you think this through."

I looked around. One of the men was wearing a bride's dress and pirouetting around the room, but most of them were quiet and ghostlike. I thought about my dreary hotel room. I shrugged and said okay.

"Get a can of chili or something out of the pantry and heat it up on the hot plate. Randy, Gus, somebody show her where everything is."

Randy, a pale wisp of a man covered with tattoos, shuffled over, a cigarette bobbing from between his lips. I guessed him to be in his early thirties. He jerked his head for me to follow him to the pantry. I opened it, he pointed to a can of U.S. Govt. Surplus ravioli. I hadn't known they made cans that large, that they could make them that large. He got it down for me and I wrestled it with a can opener. I told myself to get into the spirit of things, that this was sort of like camp.

We scooped the ravioli into a pot. I held my breath at the

odor, trying to think of something that smelled good, like the dumb little petunias I'd planted on my patio under the cactus, and a lovely, aching homesickness washed over me.

While we cooked, the men set up cots. On each, Antonia set an institutional bleached-whiter-than-white sheet. I pictured Ben climbing into one, his long, stiff legs hanging over the end as he lay there. Then I pictured him climbing into beds as a child, his thumb in his mouth, half the time scared out of his wits because there was a screaming match going on in the living room.

Randy and I got out plates and plastic silverware. His tattoos, blue on pale flesh, reminded me of the grading stamps on meat. Up close, I could see that they were typical adolescent boy-pictures—fanged bats, charging bulls, knives dripping blood. Many of them were obsolete clichés of our generation—a peace symbol, Playboy Bunny ears, "Disco Sucks."

"I did some myself," he said. "I did tattoo work to support my real work. I'm an artist."

"Where do you work?" I said.

"Nowhere now. There isn't all that much call for the tattooing now anyhows. And my hands ain't steady like they used to be. I had a bout with drugs for a while. I still sketch, though."

"Will you draw something for me?"

He took a few sheets from a stack of paper with shelter rules and a pencil from a table and sat down next to me and began to draw. Randy seemed coherent and considerate in his own way. I almost asked him to talk about my brother, but something held me back. Maybe I was waiting for Antonia's guidance, maybe I was feeling protective of Ben's dignity and privacy. Or just maybe I was experiencing a more familiar and less generous emotion, not wanting to admit to myself or to anyone else out loud that my brother was in such circumstances.

I'd read that some people like Ben become artists instead of going crazy. Ben's teachers were always raving about his mimicry ability and singing voice. Several art teachers commented on his drawing talent. Mom joked that teachers pointed out those things because they couldn't say much positive about his other schoolwork. And anyway, big deal if he had possessed genuine talent—where we came from, artistic ability was to be treated as some sort of congenital deformity, to be operated on and somehow made to conform.

Randy held up his drawing, an adventure comic-type monster done in elaborate pen strokes. "I used to sit in school and draw these instead of listening to the crap the jerkoff teachers laid on us." He made several more.

"Very nicely drawn," I said, which they were. There was no creative talent that I could see, but then neither did there seem to be craziness. Randy was something else, something different from my brother, and I felt comfortable with him, almost safe.

Randy looked at his drawing with dull eyes, then pushed it aside and said, "Play cards until supper?"

As we played an interminable game of War, I was all ready to bring up Ben, invasion of privacy or not, embarrassing or not, when two other volunteers came in toting grocery bags and plastic-covered dishes.

The men came alive for the food and for the pretty women, who were students, I learned, at Columbia University. So people like this had been helping my brother.

I felt a flow of guilt. I searched for something consoling, something to take me back to my real life. I pictured the condo I was trying to sell, with sunlight blazing in through the skylight and dancing off the pool. I had to make the calls on it as soon as I got back to the hotel. As the young women put the food out, I mentally went over the plan—get the seller, Mr. Harboil, down another fifty thousand, get the buyers, the Loebroes, up that much. All quite doable, in my estimation. I'd get my thirty-five hundred dollar commission, and with the small scholarship, my savings . . .

As a contrast to Antonia, who smelled faintly of church basement, these volunteers exuded freshness, affluence, health. And in contrast to me, they weren't threatened by these people. Yes, while I was off being a cheerleader, trying to disassociate myself from the crazies and the lowlifes, off in California peddling Mexican adobe-look condos, Ivy League women with pointed little chins and eyebrows set in delicate concern had been helping the Antonia-saints care for my brother. I watched, feeling as if I were made out of some dingy, disposable plastic that was billed as a revolutionary new material in the nineteen fifties but which became obsolete a few decades later.

One of the students placed a couple of packs of Marlboros on the table. The men scrambled for them. Antonia swooped over and snatched them up. She handed them out, one to each man. "If you must bring these into my shelter, please ration them. This place already smells like an incinerator."

The room clouded up as the men smoked. Antonia walked around waving her hand in front of her face and making little coughs.

Randy came back and plunked down beside me. "You ain't mad, are ya?"

"Mad?"

"That ya lost."

"Well, maybe a little bit," I said. "I'd like a chance for revenge."

"No problem."

As our game of War began anew, I glanced up and saw that he was looking at me with a man's eyes, not a homeless beggar's. I saw that he was probably attractive still to certain kinds of women, in a thrilling, dangerous way, with that tendony body and narrow eyes that sized you up, eyes that were still a little fussy.

Antonia sang out, "Come to dinner."

The ravioli I had heated up was surrounded by the food brought by the students: potato chips, salad, baked beans with spices mixed in, brownies with chocolate icing. The students' food looked delicious, and I hadn't eaten anything except the three-bite ham sandwich the airline offered an eternity ago when we were somewhere over Nebraska, but I didn't think I could eat in this setting.

I wasn't the only one. A man with the industrial-strength ravioli dripping off his stubbly chin offered me and then the others a spoonful of the dark orange stuff from his dish.

"I just ate," I said, almost in a chorus with the other volunteers.

I was finicky, but not compared to Ben, or at least how he used to be. I wondered how he stood it. He was so fearful of germs that for a while he wouldn't drink out of a glass that anyone else had ever touched his lips to, even if it had been washed a thousand times in scalding water, or eat off a plate he suspected anyone might have breathed on.

The volunteers got themselves coffee and brownies. I did the same. Antonia had nothing. She sat with her head back, her widow's peak defining her face so sharply under the achy-harsh light that I knew it was being etched indelibly in my memory, along with this long, long evening.

The Columbia students chatted with us all. The little dark-haired one in L. L. Bean shorts was Sally, from Boston. She was majoring in political science and planning to go for an MBA. The one in the expensive peasant dress was Becky, from Scarsdale. The men acted like puppies, though a feral yellow glimmer like the one I saw in Randy's eyes for a moment would light up their glances every now and then.

I was desperate to talk about Ben. But what would they say? Would they roll their eyes and say, "Oh my God, that lunatic?" Or tell me stories about nutty things he did that I didn't want to hear about? Laugh at me? Think *I* was a lunatic?

After dinner, some of the men drifted off to smoke or sit on their beds or play cards. I went to Antonia and, in a low voice, asked her, "Would it be all right if I asked them about Ben?"

"Go ahead."

I stood in the middle of the room, nervous. "Ben Rawson, who used to stay here, was in a scuffle in an apartment building a few weeks ago. He was with Tyrone Davis. Does anyone know what happened to him?"

There was silence and a lot of head- and chin-rubbing. An older black man over in the corner sewing a tear in his jacket said, "Oh yeah, him. Always listenin' to that Walkman, them goddamned baseball games in Pittsburgh or Philadelphia or some goddamn place. All you'd hear was the noise, the static. Yeah, he was in Bellevue, last I heard from a buddy of mine."

"He's not now," I said.

The redhead in the wedding dress, Jack, boomed out, "Yeah, I knew Ben, I knew Tyrone. Nice guy, somewhat nice guy, in that order." He got up, took his paper plate to the garbage can, dumped it, mixed himself an instant coffee, and came back to the table. "How come you're looking for them?"

All eyes, including those of the two preppies, were on me. I sat down at the table with them. "Ben is my brother."

The first expression that registered on the faces of the two volunteers was disbelief. But then their eyes softened with sympathy as they also grew distant. They began to look me over, as if I'd just walked into the room, studying my shoes, clothes, hairstyle.

Then Sally clapped her hands together loudly and said, "I liked Ben. He was sweet."

"Yes, he could be very sweet," said Becky. "This is so awful. What happened?"

Antonia joined us. As I spoke, I remembered the feeling I had had when we were new in some town and Ben got in trouble immediately for opening the school bus emergency door. He'd said he was just checking to make sure it worked. Next day, he smeared banana all over the rear window. He'd said later it was because Mom had put a rotten banana in his lunch. I said I got one of those rotten bananas, too, but I wasn't about to broadcast it. He got a final warning the day he scraped dog shit off his shoe and onto the seat of the class president.

It had been bad enough being new, but with the whole world knowing my brother was like this, I could have jumped out one of those rickety windows. For weeks after that I sat alone on the bus, no one wanting to sit next to me on that big orange-brown seat, except Ben, whom I pushed off. Every time the bus stopped and groups of girls got on, clutching their books, laughing together, I felt as if the seat next to me were a huge mouth opening wider and wider, ready to shout that I was sitting there alone and the only one who wanted to share my seat was my nutso brother in back with the blue embers for eyes. I'd spent a lifetime proving to people that I was normal, super-normal, and I was ready to get out of this place and go back to the super normal world of California, but—I reminded myself—I had paid six hundred dollars to discuss Ben, so I continued.

"Maybe you should call the police," Sally said.

"Have you tried the hospitals, other shelters?" Becky asked.

I told them that I had, that I was planning to talk to several agencies, that I suspected that it was Ben's acquaintances who were likely to be the most help.

This was like being at the doctor's office. You don't want to tell the receptionist what's wrong. It's too personal. You don't even want to fill out a form she'll read. I wished these preppy-girl receptionists would go away so I could talk to this table-ful of doctors.

"Ben's sister, huh," Jack said, shaking his head and looking at me with his perpetual-surprise hazel eyes. "Hey, I got a sister too. I've got a family in California. My mom's a psychiatrist, old man's an Episcopal priest." He drank about half the coffee that was in his cup in one long slurp.

Sally and Becky cleared the dishes. "If I can do anything, let me know," Sally said, and went to her purse and got out a pen and paper. "I'll give you my phone number."

"Mine too," Becky said, writing hers down.

It was hard to continue disliking them just because they had a low-luster Ivy League polish I'd never have, former cheerleader or not, future USC Law Review editor or not. And it was hard to dislike people who did something nicer than I'd ever do, give out their phone number to a stranger from halfway across the country with a brother who'd just had his head kicked in so that the outside now probably resembled the inside.

The students washed pans and Antonia supervised the bathroom lineup while Jack and I cleaned off the table. Some of the men returned to play cards, and I asked for more details about Ben and Tyrone.

Tyrone, it was said, was a deft operator and Ben an innocent whom he both protected and exploited.

"I heard that Tyrone had Ben on phony crutches to panhandle on subways," the black man said, carefully putting his sewing things away.

"But Tyrone always split fifty-fifty," Randy said, muscling back in on Jack to get me to play another round of War. "I seen him do that with other guys. Fifty-fifty all the way."

Jack went and sat in a rocking chair and got it going so furiously I was afraid it would tip over backwards. "Know what I am?" he said, stopping. "I'm just plain crazy."

I wondered if Ben was this far gone now. "Well, I did wonder why you dressed that way."

"I dress this way to make a statement."

"What's that?"

"I wish I knew," Jack said.

Randy leaned over and whispered, "Antonia had a sneaker for that Ben. Imagine, someone like her got the hots for someone like us."

I pulled away. He broke into laughter. The idea of Ben involved with any woman was utterly novel—I had never once seen him interested in a girl, had never seen him look twice. Nor was he drawn toward men—not that I knew of. My impression was that he was asexual or sexually preadolescent, though it may have only been a convenient assumption on a subject I didn't much care to delve into any further.

I found myself surprisingly at ease by the end of the evening when Antonia announced half an hour until lights out. Talking was helpful. It made it seem as if there was some hope that Ben was okay and maybe not to be worried about too much, that my trip would prove to have been worthwhile. And it also had become quite clear that Ben was not alone in the world—no, I thought, looking around the room, he has lots of company.

I let that idea comfort me for a while, but then as I watched the men line up for the shower, I asked myself, "Why do I think this is not something to be worried about too much?"

The men climbed into their beds. I couldn't look at Jack or Randy. Children should be supervised as they go to bed, tucked in and given their teddy bears, but not grown men. I didn't want to remember them this way.

Antonia worked her way over to me with a cup of tea in each hand. We sipped as the men pulled their sheets up over them, and she said, "Now, about our Ben."

1959

D AD WAS SHAKING his Manhattan pitcher and he and Frank were singing "High Hopes."

Dad turned and said, "Hey, Vera, I got an offer from American Tires. Of course we'd have to move to, uh . . ." He took a sip and then exhaled loudly. "Ten percent salary increase, Christmas bonus, new company car. Not bad for a fellow from . . ." He took a long drink. "Hell, not bad for a fellow from anywhere."

Mom turned the TV up louder.

Every now and then Dad slipped up and referred to his childhood. Sometimes he could joke about it, but you had to let him be the one to mention it. If you brought it up, it was your funeral. Or if Mom did, it was everyone's funeral.

I was awakened at a quarter to three in the morning by a loud crash, some loud thuds, and then the sound of Dad hopping around the living room and shouting "Son of a bitch, son of a bitch, son of a bitch."

Mom said, "Okay, forget what I said about your mother. She's a goddamn debutante. She's Mother of the Year."

"Leave her alone, I said. Son of a bitch. I sprained my ankle. Maybe broke something."

I could hear him hopping around some more, and when he got near the hallway, I could hear the floor shaking. When he bounced toward the front of the house, money on the tables announced it, and when he got near the kitchen, the dirty dinner dishes on the table rattled and a spoon hit the floor like a warning alarm to the world that the house at 10967 East Tamarack Circle Way was about to go off like the atomic bomb.

Soon Mom's voice was frantic. "I'd better call a doctor."

"At this hour? Son of a bitch, son of a goddamn bitch. I'm going to have to go to the hospital. Find out where it is."

Dad kept hopping as Mom rustled through drawers to find a phone book. Finally she said, "Here's a phone book for . . ." and she read off the names of a bunch of towns. "Wrong book. Here's ours." A few minutes later, she said, "There's no hospital in this town. What's nearby? Grange Pointe Park? Willow Valley Farms?"

"Son of a bitch. How the hell would I know?"

Mom called a bunch of hospitals to ask if they were nearby. "Harvard Valley Manor's so new, they don't even know where it is."

"Harvard goddamn *Hills* Manor. Call the police."

"It's so embarrassing."

"Son of a bitch."

Mom got directions from the police. There was a lot of commotion with coats and keys and doors. You could hear the arguing all the way out to the car, then, with the sure slam of the car doors closing, the arguing noise went quiet.

"Chr-r-rysler, Chrr-r-r-r-r-rysler," the car went as it tried to start, and then it cleared its throat to say, "I'm off," and took a firebreathing deep breath as it backed down the driveway in preparation for the charge off to find a hospital.

When I thought of them in the car, I pictured poor Mom driving with that wide-open blank look she sometimes got, and Dad with that expression that said half the time he hated himself and his job and his boss and his life and maybe even his mother.

I felt like I'd just swallowed a sink full of dishwater. I wasn't going to cry, though, because I was afraid I wouldn't be able to stop.

Ben appeared in my doorway. We looked at each other. I began to feel the wonderful silence inside the house, a silence that felt like someone had just washed and put Unguentine and a Band-Aid on the swearing and yelling and crashing and hopping. I laughed and then said, "Hey, Benny Bear, they'll probably be gone for a long time. Let's see what's in the cupboard."

In the living room, we saw what had crashed—there was a huge, jagged hole in the screen door. They'd left the front door open and a couple of moths were trying to work their way in. We stared for a moment. "The hole is at kicking height," I said. "Maybe she locked the door while he was out, and then fell asleep."

Ben cried, "Look over there."

He was pointing at the hi-fi, whose front was smashed in, too. The wood was splintered and a speaker was all askew.

"It looks like it's talking out of the side of its mouth now," Ben said.

I was sick and sad for Mom and even for Dad; I was nervous for Ben and me. The only thing to do was just forget it, I told myself, and I inhaled about a gallon of air.

We went through the kitchen cupboard. There was no candy, but there was a marble cake mix. We made it—300 strokes by hand, I had Ben count for practice—and we stuck it in the oven.

We turned on the TV. There was an old black and white movie with people in evening clothes. I knew who the one with the squeaky voice was—Jean Harlow. She wore a silvery slinky dress and an ermine stole. I'd have an ermine stole someday, maybe, when I had my penthouse in the sky.

Happiness came over me as I thought about how many interesting old things there were—like this movie, and interesting new things—like towns and houses and schools. Then I felt a little sorry for Ben, because the more I expanded my mind to deal with it all, the less he seemed to grow—mentally, that is.

I put that worry out of my head along with my sick feeling about Mom and Dad. Maybe things would turn out fine. The question was, when did you know they'd turned out fine?

I decided I'd better get Ben interested in the movie. I

looked in the paper to see what year it was made. Nineteen thirty-two. I told Ben, "That's what it was like when Mom and Dad were kids."

"Did Mom wear dresses like that?"

"No, she was still a kid."

"That looks like Mom's hair."

"Mom's hair isn't that light. Jean Harlow's was platinum blonde. Mom said Jean Harlow dyed her hair." I didn't tell Benny that Mom dyed hers, too. If he knew, pretty soon the whole world would. "She said no grownup has hair that light naturally."

"Is my hair dyed?" Ben said.

I gave up on him as a conversationalist and just watched TV.

"I think Dad hates it when he was young," Ben said. "He wants to be like people on TV nowadays."

I didn't feel like thinking about Dad just then, but I couldn't force him out of my mind. The thing I really didn't want to think about with him kicking the hi-fi was that four of his toes were missing. Mom told me about how it happened. She said Dad's mother went out a lot, and one night she never came home. Dad was locked out. There was a snowstorm, and he didn't have boots or a hat. His toes and his ears froze that night. He fell asleep on the porch. In the morning, he walked all the way to the hospital. His ears were okay once they warmed up, but his toes got gangrene and the doctor had to cut off four of them. Now Dad wore socks all the time and made excuses not to go swimming.

The movie didn't make much sense, but it was still interesting because you saw how people were in the old days. Finally a commercial came on and there was a nice, happy woman who reminded me of the mother in Dick and Jane books.

"Middle of the night commercials remind me of driving through a scary new town and suddenly you see a happy neon sign," Ben said.

Another ad came on. It was for a floor wax. There was a big shiny house and happy kids and a Mom who thought scrubbing the floor was boring but necessary. "That's what Dad wants our house to look like," Ben said.

"Yeah," I said, enjoying the commercial. The house was so

pretty and neat. None of the doors were kicked in, and all the stuff was put away and no one looked confused.

Ben sat in the armchair next to the window and it was his job to watch for Dad's car so we could ditch the cake out the window and run to bed if necessary. In Dad's state of mind, he'd really kill us. Mine was to watch the cake and serve it.

There was no pop or milk, so I made us cocktails with Dad's soda water and Hershey's chocolate syrup and maraschino cherries, and we drank those and watched Jean Harlow and waited for the cake to bake.

$\approx$

E L E V E N

T HE MOONLIGHT through the barred openings made long stripes on the supply room walls. Antonia and I moved over by the window so we could see each other. A couple of the bars went across Antonia's face.

"Do you know where Ben was beaten up?" I said. "The police told me to go to the precinct stationhouse where the assault took place."

Her look said she didn't like me. But it was nothing personal. She didn't like anyone. Love, maybe, but not like.

"The Upper West Side was all he said, in an area of expensive brownstones. I'm sorry I didn't question Tyrone more carefully, but that's what happens, you become forgetful when you have to do the work of five people at half a person's salary." She composed her face into neutrality, and said, "You should be looking for Tyrone, too. He might know where Ben is."

There was a knock at the door. "Must be the all-night volunteer." She looked at her watch. "Late. Probably out partying somewhere." The word *partying* practically exploded out of her mouth. She opened the door to a young man who appeared, like the others, to be a student.

Antonia gave him a leisurely once-over while he pushed a rollaway bed out of the supply room and into the hallway to the room where the men were sleeping. He slipped under the blanket, clothes and all. Antonia turned out the lights and surveyed the scene with a satisfied face. "I used to have the same feeling when I put my dolls to sleep," she said quietly.

We went into the back room again and she sat down at a wobbly metal table and pulled out an address book from her purse. She wrote down names of people and agencies who dealt with the homeless.

"When I think of Ben," she continued, a tightness in her mouth suggesting a smile. "I think of that radio."

I grabbed for whatever that smile was offering. "His way of tuning into something he could relate to. Baseball was about the only way order ever registered itself in Ben's head."

She stopped writing briefly, as if she were going to comment, but then went on.

"What was Ben's mental condition when you last saw him?" I asked. "I guess you know that he had a pretty busy psychiatric history."

"A lot of our guests have psychiatric problems. Does that mean they deserve to rot on the streets?"

I had it now—it was my fault that those people were out on the streets, my fault, the fault of people like me, ordinary people trying to muck through their own lives.

She gave me the list, three pages in her big, messy handwriting. We went outside and stood by the door. The moon was small and fuzzy, the air cooler now, clammy even.

"No, they don't deserve to rot on the streets. If I thought that, I wouldn't be here."

She looked at me. That ant must have been crawling around on my face again. "Your brother seemed to be doing okay. A social worker at one of the agencies helped him find a job as a night watchman."

"Ben had a job?"

"For almost a month. The problem, of course, with those kinds of jobs is that they pay only four dollars an hour."

We began to walk. I was sorry but I was also impressed that he'd held down a job for a month. "Ben is still pretty coherent, then?"

"He had that job. He was fired, however, for not showing up a few times."

"It seems, then, that you think there was—is," I fumbled, "some hope."

"There's always hope. As far as I'm concerned, he may have a chance of making his way back to self-sufficiency, to a normal life. But then, I'm not a psychiatrist."

We walked in silence, then I said, "There really wasn't much normal about his life ever. Our life." Antonia and I may not have had chemistry, but she was the kind of person you could be honest with. She already disapproved of you, and yet there was something in her that would tolerate you no matter what. "On the other hand, sometimes I think it was hypernormal, if that makes any sense."

"No, it doesn't."

"It was so typically American, midwestern, suburban, postwar, any baby-boom adjective you want to throw at it, and yet it was anything but normal on the inside."

She made a barely audible sigh. "Was anyone's?"

For a moment she had me, but then I thought of Claudia Cauliflower, and I thought of Dean.

Yes, there are families that don't have brothers who flunked everything in school but could recite the beer commercials for every brewery between the Appalachians and the Rockies. Families that don't move every time the carpet gets a dirty footprint. And, I thought happily, there is a graduate of one of those families out there who wants me, who thinks I'm sensible and funny and cute and smart, who's so real and normal that he might actually run for public office and become a bona fide representative of a majority of the people, not the nut cases and misfits, but the real, average, normal people. And I missed my Dean-O so hard I almost couldn't breathe for a moment.

But Antonia didn't want to hear about people like Dean, so I hung my head and said, "I guess not."

"Don't get me wrong," Antonia said. "There were periods when Ben wouldn't talk to anyone. Weeks when he'd come in looking blank. It may have had to do with medication. Anyway, his friends on the street said he sometimes hallucinated, talked to himself. Couldn't stand to have anyone touch him. Complained that the sun hurt his eyes but wearing sunglasses hurt his head more. But everyone liked him, rational or not. He was on a friendly basis with a cathedral priest—he even had Ben help out in some of the services."

"Ben never had anyone like that, never had a teacher who took an interest in him, never had a friend, really."

She looked at me as if I'd just made a catty remark about him.

"Just me," I said.

"Well, he has friends now," she said. "You know, if you can find out where he hangs out, you can actually go looking for him. The men often have favorite streetcorners, parks."

Our feet scraped against the driveway, echoing against the walls of the mountainous cathedral.

"So," she said, "You sell real estate?"

"Yes." Why did I immediately feel that I owed her an apology? "But I'm going to stop when I'm in law school." Then I thought, dammit, it's honest work. "I'm pretty good at it, even if I don't much like it. My father says I'm a born saleswoman. My Mom says I'm a born phony."

"Well, just don't get me started on real estate," she said. "I have some pretty definite opinions."

I wasn't at all anxious to get her started. "Is this—the shelter—your full-time job?"

"No, I do private counseling and I teach a class at City College. I like to think that I'm doing the world a little bit of good." She looked over at me, "Of course, some people don't care about that. But there are enough of us old-fashioned sixties types left who do."

I'd had enough of the sanctimonious Antonia P. Williams for one night, but we had another hundred feet or so until we got to the street. The cathedral from this angle was almost frightening in its grandness. "How long is the scaffolding to be up on the church?" I asked, to change the subject, to get us to the street.

"We feel that spending money on the appearance of the cathedral is wrong while there are still homeless, hungry people in New York. So it will stay up until the poor are no longer with us."

"That's very admirable," I said. Another twenty feet to the

sidewalk, then freedom. "It's a shame, though, that the beauty of the building is hidden," I said to make conversation.

Her upper lip wrinkled. "Are you saying that you think a building made of stone is more important than people? Than feeding and sheltering people? If so, it's a pretty despicable attitude."

I thanked her for everything and hurried off, the list tight in my hand, hoping I wouldn't have to see Ms. Antonia P. Williams, bitch angel, again.

1960

≈≈≈
T W E L V E

A FTER I FINISHED fifth grade, Dad was fired. He quickly got another job with a company that made electric garage-door openers and we moved to Sandalwood Springs, near Columbus, Ohio.

Since we didn't have any friends here, Ben and I just hung around the house watching marathon television. We watched shows like "Beat the Clock" and "Who Do You Trust" because we thought Bud Collier and Johnny Carson were funny, and soap operas not so much because they were entertaining as because they gave the day a sort of rhythm in their predictability and slowness. Mom watched them too but made fun of the acting all through the shows and just about ruined them for Ben and me.

She also made fun of the singers Dad and other people her age liked, respectable ones like Pat Boone and Andy Williams. She loved the sexy teenage stars—Elvis Presley, Frankie Avalon, Jerry Lee Lewis—so most afternoons she was slumped on the davenport with me as "American Bandstand" jitterbugged across the TV set.

One morning when Mom was listening to the radio and putting the dishes away in the cupboard, one of her and my favorite songs, "Turn Me Loose," by Fabian, came on.

Ben said it sounded like a lot of shouting. Mom said, "Wait until you're a teenager. It'll sound like a symphony to you then."

Ben nodded. "Will I like it better than Mozart's symphonies?"

That one really threw Mom for a loop. "What?"

"Mozart, that guy that composed 'Jupiter.' "

Mom and I burst into laughter. Mom explained that Jupiter was a star or a planet or something and not classical music. Ben started humming what he said was the *Jupiter* Symphony.

"Where'd you ever hear of someone like that, anyway?" Mom asked.

"In my last school. Mrs. Benson played one of his records."

Mom didn't argue about the title anymore, but said, with both disbelief and belief in her voice, "You liked it?"

"I told the teacher it made lacy lines inside my head. She said that's what it's supposed to do."

Mrs. Benson had told Mom that Ben was good at the flutofone and should take a real instrument. So Mom had actually let him take violin lessons, since they were free. But you could tell she wasn't expecting something like *this* to come of them.

When we moved in, we got the usual greeting note from the milkman and garbage man and paperboy. We also got one from an orange-juice man.

We'd never heard of having orange juice delivered before, but Mom said it was a good idea because orange juice had vitamin C and they'd discovered that vitamin C prevents colds.

"I think we should do it for the kids' health," Mom said to Dad.

"What's that?" Dad said. His face was wrinkled in concentration as he tried to hear Chet Huntley over her talking and read the bills at the same time.

She showed him the printed note from the orange-juice man. He had signed it, "Your personal delivery representative, Clarence T. Dubeaurivage."

"Tell Clarence he's going to have to be someone else's personal delivery representative," Dad said, and went back to Chet and some bills that had been forwarded from Harvard Hills Manor.

"John, would you please listen to me?"

"We can't afford it," Dad said.

"Oh, we can't afford it. I spend half my time looking for sale signs. I could get through life not being able to read any word in the English language other than *Sale—On Sale, Big Sale, Fire Sale, Clearance Sale.*" Mom didn't really sound mad; she was just muttering to herself as she fumbled for a cigarette. "What am I supposed to do? Wait for a sale before we can drink orange juice for breakfast again?"

"Maybe he'll have a Clarence Sale," Ben said. We all cracked up at that, and it put Dad in such a good mood that he said okay to the orange-juice delivery.

And then Ben said, "Dad, why do you like Shit Huntley?"

He had that look in his eyes. Dad jumped up out of his gray chair and swatted Ben. Everyone went back to their corners and that was the end of one of the few good moods everybody had had together lately.

Clarence wore a white shirt with his name sewn on the pocket in script, and black pants that had been pegged—you could see the big stitches in thread that didn't match. His hair was slicked back on the sides so that it looked like he had wings on his head.

Twice a week now, Clarence and Mom would chat in the doorway, Clarence's foot keeping the screen door open, Mom's long arms awkwardly holding three half-gallon bottles of O.J.

One morning, Mom brought up his accent. "Most of the people around here sound like southerners to me," she said. "And I find that it's rather charming."

Clarence said, "Mrs. Rawson, you have a most interesting accent, too, if I might say so. May I ask whereabouts you moved in from?"

"You name it," Mom said, laughing.

"You're gonna make me guess, I expect." Clarence said, laughing, too. "Well, now, if I had to say, what with that blonde hair and all, I b'lieve I might say 'twas Sweden, or Minnesota."

Mom laughed loud, but there was something else in that laugh.

"Am I right? One of them Scandahoovian countries, huh?"

"Well, you're in the right latitude, anyway," I said.

He gave me a surprised look, like he'd just noticed me. Then he pretended to be perplexed and scratched his head. "I can tell you go to school, little girl. Straight-A student, am I right?"

Ben was getting irritated. "Mom, can we have lunch now?"

Mom started looking nervous and Clarence straightened. "Well, Mrs. Rawson, you have an extremely fascinating accent, and I'd like very much to put your voice on my tape recorder."

"Goodness, whatever for?"

"Maybe you could get a job doing radio commercials. Or TV. Maybe I could take it to our advertising department. Yes, a nice way of talking. Re-al pretty." His voice had developed a really thick twang now.

"Wanna do my voice?" Ben said.

He looked at Ben like Ben had just asked what the square root of ten million four hundred and thirty-three was.

Finally he said, "Why, uh, you're not old enough to have yourself a accent yet, young man."

It was true that Mom had a few speech peculiarities that Ben and I didn't have, because we'd never lived anywhere long enough to start talking the way the locals did. Mom had a north midwestern accent, and pronounced "a" and some "o's" as if they were two syllables long. Around here, the "a's" were like in "hay," and certain "o's" sounded like "uh," as when they pronounced the state in which we now lived, "Uhiuh."

"What do you say, Mrs. Rawson?"

"Maybe some time."

After that, when Mom saw Clarence's delivery truck outside, she'd go into high gear and look for a lipstick, tearing bobby pins out of her hair as she rushed around. If she was still in her robe, she'd put on clothes, usually her blue pedal-pushers that made her legs look dainty, or her plaid Jamaica shorts that made her look youthful and collegiate.

After a few weeks, Clarence was closing the door behind him and stepping in when he talked to Mom. Once she asked what kind of name Dubeaurivage was. He said both his names were French. She said he looked a little like Elvis. He said his names might be French, but like Elvis, he was an all-American boy.

Finally, the big day came and Clarence actually brought the tape recorder over. It was cumbersome and heavy, with reels of tape just waiting to hear Mom's accent. He looked around for a place to put it, but all the tables were full of coffee cups and ashtrays and clothes and papers. He asked if he could "park it" on top of the TV. "Okay, if I turn this off, kiddies? Maybe you can go out and play for a while."

Ben took his thumb from his mouth and said, "No-o, Mom, help."

Mom hurried over. "Oh, no, we can't interrupt the children's television-watching."

I could see how nervous she was. I never could figure out why Mom was so thin, what with all the bridge mix and other goodies, but the tendons in her wrists stuck out like banjo strings as she protected the Off button, and her neck got long and skinny as she raised her chin. Mom's face looked like a scared little kid's. It was a lot like Benny's face sometimes.

Clarence laughed quietly down at the floor and said, "Well, now, maybe we can do it in the kitchen, then, Mrs. Rawson."

"I don't think," she began, but just then she was saved by the phone. I'd never heard her so eager to talk to Grandma. She stayed on for a long time, and finally Clarence grabbed the handle of his tape recorder, grunted as he picked it up, and left.

The day did come when Mom said all right he could tape-record her voice. So the following Tuesday, Clarence hauled in that big tape recorder and told Ben and me to go out to the truck and drink all the orange juice we wanted.

"There's some paper cups for free samples right next to the driver's seat," he said, not even looking at us. "Just be careful you don't touch any thingamabobs or jobby-doos on the dashboard."

In the truck, Ben and I made believe we were the orange-juice man on his delivery route. "It's neat to drive standing up," Ben said, twisting the wheel. "It makes you something special."

We climbed around in back and as we drank grape and orange juice, we counted all the bottles. It was cold like winter and we chased each other around the cartons, pretending they were ice forts. Then we went back up front. As I pretended to drive, Ben reached to the floor for a clipboard of papers with check-off marks for deliveries. We wrote a bunch of extra checks, and then Ben picked up the other papers on the floor and found some magazines under them.

At first I couldn't believe it. They had pictures of naked people playing volleyball and you could see the women's saggy boobies and hair and the men's things. I felt like I was going to throw up. Ben just kept turning the pages. I was so upset I almost cried.

I had to get inside and warn Mom about Clarence. I ran up to the door. Mom was in a corner with Clarence giving her his Elvis look and acting like he was going to kiss her. She looked like she didn't know whether she wanted him to or not, and I nearly threw up for sure this time.

As soon as the screen door slammed behind me, Clarence turned and got an angry look and said, "Did you kiddies get all the juice you wanted out there? There's some potato chips in the doohickey next to the—"

"Mom," I yelled. "Benny drank too much and he's sick. He's about to throw up grape juice all over the truck, all over the papers and magazines in the front. And he's trying to drive the truck."

"Holy be-Jesus," Clarence shouted, running for the door.

I was too upset to tell Mom what we'd found. I didn't think I ever could, it was so creepy, and I decided to forget about it so I wouldn't think about the pictures when we played volleyball in gym class.

But leave it to good old Ben, who at dinnertime piped up with, "There were people without their clothes on."

"Where was that, Ben?" Dad said.

"In the orange-juice man's truck."

Dad looked at Ben like he usually did, like Ben was just saying dumb-little-kid things that he'd outgrow some day.

But I caught a look in Mom's eye as we exchanged glances, and nothing more was said about the naked magazines that night.

The following week, when Mom saw Clarence's truck pull up outside, she ran and locked the door and turned off the TV.

"No," Ben cried.

But she jerked his arm and pulled him to the bedroom and waved for me to follow. "Shhh. Pretend we're not at home." She dragged us into a closet.

Clarence rang the doorbell. He rang again and again, then knocked for a while. Then he went around to the side door and rang and knocked. We were all sweating, and Mom and I were trying not to crack up. Mom was her old self now, acting almost like she was a kid, too. She held her hands over her mouth, and made a muffled laughing sound. Then we heard Clarence tapping on a couple of windows in the living room and calling out, "Mrs. Rawson, oh Mrs. Rawson."

Mom opened the closet door just a bit and then froze. I looked out the crack. Clarence was peering in the bedroom windows now. When Ben put his eye to the crack and saw, he cried out a little. I thought it was all over, but Clarence didn't seem to hear.

We were all shaking and excited by the time we heard the delivery truck make that moaning noise and chug off.

"Ooooh, boy," Ben said when we emerged from the closet. His face was glowing and hot. "I never knew getting orange juice could be so much fun. Do they deliver pictures of people's weewees if you want them to, Mom?"

But she was already fogging out. "I suppose so, Benny." She came back and looked at me and said, "I guess we can go back to good old-fashioned pills for our vitamin C."

When Dad came home that evening, Ben ran to him and said, "We had a scary day. We hid in the closet from the orange-juice man so he couldn't tape-record Mom's accent."

Dad loosened his necktie and said, "Fletcher called me in. The S.O.B. told me if sales aren't up this quarter, he's letting three of us go."

He disappeared into the bedroom, then came out in his at-home clothes and his at-home face. We moved out of the room as Frank kicked on with "They Can't Take That Away from Me."

Mom was scared to tell Clarence that we wanted to stop getting orange juice, and we had to hide every time he came. She seemed relieved later when Dad asked how much the orange-juice bills were running and she could tell him it was kind of expensive after all.

Ben said, "Let's get naked pictures delivered in the milkbox instead."

"What?" Dad said.

"Pictures of people playing volleyball with no clothes on."

Dad's face got red and his forehead wrinkled. "Benjamin, I ought to warm your little fanny for talking like that."

Mom told Dad he was being a prude, that Ben was exhibiting a little boy's healthy attitude about you-know-what.

"What if he talks like that at school? That's half his problem, you let him get away with things."

"I read that it's perfectly normal for boys to ask about s-e-x."

"What the hell is going on? All of a sudden we're a family of deviates." Dad's voice trailed off into the air, showing he wasn't in the mood for an argument. So of course Ben edged into his softening mood and told about the magazines in the orange-juice man's truck.

"Vera, do you know what he's talking about?"

Mom laughed and told Dad about Clarence and his tape recorder.

Dad yelled that he was working his ass off while she ran around acting like a teenager. Ben and I slipped off into our rooms.

Pretty soon he was ranting about the office ass-kisser.

"Winklestrom's been bucking for that job ever since he laid eyes on me, his biggest rival for it. He knew I'd get it."

"Then how do you explain the fact that *he* got it?"

"He's a phony, that's how I explain it."

Mom made a stab at consoling him. "Your turn might come."

"Ah, they play favorites. S.O.B. suck-ups. They've got money. Them and their goddamn parties in their goddamn house with their goddamned backyard swimming pool with the crenulated canopy."

I thought about how goddamn hard life sometimes was.

"That swimming pool isn't big enough to take a bath in."

"It's a swimming pool, isn't it?"

"And the canopy is plastic."

"Fiberglass."

"Oh, so what?" Mom sounded tired.

"The corporation doesn't care about merit. I called Chuck Wylie at Parker Tires. He said the offer in their PR department is still good."

"You tell Wylie Coyote that I'm not moving again. I'm making a home for the first time since I left Mother's."

"I'm not making enough money."

"Enough for what?"

"Enough to keep you in cigarettes, for one thing."

Dad threw something at the wall and Mom said she was calling the police.

"Tell them to pick me up at the Holiday Inn bar."

From my bed, I heard the keys jingling, the hangers in the closet dancing frantically, the door slam, and the car back down the driveway. During these fights, I never quite relaxed until the car shifted into forward gear and disappeared down the street. It was funny, because I always knew the sound of our own car. Dad usually had a new company car, sometimes for only a few months, but Ben and I could always tell the sound of our own.

Later, Mom came into my room. She'd put on her nightgown, the faded yellow nylon one with a safety pin holding up one of the straps.

"Couldn't sleep," she said.

Pretty soon Ben was there, too, wanting to hear a story.

"Did I ever tell you about the junior prom?"

"Did you go with someone who looked like Elvis Presley?" Ben asked.

"Hardly. His name was Norman Gipson and he was very shy. He lived on a duck farm. Grandma made me the sweetest blue dress. Satin. And even though it was the Depression, Norman managed to scrape up the jack to rent a tux."

"Did he wear a flower in the buttonhole?" I asked. "Like they do on TV?"

"He had a flower all right, but it didn't do him much good. He still smelled like ducks."

She lit her cigarette and let Benny blow out the match. She threw the match into the air and it landed on the powder blue hat that she'd gotten me for Easter that I kept on a little stand on top of my dresser.

"What does a duck smell like?" I asked.

"A whole farm of them smells worse than anything. Worse than a house where they have a bunch of dogs. Even worse than cats. Mother took me aside and whispered, 'Vera, he's wearing work boots.' I looked, and sure enough, he had on clodhopper boots with soles you could sail across Lake Superior on, covered with mud and duck shit."

"Why didn't he wear shoes?" Ben wanted to know.

"I guess he couldn't afford them, Benny. So Grandma took me to her bedroom and sprayed me with her eau de who knows what. 'There, now you won't smell ducks,' she said. She kept spraying, and the atomizer got stuck. We got to laughing so hard she didn't think to aim it in another direction until my dress and neck and hair were soaked."

Mom hugged me and I felt good. Sometimes Mom was my traveling, portable best friend.

"I smelled like a French cathouse."

"What's a French cathouse?" Ben said.

Mom winked at me like I would know. "Never mind, sweetie."

"Whatever it is," I said, "It doesn't stink as bad as a duck farm."

Mom laughed to herself. All her mascara had been wiped, or cried, off, and she looked old. "I left the house like that, and he took a sniff of me, and said, 'What's that strong odor, hair pomade or antiperspirant?' And he rolled down the car window—because *I* smelled."

She and I laughed; Ben looked like he was hearing the most serious story in his life.

"I hurried in to the school gym and had the time of my life, just dancing and dancing with everyone else."

Mom got up, a cigarette faithfully burning away between

two fingers in her right hand, and said to a pretend partner, "Sure, I'll dance with you," and she started swirling around the room. You could see her still-young body as a shadow under the snagged nightgown with the safety pin in it, the cigarette smoke swirling in a trail like the special effects in a movie dance scene.

She didn't dance the new way, the rock 'n' roll way, but with her arms up like she was holding someone. Her dancing-and-remembering smile was innocent, like in the old black and white movies. Nineteen-sixties teenagers' expressions were knowing and sly. There was as much difference between her smile and that of today's rock 'n' roll teenagers as there was between the expression of Africans in the *National Geographic* and the Negroes we'd seen downtown in Cleveland.

"I danced with everyone else. And I was elected queen of the dance and I got to wear a beautiful tiara and cape."

I could see it, I really could—Cinderella Mom.

She bowed and then flopped down on the bed and talked some more. Finally, with the slumpy posture of a girl at a slumber party who doesn't want to go to bed, she got up and told Ben to go to his room.

I went to sleep seeing Mom dancing around in a shiny blue dress and sprinkling her cherry red lipstick laughter all over the room. It came to me then, the truth about Mom. When she met Dad in Detroit, he was probably a decent enough Prince Charming for her. He might have been exciting, someone a little older who wore the right kind of shoes. And if her life was all confusion and nothing had turned out the way she'd planned, at least she didn't have to be the prettiest and smartest girl in town with no one to dance with except boys who smelled like duck turds.

1961

THIRTEEN

O NE MORNING Mom found a note that had been slipped under the front door. She opened it, and as she read it, her face rearranged itself. Calmly she went and poured herself a cup of coffee, sat down, and reread the note. She looked off in the distance, her face tensed like she was going to cry. But instead, her face became contorted and stiff. She sat for a minute, whispering to herself.

Suddenly, she hurled her cigarette pack at the wall, watched the cigarettes scatter, then went and picked them up. Soon she was storming around the kitchen looking for matches. She turned on the stove and stood waiting for it to get hot, even though we had a gas and not an electric stove this time and she didn't have to wait to light her cigarette.

"Those goddamn idiots. Who do they think they are, anyway?" she said, and started calling them more names, her voice growing louder as she slammed around the kitchen cupboards in search of a box of bridge mix.

I picked up the note. It read:

Dear Customer:
   It has been brought to our attention that your refuse was once again improperly disposed of this week. Cans and bottles

are to be separated from other items; paper will not be picked up and must by city ordinance be incinerated in a legal receptacle.

This is a <u>second</u> notice. A <u>third</u> notification will result in immediate discontinuation of pickup service.

It was signed by the president of Rick's Scavenger Service.

"God damn them," Mom said, picking up the notice and waving it as she stomped over to the phone. She cleared her throat loudly, then with a shaking voice asked the operator for the number of Rick's Scavenger Service, even though it was on the note. She was put on hold and was hysterical by the time she was transferred around to the right person.

"Do you think I have time to worry about stupid things like garbage? That's your job, not mine. I have more important things to think about." She took a couple of mighty puffs of her cigarette, then added, "And you have a damn monopoly on the town anyway, so you've got to pick up the garbage even if I empty the goddamn contents of my refrigerator all over the lawn. It's my right as an American citizen. Believe me, if there were any other garbage company, I'd have gotten them long ago." She threatened to sue them, and hung up.

Mom started leafing through the yellow pages under Attorneys. Ben came out of the bedroom. "Crosby," he whispered, "Is the garbageman mad at us again?"

I nodded and went out for a walk because the whole thing was making me depressed.

Problem was, I knew how Mom felt about garbage. It was more than just being in trouble with Rick's Scavenger Service that got to Mom. It was that not knowing how to throw out the garbage marked you as an outsider, as a dirty, un-middle-class, un-American outsider. Mom knew she didn't want to be considered dirty and low-class, but I don't think she was absolutely positive that she wanted to be middle-class American squeaky-clean. She was confused and frustrated as much as she was insulted.

The garbage was about the most sensitive issue there was for Mom. Wherever we went, it seemed we were in trouble with the garbageman. The rules changed everywhere. In Heather Wood Villa, you'd had to wrap the food and other perishables separately from the cans and bottles, and you were limited to three bags. In Upper Sterling Meadows, you combined everything, but you had to have a specific type of can and you could only have two and they had to have the lids on tight or you'd get fined. In Crestwood Valley Cliffs, you were allowed an unlimited amount of refuse, but it all had to go in bags and be out on the curb by six A.M. the day of pickup. In Harvard Hills Manor, you had to put leaves and grass clippings in a specific bag and regular garbage in cans and there were two pickup days a week and you could put the cans and bags out any time you wanted. In Tower Brooke Estates you couldn't use bags at all, and in Park Villa Manor, you could do anything but the catch was you had to give the men a tip or a six-pack of malt liquor or they'd conveniently forget to pick up your trash or else spill it all over your lawn and leave your cans dented and lying on their side.

I didn't have time to let myself get down about this, I decided. Things like putting out the garbage automatically and not having to think about it were luxuries we just weren't able to afford in life yet, and I was going to have to face it. When I grew up, I probably wouldn't know how to do it either, since I wouldn't be a native of anywhere. But then my personal maid could worry about separating garbage and getting it out on time, and that would be a tremendous load off my mind.

Dad tried to tell Mom that it didn't matter, that not knowing the territory was sometimes the price of trying to get ahead in life.

He also said we should occasionally try to get a little culture. A *little* bit.

One Saturday afternoon in the grocery store Dad told Ben and me to pick out two things each. He and Mom were going around laughing and joking and getting unusually good things, like fresh Italian bread, steaks, corn on the cob, and real butter, because he'd gotten a good commission the day before.

At the checkout, he noticed that they were giving a big discount on classical records. Each week they offered a different selection. That week it was Schubert's *Unfinished* Symphony. Dad picked it up and looked at the cover and read

about Schubert. Looking at him, his face all concentration,
sort of innocent, I felt a big surge of what other people called
love but which our family didn't know what to call.

"You know what, Vera, we should get these. Dave Dough-
erty has a big collection of classical music."

"How do you know?"

"I know because it impressed the hell out of Chuck Lines-
lyme when he and his wife were invited over for cards."

Mom took a carton of Viceroys off a shelf, pulled out a pack
and opened it. "What's going to happen to Sinatra? Is he
getting the boot?"

"No, I mean it, Vera. Ben has an aptitude for classical
music. We should get him a piano." But that trailed off, because we could never afford a piano and even if we could, we
couldn't afford the lessons, and even if we could afford them,
there were other things we needed more, and even if we got
those, I could just see Mom getting Ben off to lessons and
then making him practice regularly.

"Anyway, it will help him appreciate it more. Crosby, too.
And I like the stuff for relaxation."

Mom pulled a cigarette out of the pack and lit it and threw
the match into the gum display. Dad took the record and put
it on the checkout counter with the groceries he was taking
out of the cart.

"There's one born every minute," Mom said.

Dad's face got a little red and his acne scars flashed, but he
didn't respond.

At home, Dad put the record on the hi-fi. It was real
gloomy-sounding. Even Ben didn't like it. Dad played it as he
drank Manhattans and made marinade for the steak and ran
inside and outside to check on the charcoal fire.

Mom was trying to watch TV. "John, I've had enough of
that record. It's so dreary I could kill myself."

"You don't know beautiful music when you hear it." He
picked up the album, reread the label, turned it over.

"What's it called?" Ben said.

"Rawson's Death Dirge," Mom said.

"Schubert's *Unfinished* Symphony," Dad said.

"Well I can sure see why he didn't finish it," Ben said.

Dad laughed and turned it up louder. Mom turned the TV

up louder. Pretty soon the house was like a carnival, with the TV blasting, Cheyenne Bodie—whom Mom had a crush on—threatening to shoot a bad guy, women screaming and the bad guy saying you can't run me out of town, the violins screeching and horns blowing like it was doomsday and then shooting and cattle stampeding. Mom and Dad both went and turned their stuff up even louder, and the windows started rattling and I was afraid they'd break. I ran to close the back door after Dad went out, so the neighbors wouldn't hear.

The next thing I knew, the door boomed open and Dad came in and said, "Bud Thompson came over and asked if we could turn it down. Goddammit, Vera, you and your cowboys. With all this confusion, how do you expect me to get dinner finished?" He hurled the barbecue brush at the TV. A red smear traveled down Cheyenne Bodie's face—he looked like he'd been shot.

Mom jumped up and shouted, "I'm tired of you and your phoniness. I don't care what the neighbors think, I don't care what your boss thinks, I don't care if you finish dinner, and I don't care if Schubert ever finishes his goddamned symphony." And she went over and ripped the needle off the record and sat back down.

With that, Dad grabbed the record off the hi-fi and took it outside and threw it into the barbecue.

I went to my bedroom and Ben was in there already. He was on the bed, staring up at the wall.

I lay down next to him, hating Dad. And yet I couldn't help feeling a little sorry for him, too, because after all he was just trying to get ahead in life and wasn't getting any help at all from the rest of us.

≈≈

F O U R T E E N

T HERE WAS A BIG blowout fight over whether we could afford to have the davenport recovered, and Dad left in a torrent of gravel.

Next morning, Ben woke me. He grabbed my nightgown sleeve and said in a hoarse voice, "He killed her."

My heart started thumping and my stomach compressed. "What?"

"He killed her."

"Mom? Dad?"

"Yeah."

"How do you know?"

"There's blood. Everywhere."

I didn't really want to see it, but then Ben was always mixed up and I mostly didn't believe him. On the other hand there was something smart, intelligent, about Ben, too. I got out of bed and cautiously followed him to the hallway.

Sure enough, there was a trail of blood leading both ways down the hall. Big blobs of bright red blood, in perfect round spots the size of pennies, which left an almost perfect pattern. It stopped at Mom and Dad's bedroom door.

Without breathing, I turned and followed it to the living

room. Ben walked behind me, doing the opposite, exhaling noisily as if he were breathing for me. In the living room, the blood beaded in tiny blobs because we had a nylon carpet now.

I stood very still. It felt like someone was watching us. And yet it felt as if we were on another plane, up in an atmosphere of light and unreality, where we would not feel pain if the fiend stabbed us, too.

Ben was looking up at me, and I suddenly didn't feel frightened, I felt light, superhuman, standing on a foot of cushioning air. Then a sweep of nausea went through me. The morning sun was shooting in through the low windows. It became a spotlight on the crumbs that littered the dingy, unvacuumed carpet, on the perfect little balls of blood here and there. I looked up, facing the sun which was forcing me to see. Then I noticed that snow had fallen the night before, and great hunks of the brilliant, too-white stuff sat on our window ledge and our neighbor's, dazzling like costume jewelry. It hurt my eyes so penetratingly that my brain ached.

The snow made everything seem quieter than normal, even for a Sunday morning. The fiend was so quiet that the sun had overpowered him, too.

A car went by with snow chains clinking. A normal, happily jingling family going by. Even with the disaster here, life would go on outside. Yes, there was a life outside. I felt a big flow of oxygen.

I got up my nerve, and followed the trail of blood to the kitchen.

The red blobs were bigger there. I dared to look up, fully expecting to see a deranged killer ready to strike—whether the killer was Dad or not didn't matter. But I didn't see anyone, just the butcher knife on the counter, covered with red blood.

But that wasn't blood. It looked too sticky, too red to be anything real, anything as natural as blood. And then I saw that it was only cherry pie. I laughed nervously, then Ben joined in as he saw the pie on the counter.

It was the kind of pie that's artificially red, with waffly whipped cream on the top. The kind of pie you buy at the grocery store in a box.

A thick pool of the "blood" covered the spot on the aluminum pan where a piece had been cut out. Then I saw the cut-out piece in the garbage.

We stared for a while. Mom was usually the one to get the urge to go out late and get something sweet and gooey.

"Mom didn't cut that pie," Ben said.

"How do you know?" I said.

"Because the slice is too small and neat."

Mom usually took a slice with whatever was handy—a table knife or the edge of a fork, even the edge of a plate—and her slices were always big and jagged. So he seemed to be right. But now we were stumped, because Dad never ever ate desserts. He worried about his weight. He even did push-ups on weekend mornings, and he played basketball a couple of times in towns where he met other guys to play with.

Finally, I thought I had it. "He bought that pie for Mom— she loves cherry pie, it's her favorite. And he cut a piece to take to her."

"Yeah?" Ben said sloppily, sucking his thumb now.

"That's why the trail leads to the bedroom. He must have come home late at night with that pie and tried to make up to her."

"Yeah."

"After the fight."

"Yeah."

We thought some more. Ben said, "But Mom would just make fun of him for doing something nice like that."

That was true. She wouldn't think the pie was enough, not for all the things she was mad about.

But I thought how nice it was of Dad to at least try. Things were changing around here. Not necessarily for the better, to be sure, but things were changing and starting to catch you off guard.

I cut myself a piece of the pie, and asked Ben if he wanted one. "I'd throw up if I ate that pie," he said.

I just laughed as the drippy, gooey cherry stuff dripped onto my arm. "Augh, he just stabbed and killed me," I said, laughing, but not loud enough to wake Mom and Dad.

A few nights later after we were in bed, I was awakened by Mom shouting and crying on the phone, then she called to me, "Crosby, are you still awake? Crosby?"

I came out, Ben shadowing me. Mom sat there looking pale against the bare, unpainted wall. There was a big crack in the plaster where she'd driven in a nail to hang a picture but didn't finish because the frame fell apart and she didn't have the stuff to fix it. Whiter-than-white snow lined the living room windows, and everything was so colorless it was like the whole world had been sucked of its blood.

"Ben, go back to—oh, you might as well stay and hear, too." She put her chin high in the air and looked at me like I was another grownup.

"Crosby, Ben," she said, trying to sound mature. "Your Dad and I are getting a divorce."

The next night, in the middle of the night, I woke up from a dream where the world was on fire and we were all running from it. Mom and Dad were holding hands and running with us, and the fire didn't seem so bad.

But after I was awake for a minute, I realized it was really smoke. I sniffed. I sniffed again and an alarm went off in my head.

I flew out of bed and yelled for Mom. I ran to the living room and there was smoke, gray, serious puffs, and the air smelled like death. I heard Mom's light footsteps behind me. I ran through the smoke into the kitchen. There was Ben, standing by the sink and throwing a glass of water on a snapping fire on the stove. The cupboard over the stove was on fire and flames were reaching out their pointy fingers at Ben's hair. I screamed and screamed and Mom ran in and grabbed Ben. I felt her pull my arm and I felt myself running and then I was out in the snow in my bare feet and Mom was squeezing me and running some more, holding me tight with one of her skinny, soft-as-boiled-chicken arms.

~~~

FIFTEEN

M OM GREW MORE and more nervous and lost interest in food. She'd just pick at her dinner, eating only the onions, throwing what was left in the garbage. She became so thin that her cheeks sank in and her teeth protruded.

To set an example for Ben, who was smoking the night of the fire, and to gain weight, she tried quitting cigarettes. That lasted for about six hours.

By spring, she said she was going to have to take Ben and me to stay at Grandma and Grandpa's up in northern Michigan.

"Just until I figure out what I'm going to do," she said, looking sad, but not quite as sad as before she got the idea, and not nearly as sad as Dad did when we last saw him.

The first morning at Grandma's, I heard Mom talking to Grandma in that tone that people use only when talking to their mothers—bored, slightly irritated, comfortable in an uncomfortable way. All that ever changed were the proportions of each ingredient. Right then, comfortable was dominant.

"I have to get a job, of course, but I'll look into nurse's

training part time. Who knows, maybe I'll snag a rich doctor."

"I still think you two should set down and try to . . ."

"Oh, Mother!" Irritated took over, and within half an hour, bored had won and she was making for the back door with quick steps and calling out, " 'Bye, kids, I'll call soon."

Watching Mom back down that gravel driveway flicking a cigarette ash out the window made my stomach feel like a piece of chewing gum. When she shifted gears and drove off, I ran into Grandma's bedroom and flopped down on the bed and cried myself into a headache. Pretty soon, Ben was sitting next to me, that scared look in his eyes.

"What are we gonna do now, Croz?" he asked.

I looked around, at the gauzy curtains in the breeze, at the trees out in back, at the smoke billowing into the air from the factory down the way. I'd adjusted to new situations before, but this was too much. Mom and Dad may have been chaos, but there's security in chaos if you get accustomed to it.

And this town was different from anywhere else we'd lived. Birchville had old houses and lots of different kinds of people. It was surrounded by woods. I'd liked it the few times we came up here for Christmas or the Fourth of July. But I wondered if I would ever fit in here. Traveling over all that brand-new concrete had worn me into a different kind of pattern, or into no pattern, smooth and fast, almost as if I were one of Dad's tires rolling through an endless succession of suburbs.

Well, we had to adjust—it wasn't as if we had any choice. "Look, Ben, when things get too depressing, you just pretend you're pretending that you're doing what you're doing," I said, trying to figure out a way to survive this. "We're really at home, we're just pretending we're at G&G's."

Ben nodded. We sat on Grandma's saggy-soft bed with the hardened cotton lumps in it. Now I was glad I had Ben for a brother, even if he was weird and was going to have to repeat third grade. At times like this, he certainly was better than nothing. "Do you wanna play checkers or watch TV?" Ben said.

Freckles, Grandpa's springer spaniel, came in and put his

nose up on the bed. I liked him because he had more freckles than I did, and floppy ears that felt like bath-powder mitts.

The first Saturday morning we were there, we got up and went through our usual ritual—turning on the cartoons loud enough so we could hear them in the kitchen, and then going to get some cereal. All they had were bran flakes. I looked in the refrigerator and found eggs. "Scrambled or boiled?" I asked.

"I want Sugar Pops," Ben said.

"We'll just have to make do," I said. I turned the fire on under a frying pan and put some butter and Crisco in it.

I was so busy I didn't notice that Ben had left. After a while, there was a knock at the back door. I went down the stairs to answer it, and there was an old lady with her hair in pincurls and a hairnet standing with Ben.

"I live just down the way and this boy was asking if we had something to eat. I come to see what the problem is. Are you Etta and Wendell's grandchildren?"

I nodded. "He's just being belligerent. He doesn't want eggs."

And we started talking about the different ways to cook eggs, and the next thing we knew, Grandma was shrieking and the dog was barking and Grandpa was yelling. The neighbor and Ben and I hurried up the stairs to the kitchen, where a fire was blazing from the stove. Grandma dug a box of baking soda out of the cupboard and dumped it on the frying pan and the flames went out.

"Now, young lady, I've a notion to take a switch to you," she said, shaking my shoulders. Her mouth was so tight you couldn't see her lips, and it turned down at the corners all the way to her jaw. She made a half-smile at the neighbor, who told what Ben did, said something about if they were her grandchildren, and left with an superior smack of the screen door.

"Why, you," Grandma said, shaking Ben's shoulder now and looking down through her bifocals. "Now that you're living here, you're not going to behave like a wild Indian any more, do you hear me, young man?"

She told him off some more until Grandpa made a wheezy cough and said, "Christalmighty, Etta, where's my breakfast?"

Grandma cooled down and put on her apron and took Canadian bacon out of the refrigerator and put it in a pan, and then put an old iron contraption on the stove. She lit the fire under it and said, "Now, you kids, let's have breakfast. I made the batter last night." She took a bowl out of the refrigerator and poured from it into the contraption on the stove. It sizzled. "Blueberry waffles, with butter from the farm. How many, Ben?"

"I can eat about eight," he said.

Grandpa put down his pipe that he'd been scraping, and said, "Holy mackerel. Then I'm entering you in the waffle-eating contest over to the Pine Tree County Fair."

"I'll give you two to start," Grandma said. "And you can have as many as you want, soon's you finish what you got."

Grandma told me the contraption was a waffle iron. I told her I'd never seen a pan that was only supposed to do one thing, that we just had general things like frying pans and pots.

Ben just about croaked when he saw how big and fat they were and how much butter and thick syrup she put on them. He was used to frozen waffles with Mom's tiny swab of burnt toast-flecked margarine and some Log Cabin if by some miracle we happened to have any in the house. Ben ate two waffles and I ate three.

I had to dry dishes and Ben had to feed Freckles. I told Grandma that I'd never done dishes before. As she got the garbage ready for Grandpa and Ben to take out, I told her about our troubles with garbagemen. She shook her head as I spoke.

It was reassuring to watch her, she was so slow and deliberate, dumping coffee grounds into a newspaper, adding bits of waffle and the little packet that her saccharine came in, pouring the grease into the orange juice can. She was in charge of her garbage instead of letting it be in charge of her, unworried about screwing up, accepting of the fact that she had to do this chore, unlike Mom and Dad who wanted to get things over with so they could return to whatever was worrying them.

"Sometimes I don't think a divorce is as bad as they say it is," I said to Ben one day.

"Yeah? Me too," he said, but I noticed he also was asking me all the time, "When are we going home, Croz?" And I'd joke, "What home?" Jokes lately were wasted on Ben. He just watched to see if you laughed, and if you did, he did.

All I could think was that maybe Ben wasn't a total hopeless loss, not completely crazy, because I wasn't crazy, and I'd accidentally started a fire. That's the way it was with Ben, you were never totally sure that he was nuts.

$$\approx\approx$$

SIXTEEN

OFFICER ROSSETTI slumped over the computer and punched some keys. "Okay, here's what we got. This Benjamin J. Rawson has on his record two arrests, two convictions—one last June for loitering, for which he received a suspended sentence, another in July for drunk and disorderly, for which he spent one night in the lockup."

He looked at a computer printout. "Here's something else. Oh, never mind."

"Never mind what?" I asked.

"He was charged with creating a public nuisance, but that was later dropped."

"What did he do that time?"

"It seems he erected a shelter in a city park." As I was about to ask why that was a crime, he said, "You can't put up a residence on public property. You can sleep on a bench, but not put up a tent or cardboard boxes or anything to sleep in."

"When did this happen?"

"August six, in a sweep of Tompkins Square Park in the East Village."

I checked the calendar on his desk. "That's two nights after he stopped showing up at the shelter, one night after he was beaten up. Well, it means he's alive. Or was. The guy in the brownstone didn't kill or completely incapacitate him."

Officer Rossetti gave me his half-opened-eyes deadpan expression.

I wondered how far I could push. Having established that Ben had not been in jail or been reported as an assault victim in the past month, I got the message that if I received any more help from the police, it was going to be because someone was in the mood to do me a favor.

"But then he still might have been hurt, though, couldn't he have, and the doctors just didn't report it? Or he might not have even received medical care?"

He threw his hands up. "Whatever happened to him, if he isn't carrying I.D., he's extremely difficult to locate, and most of these homeless individuals fail to carry identification of any sort."

"Well then, I guess I'll go ahead and report him as a missing person."

"I hate to disappoint you, but I don't believe we can help you there."

"Who do I see, then?"

"A private detective."

I looked to see if he was kidding, but Officer Rossetti seemed to be without guile. "Wouldn't that be expensive? Don't the police look for missing persons?"

"Crosby—I can call you Crosby?—Crosby, I could take you in to see a missing persons detective, but he'll tell you no way he's gonna go pursuing a vagabond."

I straightened at hearing Ben called a vagabond. Homeless was sounding good now. A good catchall euphemism that, homeless. "Well, I must say, that seems discriminatory."

"You want to hear it from a missing persons detective? Let me see if Detective Skovick is in."

After he disappeared down the hall, I went back out into the lobby and called my prospects, the Loebroes, to see if they were getting along with Sarah. I thought they sounded a bit distant, but then we were three thousand miles apart. I called my client, Mr. Harboil, who last night had given me the depressing news that he did not intend to reduce his asking price. I told him the buyers were not likely to stay interested. He said to wait and see.

I sat down on one of the greenish aqua plastic seats attached to the wall and watched the people coming in and leaving. What a city my brother had come to, what a precinct he had gotten himself beaten up in. People in baggy silk pants and designer "eyewear" stepping out of brownstones with walls painted the color of chocolate milk, and their police have to work in a place with checkerboard orange-and-brown tile walls and green chairs, a building that looks as if it had been decorated by Howard Johnson on an acid trip.

Officer Rossetti motioned me from the hall and we went to see Detective Ken Skovick.

Detective Skovick finished a phone conversation, answered a call and put it on hold, and then looked up at me. "Go ahead, it's your nickel."

He listened carefully, pulling on a rubber band as I explained the situation. When I had finished, he said, "Tell me something. Where is your brother missing from?"

"He's missing from the shelter." But as he questioned me, I had to agree with him that it wasn't exactly Ben's permanent address he was missing from. I tried again. "But he's really missing from home, back in the Midwest."

"Do you know how many thousands of people flee small towns and families to come to New York each year to get lost in the crowd?" the detective said. "Do we have a right to track them down for their families?"

The phone rang. He answered, settled back, and swung his chair around to face the opposite wall. Officer Rossetti and I went back to his desk.

I gathered my things, upset that the police wouldn't look for him, but relieved that Ben hadn't appeared in any of their current files. I shook hands with Officer Rossetti. "You've been great, thanks," I said. "I guess I seem overly worried, but Ben's so awfully naive. I just hope I find him before I have to go back to California."

He made a squinty, friendly smile. "Must be a boyfriend makes you so eager."

"No, actually I have to start law school."

"Just what this world needs, another attorney settin' criminals free. Just kidding, seriously, just kidding." He sucked in some air and his chest expanded. "Listen, seein' you have to get back to the coast, what I can do is I can put out your brother's description as a person with a mental problem in need of medication. They're not going to tear the city apart looking for him, but who knows."

I gave him a grateful smile as he situated himself at the computer again.

He read off Ben's description and asked if I could update it, but my description of Ben would be seven years old. "The only thing I could add is that he might possibly have a head injury."

His fingers made the computer keys crackle. He turned to me again. "I got your home number. I need a phone where you can be reached in town."

I gave him the number of the Royale Payne. "Not exactly the Ritz."

His soft Italian eyes were still sympathetic, and now mildly curious. "Just how long are you figuring on being in the city?"

Suspecting that his interest in the case would diminish if I told him two more days at the most, I said I wasn't sure.

"Oh, and one other thing," I said. "Do you have a Tyrone Davis anywhere in your computer? He was my brother's companion that night, the last time anyone saw him."

Officer Rossetti checked. "I got eleven Tyrone Davises, ranging from a cabbie charged with murder and found driving around with his decapitated father's head in his trunk, to a parking scofflaw with forty-three outstanding violations."

I said that I thought we could rule out those two, but I couldn't tell him any more except that Tyrone was black and in his early twenties. "He doesn't have an address. He's homeless."

"That helps a lot."

I thanked him and went to leave. As I opened the door of the station house to leave, he called out, "Hey, if you find your brother before we do, be sure to tell him that warrant for his arrest was dropped. He might not know that."

I ate a deli roast beef sandwich in my hotel room and watched a silent "Sesame Street" as the phone rang and rang at Bellevue Hospital. When I finally got through, I asked for Charlene Franklin, the supervisor I was told might be helpful.

She checked records. Ben had not been there within the past two weeks—the time since the brownstone incident—as a medical patient. I told her what little I knew about his past hospitalizations. She put me on hold. When she came back to the phone, she said, "He was here as a psychiatric inpatient last year, discharged in November. He was an outpatient after that, and was supposed to come in for medication."

November 27. Thanksgiving time. I pictured Dean's family, his sister with her fan of orange hair playing show tunes on the piano as we sang along over our after-dinner stingers.

"Is he still an outpatient?"

"He stopped showing up in the middle of July."

"What happens if he stops taking his medication?"

"You'd best talk to a physician, Dr. Rosenfeld or Dr. Chin. But they're on vacation. Maybe a nurse could tell you more than I can." Her hand went over the phone, and I heard some fumbling, clinking, then I heard voices and laughter for the next fifteen minutes as I watched Oscar the Grouch and the Count and the other muppets. I wondered what would have been different if Ben and I had watched "Sesame Street" instead of "Howdy Doody." Nothing, probably.

A woman who sounded Puerto Rican got on the phone. "How can I help you?"

"My brother, Ben Rawson."

"Yes, I know who he is."

"Can you tell me about him? The medication, how ill he was? Can he take care of himself?"

"Maybe you can come to the hospital. I could talk to you when I have my break this afternoon."

I sat on the subway trying not to make eye contact, which seemed the thing to do. Staring me in the eyes on the wall was a huge condom on a poster warning gay men about AIDS, the little flaccid tail limp but ready for action. No doubt about it, Crosby, this is no longer the New York of "My Little Margie."

Just after we passed Forty-second Street, a beggar in army

fatigues came through, holding the stump of an amputated arm out as his other hand held a jingling cup. For people like me who didn't donate, he stuck the arm in their face. Ben did this, begged for money, according to the men at the shelter. What did he stick in people's faces—the crazy look in his eyes?

When I emerged from the subway, it was raining. I bought an umbrella and worked my way over toward Twenty-ninth Street and First Avenue.

The last part of the walk was through a park. The rain had driven people away, but sparrows hopped daintily among dozens of empty quarts of Budweiser and pints of Smirnoff vodka and Thunderbird wine. The wind began to blow and I felt as if I were entering hell. By the time I was able to see Bellevue Hospital, the skirt of my dress was soaked and dotted with black mud, my face was dripping.

I tried to convince myself that it was the rain that made the hospital look depressing. But the architecture, dished up by a government like the one responsible for the previous night's ravioli, screamed out, "Mental hospital." The windows were long, morose openings into psychotic blackness. I shivered and thought of how the sun came up over my mountain back home, and went on.

I felt somewhat relieved when I got inside; the lobby was a perfectly nondescript remodeled modern nothingness. I followed signs pointing to "Psychiatric Emergencies," and found Henrietta Velez.

She took my arm to lead me to the cafeteria. "Your brother, Ben, I tell you, if he have fifty cents in his pocket, he would want to spend it on you."

We got coffee and fended off ragged people begging for cigarettes as we searched for seats.

She had looked up Ben's record for me. He first came to New York when he was discharged from a Long Island mental hospital. His release was part of the deinstitutionalization of patients, considered an enlightened move by mental health experts. He then came into New York City and lived with a couple of friends.

"They got lucky and lived in an SRO."

"SRO? I assume you're not referring to theater tickets."

Her eyebrows, thin-pencilled arches, rose. "Not exactly. Single Room Occupancy." She poured a long stream of milk into her coffee. "Except sometimes the real translation is flop house."

"Ben wasn't all that fussy."

"No, and sometimes they are very happy in SROs. I know because I have a ex-brother-in-law who lives in one. Oh, that Ben, though, he was so kind. One time he told me that he has rats, and wondered if I could recommend something to get rid of them. I told him he should get a trap. I gave him one to borrow, but he told me he wouldn't use it. I asked him why, and he say because he don't want to hurt a little animal. So I laugh and tell him he will just have to live with them, and he wanted to know if I have a cat he can borrow to scare them away. I told him yes I have a cat, but it likes to eat mice, not just scare them. So the next time I see him he tells me he has put cheese in the hallway for them to eat, so they won't come in his room. And then he tells me he eat only Hostess cupcakes in his room, because he has heard of a scientific study that those cupcakes are so artificial that rats don't recognize them as food."

We both smiled and shook our heads. There was, after all, a certain kind of logic operating out of Ben's head sometimes. I found it comforting to talk to Henrietta about Ben; to her, his behavior was everyday mental patient, and at least in some way he was normal.

"This SRO thing sounds like it was working out. What happened?"

"I think they tore his building down. He had nowhere to stay then, but a new program began, outreach teams. One of the teams brought Ben in because he had slept on a pier with some other homeless people and got a severe sunburn. You see, when they take medication, sometimes they get sunburned more, and Ben he has such fair skin anyway—he had blisters that got infected. And he said he didn't feel it."

He was readmitted as a psychiatric patient. Put on some new medication, he began responding.

"He had a handsome smile when his skin healed. Oh, he is a good-looking man, that Ben."

When he was released from Bellevue, he went to stay at

various shelters, including St. John the Divine, coming back to Bellevue for outpatient treatment once a week.

"But I didn't see him now for a couple of months. I was on a different ward, then I had to take some time off because my sister had surgery on her feet and I had to help her with her children—she has five boys, one retarded, and three girls, one of them fourteen and with a little baby—and then her husband got arrested for grand larceny."

"I'm sorry to hear that," I said. Poor woman. Crosby, someone else in this world has problems, too. Odd that the people with difficulties I can relate to, the people who can relate to my problems, are often minority people. If I have to endure sympathy from anyone, I prefer theirs over that of my demographic peers. "How is your sister?"

"She lost her job." As she told me about her family and its various messes, I thought she was probably able to be so philosophical about it all because she got everything off her chest by talking to people, talking about matters that to most people would be locked-up family secrets.

"Tell me about Ben's medications."

"He was put on several different drugs with various successes. The last was Thorazine."

"What's that for exactly?"

"Oh, sometimes he has erratic behavior, depression, paranoia. But there are side effects. It can make patients sleepy. And it can make their tongue wag a little bit. Like a lizard." She flicked her tongue in and out to demonstrate.

"What happens when they go off the drug?"

"They might hallucinate. They might get depressed or do bizarre things."

"Bizarre things like what?"

"Well, I think Ben tried to commit suicide with pills."

"It wasn't the first time," I said. I didn't find out until more than a year later when Grandma mentioned it, assuming I had been in on it in the first place. The only reason she knew was because she had been there when Mom got the call.

Ben apparently had been depressed and stopped taking whatever medication he was on. He decided to kill himself by jumping from the window of the fleabag hotel he was staying in.

What saved his life was that transistor radio of his. The wires to the earphones had gotten tangled around his arms and neck and caught on something on the window lock when he jumped. In twisting around, his clothes caught on something else. He was stuck so securely that it took three firemen to get him free.

And Mom didn't even tell me, never mentioned it, never suggested I visit Ben in the hospital. That's how much it meant to her, that's how much she thought it meant to me, and I wasn't so sure that *wasn't* how much it meant to me. I was busy being a cool cheerleader, and having a suicidal brother was definitely an uncool thing to have.

"His condition—what exactly *is* wrong with him?" I said more to the heavens than to Henrietta.

She raised her pencilled eyebrows. "Ben is diagnosed schizophrenic. You mean you didn't know?"

I recalled the first time a doctor said Ben might be schizophrenic. I went to the library. I read book after book on the subject until I felt a strange emptiness.

"Yes, I knew. Sort of."

I stopped going to libraries, but couldn't avoid whatever was in the newspapers, magazines, about the disease—not that there was much. When I read that the predisposition might be hereditary, I stopped reading about it altogether. I've walked around since trying not to wonder too much about the schizophrenic gene I might be carrying.

"I knew he was schizophrenic as much as anyone else did, and I sometimes doubted it as much as anyone else did," I told Henrietta. In his early twenties he was deemed by one psychiatrist to be definitely not schizophrenic. A year later, another shrink was convinced he was and put him in a hospital. Since then, he'd been diagnosed variously as depressed, alcoholic, drug-addicted, personality-disordered, pathologically this and borderline that, and then there were the less scientific theories, that he was spoiled, that he was neglected, that he was evil, that he was a saint.

"To be perfectly honest, I didn't want to know. My parents probably know more, but they don't believe any of it, or they believe all of it. They just think he's weird, or stubborn, or they don't want to know. They don't like being blamed. And I'm not sure they should be. They feel guilty, they feel helpless. Their assessment of it has often been that there's nothing wrong with him that a good swift kick in the pants wouldn't cure."

"I think he is a schizophrenic, and I don't think people's families make them that way. I think sometimes a person can go either way and what kind of life he has can steer him in one direction. But maybe you should talk to Dr. Rosenfeld when he comes back from vacation. Now I have to get back to work," she said, pulling out her mirror and lipstick.

"I'll call him next week from home. Now I'm worried about the medication along with the head injury. I wish I knew where he spent his days."

"I know he had a favorite food pantry, if that's any help."

"It certainly might be."

"Let me write down the name and address for you. And if I were you, I wouldn't get panicked about the medication," she said, patting my knee with her cool nurse's hand. "He went for many years without it. Sometimes they can get along okay. It's still very controversial, you know, the medication. And Ben, he seems to be a survivor."

It was four-thirty when I got out of Bellevue. The rain had turned to misty drizzle. I felt so lonely that I wanted to call Dean and tell him everything. I got back on the subway and tried to clear my head to plan the rest of the day. I'd start on this list of city and church shelters, then get to the clothing banks and medical clinics that serve the homeless.

When I got back to my room, tired, defeated, ready to lie in bed and fondle my law school catalogue, there were three messages.

One was from Dean—"Hey, Love of my Life, found out where you are. What's this phony aunt business, anyway? What the hell's going on?"—with his Washington phone number. But by now I was thinking better of letting him in on all this, and I put the message aside.

The second message was from Antonia saying one of the

volunteers had cancelled and could I possibly fill in that evening? I crumpled that one up.

The third was from Sarah. "Condo sale in trouble, call ASAP."

1961

SEVENTEEN

O NE OF THE MOST amazing things about Grandma and
Grandpa's was that when you needed them, the scissors
were always in the same place, middle drawer of Grandma's
desk, in the box they came in. Everything, from bread in the
metal bread box in the kitchen, to Grandpa's penny collection
in the cigar box on his dresser, seemed to have been *born*
where it was at G&G's, and if you tried to put something in
a new place, the whole house would probably collapse.

You could spend hours just looking around and daydream-
ing in Grandma's kitchen. There was a set of canisters she'd
gotten as a wedding gift. They had illustrations of pouty-
mouthed ladies wearing sacque dresses. I tried to imagine
Grandma in one of those, with the dark spit curls. It was
impossible. Grandma was plump and she wore her yellowy-
white hair in tight waves all over her head. I got the feeling
that Grandma had always thought there was something immoral about being too stylish. It was okay to envy and admire
people who were rich and beautiful, but to be that way yourself was wrong. Cooking was where you were to excel, and
in Birchville, any woman over the age of twenty who wasn't
obese was suspected of being vain.

Grandma's cupboards were quiet sanctuaries where order reigned. All her dishes matched and sat in neat stacks instead of being stashed any old where, and the cups hung from hooks. The glasses were put in upside down, like someone loved them enough to carefully put them to bed on their stomachs. G&G weren't rich, not even average, but their dining room was elegant, especially the china cabinet with Grandma's teacup collection—I could entertain myself while waiting for an interminably slow dinner to cook looking at those cups and deciding which was the most beautiful.

The furniture in the living room never had nicks out of the wood or spills and cigarette burns in the chairs and couch. There were doilies everywhere, with pins in them so you always had to watch it and they stayed neat, and lots of pictures of Mom, the only child, in nineteen thirties and forties clothes with funny collars and shoulders.

G&G had separate bedrooms. Grandma's was crowded and smelled of potpourri sachets and Christmassy dusting powder and the faint sewery smell from the bathroom it led to. Grandpa's was brown and spare and had the odor of not-yet-washed clothes in the closet, pipe tobacco, shoe polish, and oil from next door, where the people were always fiddling around repairing a car or a motor of some sort.

The whole house, in fact, was full of aromas, from the cleaning fluids in the hall closet to the sickeningly sweet African violets next to the picture window, to the cloves and allspice of the kitchen, to the mildew and mud damp of the back stairs that led to the driveway and to the basement. You could lead me blindfolded through the house, and I could tell you which room I was in. In any of our houses before, the only place with its own special odor was the garage.

As I was putting my clothes away the night before the first day of school, Mom called. Her voice was cheery and light and more refined than the other voices around G&G's that I'd gotten used to. I wondered if Mom used to talk like they did around here before she "went over the wall," as she put it, and left Birchville.

"I'm in nurse's training at a hospital over in New Kenmore Acres, a little town nearby. I'm going to come up and get you two kids before long. You just start school there and be good. And don't worry."

Ben didn't show his emotions—if he had them—and he acted like talking to her was something he did all the time, every day, still, and went back to watching TV after he was done. I got a stomach ache because suddenly I missed Mom more than anything. After a while, I even missed Dad, too.

Grandma had a cherry tree out in back. The cherries were translucent, sour if eaten raw, frequently wormy, but they made a pie with a flavor that hit you in the back of your throat, where it seemed to stay longer.

We picked them from the stepladder in July. We canned most but kept enough for a cherry pie riot. We'd make half a dozen pies at a time, some for us, some for neighbors and relatives.

We'd work like crazy, sifting flour and salt and mixing in the lard and butter. Grandma would ask Ben if he wanted to help by measuring the sugar, but he usually just sat at the table staring off at the stove as if it were a TV.

These were real cherry pies with big, full, protective crusts that were so hard you could thump on them and they'd respond by promising you that deep sweet secrets were inside.

The cooked cherries weren't at all like the impossibly red ones in the grocery store pies, the kind that go straight for your glands. These cherries turned their own shade of red, sort of rosy burgundy, and had a mellower, longer-lasting taste. Cooling on the kitchen counters, the pies looked like a row of sculptures, each a variation on a theme.

Ben wouldn't eat them. I knew why but I didn't tell Grandma, even though she was bewildered about it. I didn't tell her because I didn't want her to know about the blood that wasn't blood and the perfect grocery store pie and Mom and Dad fighting all the time. I didn't want Grandma to know that Ben was always ready to believe that Dad would kill Mom and that I was half ready to believe it. I let her go on thinking that underneath it all Mom and Dad loved each other more than they hated each other, which was probably the truth anyway.

The school here wasn't new like the ones we usually went to, the flat kind with new light desks and cement block walls. This was the school Mom had gone to—a three-story red brick building with creaky, sinking floors. The desks were dark and had inkwells. The blackboards, like the ceilings, were high. The giant windows had wavery glass. Outside, instead of the usual mowed lawn surrounded by a chain link fence, was a playground full of bare spots and a thick forest. When things got boring, I could look out and pretend I was a wild animal in the forest. Other than at the zoo, most of the wild animals I'd ever seen were dead on the side of the road, smashed by cars. Here I saw chipmunks, rabbits, deer.

I'd worried too much about fitting in here; the students were real friendly at the school. They were pretty different from the kids I was used to—here, faces were rounder, softer, showed what the person was thinking.

Ben was quiet and was getting quieter. "Oh, he's bright enough, I guess," Grandma would say to people, brushing back Ben's baby-doll hair and bringing his face up so people could see him better. "But you can't get a peep out of him about school. That September-Crosby will talk you blue in the face, but Ben don't feel like he has too much to say, I guess."

I can't honestly say that behind all the silence lurked a happy Ben. Every time I turned around, he'd be right behind me drawing on that thumb with that queer look in his pale eyes. And I began to wonder if he was just temporarily confused or if it was becoming a way of life for him, a way of making his statement, because right away he stirred up trouble at school.

It all began with the baby toads. Actually, I wasn't sure if they were toads or frogs—I didn't know that much about amphibians—but they were ugly enough to be toads. And there were millions of them in the woods near the pond.

That ugliness was a challenge, so I made myself pick one up and pet it so I wouldn't be afraid. As it turned out, they were cute, so soft it almost felt obscene. At recess I'd catch them and put them in a box for later, but they always got out. So I had this idea to keep a toad in my desk as a portable friend. I told Barb Henderson about it.

"Ooooh, that's a good idea." Barb was one of those people who never have original ideas and think you're a genius if you do.

She rounded up a bunch of kids, and pretty soon the playground was lousy with sixth graders catching the little toads and putting them in anything they had—paper bags, boxes from the dump, coat pockets, hats and scarves, lunch boxes. There we were, running around, shrieking and laughing and scaring each other with our toads. When the bell rang, we went in with our bags, planning to put them in our desks. The toads hopped and made little crackly sounds.

"Shhh," I said to everyone as we passed the third and fourth graders coming out for recess. This was our own big secret.

But when Ben went by I thought, hey, this might be a way to help him be more popular. I opened my bag and showed him my four toads and said, "They're all over the woods. Get all the third graders to catch them and put them in paper bags or lunch boxes, then hide them in your desk."

"Yeah, Miss Stine wouldn't like that," Ben said, trying to look wicked. "It'd pay her back for yelling."

"No, the idea is to not get caught. It's a secret joke among the kids, get it? If the teachers find out, it won't be funny."

Ben got a really serious look on his face and nodded. Then he said, "Will you walk home with me after school?"

"Can't. I'm going with Barb for Fudgsicles."

That afternoon, there was a knock on our classroom door, and it was Ben's teacher, Miss Stine.

"I'd like to see Crosby," she told my teacher, and right away I knew there was trouble.

She led me to the school nurse's office. The nurse was so angry she was barely able to control herself. "Your little brother says you made him eat some frogs out on the play ground. Is that true?"

She looked like she really believed it. I explained the real story, which sounded dumber and more unbelievable than Ben's lie. She put her hands on her hips. "Whether or not that's true, you ought to be ashamed of yourself."

"Are your parents, er, together, Crosby?" Miss Stine asked.

"No, they're divorced." I knew what she was driving at, so I said, "But Ben was already weird before that."

"Hush," the nurse said. "Benjamin," she called out, "How are you feeling, dear?"

Ben made a retching sound. I went around the corner and found him in a little room lying on a cot. His eyebrows were up in a scared position.

"Ben, be honest. Did I tell you to eat the toads?"

He made a series of burping noises and wouldn't answer.

I could have axe-murdered him right there if we hadn't had witnesses.

"There, there," the nurse said, feeling his forehead and giving me a look.

The next thing I knew, Grandma was there. She had put on her powder and lipstick and good navy blue dress, so I knew I was in serious trouble.

"I pretty near was out the door to do some marketing when I got your call," she said. Her face was white from all that powder and she looked a little sick, too. "I thought I'd best come in and see what this is all about. These two don't do things like that at home. This just don't sound like September to me."

I noticed she didn't say it didn't sound like Ben to her.

They talked for a while and Grandma assured them that she and Grandpa were giving us a decent place to live. And the next thing we knew, Ben was in the bathroom throwing up. The toilet flushed, and he came out and said he felt better.

Grandma took Ben home and I had to go back to my class room. There was an announcement over the loudspeaker that everyone had to go out and let their toads go. It was something to see.

The rest of the afternoon, I tried not to wonder if there had been toads hopping around in Ben's puke. I never found out if he did eat them, and no one else seemed to know for sure. But I wouldn't have put it past him, and I have a suspicion that he did do it—just to get attention, just to get to me, just to, just to be Ben. I know one thing. I never treated him as normal after that.

1962

~~~

EIGHTEEN

A s we got ready for church one Sunday morning, I told Grandma about some of the ones we'd been to. Her mouth got all pursed up as I talked, either because she didn't like what I was telling her or because she was trying to get the veil of her hat to come down over her nose and it kept popping back up.

I wondered if it would be like the ones Mom and Dad always took us to, where people had smooth clothes and looked around all the time to see who was there. "What denomination is your church?" I asked. "Presbyterian? Methodist or Lutheran?"

The biggest problem with those churches was that they were so godawful boring. The only religion that I'd seen so far that wasn't dull was the Catholic religion, I told Grandma. Her face immediately unpuckered and she snapped, "Now listen here, young lady, we're not Catholics. And for now, you're not anything except what we are in our little town. And that's enough of that kind of talk." And then she patted my head and said she had cinnamon rolls made from leftover pie crust heating in the oven.

In the suburbs, you had to walk a careful line between

being too religious and being a Communist. I personally thought religion could be more than our family made of it, but I knew it was a subject that was a lot like sex and not to be discussed out in the open. So I didn't tell Grandma about the time we moved into a house with a little statue of Mary out in the backyard.

Mom told me she was going to have the garbagemen haul it away as soon as they could. I thought it was exotic to have it out there and if there was a God he might get mad seeing it trashed.

From what I'd seen on TV and read in books and heard from friends, the Catholic religion was good because Catholics knew exactly what to do. It was all spelled out for them in church, and most of them made a reasonable attempt to follow their rules. The best part was, even if a Catholic did something wrong, a mortal sin or something, he still could get out of trouble by confessing to a priest and saying a rosary in Latin.

I wished we had something like that. Before the Mary statue was taken away, I'd tried my own version. A neighborhood girl and I had been teasing Ben, asking him why he didn't have any friends and then imitating him sucking his thumb. Ben hadn't responded, just looked at me like he couldn't understand why we did it. That look bothered me for a day or two, so I took him out to the little Mary statue in back. I told him to mumble things in pretend Latin. "If you do, you won't be loony anymore," I said.

But of course it didn't work, maybe because we weren't real Catholics. It at least got me to thinking about the problem with being a Protestant. The problem with being a Protestant was you were always going around feeling like you'd done something wrong, and you didn't quite know what to do about it. The church said you'd do it again, because you were human, but that you were supposed to try not to, even though you would.

With Mom and Dad, we went to church when we first moved somewhere, once, maybe twice, again at Christmas or Easter if we were still living there, and that would be it until the next move.

Sometimes, though, Dad would get the bug and decide that

we had to go to church in March or October or something—
usually it was because someone at his office was a bigshot at
a church and Dad thought that might be the key to success.
I have to add, though, that underneath it all, there was something sincere about Dad's interest in church, though Dad said
he wasn't brought up in any church so he didn't quite know
exactly how to go about doing it right without looking ridiculous.

It was always embarrassing, because we'd have to come in
in the middle of the Sunday school term a lot of the time, and
we never could catch up. It wasn't like making an entrance
in the middle of everything with real school, because I read
so much outside stuff that I never had a problem with non-
religious subjects.

Grandma said it was time to go. Grandpa grunted and got
up out of his La-Z-Boy. He looked serious and dignified and
pale in his navy blue suit.

As Grandpa drove us over to the church, the Sunday
schools I'd been to ran through my mind and I started getting
that slow sickening feeling in my stomach again.

It was always the same: you'd come into church, and Mom
and Dad would ask where the Sunday school classes were.
They were either in a suffocating upstairs room with a lot of
notices on the wall that were about things that were impossible to understand, and even if you could, probably boring as
hell, or else in the basement, which always smelled of paste
and Kool Aid and mildew. You'd go into the classroom, and
everyone would stare at you like crazy while some incredibly
polite teacher would introduce you. The kids were all dressed
up in clothes that were for Sunday school only, while we
clumped in wearing our boxy school clothes, and you took a
look at them and were sure that they all knew so damn much
more of that Bible crap than you did.

Then the teacher would say to you, "The class had a homework assignment. We'll just sit you down over here to the side
and let you do it, and while we wait we can sing a few fellowship songs, and then we'll all go over the homework together."

They'd use a lot of words like *fellowship* that neither they
nor the dictionary ever explained clearly enough for me.

There were two possibilities about words like *fellowship,* along with *stewardship* and *salvation* and *redemption* and *grace:* they were either tremendously complicated and wonderful terms, or else they were come-on words which seemed to mean something really important but in reality were only tinny little ordinary words that made you feel cheated.

And they'd talk about places I couldn't get straight, like Galilee and Judea, which through history changed their name and became something else and then became something else to where I couldn't keep up with them. It could almost make you grateful for suburbs with names that were interchangeable. It was all very confusing and creepy; I really appreciated the Catholics' luck in having it all in Latin. They had a good excuse for not having God all figured out.

So you'd look at this assignment the teacher had given you to do. Memorizing some Bible verse that for the life of you you couldn't understand, and if you had to repeat it out loud you'd about die. Or reading some story, like about Jacob's ladder or Joseph's coat of many colors. That part was okay, until you had to answer questions about it, which you couldn't do because you were sweating under your arms and could hardly concentrate, because people were looking at your shoes, which were school shoes and they all wore patent leather Mary Janes. Or else your Mom had finally gotten you some Mary Janes and all the kids here wore loafers or saddle shoes and thought dress up shoes were for hillbillies or hoods.

What really scared you was you might have to say some goddamn prayer out loud. Worse was when you had to match up some Bible verses with characters, and you never learned that stuff, so you had to just sit there like an idiot during the whole goddamn hour half-holding your breath. And then you'd wonder how many of the kids really believed all this stuff, and which just acted goody-goody while they were there and then acted snobby at school.

And then they'd always do some group thing, and the kids all knew each other in the groups, and knew the damn Bible stories, so you'd feel even more like an idiot, because you couldn't help figure out what your skit was going to be, or your collage or whatever the hell it was you were doing. And inevitably, there'd be some craft—pounding out praying hands on a piece of metal or making a church and steeple out of Popsicle sticks, and I was never good at that stuff. My praying hands looked like lumpy fists, my churches with steeples looked like fists giving you the finger.

The most horrible moment was when they passed the plate around, and everyone had a white offering envelope with their name on it, and you didn't have an envelope because you hadn't been a member when they made them up. So you had to put your dime in, and then everyone else saw it when they passed it around, your naked little dime that said "In God We Trust;" a dime that refused to sink to the bottom, but sat there bright and shining and winking at everyone else, who had one of those beautiful white envelopes with their name machine-printed on it, an envelope that shouted, *"I belong."*

And you'd dread the end of class, too, because that's when the parents showed up. Almost everyone else had parents who were really reverent acting and were involved in things like the greeting committee, and they'd talk about it while the kids were gathering up their projects to take home. Mom and Dad would just show up and give people nervous phony smiles and then scoot us out of there as fast as their legs could carry them. They never figured out that if *they* didn't fit into the church, *Ben and I* sure as hell weren't going to. No, I knew that I would never be a part of these groups, even though for some unknown reason, I sort of believed in the Bible stuff (though that seemed to be secondary to what the church was for—it seemed mostly to be a place for people who never swore and yelled to get together.)

You'd think all the Christians' Christian charity and humility and kindness would make it so I felt welcome, but it was just the opposite. The churches we went to attracted people with perfect, dull lives. Let's not even talk about Ben; what if they found out about Dad kicking his foot through things and quitting jobs? And how did you explain someone like Mom? I can tell you what—we'd be on their list of people to help out. It looked to me like Christians believed in helping people out, but they also believed in not spending any more time than you had to with people who needed helping out.

It made it a little more interesting, though, that G&G's church was a whole different world. I could see that the minute we got inside. Our other churches had always been too bright—the worst were the white ones with red carpeting that hurt your eyes so early on a Sunday morning. They always smelled like a funeral had just taken place, flowers and dust. But this church was real tiny, and the altar looked more like a stage. There was wood everywhere, so that when you walked there was a hollow sound, like Hell was just underneath so you had better watch your step. It had that dusty, damp, closed-up smell that I remembered from a horror house at a carnival Mom once took us to. I'd had nightmares for a long time.

Grandma said we didn't have to go to the Sunday school, just sit in church with them. G&G's minister didn't wear a robe, just a brown suit, and people in the audience said "Amen" all the time. He acted alternately really nice, too nice, and mean, yelling and waving his arms around.

I never did figure out what point he was trying to make. Every time it looked like he was going to come to one, he'd start chanting out Bible verses. Finally, though, it gave me a headache. I slunk down a little bit, because every now and then he'd point at someone and yell at them.

After he was done preaching and a choir sang and the organ ground out a bunch of hymns, they took up the collection, and it felt good for a moment, because G&G had envelopes with their names on them, and I sat up straight again.

But then something really creepy happened. They drew back the maroon curtain, and a musty smell waved over toward us. There was a big tank of water on the stage, and I expected to see fish or maybe some carnival act. But Grandma leaned over and, with a rather nasty smile, told me someone was going to get baptized.

Three people came out with robes and shower caps on, and they looked nervous and scared, and I got nervous and scared, because the minister had been asking if everyone in the audience had been saved and baptized.

Then the three people had to climb some steps and get in the tank. The minister pushed the people's heads down in the water, raised his hand and yelled some stuff, and then the people came up all wet and I felt my heart pounding and I started praying to God to please not make me get baptized.

I looked at Ben to see if he was scared—it was hard to tell when he was frightened or just looking normal.

"It's okay," I whispered to him. "Don't be afraid."

His eyes were big, staring at the scene on the stage. Finally, he said, "Croz, remember when you told me it was okay to go to the bathroom in the swimming pool?"

"What?"

"That time when I had to . . ."

A couple of people in the pew in front of us turned around and said, "Shhhh."

I looked at G&G. Grandma had a puckered, almost smug look; Grandpa was looking, but he seemed to be thinking about something else. "Quiet," I said.

"I just wanted to know, Crosby, can those people on the stage go to the bathroom in there?"

Grandma's head turned in a split-second. "What's that?" she hissed.

"Nothing," I said.

"I said can they go to the bathroom in that water?" Ben said.

"Why, you," Grandma sputtered. "You mind your manners." There was Grandma, expecting Ben to act normal.

At first I thought it was cranky of Grandma to get so upset. But I realized pretty soon that she thought we were making fun of her church. I'd heard her criticizing Mom for making fun of Birchville, and Grandma said she wasn't going to let her grandchildren do that. Maybe Mom had her fooled—maybe she thought we were regular, envelope-carrying members of one of those big churches we showed up at from time to time, chuckling with everyone else as the minister told polite jokes about the football team during "Announcements" before he started his sermon.

I wished I could explain to her first of all that Ben didn't have the glow-in-the-dark mean look in his eyes, so he really was wondering about the bathroom stuff, and probably was not trying to be mean. He was in his dumb, not his vicious, mood. And I thought later I'd better tell her the truth, that we never felt a part of a church, that I never even knew what

particular kind of religion I was supposed to belong to because we went to whatever church was nearest, as long as it
was a mainstream church. That was the important part, that
it be mainstream, mainline. When I needed to put it down on
the emergency card at school or when someone asked me, I
wasn't sure what to say. I asked Mom, and she told me to just
say "Protestant," to make sure they knew we weren't Catholics or atheists or some religion that was so far from Christian that you'd get in trouble for just mentioning it.

But it was like everything else in our lives, here we were,
sort of Jane Parker/A&P-brand Christians in a world of
name-brand churchgoers—Presbyterians, Baptists, Method-
ists, Lutherans. At least Grandma could say what she was—a
United Church of Nazarene Brethren.

I peeked at Grandpa, who looked stiff and bored as hell, but
somehow peaceful, too. Normally, he wouldn't like having to
give up a whole morning of TV watching, but there wasn't
anything good on on Sunday mornings, anyway. And I sort
of guessed he felt that enduring church was a simple, passive,
Protestant way of getting your sins forgiven—a punishment
for things you'd done for fun. And unlike when you went to
church with Mom and Dad and you walked out feeling emp-
tier than when you went in, here you actually felt better for
having gone to church, because these people didn't look
down on you. This church was something you went to in
order to get your soul cleaned and repaired. You came out
with the same feeling as when you went to the dentist.

$\approx$

N I N E T E E N

O NE EVENING IN APRIL, while we were in the kitchen, Grandpa and Ben sorting through fishing tackle for a trip up north and Grandma and I cleaning the camping dishes, there was a flash of car lights in the driveway. The circles of light on the garage door expanded, then burst onto the trees and grass around it so fast I knew it had to be someone from out of town driving. The brakes screeched to a stop a split-second before the headlights went though the garage door. I flicked on the porch light and saw Mom's long legs swinging out of the car.

Ben yelled out the window and then ran down the stairs and out the door. The two of them walked in together. Mom wore a yellow shirtwaist dress and looked so very slim and modern next to Grandma.

Mom sat down on the davenport and Ben slumped down next to her. Mom stuck a cigarette in her mouth and looked for a lighter in her purse. Her nylons made a scratchy sound as she crossed her legs. She wore light-colored mesh hose. Grandma still wore shiny dark hose with seams in them. Her legs were thick and straight and her hose bagged around her ankles.

Mom had gained a few pounds. She also had gained some hair. It was no longer in a pageboy but in a bouffant flip. When she kicked her shoes off, you could see a big hole in the toe of her hose that had started to run. Grandma never had runs. I bet she'd had the same pair of hose for twenty years.

Mom made a big smile. "I'm taking you kids home."

I clapped my hands. "Where?"

"Toledo. North Ridge Gardens, to be exact."

I jumped up and down.

"I've got a good job," she said, puffing long and importantly, "At a bill collection agency."

"Oh?" Grandma said. "What happened to nurse's training?"

"Couldn't hack it. I'm too damned old and I have too much else on my mind."

"Oh?"

"Don't give me that sanctimonious 'oh,' Mother."

Grandpa grunted and got up and went to the kitchen.

"I just wondered if you'd got that notion out of your head, that's all," Grandma sniffed.

"You hoped. You know I always wanted that. To go down to Kalamazoo for nurse's training. I should have gone ahead and done it when I was eighteen. I've been thinking about it, Mother. You were against it because it was a waste of money."

"I knew you'd find a husband."

"Oh, Jesus." She blew out a big puff of smoke.

"Now, listen you here," Grandma said, the sound of her knitting needles punctuating her words. "I told you you could go to nurse's training nearby, maybe in Traverse City or somewheres. But, no, you had to go down to the big school in Kalamazoo or nothing, or else be a fancy secretary in Detroit."

Grandma dropped the ball of yarn from her knitting and reached over to pick it up. Mom stuck her tongue out at her. "Well, I'm getting meaner in life. Being on my own has opened my eyes—I kid you not. And forget nursing—I've concluded that there's no money in any job that helps people."

"Doctors help people," I said. "And they're rich."

"Yeah, Mom, you could be a doctor," Ben said. "Or Dad

could. Or Crosby could." I noticed he didn't say *he* could, and no one else added that. Maybe he was smart enough to realize how dumb he was, or sane enough to realize how crazy he was.

"Benny, ladies don't become doctors," Mom said.

"How come?"

"Oh, I don't know. Anyway, you have to be rich and really smart to go to medical school."

"A lady doctor came to our school," I said. "But she was Chinese."

"Well, I'm not Chinese," Mom said.

"Doctors, rich bitches," Grandpa said, coming back from the kitchen. He was talking louder than usual. I could tell he'd had a sip from the bottle in his fishing waders in the garage.

Grandma's eyes followed him as he made an unsteady trip over to his La-Z-Boy. "Now don't you get tight, you, just because you're tickled that Vera's here."

Grandpa glanced at Mom and turned on the TV. I guessed the fishing trip we'd planned for that summer was off.

"The job is funny," Mom went on, patting my knee and giving me her "you-and-me" look. "I call up people and say, 'Hello, is Mrs. So-and-So there?' And when they ask who's calling, instead of admitting I'm with Geiger Collection Agency, I say what my boss told me: 'This is Vera Rawson,' so they won't hang up on me right away." She giggled and squeezed Ben. And then a scary thing crossed my mind, that Mom was a little kid trying with all her might to live in a grownup's body. That was her way of dealing with things. It came to me, too, that maybe G&G knew and tried to pretend it wasn't so, or maybe the opposite, that they were so simple and ordinary that they wouldn't know a crazy person if she walked in wearing a straitjacket. Yes, sometimes Mom had the same expression that Ben did, I thought, and then I felt like I had just looked directly at the sun. I closed my eyes quick.

"Why do they hang up?" Ben asked.

Grandma shook out the scarf she was knitting. "Some people don't like to pay their bills."

"Yeah, like me," Mom said. "Don't ask how many times my

phone and electricity have been shut off." She put another cigarette in her mouth and lit it. When she took it out, it had the usual red ring with little lines where her lips wrinkled around the filter. It felt comforting to see that again.

"You know you can always move back home," Grandma said.

"No, I'm off to seek my fortune." She puffed and looked at her high school graduation picture on the wall over Grandma's sewing machine. "Like I did eighteen years ago. And boy, did I hit the jackpot." She frowned for a moment, then burst out laughing. "Joining John Rawson's traveling salvation show."

Ben jumped up. "Know what Great-Aunt Nora Beatty said? That you had to get out of Birchville and be a bigshot."

"That sounds like her. Aunt Nora Nobody." Mom sat on the davenport rocking Ben and smiling at me like a naughty child.

On the drive in the rain down to Toledo, Ben and I sat in the backseat. We felt quiet and a little sleepy.

It was nice and cozy back there, and I felt like there was nothing in the world to be afraid of. But Ben was worried because Toledo didn't have a major league baseball team, only a farm club. He'd spent most of his time at G&G's watching baseball and in the winter playing with his baseball cards, the way girls play with dolls, putting them to bed on Kleenex boxes and covering them up with the tissues, things like that. It had been good for Ben because Grandpa liked baseball on TV. Dad liked playing some sports, but not watching them. Ben still occasionally had this thing about Mozart and a couple of other composers, and Grandma got him the transistor radio Mom never got him so he could listen to the classical music station from the college over in Piketon. Those had been the two things lately that made Ben feel secure—baseball and Mozart.

"Don't worry, you can listen to Mozart in Toledo," I said.

"Ben, when are you going to get off that?" Mom asked.

"I like music sometimes," Ben muttered.

"Oh, baloney. You're just trying to get attention. You wouldn't know Mozart from the man in the moon."

"You'd be amazed, Mom," I said. "You'll see. He really understands it. He listens to music like you and I do ordinary things. He hears parts that sound like other parts, and he can even tell the difference between a pause in the middle of a record and when they're really at the end."

"Oh, Benny Benny Benny," Mom said, reaching over the seat and shaking his foot.

"I'm glad I'm coming home, but I'll miss Freckles," he said.

"Freckles? Grandpa's dog?" Mom asked, smiling into the rearview mirror, her lipstick mouth wide, her teeth large and white. She was pretty, until cars passed us and the lights went all weird and she looked grotesque, like she was laughing at us from some different angle, like she was someone new.

"Freckles smiled at me all the time," Ben said.

Mom stared into the glary rain, then she brightened and said, "I'll tell you what. We'll get ourselves a dog. A dog named Spot, like in Dick and Jane. First thing in the morning, we'll go to the dog pound. Okay?"

Ben and I weren't sleepy any more and played license-number games all the rest of the way.

As we drove into the apartment complex over the speed bumps, Ben and I shook each other in excitement.

"Look—a pool and tennis courts," Mom said. "Tomorrow you'll see them better. Pool opens on Memorial Day, a little over a month away."

The apartment complex was called "Chateau du Nord." We lived on Rue de Rivoli.

"Can you remember that?" Mom asked. "Rue de Rivoli?"

Ben said, "I'll just think of Franco-American ravioli."

In the lock, the keys sounded tinny and foreign, like someone else's. Inside, it was dark and shadowy. When the lights burst on, a lot of things were familiar—a wall mirror, a metal magazine rack, other pieces of furniture that had survived the fire, though it looked like the furniture was all cold and uncomfortable because it was in a new home. But, I quickly reminded myself, it always did at first when we moved.

"Everyone in the apartment complex has either gold or green carpet," Mom said. Ours was green, sort of pea green, with kitchen linoleum to match. "Gold carpeting is such a common thing in decorating now, so we have something a little different. And see the wrought iron here between the living room and kitchen? That's French, like in New Orleans. I guess that's why they gave the complex a French name." Mom got another funny look on her face, the grownup look, the one I liked best, and said, "Kind of pretentious, isn't it?"

Ben was to sleep on the air mattress—like a soldier camping out—and I got a sofabed in the living room. The apartment was overheated and too dry, and shadows climbed across the ceiling all night, but I finally got to sleep thinking how glad I was to be back with Mom.

The next morning we got up early because we were so excited about getting the dog. We didn't have any encyclopedias, but I drew pictures on the back of paper placemats we'd taken from Howard Johnson's of the various breeds for Ben and told him about them. We went outside and saw the pool and tennis courts. They looked little and silly and vain in the April morning gloom, with rusty puddles in them and the paint chipped. We went back and explored the apartment, trying to make enough noise to wake up Mom, and yet not so much noise that she'd yell. I tried to straighten out the dishes in the cupboards like Grandma did—Mom had just stuck things in helter-skelter, the only separating being food from dishes—but it was hopeless because the plates were different sizes and styles and wouldn't stack right.

Finally she came out of her bedroom. "Sleep well, sweeties?" she said, making coffee.

We didn't say much of anything for a while. We were waiting for her to bring up the dog. She made toast—burnt, the way she liked it. "No margarine," she muttered as she peered into the near-empty refrigerator. With two arms, she lifted a great big jar of peanut butter out of the cupboard, slathered some on the toast, and sat munching and reading the paper while Ben and I horsed around quietly.

"Oh, this is terrible," Mom said. "The poor little thing. Listen, a little baby's ear was bitten off by rats. I wonder if they were poor people, colored people. Jones Avenue, I wonder where that is. See, if I were a nurse . . ." She munched and stared off into space and I got nervous and couldn't stand it any more. "Mom, when are we going?"

"Going? Where?"

"You know . . ."

"No, I don't know."

I could hear Ben's breathing. It irritated me. I couldn't bring myself to come out and repeat her promise about the dog. I just couldn't. If I didn't say anything, then there wouldn't have been a promise, and there wouldn't be a disappointment. But Ben, of course, had to open his yap.

"Mom, we're going to get Spot, remember?"

"What?"

"Spot—a dog, remember?"

"Oh." She looked like she'd been worrying about other things, and that was why she forgot, not because she was mean. "I don't know if the pound is open on Saturdays. And, honey, I don't know if they'll let us keep dogs in this apartment complex. What if they don't?" She looked at me like I was supposed to figure it out. "It's so nice, you'd hate to leave it, wouldn't you? I mean, it wouldn't be worth it, would it?"

I just looked down at the green carpeting. I couldn't talk. Ben didn't say anything either.

About an hour later, after she'd had several cups of coffee, she said, "Okay, I'll call and see if the pound is open."

Ben and I danced around the room when we heard her on the phone saying, "All right, until five, you say? Thank you. Er, is there a charge? Uh-huh. How much? I see."

"Can we go?" Ben said.

"I almost forgot, I have to get the manager of the apartment complex on the phone." She looked in the phone book, then dialed a number. "No answer. Look, kids, I promise you, we'll get a dog if the management says it's okay. But I might not be able to get ahold of the manager until next week."

"I can't wait that long," Ben said. "It's boring here." He looked around the room, where green seemed to have swallowed up the few pieces of furniture.

"Benny, I don't see what the big deal is," Mom said. "I never had a dog. Dogs make a mess. And the expense . . ." She wound a clump of hair around her finger and frayed it, looking for split ends. "Oh, don't worry, kids, we'll get one sooner or later. I just don't see what the big deal is, though. Let me see what the management here says." She said it automatically, like she was thinking of other things that she had to get out of her head before she could deal with the dog.

"I don't give much of a shit," I told Ben, and I opened the book Grandpa had gotten me about Arabian horses. Ben turned on the TV. Mom drank coffee and looked at the bare walls.

For dinner we had Franco-American ravioli, in honor of the new apartment. Then Mom said, "Hey, how about a movie?"

We went through the paper, and the only movies playing at our neighborhood theater were *Fantasia* being rerun and *Psycho.*

I voted for *Fantasia,* which we'd seen at G&G's but which I'd gladly see again for the dancing hippos, but Ben said he got scared seeing a movie with Mickey Mouse being serious. Mom said all she knew about *Psycho* was the ads always showed a woman in her bra and it looked like some depressing mental-breakdown movie and it wasn't even in color. But then I said maybe it was good because it had been playing at the theaters for a long time. That made sense to everybody, so we all agreed on *Psycho.*

Well, you can imagine how surprised we all were when the shower scene hit. I just about fainted and Mom nearly crawled under her chair. But old Benny, he just sat there, chewing on his Sugar Daddy and watching. The same with the stabbing on the stairs. By then, Mom and I had had it, and Mom wanted to get up and walk out. But Ben wanted to stay, and something icky inside me wanted to stay, too, so we did.

Mom and I managed to cover our eyes in the scene where they run to the basement and turn the chair around. All I knew was there was a siren or screaming or something.

The fright made us ravenous. Mom suggested we go for hot fudge sundaes. We went to Fannie Farmer's and sat at the counter. We told Mom about things we'd done at Grandma's.

Ben and I twirled around in our seats and watched the people coming in. Finally, I just had to ask Ben what it looked like when they turned the chair around in *Psycho.*

"Yeah," Mom said. "How bad was it, Benny?"

Ben twirled in his chair, feeling important.

"Come on, Ben," I said. "Tell us."

"Nope."

Mom and I laughed, and Ben twirled some more.

On the way home, Mom let us listen to a rock music station and a teenager drove up next to us and smiled at Mom and gunned his engine. Mom turned and looked at me and laughed. Most Moms weren't as much fun as mine, I knew that.

"Ben, I'm giving you one last chance to tell us what it looked like," I said.

Mom looked at Ben, a thin smile across her face.

Ben never did tell us what it looked like, and I had to wait until I was a little older and saw the movie again to find out. But I have to say that I heard him tossing and turning on that air mattress all night, and he got up about a million times to get a glass of water or go to the bathroom, and he didn't want to go to any movies after that, not that I can remember.

1962

≈≈

T W E N T Y

T HE FOLLOWING MONDAY was our first day of school here.
I got up early and made some hot chocolate out of Hershey's Cocoa, a packet of sugar from Howard Johnson's, Cof-
feemate, and hot water.

It hadn't really hit me until this point that there was almost
no furniture. A lot of it had been lost in the fire, and some was
at Dad's in St. Louis. All that was left were the bare essentials
that let you know you were for sure in the Vera Rawson
household.

I piled up decorator pillows and made myself a little seat
for watching "The Today Show." I leafed through the only
reading material in the house—*Ladies' Home Journal.* An
article on child psychology caught my eye. There was advice
on dealing with kids who won't eat their vegetables or who
have bad dreams, nothing on what to do when they score in
the 93rd percentile on the California tests but flunk a year in
school and set the house on fire.

Just as I was getting into the "Can This Marriage Be
Saved?" column, Ben came and sat down right on my magazine.

"Get away," I said and hit him in the face with a pillow. He fell backward and started to cry, but then grabbed another pillow and timidly tossed it at me. I dodged, jumping up onto the sofabed. I grabbed a pillow from the sofabed and began beating him over the head with it. Pretty soon we were both laughing and shrieking, and then Mom appeared in the doorway in her bathrobe, fumbling for a cigarette. "What are you kids doing?" she managed to say while sticking the cigarette in her mouth. Ben accidentally threw a pillow at her, knocking her cigarette across the room.

We were late for school that day, but it didn't matter, since we had to go to the principal's office to register. It was lonely, walking into that school, another almost-new one with lights on the ceiling that looked like ice-cube trays and gave the place a cold and lonely look.

Since we were entering this school in April, I was going to feel like something that fell out of the sky and landed in the middle of a classroom. I figured I'd just look for that light above my head that I used to feel when I was little—that would steady my stomach. For all the stuff I made myself believe about not being scared of anything, my stomach sometimes called me a liar.

Ben didn't act like it bothered him at all. Mom said she picked this town because the schools were supposed to be good. I never knew for sure what "good" meant to adults—to me it meant a school where the kids had more expensive clothes than we did.

It was so modern and brightly lit, I felt it was making me even more conspicuous and I just wanted to sink into the ground because there I was, brand new, and all these kids were walking around laughing with each other and horsing around and I was feeling a hundred feet tall with a spotlight shining on me. And then the assistant principal decided to take me to class while it was going on, instead of having the decency to wait until the bell rang so I could at least walk anonymously into a room with the other kids.

"I understand you have a brother," the principal said as we made that long walk down the hall.

"Yeah, he's in fifth grade."

"Over at Washington?"

"A lot of elementary schools are named after presidents,

aren't they?" I said, chattering nervously so as not to think. "Like in Heather Wood Villa. Our school there was Dwight David Eisenhower Elementary," and I told him about some of the others I'd attended. "It's too bad there weren't any girl presidents, so there'd be schools with girls' names, too."

"That's a very good point," the principal said. "Maybe you'll run for president some day and change all that."

We stopped in front of the door to my civics class.

"How many schools have you attended? Your mother just gave me the report card from your school in Michigan."

"Maybe half a dozen, maybe more. I'd have to stop and figure it out. Anyway, my parents are divorced now, so we're not supposed to move again."

"I see. I'm awfully sorry. We have a guidance counselor you can talk to."

"Maybe my brother would want to, but I'm okay," I said. I was just about to add that he could help by waiting until the next class change to make me start school, when the teacher spied us through the door's window and came and opened it.

"A new student," the principal said, leading me in. "This is Mr. Whitehead, and this is Crosby Rawson." Then he turned to the class. "Class, meet Crosby Rawson, from—" he stopped to look at one of the papers he'd been carrying, "from Birchville, Michigan."

There was an absolute dead silence. I decided I'd get through the day by thinking about the new puppy we'd get after school. When the principal left the room and I was still standing up there, a girl said, "Crosley. What kind of a name is that? What kind of town is Birchville?"

There was some tittering, and a boy said, "That town's where they stick the tube when they want to give the world an enema."

Mr. Whitehead sleepily tapped his desk with his ruler. "Take a seat, Crosby."

As I passed by that kid's desk, I said, "I'm not surprised that you're an expert on enemas, since you're such a big asshole yourself." The entire classroom roared.

I made friends with a girl who lived in another part of town, so I had to walk home alone. It had been raining off and on all day. Now it was a drizzle that stopped, then started.

There was a glare from the sun that hurt my eyes, so I tried walking with my eyes squeezed shut part of the time. I ended up in a neighborhood with long stretches between driveways, where there weren't any sidewalks. I got my shoes all muddy. Then my socks got soaked, and they made a squish as I walked. Some man driving by stopped and asked if I wanted a ride. I ran away as fast as I could with my reluctant, muddy shoes and socks talking back to me, saying "suck suck suck suck schmuck schmuck schmuck schmuck," and then I realized I was lost.

I slowed down to a walk and wandered around some more. And then, of all things, I found myself out in front of Washington School, and they were just letting out. I waited, and finally I saw Ben, carrying his lunch box like some worn-out factory worker. There was the closest I've ever seen to tears in his eyes.

"What's wrong?"

"They made fun of me."

"Me too, but after a while it wasn't so bad," I said. "We did essays on our favorite planet. Mine's Venus. Did you do anything interesting?"

"Nope."

"No recess, games?"

"They played that son of a bitch Seven-Up game."

I knew what he meant. That game was tough on you when you were new, and it was tough on kids who weren't popular, even if they weren't new. I was afraid to know, but I asked. "Did you get picked?"

He didn't answer.

"Don't worry, there were times when I was never chosen, too." I really hated that game—where the teacher appoints seven kids to come up to the front, while everyone else puts their head down on their desk. The seven kids go around the room, and each taps one person on the head and then returns to the front. Then everyone puts his head up and has to guess who tapped him. Fat kids and kids with polio braces never get tapped, and kids with new clothes get picked every damn time. I never did figure out why teachers made kids play that game, unless they were somehow in cahoots with the popular kids.

"Someone knocked me on the head with a paperweight while I had my head down." He bent his head and showed me a lump that looked like Silly Putty.

We walked silently for a while. I didn't know whether I loved him more or hated him more because kids were mean to him. When the part of me that loved Benny stopped aching enough for me to talk, I said, "Did you tell the teacher?"

"Yeah. She told the kid not to do it again, and everyone turned and looked at me. Then they kept on playing."

If you let these things get to you, you could start feeling bad and never be able to stop. "Hey, cheer up," I finally said. "We're getting Spot."

"Yeah," he said. He looked happy now. We walked in the wrong direction and got lost again. Pretty soon we were in a creepy part of town, or another town, I suspected, and there were some dark-skinned people gathered around a car drinking beer. They stared at us. But I was desperate, and with Ben I couldn't be scared, so I went over and asked if they knew where Chateau du Nord apartments were.

The guy looked at me, then Ben, then jerked his head in one direction and said, "Six blocks, then turn right, then straight."

A few blocks away, a truck driver pulled up and asked if we wanted a ride.

"No thanks," I said, and I whispered to Ben, "Don't talk to him."

The truck driver drove slowly next to us. "Hey, girlie, you like candy? How about the little boy? Does he like chocolate ice cream?"

"Just Neapolitan," Ben called out.

There was no place to run to, because we were next to a big open field. He followed us for about five minutes, and Ben called out to him, "Can you tell me where Chateau apartment is? I live at Five fifty-two Rue de Ravioli. That's since my Mom got divorced and Dad moved to St. Louis for a new job."

I just about ditched Ben then and there. I just about did. But he was just little, and besides, I didn't have anyone else or anywhere to run to. "Yeah," I yelled to the truck driver, "But her boyfriend lives with us and he's a cop."

"That's not true," Ben said.

"Mmmm." The truck driver drove alongside us for another

few minutes, then shifted gears and shot off down the road, spraying us with mud and gravel.

I kicked Ben and walked ahead of him all the way home. Mom wasn't there yet and the door was locked. So we sat on a bench in the wet, puddly tennis court and waited for Mom.

She arrived three hours later. She was thinking about something as she walked toward us, but when she saw us she smiled, then looked surprised. "Goodness, your clothes are filthy," she said.

Home had never looked so good. I took off my shoes and socks and wiped my feet on a newspaper, thinking how our new dog would tickle my toes when he got used to us.

"I forgot about the key. I'll have keys made for you kids, soon as I can," Mom said, kicking off her shoes and flopping down onto a throw pillow. She didn't say anything about a puppy. So I pretended the whole idea had never come up, but Ben said, "Mom, did you ask about Spot?"

"Oh, uh, I will tomorrow, sweets. I was too busy at work today."

You couldn't really get angry at the only real person in your life. You had to pretend everything was okay, or you'd go crazy. We just tried to forget about the dog, and let it slip into the big box of disappointments and confusion that was dragged behind us but which we all tried to ignore. After all, having a dog was something other people did, not us Rawsons, and something Dick and Jane did. And we could always still pretend.

We got into a schedule of sorts. After school, we raced home, got the key from under the mailbox, and settled in to watch "The Three Stooges," "The Little Rascals," and "Rocky and His Friends." Ben and I fought a lot because he liked watching TV with the sound off. He said he couldn't watch and listen to something at the same time.

We sat on my sofabed and tried to have on hand whatever candy or cereal they advertised for each show—Kix or Maypo or Clark Bars or whatever. We sometimes could only have BLTs or egg salad sandwiches or Lipton noodle soup for dinner because Mom didn't have enough for real dinners, but she got us our goodies no matter what.

Ben said he was happiest here. "We don't *have* to make friends at school, do we Crosby?"

"Not until fall," I said.

"Then I hope it's always spring."

We ended up, Ben and I, practically living in that bed, having breakfast in it, playing marathon Monopoly, having to-the-death wrestling matches, then eating dinner and watching TV until we dropped. We found out there was a bus that picked you up in our neighborhood, but we missed it about half the time, and then it was too late to walk, so Mom would get in the car and drive us, going about ninety miles an hour, her hair up in big sponge rollers, but her lipstick on. She'd laugh and sing along to the rock music radio station.

1962–1963

~~~
# *T WENTY - ONE*

A T TIMES, I thought the divorce wasn't working out so well.
Despite her constant talk about nursing school, Mom
didn't have all that much ambition and spent most of the time
watching TV with us.

Ben and I had to answer all the phone calls, because collection agencies were calling and Mom knew all their tricks.
Then one night they turned off the electricity, and Ben fell
down the basement stairs on his way to get candles. He cut
his ear and Mom couldn't see in the dark how bad it was. She
had me light matches in the bathroom so she could make it
stop bleeding, and washed and bandaged it.

"See, this is what happens," she said.

"What happens when?" I said.

She didn't answer.

The next morning, the ear didn't look great, but Mom
figured it was too late to prevent a scar.

"It'll probably leave only a tiny scar, anyway." She patted
Ben. Ben couldn't have cared less. "See, if I were a nurse, I
could have prevented that scar." She looked at me. "Tell your
father that next time you sit talking to him on the phone for
half the night."

That was another reason the divorce wasn't working out too well for me. Despite his shortcomings, I missed Dad.

He called about twice a week from St. Louis, and mailed presents every now and then. He sent things like an electric hockey game for Ben and an autograph hound for me, a paint-by-number set for each of us (for Ben, though it was wasted—he just painted the pictures any old way he wanted, over the numbers and lines). Ben especially loved the baseball mitt Dad had gotten autographed by Stan Musiel. He stuck it on his hand, and instead of going out and finding some guys to play baseball with, he lay on his bed and listened to the Cleveland Indians on his transistor radio. Sometimes he pretended they were in the same league as the St. Louis Cardinals so he could make up a whole game with Musiel hitting homers and using the mitt to catch fly balls to save the game.

Ben would lie there for hours, announcing games and even doing commercials and the banter between the announcers. His best was Bob Prince for the Pittsburgh Pirates.

One night Dad called and told us he'd gotten a big promotion. Mom held the receiver and listened along with me, and the next day she called a lawyer to see if she could get the child support raised.

"Honey, things are getting bad," she said to me after calling the lawyer. She looked embarrassed or guilty. "It's all a big mess because the divorce was in another state and we're living in two different states now, and he won't voluntarily increase it, and it's so expensive to live . . . I just don't know."

One time Dad came to Toledo on business. He was going to rent a car and pick us up. We had to watch for him because Mom wouldn't let him in the house. It was a funny feeling standing there and watching for a car we wouldn't recognize, looking at the drivers to see if they held their head in the same erect posture Dad did.

I told Ben Dad would have to act differently now because he wasn't allowed in the house. "He won't kick anything in or anything like that. He can't, because we could just leave."

"How could we leave?" Ben asked.

That was a good point. Mom wasn't much protection, and if she couldn't stop him from kicking things in when we lived

with him, how could she stop him when we didn't? And yet
I had predicted right—Dad *was* different with us now,
strained, formal, nicer.

We stopped and got hamburgers from White Castle and
brought them to his motel room. We had the large-size Cokes,
something Mom would think was outrageously extravagant.
The three of us polished off ten hamburgers. Then Dad noticed Ben's ear, which had healed but bore a puckered mark,
and asked what happened. Ben wouldn't tell him, so I did.
Dad got mad for a little while, I wasn't sure who at—the
electric company for shutting people's electricity off so their
kids fall down the stairs, Mom for not paying the bill, himself
for not giving her more money, or the both of them for not
being able to get along. "You kids need," Dad started to say,
but he just got up and stared out the motel room window. I
turned on the TV. Ben wanted to watch with me, but Dad
said, "Ben, we need to toughen you up. It's time you started
playing sports."

So I got to vegetate in front of the TV, but Ben had to go
with Dad to look for a park and play catch with a football.
Then Dad made him go for a swim—alone, because of Dad's
feet—at the motel's indoor pool. When they came back, they
were all tense. It was a damn relief to be a girl.

As far as I was concerned, there wasn't a thing in the world
wrong with Dad trying to teach Benny how to play baseball
or football or getting him to learn to swim. But Dad honestly
didn't know that you can't teach that in an hour on a Saturday afternoon when the kid is almost in junior high. At least
Mom knew all that, and just sort of gave up and made us
happy in our own little cocoon of a house.

"How about a pizza for dinner?" Dad said.

Mom couldn't afford to get pizza, so this was a rare treat.
I clapped and said I'd love it, but Ben, who I expected to
imitate me like he always did, just sat there.

When Dad went out for the pizza, I asked Ben what was
wrong.

"I can't do it, play football."

"How come?" I said, but I knew why. He just didn't have
the mental energy for it.

"I can't figure out why anyone would want to do it in the first place," he said.

"Why don't you tell Dad?" I said, but I knew the answer to that, too. Dad said that's what got him out of a miserable childhood, playing football, and he thought what applied to him applied to everyone.

It seemed like all this craziness was looking for its own ending, and as we were leaving for the last day of school that year, Mom came and sat on the bed with Ben and me and said, "Kids, I just can't do it anymore. We're broke." Her eyes were puffy and watery.

"What can't you do any more?" Ben asked.

"Take care of you kids."

"Even if you got the child support increased?" I asked.

"Our problem is money, all right, but it's other thing, too," she said. "I'm not just broke, I'm broken. I can't seem to figure out how to raise kids all alone with no money in a world that doesn't act the way it used to."

So it was back to Birchville for Ben and me, back to G&G's, just when we'd gotten used to Mom and Dad this way.

*1963*

~~~
T W E N T Y - T W O

B EN WASN'T THE ONLY baseball nut around that next summer. I started a scrapbook of all my new friends, the
Detroit Tigers.

Unlike Dad, Grandpa was a baseball fanatic. The three of
us would sit in front of the TV and swill pop—Squirt, Vernor's, Orange Crush—and get ourselves all worked up over
every game; we lived and died for those Bengals.

I loved them all: Stormin' Norman Cash, Rocky Colavito,
and especially Al Kaline, who seemed like the team intellectual to me. I'd sit next to Grandpa's La-Z-Boy and keep a very
scientific scorecard that Kaline would approve of. But I have
to say, the more I got interested in baseball, the more I could
see that Ben's mind drifted a lot and he didn't always have all
his circuits tuned in to the game. Ben would sit behind me
and tap me on the shoulder every now and then to ask a
dumb question about the game because he couldn't see and
hear it at the same time, or he'd out of the blue ask when we
were going home.

Dad visited once that summer and I went out and played
catch with him while Ben moped around the house. Dad
joked that I would have made a damn good boy, then imme-

diately apologized and said I'd be a "very intelligent, very personable" woman. I wasn't worried. Somehow I knew that when I got to be a teenager, I would want to be instantly feminine and grownup, so now I was resisting all that turning thirteen meant with all my might, trying to squeeze out every last drop of my childhood.

Grandpa was taking us to a game down in Detroit as a present for my birthday. He told me he had an old friend who was an usher at Tiger Stadium who maybe could get some of the Tigers to autograph my scrapbook, too.

Grandpa seemed a little nervous about the whole thing as June 15 approached. First of all, he'd written to his old friend the usher, and a woman wrote back and said the guy had died nine years ago.

That evening, after a few trips out to the garage, Grandpa said, "Oh well, I'll just have to go down to the dugout when we're there and speak to someone myself about autographs."

He hadn't been in Detroit since he saw Ty Cobb play. I reminded him that Al Kaline was being compared to Ty Cobb, and that made him more eager. He sat down and told me about how mean Tyrus Raymond Cobb had been, how he spiked other players when he slid into base, how he soaked his hands in oak brine to make them tough. "And not just for batting," Grandpa said, making little "puh-puh" sounds on his pipe and looking like he was trying to remember why it was ever important to be a tough guy.

Grandma wouldn't go to the game with us. "You couldn't get me to Detroit if they was giving away hundred-dollar bills at the city limits," she said one night as she and Ben and I stemmed strawberries. We were going to have them with shortcake and homemade ice cream while we all watched the game.

"Why not?" I asked.

"What was it like when you were there?" Ben asked.

"Oh, I don't know."

"Were there tall buildings?" I asked. "Glamorous ladies in jewels and fur coats? Millionaires riding around in limousines?" I wanted to see a big city like there were in movies and on TV.

"Oh, maybe."

"When were you there?" Ben asked.

"Did I say I was ever there?"

"You never went to Detroit?" I said.

"Never been there and hope I never do."

"Well, I want to see it. I'm going to live in a big city when I grow up," I said. "And I'm always going to have my scrapbook with me. It will be my souvenir of the first time I was actually inside a big city. And I'll have all the autographs of the Detroit Tigers."

"Me too. And I'm going to have an autograph book, too," Ben said.

The morning of the game, it looked like rain, and Grandpa was so nervous I was afraid he'd use the bad weather as an excuse to not go. I kept looking outside every five minutes to see if it looked a little brighter, but it didn't; if anything, it was a little darker each time. Grandpa looked, too, and puffed on his pipe and said, "Oh, I don't know."

But finally, just as I was about to give up and go back to reading *Little Women,* he said, "Aw, hell, I already spent all that moola on the tickets. Might as well chance it."

So Grandpa got his fedora from the high shelf in the closet and put it on in front of the mirror. He adjusted it, looking at his image like he wasn't completely pleased but he wasn't entirely displeased, either. "Twenty-three skidoo," he said, and we all piled into the old Studebaker, me with my scrapbook, Ben with his thumb. We had rain slickers and a sheet of plastic to put on the bleachers, and a basket of supplies to eat on the way down—oatmeal cookies, what was left of the season's strawberries, baloney sandwiches, a thermos of coffee, two pint cartons of chocolate milk, and a couple of bottles of Squirt.

It was a three-hour drive and after a while Grandpa looked as if he wished he could change his mind about going. He watched the road as if he were afraid it was going to jump up at him. I knew Grandpa wouldn't do anything like this for anyone else in the world. He was so quiet that I thought it a good idea not to talk for a while. So I picked up *Little Women* again and turned on the radio. Rain was forecast for the entire lower peninsula, the announcer said, then immediately played a Chuck Berry record, as if he hadn't just ruined my entire day.

I tried to let "Johnny B. Goode" cheer me up. At least Grandpa let us listen to rock 'n' roll stations as long as we kept the radio low, unlike Dad who went nuts when anyone played rock 'n' roll. The three of us, Ben, Mom and I, had always been kind of glad when he left so we could play it. When I remembered that, I felt guilty. Dad was only trying to be high-class and to make us high-class, too. He said it was because no one would ever take music beyond where Frank Sinatra had taken it. "I've been around the world in a plane . . ." I'd hear from my bedroom, and I had to admit sometimes it got me to thinking the way it probably got Dad thinking, too.

Remembering Dad didn't make me miss him, I noticed. And yet, I was glad I had Dad somewhere in the world, glad I was going to be seeing him again, because he was the only person who made me feel like there was something special awaiting me in life when I grew up, something I'd do really well that would make me feel important. Say what you would about Dad, he thought I had "a lot on the ball," and G&G and even Mom didn't seem to know too much about all that. Having a lot on the ball, that is.

I thought about the first time he said that—I had won an essay-writing contest on how I convinced my family to get rid of fire hazards around the house. Even though it was all a bunch of lies, Dad clapped when he read it and said, "Crosby, you've got a lot on the ball."

Ben just sat and listened and said, "Croz, are you allowed to make up pretend stuff at school?"

Dad never said Ben had a lot on the ball.

"Looks like the sky's a little better down here," Grandpa finally said. "Maybe we oughta eat our sandwiches now, hey, Chickie? Pour me some coffee and put in three sugar lumps."

Both Ben and I brightened and took a bigger interest in what was outside. We were getting closer—the countryside had given way to houses all alike in rows, like in Monopoly, everywhere you looked.

"Oh, I know where we are," Ben said. "We used to live here."

"We did not, dummy," I said.

"Or else nearby."

Then we got on a big expressway. It was funny how being on a crowded expressway made me feel real important.

"We never lived here," Ben said.

"Ben, I'm not listening, so you might as well be quiet."

The traffic slowed down and Grandpa for the first time stopped gripping the steering wheel with both hands and reached for his pipe. "Uh-oh, traffic jam."

"Grandpa jam, Grandma jam," Ben said.

Grandpa was getting nervous again. "What's that?" he said, with the tiniest bit of irritation in his voice.

"Grandma makes jam, and you get into it," Ben said.

Grandpa lit his pipe and rolled down the window. It started to rain so he rolled it up most of the way. The pipe smell was making me nauseous. The rain drummed its fingers on the car roof, trying to decide whether to stay or let the Tigers play baseball in honor of my birthday. None of us said anything. It was stop-and-go traffic for a while. Then when we got into Detroit, it seemed like there were colored people everywhere. Grandpa's chin jutted out and stayed like that. I pressed my face up against the window to get a better look. The rain slowed to a few sprinkles on the windshield. I turned the radio on to the Tigers station and the pregame show was on, so we figured the game was going to be played. A bunch of colored kids wheelied their bikes right straight toward the car and Grandpa slammed on the brakes. Now I could see why Grandma didn't like Detroit. She had no sense of adventure, and you had to have one in a place like this. A constant stream of colored men came walking in front of the car, and one of them slammed his hand onto the hood of the car.

I rolled down my window and yelled, "Will you let us through, dammit?"

They started laughing and our car leaped forward like a crazed rabbit and Grandpa found his way to a faster street. We all felt a little better as we started seeing baseball fans of all colors walking, carrying their plastic and their raincoats and wearing Tigers caps. The sky got glary and the sun tried to break through.

We had to pay two dollars to park the car, something Grandpa hadn't counted on, so we'd have that much less refreshment money. Then as we walked toward the stadium we all saw a place for a dollar seventy-five. Grandpa and I pretended we didn't see it, but Ben's big mouth had to announce, "Look, we could have paid less."

Grandpa was getting quieter and quieter. I clutched my scrapbook.

There was a lot of excitement in the air, but I noticed that things were a lot dingier than they looked on TV. And I was about as confused as Grandpa looked by the size of the stadium and the people pushing us on all sides. There were all kinds here—people like us, average types, but also colored people and others who were dark-skinned and had rounded features but weren't colored. They seemed to have large families and to ignore everyone else. I watched and watched, giving my eyes some real exercise. I was a bit nervous, but I liked the mix of people, a bigger mix than I'd seen in one place before, even Birchville. There were some older men with jackets that zipped up in front, the kind little kids like Ben wore, and they reminded me of tough guys in movies. I did get to see some rich people, too, and they looked like they do on TV and in movies; one woman had platinum blonde hair in a huge beehive and a tight dress that showed the tiniest waist I'd ever seen on a grown lady. The men wore suits and no ties. They got out of the first limousine I'd seen and walked in a tight little group and disappeared through a door that nobody else was going in.

We found our seats and put the plastic over them. This was the highest place I'd ever been in—it seemed like if you leaned forward, you'd fall all the way down onto the field.

The game in person was a whole different experience. The players looked so much less significant on the field that at first I thought that they were a practice team. You couldn't see their faces, and everything was so much slower. When anyone got a hit, you couldn't tell because there wasn't a commentator. I told Ben we needed him as an announcer now, but he could only do that when he was listening to a game—watching it confused him.

But I slowly got myself into the spirit of things, and as soon as someone got the first base hit, I turned to Grandpa and said in a too-cheerful voice, "This is great."

"Yep," Grandpa said. By the look on his face, he didn't think it was so great, either.

The refreshments were horribly expensive, so all we got were peanuts and Fritos and Ben and I had to share a syrupy Coke. And Ben kept squirming until he knocked my scrapbook off the seat and onto where someone had spilled some beer on the cement, and it got soggy. I picked it up and looked inside. A bunch of clippings were wet and the writing I'd done had started to smear.

I smacked his shoulder, and said, "Just for that, I'm not letting you go into the dugout after the game to meet Al Kaline."

I turned to Grandpa. "We can go to the dugout after the game, can't we?"

Grandpa acted like he did with Grandma sometimes and pretended not to hear.

Ben blinked and said, "I can go to the dugout if I want to."

"You just try it," I said. But I was beginning to wonder if Grandpa was going to be able to take anyone to that dugout at all.

The score was now one-nothing, New York, and even Al Kaline hadn't had a hit. Grandpa got a beer and gave Ben and me a quarter each, and he got another beer and that was the last of the refreshment money Grandma had given him. His mood improved with the beer, and he started talking about using the gas money to get another, and then about seeing how to get autographs.

"I'm getting autographs, too," Ben said.

"On what?" I said.

"In your scrapbook. I'll help."

"Sure you will," I said.

I told Grandpa he could have my quarter for beer, but he said no, and Ben said he'd take it because he wanted an ice cream bar. Ben had a way of being pitiful, so I gave it to him.

You had to go down to the stand for ice cream, and I would have gone with him, but just then there was a hit into right field.

Grandpa broke down and took his lucky fifty-cent piece out of his wallet's secret compartment and bought another beer, and yelled at the pitcher, "Back to the minors, you bum." I started getting that scared feeling in my stomach and I wished Grandma were here.

Then I noticed my scrapbook was gone. I looked under the seat and under everyone's seat around us, then I realized Ben must have taken it. I hurled down my scorecard and stomped over to the refreshment stand. But on the ramp, I heard a lot of whistling and then some booing and I stood on my tiptoes to see what all the excitement was. It was a fan on the field. And then I noticed it was a very small fan, out in that big, lonely outfield, and it was Ben.

He was carrying my scrapbook. An umpire and a couple of other people went and got him, and the next thing we knew, there was an announcement over the loudspeaker asking for the parents of Ben Rawson to come to the information booth. I got back up to our seats to find Grandpa gathering up the coats and the plastic without folding it. He had a really grim look on his face suddenly, like the announcement sobered him up better than a gallon of coffee could. While we were hurrying down the ramp, the whole stadium seemed to lift into the air in a giant roar. I heard someone yell "Home run." I couldn't even tell who had gotten it.

We went to where they were holding Ben. Two security guards were with him. He was working on a Fudgsicle, his eyes lit-up and blue as those plugged-in beer advertisements with Michigan lake scenes on them, the ones in the bars Grandpa sometimes snuck us into when Grandma was at her club meetings.

After we got Ben out of that mess and were out of the stadium, there was a Tiger home run.

I didn't notice until we got to the car that we didn't have my scrapbook. I asked Ben where it was.

"I don't know," he said.

"What did you do with it?" I screamed.

"I left it down there, I guess."

"He's always ruining everything. I wish Mom and Dad were here. They'd kill the little bastard," I screamed out to the now bright and sunny sky.

"I was just trying to get Stormin' Norman's autograph."

"You idiot, you don't even like him or care about him," I sobbed.

"Maybe he wanted it for you, Chickie. For your birthday," Grandpa suggested.

"Yeah," Ben said.

Grandpa zigzagged over to the side of the road and stopped. "You want to go back and try to get it?" Grandpa asked. He looked like he didn't really want me to.

It would take forever to talk my way back into the stadium, and it was too embarrassing to explain that it was my brother out there, and I decided not to.

I kicked Ben. Hard.

Ben sucked his thumb and looked out the window.

I knew what he was doing. He wanted to make everyone think he was crazy so they'd feel sorry for him. Or that he was too little to find his way around in the world by himself. Jesus Christ, I could—why couldn't he?

I closed my eyes for a while and tried not to think about him. Somehow, the air in the car got better. We all seemed relieved to be leaving Detroit and going back to our own little life capsule in Birchville.

My mind drifted back to Ben. It suddenly occurred to me that he had only been trying to get me to like him—that's why he went down on the field. I pulled out the traveling checkers game and jabbed him with my arm to see if he wanted to play.

Ben started doing more things like he did at the baseball game. They were things that at first made you say, "Damn that Ben" and then, quickly, "Poor Ben." And you walked away not knowing what to think—you didn't know if he was honestly dumb enough to do the things he did, or if he was trying to embarrass or scare us or just get some attention. Maybe he needed more attention than most kids. Maybe he needed more attention than anyone could give.

I started a new scrapbook, but for a different reason now.

It wasn't the sport I was in love with any more. It was Tiger pitcher Hank Aguirre.

We went back to watching games on TV, and I watched for him—the only reason I watched the games anymore. I painted my toenails while I watched and dreamed of a penthouse with pink velvet curtains and towels to match, and Hank Aguirre calling me on my pink telephone that I kept right next to my sunken bathtub.

My new scrapbook was different—all the newspaper articles and pictures were of Hank Aguirre. As far as I was concerned, he was the sexiest guy on the team, maybe in baseball. I wondered what he'd think of my Champagne Taffy toenails; what if he liked Pineapple Yum Yum or Platinum better? I fretted.

Ben didn't understand at all now. "So what if he's handsome?" he'd ask. "I'm handsome, and you don't like me."

"You're half right. I don't like you."

"What if I was ugly? Would you like me then? What if I slashed my face up with a butcher knife and bleeded cherry juice all over the house?" And then he started imitating Dick Van Dyke walking around his nice carpeted house with his face all slashed up.

"I'd still hate you," I said, but I was laughing.

G&G just gave him that sidelong glance.

~~~

TWENTY-THREE

Y̲OU NEVER KNEW whether Ben was doing things because he was screwed up, or if he knew exactly what he was doing and, like they say about comedians, would do anything for a good laugh, or in his case, a good scare. Like on the camping trip to Trout Lake.

We'd planned it in the spring with a brother of Grandma's and a nephew of Grandpa's, and prepared for it all summer. Grandpa and I dug up night crawlers and kept them in a box of dirt in the garage. We unfurled the old tent in the backyard to check for tears, and inhaled its permanent kerosene-and-mosquito-bomb odor until we were drugged with camping excitement. Grandpa got a new trailer hitch for the back bumper of the Studebaker and we worked until we got the turn signals that attached to the rear of the boat trailer to work. The night before we left, Grandpa and I cleaned out the boat and checked the motor and Grandma and Ben went to the grocery store to stock up. By the time August 15 came, we were in pretty good shape.

We set out so early that it was cold. Ben and I slept under a blanket in the back seat. When we got to the Straights of Mackinac, traffic was stop-and-go to the bridge. It was boring, and the smell of the ham sandwiches with their mustard and pickles about drove us crazy, so Grandma got them out even though it was only ten in the morning.

Some of the other men were already drinking beer, and a guy pulled his car right up next to ours and leaned out his window and said to Grandpa, "Hey, come on over and have a brew." His stale beer-breath made it all the way to our car.

"Oh no, you don't," Grandma said to Grandpa, rolling up the window. "You're not getting tight before you've even got the tent pitched."

"I like camping," Ben said.

"How do you know? We've never gone before," I said.

"Yes I did," Ben said in his timid way.

"Where?"

"In Toledo. When I slept on the air mattress."

I burst into uncontrollable laughter. "That wasn't real camping, that was pretend camping. This time we're going to be in a real tent, with a real lake, real swimming, real boats, and real fish."

"And real bears," Grandpa said, rubbing Ben's crewcut.

"And we're going to Canada, which is real camping territory."

Ben was quiet for a while, and then he said, "Croz, have we ever lived in Canada before?"

I burst into a huge laugh again. He thought we were moving there. Grandpa just squinted at him and looked serious for a little while. I hated it when Grandpa looked serious. He was supposed to joke around all the time. Even though we'd had school here, I felt that living at Grandma and Grandpa's was fun-and-play fantasy time, this-isn't-the-real-world-or-my-real-life time. When Dad got mad it was one thing, but when Grandpa was serious or mad, it was like the whole earth had swallowed you up. Fortunately, it didn't happen too often.

We got to Trout Lake before dark and immediately set up the tent because the sun was going down over the lake fast. Grandma cooked corned beef hash on the Coleman stove, and then we ate an entire blackberry pie and drank a whole quart of milk with it.

"Tomorrow night, better make room for fried potatoes and trout," Grandpa said.

Pretty soon Uncle Rufus and Aunt Thelma and Merle came over and the boys had a few beers while Grandma and Thelma and we kids had Vernor's and potato chips and French onion dip. Then Ben and I went for a walk down to the lake. It was so mysterious, like a great big bowl full of ink. The lake, the night, the whole world seemed overflowing, so full of surprises that you couldn't stand all the happiness. You could hear the lake slopping against boats and the crickets enjoying the northern cold and the beery laughter from campers, whose Coleman lanterns and pine-log fires glowed in spots like signals that said they were glad we were all here together, one big happy camping family.

"You have to watch it when you go swimming," I said to Ben, throwing a pebble into the water.

Ben took a pebble and threw it in near where mine went.

I threw another pebble to have the last word. "Grandma says there's a drop-off, so you can't go out over your waist." Then I said I was cold and I wanted to go sit under the army blanket. Ben said okay, he would too.

There was a peculiar thing about Ben. You had to tell him when it was cold. Hot, too, come to think about it. One time he was sitting in bathwater that would have burned anyone else, and Mom screamed and got him out. His skin was all red and he just laughed about it like it was a joke.

The next day, Ben and Grandpa and I went out on the boat.

There was a haze in the air and it smelled like fish and gasoline from other boats. I was excited, but I was nervous, too, about getting into the little aluminum boat. I didn't show it, though. Ben got in but yelped every time it rocked back and forth. "It's tipping. We'll drown," he cried out.

"You want to stay here, Bub?" Grandpa said. "You can help Grandma pick berries."

"I'm going fishing."

While Grandpa and I put worms on our hooks, Ben said, "Does it hurt them?"

"No," I said. "They don't have the same kind of nervous system—brains, to you—that we do." Then, I couldn't resist.

"At least, not like mine and Grandpa's."

Grandpa didn't laugh, so my joke fell flat. I wished Mom and Dad were there. They'd laugh.

I caught a fish right away.

"Bluegill," Grandpa said. "A keeper."

The bluegill wiggled like crazy as Grandpa tried to get it off the hook. He dropped it and I shrieked and laughed as it flopped all over the boat. He had trouble getting the hook out of its mouth. "Ooops, swallowed the bait," Grandpa said, looking down its mouth. When he finally pulled the hook out, the fish's guts were dangling on it.

"It hurts," Ben yelled. "It hurts the fish."

"He can't feel it," I said. "Right, Grandpa?"

"Yup. Hey this is a beaut," Grandpa said.

Ben leaned over it and almost toppled the boat. "His eye is still open. He's looking at us."

"Naw—he can't see us," Grandpa said, holding it up for me to admire. "Can't hear, neither."

"How do you know?"

"I asked a fish once if he could see me, and he didn't answer," he said. We both laughed. Grandpa's jokes were never mean like the rest of ours. They were just meant to be funny and dumb. But the joke seemed to make Ben even more upset. He just stared into the lake and finally said, "The lake looks like grape jelly, like if you walked on it, your shoes would get sticky," he said. "Is it thicker out here in the middle?"

Grandpa and I just gave each other an "oh well" look. People in the family were always giving each other "oh well" looks over Ben. If he was aware of it, he never said so.

We spent the whole day out there on the boat, and I felt a surge of excitement every time Grandpa started the motor and we took off, rocking around in that deep old lake with our little aluminum boat.

The next day, we didn't wake Ben, leaving him instead with Grandma. "He don't want to go anyway," Grandpa said. "He just don't know that he don't."

It was a gray day, but it made you feel tougher. For some reason, the mosquitos were worse, maybe because we were staying out later that day, maybe because it was so overcast.

And I hated to admit it, but I missed Ben. I was starting to feel disillusioned with fishing.

I lost count of the beers Grandpa drank. I managed to polish off four cans of Faygo Red Pop. I had to pee in the coffee can while Grandpa turned and looked the other way. I had to turn around for him twice. But even with all the drinking, this fishing trip wasn't as much fun and I was glad when Grandpa ran out of beer and it was time to go in.

"We'll have to get Horace and Merle and Agatha and Nora and everyone over for supper," Grandpa said.

I shook off the eerie feeling I had. Horace was a good poker player and Agatha was interesting to listen to.

But when we came in to shore, we saw an ambulance and a big crowd of people on the beach. I could feel it in my toes that it had to do with Ben.

Uncle Rufus came loping over to us. He nervously adjusted his fishing cap with lures stuck all through it and said, "Couple a guys pulled him out. Little feller went way the hell out."

I couldn't look, but I had to. I elbowed through the crowd. There was Ben, on the ground with a blanket up to his neck. His head was turned the other way. I said to myself, "He's dead, and it's my fault because I didn't wake him up to go fishing."

And then the shock of his being dead hit me, and my head got all prickly and hot and I moved around to see his face. It was purply blue all around his lips. And then his teeth started chattering and I almost leaped out of my body from happiness.

"Ben!" I said.

He opened his eyes a little and looked at me but didn't say anything. I didn't want to look straight at his eyes. I sat down on the ground next to him, feeling sorry and at the same time hating him for scaring us and screwing things up. Grandma came over and led me away. "Wendell, what's the idea of keeping the child around? Crosby, you come back to the tent with me right this minute. This isn't anything for you to see."

She told me Ben had gone in swimming and, despite the warnings about the drop-off, had gone out too far.

"All forenoon he was pestering me, so I told him he could go in the shallow part, up to his bathing suit." Grandma said.

I'd never seen her looking like this—all serious and, for the first time, wondering what next.

That night, while we sat on lawn chairs in front of the tent and swatted mosquitos and put vinegar on our sunburns, Rufus and Horace came over and got into a long, lulling conversation with G&G about their plans for deer season. I whispered to Ben, "Why'd you do it, idiot?"

"I was looking for you and Grandpa. I wanted to go fishing because I made myself not care that the fish got hurt."

"Didn't we warn you about the drop-off?"

"Yeah."

"Well you know what the drop-off is, don't you? Or do you?"

"Yeah."

"What?"

"I'm not telling."

"You don't know."

When we'd gone to bed and G&G were snoring, Ben shook me. I was still awake anyway, wondering why my boobies all of a sudden felt sore.

"Know what I did, Crosby? I took my bathing suit off and wrapped it around my neck."

"When? What for?"

He made a laugh that was trying to sound evil but which only came out as unsure. " 'Cause Grandma said I could go in up to my bathing suit."

I tried to imagine him taking off that faded little bathing suit with the little rocket ships and planets all over it, then wrapping it around his neck and going in with that blazing serious look.

"That sounds like something you'd do," I said.

"That sounds like something *you*'d do," he said to me.

"I've got more sense than that."

But I did think about it as I lay in the black night. Maybe I did do such things, but whenever I did, I got away with them.

It wasn't that Ben was really stupid. Despite his bad grades, we always had to remember that he'd scored in the 93rd percentile on the verbal part of his California tests. Mom and Dad couldn't figure out if it was a mistake or dumb luck or real.

"Ben, don't do things that you can't get away with. Concentrate on getting through the day doing normal things."

"What normal things?"

"Like playing games and doing school work and watching TV."

"Sometimes my head gets too busy." he said.

"Too busy with what?"

"Cowboys. Croz, do you sometimes feel like you're watching a cowboy movie in life?"

Grandma started grinding her teeth and we waited until we were sure she and Grandpa were both sleeping.

"What on earth is that supposed to mean?"

"Everything—the things you're thinking about—is running around in different directions."

"I don't get it," I said.

"It's like in a cowboy movie. You can't always figure out what's going on, where the different cowboys are shooting from or whose side they're on."

"Is that all?" I whispered and patted his arm. "Don't worry. You're not supposed to."

"Yeah?"

"Sure. You know what's going to happen, don't you? The good guys win."

"I hate it when everything's going on all at once. I want to hit my head, like it's the TV when the horizontal hold is rolling. I want to take a hammer and hit my head where it's unhappy, I want to kill the sad things in my head."

That made me get a rumbly stomach for Ben so I told him to shut up and let me concentrate and I went back to worrying why my tits were so sore.

~~~

TWENTY-FOUR

WHEN WE RETURNED to Birchville, we found a strange car with Ohio license plates sitting in the driveway. We were met by a big cloud of smoke in the living room, where Mom sat, her legs crossed and the top leg swinging madly.

Her smile took up the whole room. Ben and I ran over to her. She stuck the cigarette in her mouth to hug us and said, "John's out getting his Manhattan mix." We sat down on either side of her. Ben played with the hem of her skirt. "When he comes back, we'll have a toast. We were married again yesterday in Lansing."

Grandma's movements got brisker and livelier as she took care of the box of camping stuff she'd brought in from the car, but she didn't say anything. Grandpa put down the sheets and blankets and pulled his pipe out from his pocket and lit it cautiously, as if any sudden movements would scare the mood away. "Hey, that's real good news, Vere," he said.

Ben's face didn't register any reaction at all.

"I tried being a mean, tough, son of a bitch single woman. And you know where it got me? It got my phone cut off again, and the dentist and wallpaper store after me to pay my bills."

Mom blew out a ferocious puff of smoke. "I did it too late in life, dammit."

"It got you to appreciate your marriage, maybe," Grandma said, sitting down in her chair and picking up some knitting.

Mom gave Grandma a dirty look. "As I was saying, it got me a boss who had me doing everything from bringing him breakfast in the morning to washing off his desk at night. I told him he ought be done with it and stick a broom up my ass, so I could sweep up while I was doing everything else."

While all the grownups started talking and things got all heated up and lively, Ben sat there sucking his thumb, his throat wobbling like a bird's. I went back to our room on the porch and started to take down my map. Birchville had two stars next to it, and it deserved them.

We were going to live in Radcliffe Heights Estates, just outside of Youngstown, where Dad had gotten transferred in his new job as a field rep for National Rubber. The company was paying for us to stay in a motel and eat out all the time until we got a house. The first night, we went to a restaurant that had white tablecloths and candles in red glasses. There were waiters instead of waitresses, and they were real polite.

The waiter kept smiling at Ben and me as Mom and Dad figured out which appetizers they wanted. Finally, Mom said she'd just have a Coke and Dad said he'd have a martini on the rocks.

"Are the shrimp fresh?" Dad asked the waiter. We all stared at him for having the nerve to say something like that.

The waiter went to find out if the shrimp were fresh. He came back and said they were frozen but there were fresh oysters.

Dad acted like we weren't staring, and said, "I'll have the oysters, then." And he said to Mom, "Would you care for some?"

"Not on your life."

"Then would you care for a glass of sherry, dear?"

She got that look on her face, the smile that took over only one half of her face. "No, *dear,* I'd just care for the Coke."

Dad usually would have jumped up and started yelling, and

I was bracing myself for that, because it was obvious Mom was taunting him. But he just lifted his eyebrows up and slowly turned to the waiter and said, "That will be all, thank you."

I didn't think I'd ever heard Dad say "thank you" before. It sounded like he'd been practicing and also figuring out when you're supposed to say it. The waiter said, "Would the little lady or gentleman care for a Shirley Temple?"

"How would that be, kids?" Dad said.

Ben said he wanted chocolate milk, but I played along with the Shirley Temple thing just to see what it was. When it came, with an umbrella on top, I felt stupid and too old for it. Dad lifted his glass and told me to lift mine, and clinked his glass against mine. "Cheers."

Mom said, "Oh ber-r-rother."

The only time I'd ever seen oysters was in the movie *Alice in Wonderland,* so I had a good look at them when they came.

"Try one," Dad said, holding a piece in his fork out to Ben.

"They look like dead eyeballs," Ben said.

"Not to me," I said, wanting to seem sophisticated to make up for the Shirley Temple.

So Dad gave it to me. I held my breath and thought about something else while I swallowed it. After I swallowed it, I was glad I did, the same way I was glad the time I stood right on the edge of the roof and leaned forward so that I almost, but not quite, fell.

"Crosby, how come you can eat oysters and not toads?" Ben asked.

I ignored him, and Mom and Dad were too busy talking about the houses they were looking at to notice. Dad said to Ben and me, "We're moving into a very nice part of town. It about broke me to get the down payment for this place, but we signed the deal today. The schools are very good, too."

"Your nice part of town and a dime will get you a cup of coffee," Mom said. "We still don't have any money saved and we're broke."

"We're going to start saving, Vera. And we're going to stay long enough to get some equity . . ." And he went on talking about mortgages and bonuses and all the stuff that always came up when he was in a good mood.

Mom's half-cheerful snottiness was slowly easing, and Dad was so optimistic-sounding that the future looked about as rosy as I could imagine it. I ordered the turkey plate and Ben did too. Then, of course, he got gravy in the salt shaker and spilled his second chocolate milk all over the white table-cloth. Dad about burst a blood vessel trying not to yell, but he didn't.

On my first day of school, I put on a skirt that Grandma had made me out of material on sale at Woolworth's. It was really, really red. When I spun around and the wind caught it, it billowed out like a huge umbrella.

We were surrounded by boxes, and I couldn't find a blouse to go with my skirt. Mom disappeared into her room, moved some furniture around, opened some packages, and returned with one of hers. It was light blue. The style and the shade somehow didn't seem to go together with my skirt.

"Oh kabloney. Red and blue are fine together," she said. "And I'll tell you something else, boys like red."

I took her word for it and climbed back into my room to get dressed. What did I know about red and blue? I was excited about school. I couldn't wait to see how this one compared to others.

But I knew right away something was wrong when I walked into my first class. The girls stared at me, and it wasn't the usual "who's the new girl" look.

At first I blamed it on the enormous blue blouse of Mom's that no one under the age of ninety would wear. But at lunch I looked around carefully; it wasn't just the blouse. Everyone was wearing knee-length skirts, mostly pleated, and sweat socks and tennis shoes. I realized what I subconsciously knew all the time, that the real offender was my enormous red skirt. My sandals worn without socks were guilty accomplices.

That was one of the longest days of my life. Even though I was dressed, or overdressed, I felt like I did in dreams where I went to school with no clothes on. I sat through the afternoon classes totally unaware of what was being said. I couldn't tell you at the end of the day what one single teacher said or looked like. All I knew was I had to get some clothes—

some normal, blend-with-the-crowd clothes, and fast.

When I got to the bus stop, Ben was there. He was clutching his sack lunch as if it were a bagful of silver dollars. I asked him why he hadn't eaten his lunch.

"There's no lunch in here," he said.

"What?"

"Mom gave me the wrong sack. This has got a pack of cigarettes and a box of Q-tips in it and the receipt from when she went to the store last night."

I looked inside. Sure enough, Mom had screwed it up. Only it wasn't Q-tips, it was a box of Junior Tampax she'd gotten me because I'd started my period. I grabbed the bag from him and stuck it in my purse.

I couldn't worry about Ben. He thought he had it tough at lunch; I'd had to sit in that huge cafeteria all by myself, listening to other people laughing and squealing, choking down one of Mom's stale cheese-and-mayonnaise sandwiches along with an apple full of brown spots. I'd almost puked. From now on I'd make my own lunch. And Ben's too, if he was nice to me.

Some girl was staring at my skirt, and when the bus came I almost knocked Ben off the steps to get away from that school, fast. I sat on the inside seat and pretended I was alone in the Grand Canyon or something. When we got home, I tore off the clothes and put on my old slacks and top and crumpled the red skirt up and stuffed it into the wastepaper basket.

I wasn't sure I was going to like Youngstown, and I wasn't sure I was going to like being a teenager. It was a lot more complicated, and a lot harder on your feelings. I tried to figure out how to get back to G&G's and even try to be a kid again for a few years until I was ready to be a teenager.

Mom squeezed through the boxes and sat down on my bed. "How was the first day? Meet any boys?"

"Mom, I can't wear that red skirt. And that blouse you lent me is so big you could see my bra through the sleeve holes."

"Oh, you must have about died. But consider yourself lucky—when I was your age, I was so flat-chested that I didn't even wear a bra—all they would have seen was an undershirt."

"The bra's not the only problem. The skirt's not in style."

"I guess we'd better unpack the clothes boxes tonight, then," she said. Her face had that naked look; without her eyebrow pencil and lipstick, she looked like one of those old Dutch paintings.

"No, I need a bunch of new clothes. They wear different things here."

Mom looked at me as if I were a snotty salesclerk or something. "What do you mean?"

"They all had pleated skirts and socks and tennis shoes."

"Honey, I cannot buy you a completely new wardrobe. We're saving money now, you know. Putting it in the bank. Why, when I was your age, I had nothing, and I was prom queen . . ."

I must have looked especially depressed, because she said, "Okay, you can make do with what we have for the rest of the week, and on Saturday we'll go shopping."

Ben was trying to negotiate his way through the boxes to get in. "Come on, Crosby, let's watch 'Rocky and His Friends.' "

"Go away," I said. "I'm tired of cartoons." I took some deep breaths to keep from crying, then got up and started ripping open boxes to find my clothes. From the living room, I could hear Edward Everett Horton narrating "Fractured Fairy Tales" and ads for cereal and candy. Every time there was an ad, Ben would call out, "Hey Mom, can we get some [Maypo, Chunkies, Bosco, you name it]?" and Mom would yell, "Yeah, yeah" from the kitchen over the noise of ripping shelf paper—she couldn't find the scissors.

By dinnertime, I'd gotten all my clothes out and sorted them and decided I'd cut off a couple of skirts and sew up the hems. That would last me until we went shopping. Luckily, Grandma had shown me how to shorten a skirt.

"Mom, where's the sewing stuff?" I said, emerging from my room feeling better.

"What sewing stuff?" she called out.

"Like needles and threads."

"Your guess is as good as mine, honey."

"They've got to be in the boxes marked for the living room."

"I don't know, I may have thrown those things out."

"Then I have to go to the store to get some."

"By yourself? You don't even know where there's a shopping center, do you?"

"I have to hem my skirts."

"Crosby, what has gotten into you?"

"Can you take me to the store?"

"No I can't. I have unpacking to do."

I didn't have a clue as to where the nearest shopping center was, but there had to be one nearby; there always was. I'd find it by instinct.

I had a couple of dollars Grandpa had given me. I felt so independent, I wasn't at all worried about going myself. After dinner, I went out and got my bike and rode until I found a shopping center. But the stores all had Closed signs up. I looked in the window of the drugstore for a minute, at the nail polishes. There were so many beautiful red, orange, pink shades. I could stand there for hours trying to decide which nail polish and lipstick shades I liked best. Winner, Revlon Persian Melon; first runner-up, Revlon Fire 'n' Ice; second runner-up, Tangee Orange; Miss Congeniality, Max Factor Pink Jade, and talent competition winner, Revlon Orange Flip. Some day I'd be rich, by God, and I'd buy any color, maybe every single shade I wanted, and have the contest while I sat in my bubble bath.

But I turned around and felt the emptiness all around me and got out of there. There's nothing more useless, I thought, or more depressing than a closed shopping center.

Saturday morning, Mom slipped into her straight skirt and high heels. She put her hair into a French twist, and her neck and shoulders looked like the stem on an ivory goblet. She blotted her Cherries in the Snow and flashed a smile. Then she clamored around the house looking for her keys. Mom never got out of the house without a big search for her keys. "Oh, in my purse," she said in a tinkly voice. She closed her black patent leather pocketbook with a "time to go" snap that made powder whoosh out, and now the air smelled of Coty face powder. As she turned, some of the powder got on the hip of her skirt. I told her and she brushed it halfheartedly and didn't get it off, which I also told her. She said no one would notice.

Dad was out of town and had the car so we got to take the

bus. At the bus stop, Mom smiled the way someone smiles when she thinks people are looking at her. Like Dad. She was trying to be like Dad now sometimes, and it was touching. Mom was making a stab at understanding this world she'd gotten herself into. But it came to me that Mom, along with Dad, was nervous around people, like she didn't quite know how she was expected to act, and wasn't quite sure she wanted to act that way even if she figured it out. Come to think of it, she was always a lot nicer and more polite when Dad wasn't around. Like he was her Dad, too, and she could act childish and bratty around him, but when she was without him, she had to be more of a grownup and if people didn't like her, she had no one to blame but herself.

At Trent's Department Store, there were all kinds of signs up for school clothes. I was a junior size now. But instead of heading for the junior department upstairs, we went on the down escalator to the basement junior department.

I tried on several skirts and blouses. My body was lumpy, my legs looked short and undefined because of all the summer freckles that still ran riot. But worse, I couldn't remember exactly what it was that everyone wore. These were pleated skirts and tailored blouses, but they didn't seem quite right.

However, they were better than what I had, so I told Mom I'd take the blue plaid pleated skirt and the yellow and green, and one white blouse and one yellow. Mom looked at the price tags. "No, you'll have to pick just one thing. That's all we can afford. We have to save money, and you're just a kid, anyway, so you don't need anything fancy. When I was your age during the Depression, I got along just fine with a few skirts and blouses. And I did all right in the boy department, believe you me. They don't notice clothes. They notice your inner beauty." I frowned at the skirt. "How healthy you are, how you carry yourself."

Next, we went to the shoe department. There were lots of tennis shoes, but somehow they didn't seem right. I wished I could transform myself back into a class at school right away and check out the shoes. But I picked out some and a pair of turquoise knee socks to go with the skirt.

"Now can we go get sundaes?" Ben asked.

"Just a few more things to buy," Mom said.

We went to the boys' department and looked around at stuff. Mom picked out a couple of pairs of pants and several shirts.

I looked at the pile, holding my thin little package. "That's enough to outfit five boys. Ben's really making out."

Ben was wild with boredom by now, but he managed to crack a joke. "Hey Mom, you made out okay in the boy department when you were a kid, and now I'm making out okay in the boys' department."

"How come Ben gets all these new things?" I asked.

"His clothes have holes in the knees, tears in the pockets. He loses his lunch money and comes home with cut knees."

"That's not my fault."

"That's how boys are, Crosby. I can't send him to school looking like a beggar. At least your clothes are in one piece."

"But he doesn't even care how he looks."

"Well, I do. You have to care how your kids look, or they'll go around looking like hobos," she said, then added, "But of course there's a point at which you have to stop. We have to save money to get some new furniture. For you to go to college. You want to be a teacher, don't you? Goodness, you shouldn't be so concerned about appearances, anyway. You should know that you aren't judged by the way you look. People—the people worth bothering with, anyway—judge you for what you are inside."

I was getting tired of that inner beauty crap. I sulked for a while, and the next thing I knew, there was a commotion behind some racks of clothes. I heard laughing and loud voices, then I heard Mom shriek. I pushed my way through the crowd, and I couldn't believe my eyes. There was Ben, eleven years old, standing stark naked in front of a set of mirrors and turning around looking around like he'd just noticed he was out in public.

While Mom and Dad had a yelling match about Ben getting naked at the department store, I tried on my new clothes in my room. I still wasn't right.

That week, I saw that the biggest problem was my shoes—the wrong brand, the wrong style. The biggest strategic error

I had made was in not noticing that you had to have pointed toes. Mine were round, dull, ashamed.

I'd come home from school and see Ben in his new pants and bright red-and-blue striped turtlenecks, and wonder why I had to have the old clothes, why Ben got the good ones and then tore and lost them on purpose. All I could figure out was that Mom and Dad felt guilty about him, because the worse he acted in school, the better his clothes got.

~~~

TWENTY-FIVE

B EN'S DOING IT AGAIN, fucking up my life, I thought as I dialed Sarah's number to find out just how badly the condo sale was falling through.

As the phone rang, I realized how ridiculous that statement was—Ben didn't ask that guy to beat him up, and he certainly didn't force me to come here, and he had absolutely nothing to do with the house sale. But as Sarah answered, I realized that it was still true anyway.

"Harboil won't come down and the buyers, oh Crosby, they're cooling off. They're talking about some condo in Sun City."

"Oh, Jesus. Why?"

"Security system and built-in microwave."

As she related the negotiations of the past two days, I wondered how I was going to keep up, grasp the details of this and Ben, too. By the time this week was over, I wouldn't know which end of a torts textbook was up.

"They asked what happened to that nice young lady with the freckles who was so cheerful all the time."

"They ought to see me now."

"They had such confidence in you, since you were recommended by that old geezer in Santa Barbara."

The truth of that had been that the seller needed quick cash because his family thought he had Alzheimer's disease and wanted to put him in a nursing home. We'd worked fast so he could escape them.

"I just wish I knew the senior citizen market like you do, Crosby, and I wish I knew more about this area. I feel awful about this."

"I'll call them. Don't worry, it's all my fault, I shouldn't have left."

"I know how much this means to you. By the way, how is your aunt?"

"Better," I said. "I still hope to be coming home tomorrow."

I called the Loebroes. When they told me about the cute little place in Sun City, I said, "I'll bet it doesn't have as nice a view. You can always buy yourself a microwave and a burglar alarm, but you can't buy a view."

Mrs. Loebroe said, "And a mountain can't cook or call the cops for me, honey. Get Mr. Harboil down another forty grand and we'll talk."

Mr. Harboil, a bit deaf, may or may not have heard me over the scratchy line when I called. He shouted that he would lower the price another twenty thousand and not a penny more.

I called the Loebroes back. No dice. When I called Mr. Harboil back, there was no answer. He was known to get into a mood and turn off his hearing aid. I dialed Sarah's number and got her answering machine.

I made some soup with my little electric water heater. Dean was going to have to wait until I could figure out what in the world I was going to tell him—he knew I didn't have an aunt in New York, and if I had my way he wasn't going to know I had a brother here either.

I tried Mr. Harboil again. No answer.

As for Antonia, I told her I was sorry but I couldn't make it.

"What else have you to do tonight?"

"Several calls. Then I'm going to a food pantry on the Lower East Side."

"I don't know that I would go fooling around in that neighborhood at night. Especially alone."

"I have to go there because I can't call—there's no phone."

"You should wait until tomorrow. Then you can come here tonight."

"Look, Antonia, I appreciate your help, your interest in my brother. But I think the request is a little out of line, to be honest. I don't live here, I didn't come here to New York to work in a shelter . . ."

"I'll be a little out of line when people are dying on the streets."

"I'm so overwhelmed right now with trying to find Ben and with some business problems at home that I just don't have any time or energy left over."

She dropped the bossy tone. "Are you having any luck?"

I told her what little I had found out. She sighed loudly. "All right. I'll call you if he or Tyrone shows up here tonight."

I hadn't thought of the possibility of their showing up. I sighed back. "Oh, good heavens. If you don't find anyone for tonight, call me back."

The room felt like a laundromat. I fanned myself with Antonia's list as I called some of the city-run shelters.

Finally a busy man answered at the Fort Washington Shelter. "No client by the name of Ben Rawson slept here," he said.

So that's what Ben was, a client, just like the people to whom I wanted to sell a condo with three bathrooms, two Jacuzzis, and a swimming pool.

"He was last seen at a park, a Tompkins Square Park. Is there a shelter near it?" I said.

"Shelter Care for Men on East Third Street."

That was on my list, too. I dialed and dialed, but couldn't get through. I figured it was like the post office, a number that was busy all the time. I'd probably have to just go over there tomorrow.

City shelters exhausted, I called churches. He had stayed at Grace Church on Fourth Street and Fifth Avenue. My heart raced until the woman said he was last there a year and a half ago.

"But I remember Ben so well," she said. "Oh, that first

night. He had been released from Bellevue in the middle of
a snowstorm. He had nowhere to sleep, no money. Someone
had told him to come here. We had no beds left. I had to send
him to the city shelter in the Bronx. He left before I could give
him a subway token. I found out later that he walked the
whole way, one hundred and fifty blocks in a blizzard. Can
you imagine?"

Yes, I could imagine Ben doing anything.

"Such a quiet young man. May I ask which agency you're
with?"

"I'm not with an agency. I'm his sister."

I said thank you and put down the phone before she could
finish cooing, "Oh, I'm so sorry."

All the talk of snow made me realize I was covered with a
thin film of sweat. The air conditioning wasn't even pretending to work now. I crawled across my bed and pushed the
window open another inch.

Here I was again, feeling resentful of people, nice middle-
class people who were trying to help. I didn't mind the work-
ing-class Puerto Ricans, the sympathetic blacks, but when a
white do-gooder got into it, I became itchy and angry. Was
I feeling guilty? Was I angry at the society, the system, the
world? Good heavens no. Not even when I was in college
could I afford to be a hippie. I'd spent my life trying to be part
of that society, that system, that sorority, that world. I wanted
to be in there, right or wrong, a part of it all, a successful part.

I called around some more, and was finally directed to
where I should have been sent in the first place—Central
Intake.

A man in the computer room asked some questions about
Ben, and I felt as I had when giving the description to the
police, as if I were discussing a corpse. The man said he
would be able to find out if Ben had been in any of the city
shelters recently, and took my number.

I spent the next hour calling churches and charities, without any luck. I leafed through the TV listings. The man from
the computer room called back.

"Yes, Benjamin Rawson, he frequently uses our facilities.
He was last a client of the Lower East Side shelter a week
ago."

Alive a week ago and able to go to another place to sleep!
"I could kiss you," I burst out. I sat back lightly against the
headboard and waited as he looked up a name there to call.
"Darryl Roosevelt," he said. "Good luck."

Darryl Roosevelt was brusque at first, but when I said I was
Ben's sister, his voice was careful not to hurt. "Yeah, that Ben
Rawson was here last Tuesday. I liked him. He sticks to
himself a lot, but he's okay. He doesn't make trouble, don't
bother no one."

"So his condition is good? He's okay?"

"He had a bandage on his head that night and some bruises
on his face. I asked him if he was okay, and he said he was
in a fight and the only thing that hurt was his teeth. He was
taking Extra Strength Tylenol for that."

"How badly hurt did he seem?"

"He seemed okay. Otherwise, I would of sent him over to
Bellevue emergency. That's what we're suppose to do."

I put the phone down feeling encouraged. One week away
from my lost brother, who was not lying in a gutter somewhere, not a living vegetable, but moving around as usual. As
usual except for coming up to the cathedral shelter. I wondered why not. Was Antonia getting on his nerves? Unlikely—for all her faults, she obviously favored him. It didn't
make sense.

Neither the Harboils nor the Loebroes were in yet. I was
feeling dreary. I wanted to talk to someone about Ben. But
he was a secret to everyone but my parents. I was so depressed I finally dialed their number.

"It's me," I said.

"Hi, Me," Mom chirped. "You caught me on my way out."

"Where to?"

"Bridge." She told me about her new partner, a Catholic
priest. She said she had a platonic crush on him and made
some joke about how she always had been attracted to a man
in uniform. Good old Mom. Don't let the serious side of life
get you down. "So tell me, are you still seeing that lawyer
boyfriend? Dad's about fit to be tied because he's a Demo-
crat."

"Yes, at least I think I'm still seeing him. But I called to say
I'm in New York looking for Ben."

"You really did go, huh? Oh, here's Dad, just coming in. Get on the extension, John. It's your daughter and she's in New York City."

"Hi, Crosby, hon." He sounded old. "What's up?"

"I've been going to homeless shelters to look for Ben."

"Oh, Jesus Christ, you shouldn't be going to places like that. And don't you know those people have AIDS?"

"No, you really shouldn't be there," Mom said.

"I'm close to finding him, I think."

"At least wear rubber gloves when you're around those people," Mom said. Now it didn't sound like she was joking.

They didn't seem interested in anything but AIDS, so I let the conversation trail off. When I was done, I lay staring at the map of Manhattan on the ceiling, feeling frustrated and a bit silly and foolish, something my parents had always made me feel, whether I was trying out for cheerleaders or attempting to go to law school or haunting the Skid Rows of New York looking for my lost brother.

It was so hot I couldn't breathe. At least the cathedral shelter had a fan.

I opened a bag of plantain chips and shook out a handful. Not only that, but my parents had always made me feel as if there were something wrong with my feelings for other people. The word *love* was not in their vocabulary. Not so much because they ignored it, pretended it didn't exist, but because they thought there was something slightly unsavory about the whole concept. Love was like sex, something vaguely dirty and maybe pretentious. It was for movie stars and socialites and black people.

But give yourself a little credit, I said to myself. Love may not have been in their vocabulary, but you wouldn't be lying here in a seedy hotel room staring at cracks in the ceiling if it weren't in yours.

I wrapped the bedspread around me for comfort and closed my eyes. The more I lay there and thought, the more lonely I felt. Antonia had bent over backwards for Ben. I went to the bathroom and sponged myself off with cold water. I looked about ten years older than I had three days ago. I supposed I should go to the goddamn shelter one more time. As I dialed Antonia's number, I had to laugh at myself—I was actually looking forward to seeing the crazy cast of characters again.

My parents' words about AIDS did make a certain amount of sense, especially since Mom had, at long last, become a nurse. I stopped at a drugstore and bought a pair of rubber gloves. Then I remembered that other volunteers brought food to supplement the U.S. surplus stuff, so I stopped at a deli and got three pounds of potato salad, five pounds of roast beef, and a dozen rolls. I didn't believe in smoking, so instead of cigarettes, I picked up a dozen of my favorite carob-wheat germ bars at a health food store.

A group of men stood in front of the shelter. No Ben, but I hadn't really expected that. One of them, Randy, recognized me. "Hey, ain't you the counselor that was here last night?"

"Volunteer," Antonia sang out, pushing through with a jingling set of keys. "Volunteer means unpaid, got that? Now come, come, gentlemen, please let me through."

Inside, Antonia surveyed the early arrivals. Her widow's peak sat like a crown on her prominent forehead in the harsh light of the kitchen. In spite of the heat, over her sundress she wore a shawl—old, ratty, but made of silk, with tassels that shook violently with her brusque movements. On her feet were buffalo sandals that looked like they had about a million miles of protest-marching on them.

"Tyrone's not here," she said to me. "Ask some of these men if they've seen him recently. He could be a big help."

I put the bag of food on the table and she looked at it and laughed at me. "You don't really have to bring food, you know. Oh, don't look so hurt. I suppose it's money going toward a better cause than it could." She rifled through the bag, smirking and shaking her head. "You can put your purse in the closet over there with the lock. While you're at it, get the sign-up sheet from the pantry. If anyone seems stoned on anything, alcohol or drugs, send him to the city detox tank."

She threw me a ring of keys and wrote down the address. As I opened the squealing metal door I was met once again with the massive cans of spaghetti and beans and chili and ravioli. I took out the clipboard with the names of men who were there last night and had earned priority tonight. I put my food in the refrigerator, then worked my hands into the rubber gloves and got to work. I checked off names, sent the men who didn't get in to the infamous city shelter on 160th Street.

I had to turn some particularly pitiful people away—a very sick young Puerto Rican man, an elderly white man with a gash over his eye from a bottle thrown at him the night before in the city shelter. Antonia and I gave them cabfare and sent them to a hospital emergency room.

Before I handled the silverware, I thought I should put on my gloves. Antonia, passing by with a pile of army blankets, said, "Planning on doing some cleaning tonight?"

"No. In fact," I said, my voice low, "I wanted to ask if AIDS might be a problem here."

"Only for the men who have it. And I don't know who does. That's their business."

I looked around, wondering who might have it, checking for the signs—purple patches, swollen glands. Nothing like that was immediately visible. I slowly removed the gloves, wondering for the first time about Ben and AIDS.

Most of the men were from the other night. New were a black man with a saxophone and a beefy white man wearing bicycle pants and a button-down dress shirt who said he was a Russian defector.

I sat and played War with the Russian while Antonia went with two of the men to get the free leftover donuts from the bakery.

I was nervous about being left alone, but the men seemed to know what to do, walking around setting up beds and taking turns in the shower. I sat down with two depressed-looking older guys.

"I saw on the news that we're in for more of this weather," I said.

One of them got up and walked away. The other grunted, "What?" and rubbed the black and white stubble on his chin, then ran his hand through his hair as if that would help to get my words registered inside his head.

"Tell me," I said, "Do you know Ben Rawson or Tyrone Davis?"

"What?" he said, looking all over my face as if he were trying to place it.

Jack, the redheaded guy in the wedding dress from the other night, got up and started spinning around the room. The man with the saxophone began to play wildly.

"Tyrone Davis?" I shouted.

"Wasn't he an actor back in the forties?" the old guy finally said.

I laughed, and a couple of the men who hadn't even heard him laughed to keep me company. A couple of men started clapping to the music. A warm glow seemed to come over the room. I joined in.

"Stop that, stop that immediately," Antonia's voice barked out. She stood in the open doorway framed by two of the men, one carrying the carton of donuts, the other holding the door for her. "There'll be no rowdiness in here."

The roast beef sandwiches were a hit and most of the potato salad got scarfed up, but the carob-wheat germ bars bombed. We ended up opening a monster-size can of minestrone soup to supplement the stale donuts as a dessert.

After dinner, Antonia and I asked around the table if anyone knew Ben's or Tyrone's whereabouts.

No one had any news. She got up and did something with some papers. Jack whispered to me, "I tell ya, she's got a sneaker for that Ben."

"I don't believe it for a minute," I said, trying to look disapproving.

"Oh, for cryin' out loud, I didn't mean she was getting it on with him or anything. But I know Antonia. I think she needs a man, but she likes men she can keep under control. That's why she likes it here."

"Sometimes, though, she does take them home," Randy whispered.

"Nah," Jack said.

"Remember that Indian incense-seller? And that massager guy?"

"Yeah, and come to think of it, she always let Ben go get the donuts," Jack said. "He'd pick out the freshest ones and eat 'em on the way back."

I seriously doubted any of this. How could someone who carried a spray can of Lysol around for door handles go through with the sex act? To change the subject, I asked Jack where he was from.

"Everywhere. My old man was a high-class preacher, but we lived like gypsies, moving from one parish to the other. If I say he doesn't send money, it's a lie. Genteel poverty, only it wasn't really poverty."

"Sounds like my family, only it wasn't really genteel."

"You know what I hated? All those dumb names of towns. It drives me nuts, trying to figure out how a place got its name and what it means."

"It don't mean nothin'," Randy said, his thin face breaking into a rare grin. "Ready for this, counselor? He's about to go into his song and dance."

"I came up with this idea that they should give towns numbers, like they do with streets in New York. Or at least letters, like in Washington."

"They'd run out of letters, idiot," Randy said.

"They could have AA and BBB and all that."

"Like bra sizes," Randy said. "Me, I want to live in Thirty-eight–D."

A couple of the men laughed. Antonia, from the kitchen, turned and gave Randy a sharp look.

"It would give some order and sense to the world," Jack continued. "There'd be so much less name pollution."

Randy made a high-pitched howl, tattoos of a butterfly and of a strongman with barbells coming to life as he hugged his arms and jiggled and laughed.

"How are you going to find Ben?" Jack asked me.

I told him I was planning to go to the Lower East Side men's shelter and a food pantry the next day.

"By yourself?" Randy said.

I nodded.

"I could maybe go with you."

"Me too," Jack said.

It was a bizarre idea, but no less so than anything else I'd done in the past two days.

"Sure, why not," I said. "In fact, I'd appreciate it."

$$\approx$$

T WE N T Y - S I X

W<small>E MOVED</small> to a split-level on a street that looked good when you wrote it down but was annoying when you had to say it—Beech Breeze Bluff. Mom said she was going to learn sign language. Ben said it took too much energy and he wasn't going to tell anyone where he lived. Not that anyone ever asked.

It was getting more and more difficult to make new friends at school. You'd think practice would make perfect, but it didn't work that way; being a kid is a lot different from being a teenager. By October, though, I had a girl named Angela French to pal around with.

Angela lived on Jackson Avenue in a two-story frame house with peeling paint and window shades stapled together in the ripped spots. Her hair was an explosion of black. She wore orangy liquid makeup and smelled of spearmint gum, and she had boyfriends who were old enough to drive.

She was the first Catholic I'd ever been best friends with. Once she got the message that I was impressed, she milked the Catholic thing for all it was worth, dangling her rosary as she searched her purse for makeup, chanting out a bunch of

Hail Marys after skipping class, throwing ritual after ritual for me to wonder about, me who had been brought up in that generic Protestant neither-here-nor-thereness.

She showed me how to cross yourself and genuflect. She told me about the strict rules for Communion, where you got perfect little round wafers that magically melted in your mouth, and real wine.

I'd complained, as we stood in the girls' room and drew black lines around our eyes, that we only got grape juice and ordinary bread, like Wonder, cut into squares. "And at some churches, we didn't even have Communion," I said, feeling that that admission revealed my entire life to have been equally slack and wishy-washy.

"How the hell many churches you been to, anyway?"

I told her I could never count them all, but described some of them, trying to make her laugh, sympathize, understand. I don't know if any of it registered or not, because her expression didn't change one bit.

Actually, I never knew if much of anything registered with Angela, because all in all, conversation with her was pretty limited. She had three topics—boys, records, and cars, and her state of mind was one of eternally bored restlessness: "Wanna go hang around Slade's drugstore and see if they got any new Supremes forty-fives?" Or, "This is fer shit, let's go see if there's any guys over at Big Boy's." Or, "There's a real fine dude with a red 'Vette that hangs out at White Castle." Or, "Got any money for a Coke and ciggy-butts?" These comments just about summed up her interests.

President Kennedy also made being Catholic pretty glamorous.

My parents didn't like Kennedy because they thought the pope would be running everything, and that echoed the general opinion around here. But most people seemed to feel really bad when he died.

Angela became more significant in my life because I was with her when I heard President Kennedy had been shot. "Want to skip school this afternoon and go look at this pet shop I found?" she had said at lunch time. "They got this tarantula there that you can buy. Wouldn't that be cool, to tell people you got a pet tarantula? Think of the guys we'd get— they love creepy stuff like that."

I was impressed with the burst of originality she showed in making this suggestion, but I said my mother wouldn't let me keep a dog in the house, let alone a tarantula.

We ended up instead at a gas station. She had a crush on the attendant, Bucky Bradshaw, and on his new Bonneville.

"That sure is a fine automobile you got, Bucky," she said. "I'd sure like to be layin' some rubber down the boulevard in that."

The rock station we were listening to broke right in while the Four Seasons were singing "Candy Girl," and the announcer shouted, "The president has been shot. President Kennedy has been shot."

Suddenly Bucky's boss came running into the garage and said, "D'ja hear that? D'ja hear that? They shot the mick President."

"Oh my God!" Angela screamed, and burst into hysterical tears. Nothing was registering in my head. Presidents didn't get killed. They were TV people, and when people on TV got shot, it was just pretend. I tried to calm Angela. She was screaming and crying and Bucky was turning up the radio.

As I listened to the radio, I tried to figure out what I felt. All I knew was that within an instant I'd stopped being a kid and become a full-fledged teenager, and there was no going back, and the world seemed to be doing the same thing.

I started coughing from the cigarette Bucky gave me. Angela went crazy. "Ahhgh. Ahhhgh," she screamed. "They did it 'cause he was Catholic. They hated him. Everyone hates him."

"What do you care?" Bucky said.

"Hey, shut the hell up and don't be so damn disrespectful," Bucky's boss said.

Angela straightened up and said, "Yeah, Buck." She inhaled jerkily and wiped her nose with the inside of her wrist, then turned to him. "You too chickenshit to treat us to a ride in that candy-apple blue machine of yours?"

"No, I gotta stay and work on my engine," Bucky said. "I don't have much time for dealing broads these days."

"You kids amaze me," the boss said, turning up the radio.

There was a lot of shouting. I felt that it was horrible, and yet I felt the horribleness impersonally; famous people like President Kennedy—Catholic or not—were another species, important places like Washington might as well have been in a different solar system.

Angela pushed Bucky away, and said, "We'll get to see the shooting part on TV tonight. I bet they'll have it on the news. I can't wait to see what Jacqueline was wearing. Come on, Rawson, let's go over to see this guy I know with a motorcycle."

The next day, Mom was all pissed off because her TV shows were preempted by the Kennedy stuff. "If I have to see Jackie's hind end climbing out of that convertible once more, I'll scream," she said. "Jackie this, Jackie that. Don't tell me she doesn't love every minute of this. If her husband hadn't been shot, she would have taken her pants off to get some attention."

I went over to Angela's, and her whole family was camped out in front of their TV. Her mom and sister were crying, her father and brothers looking angry, taking the shooting personally. This seemed like the right way to react, and I knew somehow that all this was making history, and it made me feel important to be a part of the time. And yet as I watched the pictures of the shooting over and over, the reporters feeling so important, so much more a part of history than I was, I couldn't help but think again that these were TV people, no more or less real than Dick Van Dyke and Bat Masterson and Crusader Rabbit, people, characters, who hovered between reality and unreality.

Maybe I was the wrong age to have a president assassinated—old enough to understand it, but too young to argue with Mom's assessment of the situation when she said, "Well, if you're a bigshot, some nut out there's bound to be jealous of you."

I stayed friends with Angela, but it wasn't easy having to wait after school for your best friend to get out of detention all the time. It was also not much fun to have a friend who seldom listened to anything you said, but was always listening to that inner voice saying "Worry about getting in trouble later and go have fun." But she was better than nothing, like a teddy bear for a kid who's alone. Okay, she was no teddy bear, more like something you won at the carnival one night and weren't quite sure you wanted to wake up and see on your pillow the next morning, but again, she was better than nothing at all.

Ben, meanwhile, had given up entirely on finding friends.

1963–1964

TWENTY-SEVEN

A FTER A WHILE, Angela's eternal restlessness and boredom started getting on my nerves. So while I waited for her to get out of after-school detentions or the principal's office, I'd find myself watching with increasing interest the cheerleaders' and pom-pom girls' practice. They'd sing the school fight song, which was the University of Michigan song with our words put in:

> Hail, Radcliffe Heights Estates
> Hail to our vict'rous heroes,
> We know you'll win for us
> We'll hold our heads high,
> Hail Radcliffe Heights Estates
> Hail Radcliffe Heights Estates
> Hail Hail to RadHeightsEst
> The leader and the best

And they'd do cheers, chanting:

> Two bits, four bits, six bits, a dollar,
> Everyone for Radcliffe Heights Estates stand up and holler.

Angela sneered and said they were suckers and squares, but something inside me was right out there on the football field with them.

There they were, all of them pretty, all of them sashaying around the field, kicking their bobby socks and flashing their teeth toward the bleachers that would be filled with admirers on Friday night.

One day I saw in the school paper an ad for cheerleading classes at some dance studio in town. It was being taught by two ex-varsity cheerleaders. I asked Mom if I could take the classes.

"Cheerleader," she said and looked at me to see if I was joking. Then she held her head back, took a long puff of her Viceroy, and said, "What would you want to do something like that for? I always thought they were a bunch of show-offs."

"Mom, being a showoff is considered a virtue nowadays."

"Well, I'm sorry, but we just can't afford it."

It didn't occur to me to find out how much the classes were. It wouldn't matter anyway. If they were five dollars or five thousand, they were too expensive because they weren't for people like she thought we were. She couldn't get lower-middle-class rural out of her head, even if she *had* been the Queen of Sheba there. No, cheerleader and all that was the kind of activity we couldn't afford as newcomers to this town, as newcomers to middle-class respectability, as newcomers to the world of teenagers in the nineteen sixties.

"You sound like Dad," I said.

That broke into her daze. "Look, honey, I can't afford nursing school, either. We just moved. Wait until I get the house furnished. Wait until I at least get a new refrigerator." The pink refrigerator had a big gash in its side and didn't work half the time.

Then the real truth came out. "Crosby, Ben's teacher said he needs to see a psychiatrist or some damn thing like that. I'm not so sure he needs it, and I know they're expensive. Let's wait and see what happens. His art teacher says he's fine, she says he's got unusual talent. Maybe she knows more. I'm going in next week to see the principal. Just wait until things get settled here."

But I was tired of waiting for Ben to act normal and for us to settle somewhere. So when Dad came home I said before he changed clothes, "Dad, I want to take cheerleader classes."

"That sounds okay," he said, sorting through the mail. "Vera, sound okay to you?"

Mom looked at me out of the corner of her eye. "I played the flute in the school band," she said. "That's a lot more respectable than dancing around flashing your rear end for the world to see."

"But I don't play an instrument."

"That's not my fault," she said. "You had violin lessons."

"That was in second grade. And I couldn't finish them because we moved into a district that didn't offer lessons."

"They didn't have *orchestra* instrument lessons. They *did* have band. I asked if you wanted to take flute, and you said no."

"That was in the middle of the year. I didn't think I could catch up."

"I don't see any harm in her taking the classes," Dad said. Good old Dad. If ever there was someone who would be proud to see me as a cheerleader, it was him.

So three days a week after school I put on my tough-girl sneer and told Angela, "I have to get my ass home early because my Mom needs help," and I sneaked off to the cheerleading classes. After class, I practiced in our basement. One time Mom came down to do the laundry when I was practicing. I stood tall and strong, one hand on my hip, one hand holding an imaginary newspaper in the air, "Extra, extra, read all about it, we got a team and we're gonna shout it!"

"What's that?" she said.

"It's a cheer."

"Don't you feel ridiculous?" she said, dumping a load of clothes into the washer and dropping in a piece of Salvo. "Because you certainly look it."

That stabbing feeling hit me. Mom's problem was she didn't understand how important it was. Her high school hadn't even had cheerleaders. But there was another problem with Mom. I saw it at Open House night.

Mom and Dad were sitting in my homeroom with me and all the other kids and parents, and Mr. Hildebrand was dron-

ing on about civics, and then he introduced the student coun-
cil reps, the head cheerleader, and a couple of other people
like that. Then, during the coffee hour, those kids and their
parents were circulating, and I noticed every time one of the
bigshots' parents talked to Mom and Dad, Dad gushed with
phony niceness while Mom pooched her mouth out and
edged away. If someone important talked to her, she raised
her eyebrows when she answered and looked like she didn't
want to talk. Like she didn't want the people to know that she
thought they were important. That's what being a poor person in a small town in the old days had done to her, the way
I figured it.

Practicing every morning and evening, I found little extra
twists for the jumps and other innovations.

Angela eventually found out about my cheerleader classes
and didn't even make fun of me. In fact, she showed a grudg-
ing admiration, and said if I wanted to be one of those fratty
shitheads it was my problem, not hers, and she'd do me the
favor of still hanging around with me. So I let her come over
on a practice day and watch me in the basement.

She observed me with a blank expression for a while, and
when I took a break, she said, "Rawson, you act like you want
to be friends with Sally Ann Robinson and the other snobs."

I said it wasn't true, but I wasn't so sure.

She went on, "But I got no other friends except Tina Fran-
chetti, and she's suspended for the semester, so I'll hang
around with you for now."

"Angela," I said, "I don't necessarily want to be friends with
them. I just want to be *able* to be friends with them."

Angela burst out laughing with a mouth full of Snickers.
"Yeah, that sure makes a lot of sense, Dumbo." She called me
names a lot, but I had to put up with it, since friends didn't
grow on trees these days. Besides, I knew she didn't mean it
personally. In her family, they called each other worse
names.

"I can teach you some of the cheers, then you can be a
cheerleader and we'll form our own snob group," I said.

"Ah, who wants it." She munched a second Snickers like
she was thinking, then she said quietly, "Nah."

I could tell that Angela was getting bored with me, too. That day after school, instead of sitting in the basement reading movie magazines, she stayed upstairs with Mom while I did my cheers. When I was done, I came up. She and Mom were watching "Deputy Dawg" with Ben. "Oh, I seen this one, me and my sister did," Angela said. "It's boring."

"I saw it a million times, too," Ben said.

"Is this the one where they break out of jail?" Mom said.

They were eating Hostess Sno-balls and drinking Pepsi. Angela offered me a bite. I shook my head and said I was on a diet.

They all turned and looked at me. Angela came in for the kill, and said, "They only pick the most popular kids for cheerleaders, you'll see."

Mom just stared at me. I wished Dad were there. Suddenly, I knew why Dad kicked stereos and drove away in the middle of the night. If there'd been a stereo nearby, it would have been on its way to Des Moines.

"You'll never go anywhere in life, Angela French. All you'll ever get out of it is pimples."

Angela got up, grabbed her purse, and shook her little fist at me. "If your Mom wasn't here, I'd kick your ass. When you want to hang around again, let me know, and I'll tell you to go piss up a rope."

After she left, Mom was nice and said, "She's just jealous, of you, Crosby."

But she didn't defend my cheerleading. I went to my room and tried to do my algebra.

I walked in and surveyed the panel of judges for basketball cheerleader tryouts down on the gym floor: four teachers and four students, including Sally Ann Robinson, head football cheerleader, and Larry Buttermeyer, basketball captain. Everyone sitting on the bleachers waiting to try out stared at me. It was weird, being there all alone. Everyone else was either a jock type or a card-carrying member of the Robinson snob clique, or both. With five positions to fill, it didn't look good for me.

First was Linda Westfield, who had a very athletic body and perfectly executed turns. She'd been the best in the cheerleading class I took. Marilyn Osborne was really good, too, but a little *too* athletic. They didn't like that in a girl.

Terry O'Keefe wasn't great, but she was definitely the prettiest girl in the school and would get picked for that. No one could recall ever seeing Kristen Johnson in the the same outfit twice, so she'd be in the running though not a shoe-in.

Next was Linda Riley, who was class president and got all A's. People like that never did anything wrong in their lives, so she'd get in. The next three girls were fair to middling, and the last was Carla Stevenson, a new girl from Florida, the only kid in school with a tan.

Sally Ann sat there in her angora sweater like a white Persian cat. I didn't hate her. No, I didn't hate her. I almost loved her. Yes, I wanted to possess her. I felt like a boy trying to win her. If I got out there and did well, maybe I would win her. You have to win the girls in life before you can win the boys, I had come to believe.

When my name was called, I got that chilly feeling in my arms and my heart started thumping and my stomach felt like it was pushing against my lungs.

I smiled a big phony smile like you were supposed to, and the silence was like little particles of air crackling, and then I belted out, "Give me an R. Give me an A . . ." And pretty soon I was just into it, and I was giving it all I had. And then I did my special turn with the smile, with my hands on my hips, and I thought it was pretty gutsy myself, and the next thing I knew, there were a couple of people applauding.

Next day, during homeroom announcements over the loudspeakers, they listed the finalists for basketball cheerleaders. When my name was called, I felt like my head was going to go through the ceiling. I tried to erase the image of myself in one of those little skirts from my mind; it was too wonderful to believe and I might screw up the whole thing.

A week later, when they had the second cuts, I was a whole different person standing there waiting. It was possible now. If it happened, I'd be so happy, I'd never let anything bother me again. I'd be so happy, I promised God, that I'd spend my whole life doing good things for people if He'd do this one thing for me and let me be a cheerleader.

I made the second cuts. Final eliminations were the next week. I practiced like crazy that week, and I didn't tell Mom or Dad. But the night before the big day, when Ben came down to the basement and saw me, I told him.

"Ben, you may have a hotshot, hot-shit cheerleader for a sister," I said, jumping and twisting in mid-air. "Then I can help you be popular. When your big sister's a cheerleader, life's a lot easier."

Ben thought about that for a while. He hated school now more than ever and was forever getting beaten up physically by the kids and mentally by the teachers. "Are you gonna watch cartoons after school ever again?"

"Can't. I'll have practice."

That night, I laid out my shorts and blouse to take for tryouts. The shorts were ones I'd made secretly so Mom wouldn't laugh at me. The shorts she bought me had elastic at the waist, and made me look about five years old. The other cheerleader candidates wore bermuda shorts with zippers and waistbands. I'd bought the pattern and cut up one of my old skirts. Ben still wasn't getting his head shrunk, but Mom and Dad were still "saving money," and when I asked Mom again for money to get new clothes, she reminded me that people who spent a lot on clothes were frivolous and wasteful.

But I guessed I could live through it. So far, the fact that I had round-toed tennis shoes in a pointed-toed world had not held me back. I had only one pair of socks, which I had to wash out early so they'd dry by morning—if it rained, the air would be too humid for them to dry overnight and I'd have to wear wet socks—but at least they were the right kind.

I floated through school that day, sure of myself, positive that I would do my best, and yet dragging with me the nagging feeling that somehow God hadn't intended for me to be a cheerleader, that Mom was right and we should stick together as a family unit and not try to be like other people because wherever we moved other people were too bewildering. But I shook off that feeling by the end of the school day and went into the gym, sat down with the twelve other finalists—all Sally Ann Robinson cliquers—and read my English homework. The other girls had Villager or Evan-Picone clothes and smooth hair and didn't talk to me. But I was going to win everyone over in the end.

I was reading this story and barely understanding a word when Linda Westfield got up to go through her routine. Then I felt someone behind me and I turned, and there was Ben making his way down the bleachers. As usual, his carelessness had made him a mess—his new shirt was torn at the shoulder and buttoned wrong, and his pants were slumped down so that they rested at the top of his butt instead of his waist. One of his shoes was untied, and the shoestring was all frazzled, like the crazy wires inside his head. He sat down and put his thumb in his mouth. In public. In my public space.

One of the teacher-judges turned around and looked at Ben, and then at me.

"Get out of here," I whispered.

"Why?"

"Just get out. You look like hell."

"No," he whined loudly.

I moved down to a bleacher closer to the gym floor. He followed me, dragging his jacket. The sleeve of it came to rest on a browning apple core.

Then it was my turn. I gathered myself and went out there and started my routine. Halfway through, though, they told me to stop. At first nothing made sense to me, then I thought maybe there was a fire drill because of a big commotion with people running past me over to the other end of the gym. I turned, and there was Ben, up on the scoreboard, his muddy shoes dangling down, holding his torn jacket by the sleeve, and yelling, "Crosby beats me up. I'm scared of her. She beats me up after school, and I don't know how to get home alone."

"Get that kid down immediately," a man teacher was yelling.

"He'll hurt himself," Miss Heywood, the math teacher, cried.

"Call the fire department."

Ben stopped yelling and sat sucking his thumb, gazing at everyone like he didn't get what all the excitement was about. When the fireman brought him down, there was a strange, empty silence. Ben stood for a minute looking at me before a teacher took him out. Someone asked if I wanted to go with him, that he must be sick or something, and I said no, I did not.

I did my routine again from the beginning, but my sneaker hit the floor the wrong way and make a huge loud squeak and then I fell forward and banged my nose. I got up like nothing happened, like you're supposed to, but I felt like running after Ben and banging his head against the floor about a hundred times and then burying my head in the sand until I suffocated.

That night, I clung to the wild hope that nothing would make any difference, and tomorrow when they announced the basketball cheerleaders, my name would be miraculously on the list. I dreamed that the whole incident had been a dream itself. I laughed at myself for thinking anything so terrible could happen. Everyone was laughing along with me, except for Mom. I awoke sweating and laughing, laughing so hard my eyes were squeezed shut.

But I didn't make it. The list was full of the usuals. I felt mousy and unimportant and a little foolish. I went back to hanging around with Angela.

And I also started beating up Ben for real. I kicked the shit out of him after school when I found him waiting outside my door.

I don't know if that had anything to do with his starting classes at the Dawes School. That was the school for kids with emotional problems and for retarded and physically handicapped kids. I don't know. I just don't know. This was one time I really wished we'd move, but we didn't. Anyway, I'll never forget the first day of the next semester. I'd finally gotten myself elected president of the Speech Club.

I became fanatical about becoming a cheerleader, about proving to the world that there was nothing wrong, and next semester I would become a cheerleader, I just knew it.

And there was Ben going out to that dumb bus with all the retards on it, climbing on, looking so trusting underneath that buzz haircut of his. I watched from our living room window. There were some kids with their tongues hanging out, large doughy ones lurching around in their seats. But some of the kids were normal-looking.

As Ben was climbing the steps onto the bus, he turned and looked back at the window for me. When he saw me, he gave me a wave that tried to be nonchalant. I felt so goddamn sorry for him. But I ignored the wave, and turned away from the window.

I had to go back to my own problems, cheerleader kinds of problems, like whether to wear my hair in a flip or in a ponytail. And then I got mad at myself for feeling so sad and sorry, and told myself that cheerleaders couldn't afford to be nice. No, I said to myself as I looked in the mirror, they simply can't spend time to go around feeling sorry for losers, or they won't be on the winning side.

~~~

TWENTY-EIGHT

R ANDY WAS STANDING at our appointed spot, smoking and drinking coffee with the kind of life-or-death urgency I remembered in Ben. I hadn't noticed before that Randy's hands trembled ever so slightly. "Wanna slice?" he asked, nodding toward the pizza stand behind him.

"I just ate."

"I guess I'll get one. We gotta kill some time, anyway. Jack stopped to do his laundry."

I bought him two pieces of pizza and a coffee, then a third piece and another cup of coffee. As we watched for Jack, Randy told me about trying to get work as a commercial artist without any formal training and as a tattoo artist with training in a world that didn't appreciate him for either skill.

I spotted Jack with a backpack, wearing a wool plaid skirt and a tie-dyed T-shirt cut short to reveal a ticklish-looking cover of orangy red hair on his stomach and back.

"Would you like something to eat?" I asked him. "Or to drink?"

"Nada, gracias. A guy gave me five bucks to keep an eye on his laundry while he fed his parking meter. So I splurged on breakfast. I had two eggs and four strips of bacon and two halves of toast and one swipe of butter. Did you know that if you add that up and divide by four and a half, you get grape jelly?"

We were off down St. Mark's Place. I felt self-conscious in my stiff khaki bermudas and too-white tennis shoes. Randy, wearing jeans decorated with horizontal rips, was relatively conservative, and even Jack hardly got a second look. People of all ages (but mostly too young or too old for the look) slithered by in black Spandex, Day-glo Spandex, boots with vicious spurs, dog collars around their necks and all the bracelets their arms could hold. Hair was plastered up in painfully against-the-grain styles. Men showed a preference for locks bleached blond at the ends with defiant black roots; the women went in for crewcuts.

As we walked on, I could see why Ben would be attracted to the neighborhood—not only was it full of strange-acting yet presumably sane people, it was also a haven for an ever greater concentration of the mentally ill and alcoholic. In fact, it was like some bizarre, futuristic society in which you couldn't tell the crazies from the normal people.

Randy pointed out the sights and landmarks and nodded at people he knew. I scanned the faces of passersby and people sprawled on the sidewalk, stopping occasionally when I saw real blond hair on a tall man, trying not to look too closely once I saw that someone wasn't Ben. One man stared back and reached his hand out. Awkwardly, I gave him a little wave.

"Honey, got a little spare change?" he growled.

I felt sorry for him, but I was running low. "Afraid not," I said with a sympathetic smile.

He shouted so hard I thought he might tear a hole in his throat, "Well ya goddamn son of a bitch, what good are ya then?"

Randy kicked the air. "Want I should thrash his ass?" he said.

"Don't bother. Just promise me that where we're going—or rather, where I'm taking you guys—it doesn't get any worse."

"Worse? Hey, this is hot property. You know how much it costs to live around here?"

"I don't know much about New York real estate," I said.

"Except that it's pretty expensive everywhere. But I had no idea . . ."

"Hey, this is where I lived when I first came to New York. Then I had to move down to the Lower East Side, then I couldn't afford that."

"Why don't you leave New York?" I said.

"And go where?"

I couldn't give him an answer. We walked for a while in silence. I didn't entirely dislike the area. Like a carnival, it was a place you find slightly repellent and yet irresistibly alluring because you feel you could get away with just about any crazy impulse you'd ever had.

I told them that there was once a warrant out for Ben's arrest for making a tent out of a blanket in a park somewhere around here.

"Wha? Tompkins Square Park?" Randy said.

"Yes, I think that was it."

"Shit, man, he's a hero. Yeah, the cops busted the homeless people there and caused some riots."

"The homeless gotta get organized," Jack said.

"Wanna see that park?" Randy said.

"My curiosity is certainly aroused."

Randy strode ahead. At a corner he jerked his head for us to turn.

"Did I tell you why I moved to New York?" Jack said.

Randy pointed his finger at his ear and wound it around in the "he's crazy" sign.

"Why?" I asked, trying to look unruffled by the stares from some of the rougher crowd we were mixing with now.

"Because the streets have numbers. I don't like streets with names. I don't like cities with names. It's another form of word and brain pollution."

"I see."

"I wrote to the post office headquarters in Washington about it. I said if they gave the cities numbers, they could make New York number One and L.A. number Ten Million or however many cities there are that need names."

"I think I lived in all of them," I said.

"I only lived in forty-seven-and-a-third of them," Jack said.

First Avenue down here was characterized by relatively

wide streets and low apartment buildings. While it was intensely urban, the spacing gave the feeling of a European village on the outskirts of a city; it was interesting in the way a city might be after the bomb. Or you could be entering a time warp, going back a few centuries. The ultimate urban landscape of poverty. The sun blazed down on us and shot back up diffused from the white-hot concrete. It hurt to look up and it hurt to look down. We went along, the three of us abreast, and I had to admit that I was glad I had my two escorts.

Tompkins Square Park presented another extreme. The trees were blue-green giants casting the generous shade I associated, oddly enough, with Grandma and Grandpa's park.

We entered the park, lost creatures in the Black Forest, searching for another lost soul. The concrete on the walks was cracked, weedy, like that in my grandparents' neighborhood. The big difference between the two parks, though, was that Grandma's had been deserted whereas this one was teeming with the most wiped-out derelicts I'd encountered yet. They were standing or lying everywhere, like the war-wounded.

"Remember," I said, making conversation to appear less frightened than I was, "to look for Tyrone, too, or anyone who might know him or Ben."

"That oughta be easy here," Jack said, waving wildly to someone.

I spotted one blond, and my heart raced, but he turned around and I saw that he was just a boy, not even twenty. And yes, Crosby, let's face it, your brother is no kid, as Mom had noted on Ben's thirtieth birthday, making the pronouncement: "His behavior can no longer be mistaken for cute."

Jack, wearing his gumpy smile, said, "Someone at the Coalition for the Homeless said a lot of the homeless are mental patients. I told him I'm part-time crazy but I have a college degree so maybe I could get part-time work. Last job I had was canvassing on the subways in a clown suit."

Jack, I said silently, you scare me in that my brother might be as far gone as you are now, and yet you reassure me, because you're so damn happy.

And then I froze as halfway across the park I saw a tall, yellow-haired guy with a bandage over his ear. He had the high, narrow shoulders, the bouncy walk of Ben.

"Look," I cried out.

Randy squinted. "Yeah, that could maybe be Ben."

"Let's catch him." As the blond head grew distant, I took off. Walking fast, I still lost him, so I began to run past the bodies on the ground, trying to avoid the broken bottles and squashed garbage and trickles of piss. Pigeons scattered. A sniffing rat with its long naked tail twitching stopped in the middle of the sidewalk. It turned and faced me, freezing like a deer looking into headlights. As the rat began to run in circles, I jogged off onto the grass behind it. I came to a group of men drinking out of paper bags who blocked my path between the shrubs.

When I tried to get around them, two white guys, one with his shirt off, and two black guys circled me. Their boom box was so loud I could feel it in my teeth.

"Hey sugar," one of them said.

"Where you off to in such a hurry?"

"Runnin' loose, runnin' wild, smokin' dope 'til I smile," said the boom box.

"I can't talk," I said, trying to get around them, seeing the blond head bob up again and then disappear.

"You better motherfucking talk or I put your eyes out for you."

"What you got in there?" one of them asked, reaching for my purse. "Somethin' fo me?"

"Dope dope fuck fuck. Gonna fuck, gonna fuck, gonna fuck a motherfucker."

"Want to buy somethin' for your head?"

"No." I was in the middle of the park. There were no civilians around, just the war-wounded. My heart started thumping so hard it felt like it was hitting bone.

"Fuck fuck fuck fuck," the boom box went on, its beat speeding up as my heartbeat kept rhythm with it.

They took my arm and pulled me behind a hedge. I was pushed onto the grass. The boom box was in a frenzy. My eyes wouldn't focus. I blinked and I blinked again, and in front of me was a hypodermic needle. A line of deep, serious red blood sat at the base of the tube.

"Baby, you wanna try some shit?"

"Take my money," I whispered.

The man with the needle had skin like licorice. He smelled like I imagined dead people smell after a day or two.

"Oh, I'm gonna take your money, all right. I just got to decide should I give you a complimentary free sample of this or should I fuck you first."

"That's one of the executive decisions we have to make today," said the white guy, his whiskery face inches from mine.

"Whatcha gonna whatcha gonna whatcha gonna, kill kill kill kill." There was no real rhythm now; the radio and I were traveling through space. I knew not to move, not to blink. I breathed shallowly, then my muscles relaxed and I gave in to death. I lay waiting for the prick of the needle, expecting it . . . I felt now as if I'd stopped breathing. But I wished it would come more quickly, the coup de grace of a knife or a gun, not from AIDS.

A police siren approached and I heard my heart pounding in my ears. The siren got louder, drilling the air near us, then faded away. Nothing to do with us.

The boom box was laid next to my ear. "Kill kill kill kill kill kill kill . . ."

I stopped hearing it and relaxed again. I could have been drugged already. Demerol could be dripping into my veins to relax me for what was to come. Relax, count down from one hundred, and it will all be over. Your wisdom teeth will be out. No, Crosby, it's only a polio shot. I was a kid again. No, it was just a blood test. Dean and I were getting married. I half expected to feel it on the inside of my elbow, to get up and walk away with a little round Band-Aid over the puncture hole.

Voices again, arguing now. No, Crosby, you've got it wrong. You'll get up and walk away and wait for death. Tears formed heavy, wobbly pools on my eyes.

"Hey man, leave her alone," an older black man said. "You want to get the po-lice out here fuckin' with us again?"

Someone else was telling them to let me go, and then some more voices joined in.

I was freed and they attacked my purse, then my wallet. As they looked through the secret compartments, my credit cards and other papers scattered to the ground. Someone spat. AIDS spit on my American Express Gold card. I got up, picked up the purse, pulled out a wad of Kleenex, and picked up my card. I also got my Blue Cross card and my driver's license. They could have the Saks and library cards. I turned and raced out of Tompkins Square Park.

There were pay phones but I didn't know if it was safe to stop and call the police. I didn't have cab or even subway fare, and I was afraid of every human being that walked by. I had lost Ben. Out on a busy street now with cabs going by, I slowed to a walk. I was disheveled and my wrists were shaking. No one noticed me—in this neighborhood, I looked like anyone else.

I sat down on a fire hydrant. I was trembling so hard I fell off. My arms felt like flapping chicken wings.

When my breathing got close to normal, I calculated how much the junkies had gotten. Fortunately, I realized, the wallet had held only my day's allotment, minus cabfare, breakfast, and Randy's pizza; a grand total of about twelve dollars.

I guessed I was going to have to walk back to the hotel. If I saw the police, I'd stop them. But as I walked along, I thought of all the red tape I'd probably have to go through, the time wasted. I'd had my wallet stolen once in L.A. and it had been a thorough pain in the ass just reporting it to the police. They'd never found the guy, just like they'd never find these.

Gnawing at me, too, was the let-down feeling of being abandoned by Jack and Randy. But what did you expect, Crosby? They are homeless people, bums. One is crazy, the other a low-class hood with a drug problem or criminal record. They're losers, not normal. What the hell did you expect, Crosby of Sunnybrook Farm?

By the time I got to Forty-second Street, all I knew was I wanted to get on the next plane back to the Coast if I had to ride on a wing.

Not one house I'd ever lived in looked as comforting and safe as that hotel room. I fell onto the bed and let myself cry. Then, when I could talk without my voice trembling, I called the airlines. I couldn't get back that night, so I made a reservation for the first flight back in the morning.

In the bath, I examined myself for puncture wounds. I seemed to be okay, but I scrubbed myself as if I were covered with filth. I scrubbed so hard I raised welts. I wondered why I felt as if it were my fault that I had gotten mugged. Maybe because I knew what people like Mom and Dad would say— they'd ask why I was in that park in the first place. And that was the essence of my whole problem, I realized.

I sank back into the tub and thought about that.

Half an hour later when I climbed out, I felt it should be time to go to bed, but it was only three o'clock in the afternoon. I didn't even want to leave the hotel room for dinner. I'd order a pizza, maybe. I called Sarah.

"Oh God, Crosby," she said, her voice quavery. "Harboil won't budge and the buyers are backing out. You've got to get to Harboil quick."

I poured myself a glass of warm white wine and bolted it and called Harboil. Harboil said he didn't think he should deal with an agent who was flighty enough to leave town in the middle of the deal, and he didn't want to lower the price anyway, but his voice was tentative.

"I'll be flying back tomorrow," I said.

"I'll be on vacation," he said, and hung up. As soon as I put the phone down, ready to call him back, it rang. It was Antonia.

"I called to see if you'd made any progress," she said.

"I think I saw my brother," I said, the wine starting to relax me, "But I got mugged and couldn't catch up with him."

"Goodness. Where?"

I told her the story, adding that I was disappointed in Jack and Randy.

"That's scary. Are you okay?"

"I think so."

I bit my lip to keep from crying. I thought momentarily how I'd like her arm around me now, consoling me and telling me everything would be okay. She was my only friend in New York, and might as well have been my only friend in the world at that moment.

"Go to the police, Crosby."

"I just want to get out of this city."

"And I called to see if you could come in again tonight. The problem is that most of my volunteers are students, and they're away in August."

"No."

"Well, if that's how you feel." She said good-bye curtly. And that was the end of Antonia and that whole godawful mess of a place and would soon be the end of this whole godawful mess of a city.

I called Harboil back and there was no answer. Maybe I should go to the police after all. I had spotted Ben, I was almost sure, and perhaps the police poking around that park might help me find him in the time I had left. Since I was stuck here for another day . . . I called the police to tell them that I'd been attacked. They told me to go to the Ninth Precinct stationhouse to make the report.

I got a cab and headed back down to the Lower East Side and told myself I deserved a nice fancy dinner afterward.

≈≈≈

TWENTY-NINE

A T FIRST it was money from Mom's purse so I could get a pair of swizzle socks. Swizzle socks were basically ordinary cotton bobby socks, but they were one certain particular brand that you just had to have. You put them on and then you twisted them—simple as that.

As simple and basic as that, and as this rule: if you didn't have them, you might just as well put a big sign around your neck that said, "Don't ever be seen talking to me in public."

So I copped money from my Mom just to get a lousy pair of socks. It was an expense Mom said I didn't need to burden her with, an extravagance for a silly, vain reason, because when she was in school, nobody could even afford nylon hose and they all had to wear wool leggings, and God knew she did okay without a pair of "swizzling" socks.

"You should live through a Depression some time, my dear, and then you'll appreciate just having a pair of shoes. Try going through it in a farm town, too, where everyone knows everyone and you have to make sure your family is known as respectable."

"Well, why did you bring us to live in a town where people expect you to wear swizzle socks?" I said.

"Ask your father, he's the authority on why we moved here or anywhere else. And he must be an authority on swizzle socks, because he sure as hell is one on swizzle sticks." She looked a little pale, the way blondes with creamy skin can look pale and stunning at the same time. Like they're beautiful in spite of themselves.

Stealing, I knew in my gut, was wrong. But there was something wrong, too, with letting yourself get beaten up by other people for the wrong reasons. I didn't mind taking crap from other kids for things I couldn't help—saying something stupid in class or missing a play in gym and making the team lose, but I did mind persecution for something I had a little control over, like having the wrong goddamn kind of socks.

The first time I did it was the day she took us out shopping and again got Ben clothes from the upstairs boys' department and me clothes from the bargain basement. I knew why she did it—because he'd torn his good pants and shirt, and she didn't want people to think the reason he was in emotionally handicapped classes was because he was neglected. But it didn't make me any less sensitive about what I warmed my feet with. The squeaky wheel gets the swizzle socks, I said to myself, and I'd spent too much time being the other three wheels all jammed together into one worn-out, holey sock.

I started saving the money I stole from Mom's purse. I got good at it. And then, to buy a pair of the right sneakers, the right kind of jewelry, I started taking money out of Ben's piggy bank. He was so confused all the time he never knew how much was supposed to be in there. I took change Dad left on the dresser, never enough to notice, and it didn't take long at all to save up for the things I needed.

Then I stole for Lesley Gore. You absolutely had to like Lesley Gore. I actually couldn't stand her songs, but you would have pulled my tonsils out with pliers before I'd admit it, and I was more than willing to go along with the required proof of devotion, owning a minimum of two forty-fives or one album.

I worked my way into the Lesley Gore crowd one day on the toilet. Patty Henshaw came in to the girls' room crying. Patti was not exactly in, but she wasn't completely out, either.

I asked if I could do anything, and she said no, and sat down on the edge of a toilet and wailed some more. I went into the stall next to hers and sat down, feeling sorry for her and getting worried because the sobs were getting almost violent.

I'd always kind of admired her because she was so normal, so absolutely, perfectly normal. I'd have given anything to be the kind of person she was—someone who wore the in haircut, an "artichoke," even though it made her nose and chin look kind of long and pointed. It didn't occur to me that maybe she didn't know it. As far as I was concerned, she was a remarkable individual—above personal vanity, someone who understood the value of priorities in life.

Finally, she asked if I could hand her more toilet paper. Then more, then more. I hung around and kept handing her toilet paper to blow her nose on. Finally, she sniffled and said, "Did you see who was with Joe at lunch?"

"Joe who?"

"Pettington. My boyfriend."

"I don't know him."

"He sits next to you in science. He told me he copies off you."

And I'd thought he was looking at me that way because he liked me but was shy. "Yes, I know him—glasses, tuba case on Tuesdays and Fridays. Who was he with?"

"That horrible Cindy Emerson. He dropped me for her."

I'd heard talk about Cindy. It was rumored she had spiders crawling around through her hair. That was because it was teased so high and sprayed so hard it took a whole weekend to brush it out and wash it, so she only did it every six weeks. It was also said that the spiders kept laying eggs. Someone reportedly had seen a couple of baby spiders emerge from one of her ears, too, and there was speculation that the littlest ones might be able to crawl through her ears into her brain.

So far, I hadn't been in love with anyone other than a baseball player I didn't know. But I understood unhappiness.

"Don't worry, nobody wants to make out with a girl with spiders in her hair for very long," I said.

I came out of the stall. I put on some white lipstick and looped my purse over my arm and picked up my books. Patty came out of the stall. Her eyes were puffy and red. "You're smart. That's one thing I can say about you, you're smart."

I didn't know whether to feel complimented or not, but I offered to help her with her science homework, and I made a couple of funny wisecracks, and she said, "Hey, wanna come over and hang around with Maureen and me after school?"

Patty's house had shag rugs everywhere and framed needle-point work bearing slogans with the word *love* or bless something-or-the-other. I told Patty it was so cheerful it reminded me of a greeting-card store.

She had her own record player. As we sorted through her forty-fives, I said I liked the Rolling Stones.

"The Rolling Stones are too grease," Maureen said. "I like Lesley Gore and Tommy Roe. Sally Ann Robinson has all of Lesley Gore's albums and singles."

"I like Peter, Paul and Mary, too," I said.

"My father says they're reds," Patty said, examining me carefully. And then she started to cry again over Joe. " 'It's my party, and I'll cry if I want to,' " she sang.

Tommy Roe wailed out "Sweet Little Sheila." I thought I'd puke. Everything, everything my instincts told me to like, everything my parents liked, was socially unacceptable. I had to hide everything to fit in.

"Ooo," Maureen said, examining some of the albums. "You've got Bobby Vinton, too."

"Everyone has that," Patty said, putting on Lesley Gore and gearing up for a good cry.

Patty's mother knocked on the door and then poked her head in. She had a pixie haircut. "Rice Krispie treats, anybody?"

"I'm on a diet, but I guess I can go off it for now," Maureen said.

"I see you're listening to Lesley Gore," Patty's mother said, passing the plate of treats around. " 'It's my party, and I'll cry if I want to,' " she sang. "You know who Mr. Henshaw and I like better than any other singer?" she asked me. "Now this is a toughie, because it won't be the first one you'll think of."

"Perry Como, I'll bet."

"Nope."

"Andy Williams?" I guessed again.

"Uh-uh."

"Bing Crosby? Frank Sinatra?"

"My stars, no," she said. "Mr. Sinatra sings about night-clubs, and I've read that he associates with unsavory types. We don't think he's wholesome. No, we like to listen to Jim Nabors. People think he's just a funny man, but he has a beautiful voice. So deep, so moving." She took a bite of a cookie, chewed it thoughtfully and tapped her foot to the music. "You know who else we like? Have you ever heard Big Tiny Little on the 'Lawrence Welk Show'? Oh, he plays that piano so well. My, my, he's just so awfully good." Then she wrinkled her nose and giggled, "Patty thinks we're out of it."

Dad said Gomer Pyle was a New Yorker's idea of a south-erner and he made it look like people with southern accents were all dumb. And I know that Dad, at least, didn't like Big Tiny Little, because every time he came on, Dad got up and slammed the TV off. The only people he'd ever liked on "Law-rence Welk" were Alice Lon, the Champagne Lady, and Law-rence Welk, when they danced together, and I was sure Mrs. Henshaw would find fault with that. Obviously, my parents liked the wrong people, just as I did, and I decided then and there that I'd be damned if I'd have people come into my house unless I had a Lesley Gore and a Jim Nabors album out in full view.

The next day, I went out and with my savings bought the Jim Nabors inspirational album and the Big Tiny Little one. I hid them under my mattress, where they stayed until the day Maureen and Patty came over after school. When we got home, I distracted them, then I whipped out the Lesley Gore for my room, and put Jim Nabors and Big Tiny Little on the table in the living room for people to see. Mom was watching TV and playing checkers with Ben and didn't pay much atten-tion. When my friends left, I put the albums away before she saw them.

This went on for a while, until one time I didn't put Jim Nabors away in time.

Mom didn't notice it, but when Dad came home I heard, "Vera, what the hell is this?"

"What?" I heard Mom say from the bathroom.

"Jim Nabors?"

"What are you talking about?"

"Jim Nabors. Gomer Pyle. Is this your record?"

"Yeah. I just joined his fan club and bought every record I could get my hands on."

Dad laughed, then said, "Well, may I ask, then, just whose it is?"

"Good God, how would I know? Maybe it's the kids'," she yelled out.

"Kids don't listen to Gomer Pyle. Someone must have been here and left this. Did anyone come over to see you?"

"No, I told my press agent to keep the crowds away today."

"Well, someone . . ."

"Are you trying to imply something?" Mom said, coming into the living room.

"Well, I don't know." Dad's voice was still light and mocking.

"Okay, I'm carrying on an affair with a hillbilly banjo player. He and I have orgies in the living room listening to Jim Nabors and Tennessee Ernie Ford."

"You're just loony enough . . ." I heard Dad say as he disappeared into the bedroom to change. A little while later, I heard Frank and Dad singing, "She's much too hungry for dinner at eight, da da da da da da da dum."

I didn't think I could take a big blowout. I sneaked into Ben's room. Ben was listening to the transistor radio, trying to get a baseball game from Detroit. I don't know, maybe we were both loonies—I had my map of the United States on the wall with stars in the cities we'd lived in, he had a list of baseball teams and their standings in the leagues and all that. He was a fan of the cities we'd lived near, but when they played each other, his allegiance followed a hierarchy dependent on which he had enjoyed most—St. Louis was his preference over Minneapolis, and so forth. His favorite was Detroit.

"Do me a favor," I said.

"What?" He was all sleepy-eyed. He was tired a lot of the time now.

"Go tell Mom and Dad that you borrowed a Jim Nabors album."

"Gomer Pyle? Why?"

"Never mind, just say you borrowed it."

"From who?"

"From a neighbor, just to see what it was like."

His eyes got that crazy light, and he said, "Borrowed Jim Nabors from a neighbor." He smiled. "Hey, I know, from our neighbor Jim Burlington."

"Good thinking." He hesitated, so I went in for the kill. "Please, please. Otherwise Mom and Dad will have a fight."

He got up slowly and went to the hallway and called out, "Hey Dad, Mom, have you seen my Jim Nabors album? I borrowed it." He turned and looked at me, his eyes dancing with his dumb joke, waiting for them to ask whom he borrowed it from. Ben was sweet sometimes.

I shoplifted, too, and that helped. By the end of the year, I had a pretty respectable wardrobe and record collection. I had everything it took to conform to being a sixties nonconformist, and Mom and Dad had a few more Jim Nabors and Big Tiny Little albums they didn't know about.

Dad was always worrying about work or watching the news, and he would never notice my clothes. With Mom, I just raced out of the house before she saw what I was wearing, and kept spare clothes in the basement for when I came home.

For cheerleader tryouts, I had a good pair of bermudas; a matching blouse with a Peter Pan collar; expensive, pointed-toed tennis shoes; a black clutch bag; a mustard seed locket; a pearl ring; and a charm bracelet with a lot of fake hobby charms like a tennis racket and ice skates on it.

I kept at it, and I finally made cheerleaders that spring. I was to be a cheerleader for football season. I got invited to my first party—not one of Sally Ann Robinson's, but Shelly Slattery's (whose parents listened to Perry Como).

This was definitely a more discriminating crowd, in every sense of the word. With my new group, I had moved out of the Lesley Gore league into the Beach Boys. Not liking the Beach Boys would have branded you not only a Communist, but an anarchist. Their "Be True to Your School" was the hottest hit at the school dances.

We'd been to everyone's house to make chocolate chip cookies or Chef BoyArDee pizza, and eventually my number came up and I had to invite everyone over to hear my new Beach Boys album.

Long ago, Mom had started to crochet a dresser scarf to cover up the cigarette burns on my chest of drawers—I sat up half the night finishing it and put it on the dresser. I put a bottle of Tabu cologne and some Wind Song talc on top, along with a snapshot of G&G I'd stolen an old-fashioned-looking picture frame for. I stuck up magazine pictures of Europe to hide the scratches on the walls—besides our own crap theirs was the crap of the people who lived here before, who'd been hard on the walls and kitchen and bathroom fixtures.

But the rest of the house was too much of a mess. It was the same old problem—ironing board, coffee cups, lipsticks; ashtrays that you couldn't exhale around or you'd set off a tornado of butts and ashes; girdles still wearing their nylons like two flowing ponytails, with ribbons of Cherries in the Snow nail polish over holes and runs; newspapers flapping around your ankles as you walked through the living room; opened and unopened bills lying all over the place, bills Mom had set down any old where because they were too depressing to deal with; furniture Dad had kicked in, appliances he'd smashed, their brains dangling out; Ben lying around with a maniac look in his eyes mimicking crowds cheering and boo-ing—what was I to do?

I stood looking at a wad of Mom's gum stuck on the lamp base, which was crooked from the time Dad hit the chair with it because Ben had watered it once when Mom was watering the plants. "You want to ruin it?" Dad had yelled, slamming his Manhattan down. "I'll show you how to really ruin the goddamned lamp if you want to. Might as well do it right."

But neither of them had totally ruined it, so we had to live with a bent lamp because new lamps were too expensive.

Well, I had to admit that a person who spent her free time shoplifting wasn't perfect. And I had to admit that these girls liked me, and I wasn't exactly the sanest person on earth, so I guessed they'd have to accept my warts-and-all family. But the mess all over the house had to go.

I tried to do a little cleaning up but Mom saw me and got annoyed, like it was some dig at her. "Nobody's house is perfect, Lady Jane, unless they have a maid or they're the star of some TV sitcom. Don't worry, I'll straighten up."

I knew damn well that "straightening up" meant she'd put a couple of the coffee cups in the sink. "You just worry about getting to school on time," she said. She put her coffee pot on and looked for bread to make toast. What was left was moldy. She got out a box of macaroni and started eating the pieces. "I'm going over to the hospital this afternoon to see about working part time in the gift shop, Crosby. I won't be here when you get home, so keep an eye on Ben for me, will you?" Then she went to the bedrooms to get Dad and Ben up.

After school, when I saw Shelly waiting for me with the other girls who were coming over, I hurried up to her. "There's an emergency with my uncle," I said. I sometimes savored my own lies. I loved pretending I had relatives living in the same town, like we really belonged to a place, so much that we had people to see on weekends and birthdays. "Uncle Bill lives a few blocks away and needs to have me rush him medication from the pharmacy. Meet me at my house, okay?"

I gave her directions and raced home, knowing the school bus had a long, winding route and I'd beat them by a good half-hour. But when I walked in, my heart sank; Mom was plunked down, playing out some bridge hands and talking to someone on the telephone. She put her hand over the phone. "Wouldn't you know? They filled the job."

"Sorry," I said.

She went back to talking and I got out the sweeper.

She put her hand over the phone. "What's going on?"

"I'm going to vacuum the carpet."

"Can't you wait?"

But I flicked the sweeper on and pretended I didn't hear and went ahead. I vacuumed and took all the newspapers that were all over the floor and started to throw them out.

"Wait a minute, what are you doing?"

"Throwing these out."

"I'm not done reading them."

I put them neatly on a table. She said, "What's going on?"

"My friends are coming over. Okay if we listen to my new album on the stereo?"

"Oh, all right. Just don't put anything away where I can't find it."

I hurried around, putting junk in drawers, hiding things like broken coffee cups and pots and pans with missing handles. Mom got off the phone and started following me around. "Who's coming over? The queen of England?"

When my friends arrived, I made sure Ben was out of the way by giving him some of the money I'd stolen from his savings to go out and buy candy. He was so grateful he skipped out of the house. Eleven years old and he skipped. Mom, bless her, acted really nice. It made me think that there was nothing malicious about her, just messy, and totally unaware of it.

We played some records and then I asked, "Do you guys want to make pizza or cookies?" I was so damned confident, having bought not only the ingredients but a shiny new cookie sheet, compliments of Ben.

"Mmm, I don't know," Shelly said, looking at Marcella and Suzanne. "I'm in a popcorn-and-Coke mood."

My heart sunk down below the vacuumed carpet. When Mom made popcorn, it was in an old iron frying pan with a lid that was dented and didn't match.

"Good idea," Mom said. And out she whipped a real, honest-to-God popcorn maker, the first appliance made to do just one particular thing we'd ever had in our home. I was speechless. And then she offered to go out and buy Cokes.

"Your Mom's so young and beautiful," Shelly gasped when Mom left, a swirl of scarves flapping around a lean body. The other girls nodded eagerly.

"Must be nice," Marcella said. "My mom's fifty-six."

"Mine never lost the weight from having my brother," Suzanne said.

"My mom's attractive," Shelly said. "But not like *that.*"

"Crosby's a smart one. She's going to end up at Smith or Barnard or one of those swell schools," Dad bragged to some people they'd invited over for bridge one Saturday night.

Mom had recently taught Dad to play bridge. Usually he was exiled to the rec room or, if we didn't have one, the bedroom, or if that didn't suit him, a bar, when Mom had ladies' bridge. But Dad had been trying to impress some people lately here, and he'd invited them over for poker, and they'd said in a snooty way that they didn't play poker, just pinochle or bridge. So Dad learned bridge, and true to form, he was pretty good by the time these people came over.

"She scored in the ninety-eighth percentile on her achievement tests."

The women at the two tables turned and looked at me from beneath a skyline of beehive hairdos. They made pastel smiles of polite interest. Mom was the only one who still wore red lipstick, and it gave her a classy look. One of the men made a funny remark about how he was going to have me come and decipher his income tax forms.

I couldn't take all this glory, so I went to the kitchen to get a Coke to take to my room. Ben was in there pouring himself a cup of coffee.

"What do you think you're doing?" I said.

"What does it look like?"

"You can't drink coffee."

"Hell I can't."

So Ben went strolling into the living room with a cup of coffee and plunked down in Dad's chair, which was about a foot away from the bridge table. It was weird to see someone other than Dad in that chair, the darkened imprint of his head and shoulders surrounding Ben.

One of the ladies looked up and said, "Hot chocolate in such warm weather?"

"Nope, it's coffee. Do you want some?" Ben said, his eyebrows poised for trouble.

I was watching from the kitchen. I thought I was going to have a stroke. Dad looked up, Mom looked up.

"Goodness, Vera," one of the women said, "Your kids drink coffee?" Another said, "It will stunt their growth."

Mom looked like she didn't understand, and Dad looked like he wanted to cry and kill Ben at the same time.

"Ben, you know you can't drink coffee," Mom said. "Pour it out."

But Ben just sat there drinking. And drinking it really fast, even though it was hot. Like you drink a glass of milk.

"Ben," Dad said. His voice was thick. "You heard your mother."

Ben got up and took the coffee cup to the kitchen, taking a last sip on the way. Then he went to his room.

No one yelled or hit him or anything after the company left. I guess Mom and Dad decided to let the incident go.

Ben was up drinking coffee the next morning. Mom and Dad were strangely quiet about it. Ben drank two cups and then went out to play. Mom and Dad talked for a while, then—for something as relatively minor as that—decided to call the psychiatrist.

But Ben never saw that psychiatrist, and I never got to be a Radcliffe Heights Estates hotshot, hot-shit cheerleader, because Dad got transferred a few weeks later, before the school year even started.

1964

≈≈≈
THIRTY

W<small>E MOVED</small> to Edge Cliff Farms Township, near Cleveland. When you're taking algebra and biology and French, it's more difficult to pick up where the rest of the class is. But I still managed to get A's and B's in everything but phys ed and social studies. They put Ben in emotionally handicapped classes because he was in them in the last school, and Mom and Dad kind of let the psychiatrist thing drop, because they didn't have the names of any here and they decided to wait and see if the special classes straightened him out.

Lately, when I went to the library, I'd find myself in the psychology section before I made my way over to fiction. I'd read about the different ways you could go nuts—sometimes it was from things you did, like taking drugs, sometimes it was from things that were done to you, like your parents holding you by the feet out a window and saying they were going to drop you. But in most cases, no one knew how or why it happened.

Ben didn't bother to use the garbage cans lately. He started to throw things like apple cores and sandwich crusts under the bed. One time he was jumping on the bed like a two-year-old and the bed collapsed. When Dad got it together again, he found a squashed pile of garbage underneath.

Dad would jokingly bring some of these things up at work, and people would talk about how messy kids that age are, and how they have a fantasy life, so he'd half-convince himself that Ben was only marginally out in left field, and things chugged on. Ben was guzzling coffee like crazy, and Mom and Dad just gave up on that and told him to drink it in a room where they couldn't see him. Ben told me that when he drank coffee, things made more sense for a little while. I never knew if that was because of the caffeine or because Mom and Dad were letting him get away with something he knew pissed them off.

Ben next developed a cleanliness fetish. He refused to drink out of a cup that anyone else had used. Even if it was washed and spotless, he wouldn't use a glass if you'd drunk anything out of it ever. Mom had to buy him new glasses, and if anyone made a mistake and put his mouth to one, there was hell to pay. Soon that extended to silverware and then to plates— you couldn't even have touched them with your fingers or he wouldn't put food on them. Then the rule became no one could even breathe within about three feet of his stuff. I began to wonder if Ben would carry it so far he'd starve to death. But eventually we did seem to get into that system okay, Dad with his Manhattan glasses that no one else could use, Ben with his glasses and dishes that no one else could touch or breathe on.

Mom was still planning her career. "I'm going into nursing school as soon as we get a few bucks ahead," she said to Ben and me for the millionth time one night as we played cards and listened to the Beatles on the radio. Dad was in Dubuque on business. "I'm going to wear one of those snappy white uniforms with a perky little hat. Did you know that the hats are different for each nursing school, Ben?"

Ben came and sat in her chair with her and watched Mom draw pictures of all the kinds of hats she'd seen.

She and Dad were getting into fights all the time again. Dad was jealous because some of the younger guys were moving up faster than he. "But most of them have been with the company longer than you," Mom would say, like she was trying to make him feel better but ending up making a fight *really* break out.

He was out of town a lot now. He tried to make up to Mom for it by accepting more invitations to go out with people from the office. Of all their friends, Mom liked the Harveys best. They came over for bridge a lot.

Jim Harvey was handsome and funny. Doris wore very fashionable clothes in bright colors with eyeshadows to match. She had a different purse for each outfit.

She and Mom started going out shopping together, but Mom ended up having to admit that with two kids she couldn't afford to shop as much as Doris did. The Harveys were older and had no children.

Mom and Doris organized a small bridge club of wives from the office, and Doris would often just come over and practice hands with Mom.

One afternoon, I came home from school and they were at the kitchen table and Mom looked nervous. I noticed there was a bottle of crème de menthe on the table. Doris smiled at us, and said, "Crosby won't mind if we have a little winky-drinky, will she?"

"I . . ." Mom said, still looking nervous.

"Well I for one am having just an itty bitty one," Doris said, taking itty bitty steps to the cupboard in her chemise. "You'll join me, won't you hon? What do you care, huh, didn't you say John is out of town?"

"It just seems so early for a drink," Mom said. "And Crosby and Ben, I mean, it's just that women in my family didn't drink, and it's hard to get away from that."

Doris got that motherly look she often wore when talking to Mom. "My dear, cocktail hour is when the big hand is on the twelve, the little hand on the four, and I had the same kind of family and don't let any old fogies run your life. Hey, kid, if the boys can play, so can Jill."

"I suppose," Mom said, giving an exaggerated laugh.

I peeled a banana and stood and tried to figure out if I should go hang out somewhere or start my homework. I was getting nervous about French. They'd all had the past subjunctive last year, and I had to figure out what the hell it was all on my own, because the teacher said she didn't have time to explain it and I should get a tutor or go back a year in French. I knew Mom and Dad would never get me a tutor—after all, they'd never had one, and look at them blah blah blah—and they'd say it wouldn't hurt me to go back a year because I'd get an easy A. But I'd be damned if I was going to do that.

"I see you have some cocktail glasses," she said, taking Dad's Manhattan glasses out. We can have our drinky-poo in these. I like an ice cube in mine. How about you?"

Ben came in just then. We got nervous just watching as she mixed and poured. "If she breaks one of those glasses, Dad'll kill her," Ben whispered.

She sat down at the table and gave Mom her drink. Mom took a sip and then just let it sit there. Doris finished hers fast and went to pour another. I went upstairs to see what I could do about French.

But Doris's voice got louder and I couldn't concentrate. Ben was still with them. Doris was making a big fuss over how pretty his eyes were, and Mom was laughing. Loudly, now.

"Oooo, I'll bet the girls like you, young man," Doris said. "Bedroom eyes."

There was more laughing and then Mom said, "I have to admit, this isn't a bad way to kill an afternoon."

"My dear, when you live in the fast lane, you have to pull over to the side of the road every now and then and let your engine cool. And, hey, you're such a swell kid, you deserve it."

When Doris left in a trail of giggles, Mom told me to make something out of what was in the cupboard for dinner, and she went up to bed. As we were finishing our Franco-American spaghetti, we heard her throwing up. We didn't see or hear from her again until the next morning. This was scarier than any time Dad got drunk.

Mom and Doris still got together and Mom drank coffee with a drop of crème de menthe to keep Doris company. They swapped stories about moving while playing bridge.

"I know what you mean," Doris said. "It's so hard to make friends. I mean, li-i-isten kid, there are only so many people in the world that you can really talk down-and-dirty to, aren't there?"

"That's for sure," Mom said. "I'll bid one club."

"Mmmm, one spade. My best friend in Omaha—a knock-out of a redhead, married to a dreamboat of a fellow, well, he was taking his secretary out for steak dinners at supper clubs while she was beans and franks with the children. Poor kid took an overdose of pills. Pills and cough syrup. On purpose."

"How awful." Mom was quiet for a while. "Two clubs. But killing herself—isn't that a little extreme? I mean, a divorce would accomplish the same thing."

"Ha ha ha, Vera, that's what I like about you—a sense of humor. I guess a divorce wasn't enough, because her husband had just told her he wanted one anyway to marry the little tramp. Office manager of an auto parts store. Cute, but definitely lacking in the brains department. Oh but what do they care, the dumber the better, then no arguments—right, kid? Oh I tell you, my friend in Cleveland—sweet kid built like a brick you-know-what—put up with her hubby's side-line activities one after the other. I tell you, the women even called the house, can you imagine the gall? Her husband kept saying go ahead, divorce me. You leave me no choice, two no trump."

"Why didn't she just divorce the jerk?"

"My dear, she had four children. How could she manage?"

"Oh God," Mom sighed, "I pass."

"A lot of the gals have a little someone on the side, though, too," Doris said, her tongue sticking her cheek out as she nodded wisely in my direction. "If you get my meaning— what's good for the goose . . . and all that jazz."

Mom said she liked Doris because she was down to earth. Translated, that meant she wasn't a snob like a lot of the people Dad worked with, like the people Dad tried to cultivate. She didn't like people who just sat around and said polite things all night. She liked people who said what they thought.

When the Harveys were transferred to San Diego, Mom was pretty upset. She had to find a fourth for the Wednesday night bridge group, but it was never quite the same, because it was someone whose husband had just been transferred in and she was one of those phonies who acted like everything was just perfect. Her husband got promoted to national sales manager in almost no time, and they were transferred to the head office in Syracuse. Mom wasn't sorry to see her go, but Dad was furious about the whole thing, saying Mom should have been friendlier to her.

They got divorced again that December. Dad got an apartment and Mom and Ben and I moved into a two-bedroom duplex in another suburb, Oak Terrace Park.

Our new place was nothing fancy. It was green stucco and had no lawn yet, just dirt where they'd bulldozed the trees down to clear space for the subdivision. They promised to lay sod in the spring. An Indian couple and their baby lived on the other side. They were pretty deferential and didn't seem like people you had to impress, so we could relax and play the radio loud and go out in the backyard in our p.j.'s, as if we lived in a regular house.

Mom and I were to share one bedroom, Ben would get the other. That night she lay in bed, trying, I could tell, not to cry. "I hate that man. I really hate him," she said. "Always chasing something." She smoked for a while and Ben came in. Mom sat up and turned the light on. "He's always trying to be something he's not," she said to Ben, and hugged her knees like a little kid. Ben lay on the floor and tossed one of her jumbo rollers up in the air and caught it. Mom talked and he kept tossing the roller. I felt a little hope. When things were awful, Ben never acted like it. It was true—when things were okay, he was horrible, but when they were bad, he just acted normal.

Mom broke down and cried. She cried half the night, and the next day she went out and got a job as a gal Friday at a ball-bearings factory.

Just as I was starting to relax with the idea that there was something wrong with us, all of us, as a family, that we weren't like anyone else, Ben was tested by the school counselor and was found to be normal. The principal told Mom that Benny was going to be "mainstreamed" and assigned to the regular school. It made us think that everyone before had just been overreacting.

"See," Mom said to Dad on the phone. "Ben is fine, as long as you're not here shouting at everyone." But as soon as she said that, her voice got apologetic and she said, "Sometimes I wish that we could get along better. Families are supposed to stay together. That's what they're meant to do, wherever they are. I mean, look at us, all we've been through just to stay together. Oh, I don't know."

$\approx$

THIRTY-ONE

D AD SENT US a little pocket money each week. I'd spend mine right away, but Ben put his in a bank, like he was told to. I regularly stole twenty percent of what Ben put away in his bank.

There were times when I'd feel a little haunted by the image of that bank—a "graduate" with cap and gown, to symbolize college savings, I guess—that he got for Christmas from some aunt on Dad's side that we never saw. (She'd sent me a ballerina bank, which got lost in some move—the only reason the graduate survived was because Ben pretended it was a magician or Count Dracula or some damn thing, and he kept track of it all the time so he could put it on his dresser to scare away the faces he said kept looking at him as soon as he tried to go to sleep.)

I had pretty nice clothes, but I was finding that it was girls who were attracted by your clothes; boys were attracted by something else. At any rate, I needed a date for the Homecoming Dance, and my prospects looked dim. Ben came into my room while I was trying to come up with a plan to get asked to the dance.

"Flipper's on," he said.

I told him I had things to worry about, like a date for the Homecoming Dance.

"Can't you go alone?"

This was hopeless. A brother who'd never had a friend in his life was not the best person to discuss your love life with. "No," I said irritably.

He thought about this, looking off at my map on the wall, and then his eyes lit up, like he'd come up with the most brilliant idea, an obvious solution that had just been sitting there waiting for him to notice it. "I'll go with you, Croz."

Oh, you poor slob, you poor little slob, I thought, what's to become of you? I could feel a collision inside my chest, a collision of the urge to hug him and the urge to squash him so he couldn't make me feel sad. The irony of it was that girls were noticing him now, I could see it when we passed them, and the joke was on them because he had absolutely zero interest in them. It was too bad Ben wasn't a girl so that he could just go and marry someone and have everyone think, hey, what a knockout, what a lucky guy she's married to. And in reality all he'd do is sit at home and listen to baseball games and watch cartoons, and no one in the outside world would notice the difference. I guessed if you were going to have to be good-looking and crazy in this life, you were better off being a woman.

At the last minute, I managed to dredge up someone to take me to the dance, Gordon Artfinger.

Gordon was nice enough, but he carried a briefcase and wore white socks. I figured for that one night what the hell, he was better than nothing, and I had the sneaking suspicion he felt the same way about me. He got his friend, Ralph, to invite my new best friend, Ingrid Olsen, so that we could double.

Problem was, I needed a dress and had very little time to get the money for it. I didn't know what to do. I had only eleven dollars and you couldn't get anything for less than thirty.

That night, during a study break, I asked Mom if she wanted to play a little bridge. She leaped at the opportunity. While I was dealing, I said casually, "Mom, I got invited to a dance."

"Oh, that's nice. So you have a boyfriend, huh?"

She looked pretty but a little tired from her new job in the state driver's license bureau. I thought she must be in a good mood because I'd heard her talking on the phone to a man from her office, and she sounded all tinkly.

"It's not someone I'm madly in love with." I said.

"I don't think you have to be madly in love with someone just to go to a dance with him, do you?"

"I suppose not. The only problem is, I need a dress."

"Oh Crosby, I don't know if I can afford it. I can't even get any decent clothes to wear to work. And it's a job where that's important if I want to be promoted."

I sighed and said, "Maybe Dad would give me the money."

She looked up sharply. "That cheapskate?" And then she seemed to think he might, and said, "If he sends more money, it's got to go into the car. The car isn't safe with those tires. And it needs new brakes. And there's the dentist, I have to take you kids, Benny has a cavity and, oh, Crosby, I just can't let you spend precious money on a dress you'll only wear once."

I didn't say a word. I knew she wasn't done. Each hand had only twelve or thirteen points, so we threw them back in.

"Oh, honey, I'll make it up to you," she said, shuffling like some supersonic machine. "You'll live in the same place from now on, and you'll have some stability, and it'll all work out. I promise you." She dealt out the cards again. "Someday, if we play our cards right, you'll have a mother who's a nurse, and you can tell people that. You'll be so proud. I wish I'd had a mother who was a professional. Do you want to hear a confession? I was always a little ashamed of my parents."

I wished I hadn't heard that; it was almost like my grandparents could hear it, too. Or maybe they had already heard it. And then I thought maybe Mom felt I was ashamed of her, even though it wasn't true, and that's why she didn't want me trying to be a cheerleader or something special.

A few minutes later she said, "Hey! Can you borrow a dress from someone?" She looked at me as if that were the most brilliant idea in the world, same way Ben had when he was thinking he could be my date.

"My only real friend is Ingrid, and she's a lot taller and

wears a size fourteen. Anyway, she's going to the dance, too, and only has one dress."

"Then quick, go make friends with someone your size," Mom said, laughing. "Wait a minute, I have an idea. Look who's your size—your elderly old mother. This little old lady here . . ."

"Mom, you don't have any of those kinds of dresses. Just that black thing you wear on New Year's Eve, and if I wore that everyone would think I was a hood."

"But you know who does have a prom dress?" she sang out in an opera voice. This was the old Mom, the pre-divorce Mom. She jumped up and went to the phone. As she dialed, she said excitedly to me, "Grandma has my old prom dresses. I was just your size when I was in high school. I only wore them once, so they should be in perfect condition."

She called Grandma, and Grandma said yes, she could probably find Mom's old dresses and she'd send them right away.

When Mom hung up, she said, "Oh, I can't wait to see them. There was the lovely blue taffeta with little cap sleeves that I wore to the junior prom. And a pink satin with an adorable peplum that I knocked 'em dead in at the senior Christmas formal. Oh Crosby, you'll love them."

I figured a prom dress was a prom dress, and Mom said if I wore one of her old gowns, she'd give up lunch for a week and buy me some high heels that we could dye to match the dress and above-the-elbow gloves. The only worry was whether they'd get there in time. There was one week before the dance.

Ben was getting up in the middle of the night and not going back to sleep because faces were staring at him from the plaster swirls on the ceiling. That night, when Ben said he was afraid to go to his room, Mom for some reason remembered the promise of a puppy. "Would you be afraid of your room if you had a nice big dog to protect you?" she said.

"Maybe not," Ben said.

"All right. I absolutely guarantee you you'll get one this weekend."

On Saturday I lay in bed imagining the dresses that were to arrive: pink satin, blue taffeta. I couldn't guess which I'd wear. It was actually kind of neat, the idea of wearing one of Mom's dresses. It was something rich people in books did, wearing "ancestral" gowns.

I heard some commotion in the kitchen, and then Mom singing "Goin' to the dog pound and we're gonna get a puppy" to the tune of "Chapel of Love." Ben, whose voice hadn't yet changed but was different, sang along.

"Hurry and get dressed, Crosby," Mom called out.

At the pound, we narrowed it down to a hound of some sort, a spayed female terrier that we were told had a habit of nipping; a half-collie, half-something else that was a little too old; a black cocker spaniel; and a yellow Labrador retriever puppy.

"The little retriever is the cutest," Mom said.

"Yeah, he'll get a home easily," I said.

"Then let's take him, before someone else does," she said.

"Maybe we should get one that won't get a home," Ben said. "I want one that looks like Spot. Remember Spot, Crosby? We can pretend our life is like Dick and Jane's again."

We argued for a while: he wanted to get the collie, I wanted the terrier, Mom wanted the Labrador. As a compromise, we settled on the cocker spaniel. The ride home was joyous. Even though she was all black, we named her Spot.

That afternoon, as we waited for the package of dresses to arrive, one of Mom's new friends who was a hairdresser set my hair with Jello to make it stiff and rolled it on orange juice cans to get the curl out, because not even jumbo rollers did the job.

Mom and Jean listened to a top-forties station, singing along and drinking vanilla Cokes.

Ingrid and I went over to the shopping center to hang around and model our hair up in rollers and cans, an advertisement that you had a date that night.

When I went home, I opened the door nervously, expecting to be disappointed, to be told the package hadn't come. But no, there it sat in the middle of the floor like an important package that hadn't arrived until Christmas Eve. Mom was so excited, she could hardly stand still while I opened it. I dug through the tissue paper that Grandma had so lovingly packed them in and held up the first dress.

I couldn't believe my eyes. It must have been the blue gown, but it was so faded, I could hardly tell. And the style was—well, it was a cross between those Cinderella Halloween costumes you get at the dime store and an old nightgown. To top it off, it looked about four sizes too big.

"Sizes were different in those days," Mom said, getting up and holding it in front of me.

I was speechless. I turned to look in the package, praying that the pink one was better. But it wasn't. The top was floppy and too low. It had ridiculous sleeves that looked like deflated balloons, and two faint but definitely noticeable semicircular perspiration stains under the arms.

"Mom, everyone's going to be wearing knee-length spaghetti-strap dresses, and I've got these long faded things that went out of style a hundred years ago." Somehow I just simply hadn't pictured Mom in limp, out-of-style dresses. Not the queen of the prom, for God's sake.

Ben came up from the basement with Spot. "Mom, she just crapped on the floor and there's worms in it."

"I can't stand this," I said to Mom. "I can't stand this. Here I am, standing in a house furnished with boxes, with dog shit on the floor, and a weird brother, and a dance to go to in six hours and nothing to wear. I wish I were dead." Tears rolled down my face. "I give up. I really give up. This is it. I just plain give up trying."

Ben stared at me. He looked frightened. It was like if I fell apart, the whole goddamn thing was going to fall apart. Mom stood there looking like a little girl who didn't know it wasn't okay to write with crayon all over the wall. I didn't know if I could stand it. I really didn't know.

The next thing I knew, Mom's car keys were jingling, and she was putting on her lipstick without using a mirror. "Come on, Crosby. We're going out to Evans' to get you a dress."

We all piled into the car, Ben and Spot eager and nervous—as if it were their dress and their dance—in the back seat, me in the front. As we got closer and closer to the shopping center,

I began to feel guilty. Mom didn't have any money. She didn't have a husband, and when she did he was a screwy husband always chasing after some mirage—a better job, a better boss, a better town to live in, trying to get ahead in life and just botching it all up. And Mom herself was caught up in that and didn't really have much interest in anything except settling down to the same house and getting a little bit of a paycheck so she could go to nurses' training school and feel like a bigshot, or at least feel like *something*. And Ben . . .

"Oh forget it, Mom," I said, "Let's turn around. I don't want the dress. I really don't." I thought for a minute. "You know what I can do? I can shorten the blue one, plump it up with one of my petticoats underneath, and wear that old lace jacket Grandma made me. If you'll lend me your heart pendant, I won't feel so bad about it all and things will be all right. But we have to hurry home now, or I won't have time."

She took a puff of her Viceroy, looked at me to see if I meant it, and then raised her eyebrows. "I said I'd buy you a new dress. This is your last chance."

I hesitated a moment, an eternity. Then something I couldn't put my finger on made me change my mind. "Let's get the dress."

I picked out a pink satin scoop-neck with an empire waist. I stood looking in the department store mirror at myself in amazement. There was enough wiring and padding and space in the dress's bosom to hold a couple of footballs. The pink made my brown hair look sleek, my eyes sparkle. I had Mom's creamy skin when it wasn't freckled, and I'd always had good shoulders and legs. Looking at me in the mirror, Mom seemed perplexed. "Crosby, you look . . . actually . . . pretty enough . . ."

She'd never told me I was pretty before. Whatever effect it had on me, it had triple on her. Acting like someone on drugs, she raced me around the store to get the accessories; we bought above-the-elbow gloves, shoes they did a rush dye job on so they'd match the dress, nylons, a bunny fur cape, some dangly pearl earrings, a little purse with pearls all over it, and a rhinestone tiara. She put everything on her charge-a-plate and gave me ulcers worrying how she was going to pay for it all.

Gordon looked at me as if there was something wrong, like his pal in plane geometry had turned the tables on him and become a girl.

After the first look, he sort of refused to look at me at all, and beat me by about fifteen paces to the car, where his mother was waiting. Mom and Ben waved to me from the doorstep as if I were going away for a year. All evening they'd treated me like I was more important than I was. Maybe this was what it was like to be beautiful. I wondered what it would be like to be beautiful all the time and decided I wouldn't like it—you'd be thinking about yourself constantly just like everyone else was, and couldn't go around being anonymous and doing what you wanted.

Ingrid and Ralph were in the back seat. Mrs. Artfinger asked us where we went to church and what our hobbies were. I said my hobby had been polo before we moved here. Ingrid said she didn't have time for a hobby because she was enrolled in Saturday classes in charm and modeling at Sears & Roebuck's.

I wished I were in those classes. But if Mom considered cheerleader lessons ridiculous, I could imagine what she'd think of charm school. Out the car window I watched the autumn evening start to erase the day, and I thought about what it would be like to have a mother who wanted to send you to charm school. After some more thought, maybe I was sort of glad I didn't have a mother who wanted me to go to charm school; maybe what I'd like would be something in between.

As soon as Mrs. Artfinger drove off in her station wagon, Gordon and Ralph started doing Three Stooges imitations and discussing the different kinds of farts they'd encountered in their fifteen years of experience. Ingrid and I linked arms and walked ahead. I told her she looked pretty.

"You don't think this dress makes me look too tall?"

"Not with the low shoes," I assured her. One thing about being tall was that when no one asked you to dance, you could always blame it on that. I wished I had an excuse. And then I remembered I had Ben as an excuse for a lot of things, Ben who at times was an even better excuse than being five-eleven and a half.

The gym reminded me of a boy dressed up like a girl, the bleachers and basketball hoops and circles on the floor hopelessly undisguisable, like telltale hairy, sinewy limbs poking out from the chiffon of crepe paper and the jewelry of tinsel. As you circulated through the aroma of damp hairspray, you found pockets of air that smelled of sweat and rubber basketball shoes rising from the floor.

Suddenly it hit me that there was something really new going on in my life, and I felt I didn't belong, wondered what I was doing here. The Supremes' song "Kiss of Fire" blared over the speakers, and I was confused, almost frightened as I watched couples dance. Gordon, his porcupiney growing-out crewcut visible off in a corner with the other class nerds, had forgotten me for Ralph. Ingrid and I turned and watched the dancers with big, fake smiles.

Our fake smiles dissolved into hungry looks as we watched Dick Walters dance by with Carol Cunningham, homecoming queen and, of course, head cheerleader. I wondered if he would like me if I were a cheerleader. I looked down at my bright pink pointed-toed spike heels, which were now curling up in the front because they were big, shoes that represented three work lunches for Mom, a cavity filling for Ben. I didn't know if Dick would like me if I were a cheerleader. I'd be the same person, wouldn't I?

But dammit, what did I care if Dick Walters liked me or not? He wasn't the only boy in school. I glanced back at Dick, and he was staring at me. I looked away quickly so I could imagine that he was still looking. Maybe someday someone like that would do more than look at me. When I peeked again, my eyes met his again.

Ingrid and I went to the girls' room. My face was pink, taut, my eyes shining. I really wasn't that bad-looking, in spite of what Mom always said. In fact, a couple of people had been commenting lately on my looks, and I'd thought they were just being nice. Like Mom always thought about herself, though I knew I wasn't anything like Mom.

We put on more eyeliner and sprayed Aqua Net until we had to leave the girls' room to get oxygen.

Coming out, I felt a bold, strong hand grasp my arm. The feel of a boy—not Gordon, but a potential-boyfriend kind of boy. I turned to find not butterscotch-colored Dick Walters, but black-eyed, black-haired Jackie Swearingen, the class hood.

Jackie's face was total recklessness. While other boys were getting into Beatle haircuts, he still had a slick D.A. He sat in the back of classrooms, his long legs crossed at the ankle, his black eyes jumping with amusement and all the patience in the world for when he'd be able to drop out of school. There was nothing intelligent in his look, but then, intelligence would have ruined him.

I waited to see if he'd made a mistake, but his beautiful face knew what it was doing. His eyes were full of some kind of joke that I wasn't in on, but maybe could be. There was a light with something else in them, something that had to do with me. I felt power surge in my breast like eagle wings.

Without a word, this Jackie Swearingen took my bare arm, his thumb touching a nerve that ran up through my chest and into a ticklish part of my neck. He led me to the stand-off circle on the gym floor and we began to slow dance to what was left of "Bright Elusive Butterfly of Love" and then fast danced, appropriately enough, to "Louie, Louie," which was reputed to have dirty words that nice girls were careful not to learn.

I inhaled the once-again sweaty air of the gym and felt giddy with the realization that there were years and years and years ahead of me, that I was my own person, that I was not anyone else in my family and I didn't have to be like the rest of them and if I worked at it, really worked at it, I wouldn't be. That realization really knocked me in the head, and I felt the interested eyes of other girls as I danced several more dances with Jackie, class (in both senses of the word) hood.

The Beatles were singing and my petticoats swished teasingly on my legs. With his head back, he pulled me against his chest. I could smell the starch on his rented shirt, the English Leather under his arms.

"I hear there's a party in the janitor's closet," he said to me, his jaw down as if to keep from bursting out laughing uncontrollably at this whole stupid, shitty, dumb world of straight people.

Marsha Lightburn came by, her dress hem obviously taken up several inches beyond where the store she bought it from deemed respectable, her hair teased and shaped into a perfect *omega.* She winked at Jackie. Jackie ran his tongue over his lip and watched her, then turned back to the bird in the hand.

"I hear there's some Southern Comfort and Seven-Up in that party in the janitor's closet." His low, boy's changed-voice resonated on my ear, sending a vibration down the sensitive part of my collarbone.

I'd never tasted Southern Comfort, and I didn't much care if I ever did, if it was anything like Dad's Four Roses. But I wanted to taste those lips of Jackie Swearingen's.

Ingrid was dancing with redheaded Jim Barrons, class smart aleck. On my way out under the Exit sign in the gym, I waved to her, and she looked at me as if I were about to sail off in a balloon. Gordon was nowhere to be seen.

At least a dozen other kids were in the corner of the janitor's closet or sitting on the edge of the big sink. They were friendlier than they'd ever been to me before. Russ Wolinski had on the janitor's uniform over his dinner jacket and was scrubbing the ceiling with the broom. Darlene Davis, the principal's daughter, was smoking a joint and drinking Southern Comfort out of the bottle. Jackie's date, Ruth Parker, was giving a hickey to a guy drinking beer out of a mason jar.

Jackie held another bottle for me to drink, and I felt a loneliness at the pit of my stomach, like we'd just moved somewhere and I wished I knew at which of my windows the sun would come up the next morning.

I shook my head no, and the lights went out and I felt a hand down the bosom of my dress. I grabbed the hand and bit it. A male voice—not Jackie's, I don't think—yelped. I got up and fumbled for the door among legs and crinolines and sticky dripping bottles, and felt a hand go up my dress. I found the doorknob and ran out into the hallway and back to the gym.

Something was very wrong. That wasn't supposed to have happened. I went to the girls' room and rubbed Cover Girl liquid makeup on my sweating face. So I was new in town, dispensable, a ship in the night, someone none of those boys had known before and therefore not a girl with—with what? A family to be concerned about? A girl passing into town and probably out again soon, like a streetwalker on a corner. If a girl hadn't come walking in just then, I would have stood there and cried in front of the mirror that had been teasing and lying to me all night with that new face.

When I came out, Jackie was there, tapping his pointed-toed shoe and looking apologetic.

"Who the hell do you think I am?" I said.

His big eyes went bigger and he shrugged. "You went into the closet, baby. I thought you wanted to have some fun."

I think that moment, then and there, I swore off sex, for at least until I was a cheerleader. "Let's forget it happened. I gotta get back to my date," I said.

"Gordon, that loser?" Jackie said. He stretched his arms out and started singing the Beatles song, "I'm a loser . . ."

I went back out to look for Gordon. He saw me and waved and came over carrying two Cokes with straws sticking out of them. He looked as good as a bowl of tomato soup. I watched Dick out on the dance floor. No, I'd stick with the Gordon Artfingers of the world until the Dick Walterses come around. I couldn't afford the Jackie Swearingens—not yet anyway. That, it appeared, was the price of middle-class respectability, which seemed to run a line between the Gordon Artfingers and the Dick Walterses, and to run a wild, crazy pattern around the Jackie Swearingens.

Gordon took me out on the floor and held me at arms' length so he could keep an eye on his feet. "Mother sent me to dance classes at the Y, but it didn't do much good. Sorry."

I said that was all right, that I'd never had lessons at all.

Gordon said, "Dick Walters invited us to come to a party after the dance at his house."

"What?" I almost yelled.

"That's what I said. I don't get it either. He's never wanted to be friends with me before. I always thought I was a hurtin' dude, and here someone like Walters invites me."

I gave Gordon a big, happy grin, and wished Mom didn't have to miss lunch for the next three days and that Ben didn't have to have a cavity just so I could do ordinary things. And

I knew it wasn't just lack of money that made it all like this, it was lack of something else—ordinariness, maybe. And maybe I had to work hard at it, but I was going to make myself as ordinary—in a special way—as I possibly could.

$$\widetilde{}$$

THIRTY-TWO

T HIS THANKSGIVING SEEMED like it was going to be awful. Grandpa had had a mild heart attack in October and we'd gone up to see him. Mom couldn't get any more time off to go again.

It was going to be just the three of us, and the weather was gray and dreary outside and I was already thinking how depressing Christmas would be. Thanksgiving morning I vowed to forget that it was a holiday. My game plan was to read my book, *Jane Eyre,* and watch the clock, so that pretty soon it would no longer be today and I could breathe a sigh of relief that we'd killed Thanksgiving for another year; one holiday down this season, only two to go.

Ben was sitting in front of the TV drinking black coffee and watching the parade. When Santa Claus came by, he jumped up and yelled for me to come and see and spilled his coffee all over the rug.

Mom was in the kitchen drinking coffee and listening to a rock station. "You kids don't mind, do you, if we forget the turkey this year?" she said.

I'd noticed that there wasn't any turkey in the refrigerator, but it hadn't registered yet that she wasn't planning to cook at all.

I didn't say anything, but Ben asked if we could at least have cranberries. That was just like Ben—out of all the millions of decadent things you got at Thanksgiving, to want cranberries. Mom said he could have some Ocean Spray cranberry juice cocktail in the refrigerator.

Then on the radio they announced that helpers were still needed at the First Presbyterian Church to serve the elderly. Mom came to life. "That's it," she cried. "That's it exactly. We'll go over to the church and help out."

So she called and got directions. I was so depressed I thought this would be the clincher, and I said I didn't want to go. Mom threw the pad with the directions down on the table, crossed her arms, and said, "Okay. Madame Crosby doesn't want to go, so we'll all suffer."

I put my book down. "All right, all right. At least maybe I'll get some turkey."

Ben never cared much where he went or when, as long as it wasn't school or an athletic event he had to participate in, so he put down his own special glass he'd been drinking the Ocean Spray out of and got dressed, a big red cranberry-juice smile on his wide, self-absorbed face. Mom got dressed in a pretty gray jersey that made her skin look like vanilla ice cream.

Inside the church there were a good hundred or so elderly people sitting at tables looking expectant, and a bunch of people running around looking very busy. There was a Christmas tree, a choral group singing some Christmas songs, and helpers were bursting in and out through a door bringing out food.

We stood there feeling like idiots for a few minutes, and I got worried that they'd think *we* were the needy ones, but then I remembered how good we three looked.

In the kitchen was a beautiful American sight: assembly lines of people carving turkeys, dozens of them. A few more rows of helpers were ladling cranberry sauce out of vats, mashing potatoes, or cutting pumpkin pies. The place looked and smelled like Thanksgiving had taken over the world.

Even Ben enjoyed himself, dropping whipped cream onto the pies. We did food work for a while, then served. I'd never seen Mom like this; she looked flushed and confident, and a couple of the men were eyeing her, but I don't think she noticed.

Then the head lady told us to go and eat. Ben must have forgotten about his new germ fetish, because he followed me to a group of poor old ladies and sat down and ate off plates that people he didn't even know had breathed on.

I waved to Mom. Catching a glimpse of her Cherries-in-the-Snow smile among all those sad old people was like seeing a color photograph superimposed on a black-and-white group shot.

Ben ate and stared alternately at Mom and me while I chatted with the ladies. I particularly liked one who was quieter than the others. Her name was Mrs. Elverton.

She told me about Thanksgivings back when she was a child. "We'd go out for a sleigh ride while dinner cooked. Oh gosh, it seemed as if we always had a little snow on the ground by Thanksgiving."

She made me think of Grandma, but she was daintier than Grandma; I suspected she had grown up in a more refined home.

She told us she grew up on a farm that got sold off in chunks until all she inherited was the house and the front yard. A few years ago she sold the house and moved into a private nursing home. Her own kids had moved to California and seldom visited.

"They tore the house down, I'm told, and all that's left is the water pump," she said. "Oh my, it's nice to think that it's still there. I haven't seen it in seven years."

I motioned to Mom and she came over, all enthusiasm. We told her about the farm. Mom said, "Shall we all go out to see it?"

"Oh, for law's sake, I wouldn't bother you."

But Mom insisted. So instead of helping clean up, we left while all the other helpers were carrying dishes into the kitchen. Mrs. Elverton sat in front with Mom. Mom felt important, you could tell, and she looked amazingly un-self-conscious for a change. If there was anything Mom understood, it was small towns and old-fashioned things.

When we got there, everyone climbed out of the car and walked out to the middle of a field. Mrs. Elverton walked like she was going to fall over any minute. Mom took her arm, looking awkward, maybe because she didn't like touching people.

We looked for the pump for a while but we weren't having any luck. "We'll find it," Ben said, so we kept looking, walking through the brush and weeds, getting thorns and briars all over our good clothes.

"Oh, I guess it's not here," Mrs. Elverton said, raising her head and gazing around at the gray and brown scene as if she were looking into the eyes of an old friend who had just said something only the two of them would understand.

"Well, at least we tried," I said, ready to go. It was getting cold, the kind of damp cold that attacks the parts of your body with no fat on them—feet, hands, nose.

"Let's look some more," Mom said. She took hold of Mrs. Elverton's arm and her back, too, and led her around. Snow started flittering down as the sun set. It was about the quietest place I'd ever seen. I felt like someone had stuffed my ears with empty, dead air.

I was getting bored. I wished I'd never brought the subject up. I wanted to climb into my bed and get back to *Jane Eyre.*

Finally, Ben shouted, "Hey, Mom! Is this it?" I trudged over, and sure enough, there was the water pump.

"Oh, for cryin' out loud," Mrs. Elverton said as she and Mom stepped over. She reached down and worked it. No water came out. While she stood there looking at it, the rest of us walked around the field. Mrs. Elverton told Ben to come over and told him all about how they used to get water. Ben listened politely—I could tell by his face that he was bored, too—and reminded me of normal, typical guys his age. That thought was so scarily wonderful that I had to get rid of it before I believed it and later got disappointed.

I felt like we were a real unit then. That wide, flat sky and the snow on the weeds and the old lady hunched over the water pump made me feel more a part of the human race than I'd ever felt in my life. It was the first time we'd ever done something for someone just to be nice. It was a feeling that made you feel good but it also made you feel nervous, like you wanted to go home and roll around in your own selfishness for a while until you felt normal again.

Wednesday, August 23, and Thursday, August 24

THIRTY-THREE

A FTER FILING A REPORT with the police, I went back to my room and called the Edwardian Room at the Plaza Hotel and made a dinner reservation for one.

I put on the ruffly white sundress that I was supposed to have had dinner with Ben in, and went out to the street and flagged myself a cab.

It was the perfect place for a shamelessly expensive dinner alone; dark, with a framed view of Central Park minus the homeless through high windows, and oversized chairs to disappear into. Not that you had to—there were only a handful of people, tourists and New Yorkers who were too old—or whose money was—to be threateningly trendy.

I had smoked salmon and a glass of champagne followed by a steak with Bernaise sauce. Not daring to look at the check, I handed the waiter my American Express Gold Card, still damp from having soaked in hot soapy water.

I took a walk along Central Park South, feeling fuzzy from the glass of bordeaux, which I could still smell, and almost cheerful from a chocolate-mousse high.

Back in my room, I tried calling Mr. Harboil. This time I got his son. Mr. Harboil had gone trout-fishing in Saskatchewan and could only be reached by leaving a message at a supplies store near his camp. After phoning the store, I called the Loebroes. Mrs. Loebroe said she was in a hurry. I told her I'd be back in La Querencia the next day and we'd definitely get together on this deal.

I contacted Mr. Harboil's son and gave him the Loebroes' latest offer. He said he wasn't in favor of lowering the price, but that it was ultimately up to his father.

I turned on the TV. I watched news reports of other people being mugged, then turned off the light and sank into bed.

The phone rang a few minutes later and I jumped, thinking it must be Mr. Harboil. It was Antonia.

"Where have you been?" she asked, and before I could answer, she said, "Listen, Crosby, Randy and Jack ran after the man you thought was Ben, and although they didn't catch up with him, they got close enough to see that it definitely was him. He got on a downtown bus. They couldn't catch the bus and didn't have money to get on another to follow him. They thought he might be headed toward the Bowery or the Lower East Side."

I sat up in the bed. If there'd been room, I would have danced around. That was where I had been planning to go the next day, anyway. I told her to thank Randy and Jack for me, and when we hung up, I felt I'd almost miss her. I fluffed my pillow and turned on the light. I was supposed to go home the next day, Thursday. I absolutely had to be there Friday. What about the condo sale? Well, I was going to go ahead and register Friday. Maybe I should stay tomorrow, I thought, and go home in the evening. I could go ahead and register, and if my world caved in and the sale fell through, I could drop out and get at least a partial refund from USC.

I watched the lights of the regal New York night. Now that Ben was okay, the question "Why me?" came back. My father was semi-retired, my mother was finally a part-time nurse, working at *her* dream job, and was even taking singing lessons, of all things. They had more time than I did, and they lived comfortably enough to have tracked Ben down themselves.

Unexpectedly, anger began to fill me. It grew to rage. I felt like a pursued animal with all the escape routes blocked. I turned on the TV and tried to get interested in a starlet Johnny Carson was interviewing.

But who was pursuing me? My conscience? My past? I turned off the TV and sat on the edge of the bed. At any rate, an unresolved problem was after me. And why were the escape routes blocked? Who was blocking them? No one but myself, with a little help from Antonia, Ben, my desire to go to law school, Dean. But really, no one was in the way but myself.

My alarm went off at six the next morning. In the sunlight, my practical side was taking over and I was leaning toward rushing home and trying to salvage it all. I didn't want to burden my best friend like this, and I needed that damned money. I began to get ready for my flight. As I was trying to brush New York out of my teeth, I got a call.

"Crosley? Officer Rossetti here at the Twentieth Precinct. Seems an officer was down interviewing witnesses to the assault and robbery you reported in Tompkins Square Park yesterday. Sorry about that—I mean it. Unfortunately, no one is willing to act as a witness, but fortunately they got some possible leads on the whereabouts of your brother."

And then a call from the Lower East Side Shelter. My brother had stayed there the night before.

Was he okay? Well, yes, the man said, he had a bandaged head, but he said he felt all right.

I dug through my purse for a pen to write down the information he was giving me and I pulled out loose papers, Antonia's letter, and other things that had been in my wallet. A snapshot of the family fell out and lay on the floor. I stared at it as I talked and a warm feeling went through me. Then warmth alternated with emptiness, hunger for something that had been missing. When I was finished talking, I picked up the photograph and looked at it more closely than I ever had. I'd always kept it because I particularly liked the little puff-sleeved plaid dress I was wearing. I must have been about seven, Ben four. We were standing in front of a new company car Dad had just brought home.

The car—I have no idea what make—dominated the picture. Ben and I stood between the headlights, which stared into the lens along with the rest of us. Mom and Dad were on either side of the car. Dad stood tall and stiff, the old Army lieutenant. Mom was smiling a big, wide, lipsticked smile. Too wide. She was so pretty I'd never before noticed that her smile wasn't quite normal, that the look in her eyes was not so much cynicism as fear, fear of being found out to be . . . what? To be like Ben in some ways, a milder version of Ben? The one responsible for his genes as well as half-responsible for his environment?

No, don't get into that, Crosby. Don't stick the rap on the mother like they always do. Don't stick it on anyone in the family, or the family as a body. Remember what Henrietta Velez said. Even if they'd wanted to, they couldn't produce a schizo without some help from Mother Nature.

Too bad my family didn't know that. Too bad they would never believe it deep down even if they did know it.

I moved over by the window to get a better look at myself. Dark hair with bangs down to my thick eyebrows. A smile that didn't know any better than to be optimistic.

Ben was looking into the camera hard, as if there were something to see. Even though it was a black and white picture, you could tell he had a sunburn. He'd gone through childhood with sunburn all summer long. He had those puffy light areas under his eyes that fair-skinned kids often have. His expression was serious. Adultlike, serious eyes, eyes which seemed more and more childish as he got older.

I put the picture down. Why me? Now I knew why me. Not only because Ben needed me now, but because I must have needed him all those years. It came to me that I wouldn't have gotten through those years without Ben.

Oh yes, Ben had screwed things up. Screwed them up horribly. But if I had been an only child with Mom and Dad for parents, I probably would have ended up a nut too, only knowing me, probably a successful nut, living in a home for the criminally insane.

There I was again blaming my family. No, I wasn't blaming them for anyone being nuts. I was blaming them for not caring enough.

The only reason I'd had a shot at a normal life was because Ben had blotted up all the problems, been the family scapegoat so that the rest of us could go on pretending we were okay and it was all his fault.

Maybe families were to blame, at least partly. Yes, Ben, you screwed up my life, you screwed up your life. Mom and Dad screwed up their own lives, everyone else's, and I probably screwed up everyone by trying to be better, by wanting out. And who was I? I was far from perfect. Oh boy, Crosby, just wait until you have a kid, if ever. Mom and Dad tried to be good parents, at least sometimes. Clawing your way into the middle class probably wasn't as easy as it looked. It sure wasn't easy clawing your way into the upper middle class, as I was trying to do.

And here was Ben, one of the people who'd dropped off the hill during everybody's clawings.

I've spent my life running from you all, I yelled out, *and I'm tired.* I threw the picture on the bed and fell on top of it and cried. Then I got up and booked myself on a flight Friday morning. I'd get back by noon, in time to get in a good talk with the Loebroes in person, to show no mercy in holding back any of my charm on them, even though the condo sale was probably already fucked. I'd hunt out Mr. Harboil's son and make a last-ditch effort with him. What was one more day when my life was going to hell in a handbasket? What was one more day when it had already been—I started adding—three, four, a lifetime?

Officer Rossetti jumped up and scooted a noisily reluctant chair over next to his desk for me. "We got some leads on your brother's whereabouts."

At the park, the police had been unable to find anyone willing to testify about my mugging, but Ben was another matter. He was known by many people. That must have been something for him, someone who was a nonentity among his peers for all his life. And now, Officer Rossetti said, Ben was even better-known now because the bandage made him more visible.

"He's known to spend his days on an abandoned lot on East Third Street," he went on, "One which a number of these people are known to frequent."

That was near the soup kitchen. If I missed him there, I

could go to the Lower East Side Shelter, also nearby.

"You take care, though," he said. "Walk around where there's traffic, and leave the vicinity at dusk."

"Don't worry. I've learned my lesson."

"Some of his acquaintances say that Ben was concerned about the warrant for his arrest that was out," Officer Rossetti said, "So he was laying low."

"I still don't get it," I said. "Why should people be arrested for throwing up a blanket shelter in a park if they have nowhere else to sleep?"

"There are some people who don't like a bunch of vagrants sleeping in their neighborhood park. Using the sidewalks for toilets, playing loud music, shooting drugs and leaving the needles for kids to step on, throwing empty bottles . . ."

I conceded that he had a point.

I wasn't crazy about the idea of going back there, but it seemed I had to. I called Antonia and asked, "Just how bad is the area?"

"I think it's reasonably safe during the day. I'd go over there with you if I could get away. Let me see if I can track down Randy or Jack." She added, "Try to think of the neighborhood as a horse you've just fallen off."

So it was back to my hotel to wait for her call. I phoned Sarah to say that my aunt had taken a turn for the worse and I wouldn't be back today.

"You must really love her to do this for her," she said.

She would try to set up a meeting with the Loebroes and Harboil's son. And one other frail hope she held out to me was that she had a client who might want the condo and we'd work out a share of the commission so that I'd have some cash to start law school.

"You're really a good friend, Sarah."

Friends I had in college and during the decade or so after that were the squeaky-clean rah-rah types I'd sought to emulate in high school. As I got older, though, my friends tended to be highly independent women, many of whom came from families, like mine, which changed addresses frequently. And as adults they still tended to change addresses frequently, like me. Army brats or corporation brats, even a few preachers' kids, we all were a rather bold lot, not afraid of much of anything. We did, however, identify with minorities of all kinds, we found, increasingly as we grew older.

Sarah was something new for me. Her parents were escapees from Nazi Germany, and she grew up in the Bronx. There was never enough money, never enough peace of mind, never much happiness. As dissimilar as our backgrounds were, I felt I understood her well. She, however, never understood me, and that was part of the allure. She thought I was, for God's sake, straight out of a TV family sitcom, and I couldn't seem to convince her otherwise. And maybe I didn't want to tell her about Ben because I enjoyed being seen that way—cheerleader all the way.

"What do you mean, *friend*, Crosby? You're just like family. And we need a lawyer in the family."

I made a plane reservation for Friday morning. I gave them my credit card number on this one so that I couldn't cancel it without losing my three hundred and fifty dollars.

I leafed through the law school catalogue. I still hadn't decided what field of law I wanted to enter. Real estate law would be a natural, but I wasn't so sure that was what I wanted. A course called "Competency and Control of the Mentally Ill" caught my eye, and another, called, "Psychoanalysis, Psychiatry, and the Law."

I watched a soap opera and opened the catalogue again. A class called "Poverty and Public Interest Law" jumped out at me.

I thought about that for a while until Antonia called. Jack and Randy were going to meet me at the fountain in front of the Plaza Hotel at two. And if I didn't locate my brother, could I volunteer again that night?

"Let me get through the day before I worry about the night," I said.

Randy was wearing low-slung jeans, no shirt, a leather vest. His tattoos glistened in the sun like filigree. Jack was wearing a long white robe and a pair of expensive-looking cowboy boots.

"I heard about what happened," Randy said. "I got some leads on the guys who did it. I'll get the scumbags."

"Forget it. I don't want you to get hurt."

After we got off the subway on the Lower East Side, we walked, a tightly knit threesome, scanning the faces of men congregated on the sidewalk. This area's homeless people were different from yesterday's war-wounded. These were less violent-looking, even further gone, more frightening in a way. They were characters out of *Night of the Living Dead.* As we passed a school playground full of them, I admitted that I was a little scared.

"Don't worry, I got a weapon," Randy said. He pulled out a razor. I winced, but I had to admit that I felt better.

"And I've got three weapons," Jack said. "My razor-sharp tongue, my smile, and this." From under his robe, he produced a spray can. "Mace. My old man sent it, along with a few hundred bucks. Mace is very Episcopalian."

We found the soup kitchen. Night of the Living Dead men hung around outside. The sidewalk in front of it smelled like beef stock and loneliness. By noon, the line was all the way to the corner. But no Ben.

We got pizza and Cokes and spent a couple of hours at the vacant lot playing cards and watching the men—white, black, Puerto Rican. Some shot or smoked drugs, some drank, some laughed and talked to themselves, some stood morosely staring off at whatever. A couple of them came over and talked to us. We asked if they knew Ben. One of them, a black teenager on a walker, his legs flailing like a squashed mosquito's, said Ben came by often.

After a few hours I had to go to the bathroom. There were no public lavatories around, the pizza parlors had none, and the restaurants had signs in the windows saying you had to eat there to use their facilities. So I walked over to an Indian restaurant and ordered four dozen vegetarian samosas. As they cooked, I used the toilet.

Back at the playground some more men joined us to eat the samosas. An old guy named Elmer who had an arm missing said Ben had moved into an abandoned building on Avenue A near Great Jones Street. The neighborhood improved slightly; scattered among the derelicts were some hippies, artists, even a few families. We rang buzzers and knocked on doors, even went into one abandoned building. Fresh pink vomit lay in puddles around the room.

"You can tell the junkies been in here," Elmer said.

Back to the soup kitchen for dinner. By six o'clock, there was no Ben, and I was tired, hot, covered with soot. I had a blistered foot and had to go to the bathroom again. We walked over to the shelter and looked at the men gathered outside, but no Ben. "Time to give up," I said, but then I saw a blond head. I hurried my step, caught up with him, tapped him on the back, and he turned around. I inhaled deeply to avoid screaming. His face was greasy black, sores oozed all over. One eye seemed to be missing.

"Ben?" I said.

"Euuuh?" he said.

Rubbing my sides to keep from crying, I said, "I must be mistaken."

I hurried back to Randy and Jack. "Let's get out of here."

We rode the cab in silence. Jack finally said, "Goin' to meet us at the cathedral shelter?"

"I don't know." I got out at my hotel and paid the fare and handed the driver another ten and told him to take my friends wherever they wanted. And even though Jack told me he'd just shaken a case of lice—at least he hoped so—I hugged them each good-bye.

I was beginning to love that hotel room. I rinsed the thin, scratchy towel under cold water and washed off my face, arms, legs, rewetted it and took it to bed. I lay naked with it on my chest and throat and stared at the spot on the ceiling map where I'd been mugged. Then I found the crack leading to the soup kitchen. I found the Plaza, the police precinct houses, Bellevue Hospital, the cathedral, Great Jones Street. I reached for the law school catalogue and leafed through it, but it had lost its magic for now, and the courses looked hard. And the thought of going to the shelter was more appealing than staying in this dump.

I called Sarah. She said there was to be a meeting tomorrow at noon with the Loebroes and Harboil Junior. Since my plane was to arrive at the Ontario, California airport at ten-thirty, I'd have plenty of time to make the meeting.

Ben probably wouldn't show up tonight at the cathedral, but I could hope. And then—well, that would be the end of my search.

I waited for a guilty feeling to come. But I felt rather good, in fact. Worn out, but good. At least I'd tried. Benny was apparently okay. Maybe he'd show up at the shelter tonight. If not, I'd leave word for him to call me in California. I'd try to get him to move out there. I could help him.

I called Antonia and said I'd be there in an hour.

1965

THIRTY-FOUR

C HRISTMAS EVE, Mom and her date came in with a burst of swirling snow. The date had rosy cheeks and plumped-out skin and an easy, calm smile. I could tell that he'd never work out. Down deep inside, Mom liked people with hard-to-read smiles, like Dad.

Grandpa and Grandma were visiting. Grandpa's doctor had said he could come if he avoided excitement. We joked with Grandpa and said we'd try to make this the most boring Christmas of his life.

Ben looked up at the boyfriend and whispered to me, "This guy looks boring. Is that why she went out with him?"

The boyfriend had an eggnog with us, and we all stared in silence at the pope on TV, like you were supposed to be reverent but you weren't sure how much. The boyfriend looked even more confused after a few minutes. And a little bored himself. Finally, he got up awkwardly and said he had to go to bed early so he could get up early and drive to Lower Maple Wood Heights to see his ex-wife and kids.

Mom let him out the door without shaking hands or kissing him or anything, and then came and plopped down on the couch with us. "What do you guys think? Is he too young? I worry that when I'm out with him, people are saying that."

Grandma and Grandpa's heads turned in Mom's direction and then cocked back to look at her through their bifocals.

"How old is he?" Ben asked.

"Thirty-six."

"That's not young," Ben said.

"Thanks," Mom said. "That's all I needed to hear."

"You look young, so it doesn't matter how old thirty-six is," I said.

"Aren't you sweet. What do you think, Mother, Father? Is he too young for me?"

Grandpa turned his attention back to the TV and Grandma pursed her lips and said, "Oh, I don't know."

Dad came over the next morning to visit. He arrived right in the middle of the present-opening frenzy. He looked confused when he walked in, like he thought we would have waited for him to get there.

It took him three trips out to the car and back to carry in all the presents he had for us. They were carefully wrapped, with crisp corners and perfect points, in expensive foil papers. Mom wrapped her presents quickly, with the ends bunched up and no ribbon or name tags, the name written right on the paper. When you asked why she did it, she said she didn't know why. I suspected that was true, she didn't know, and nothing and nobody would ever change Mom, not even a young boyfriend with rosy cheeks and a calm smile.

The ribbons on Dad's gifts matched the paper and the little name tags. The names were carefully printed in big capital letters. To top it off, the present he'd gotten for Mom looked like it had been wrapped by the department store.

Grandpa started to get up and shake hands with Dad. Dad yelped, "Don't move, your heart," and almost fell over reaching for Grandpa's hand. But everyone else just sat and stared at Dad, and so he handed his presents around. Mom said, "Oh John, you didn't have to get me anything," as she ripped off the department store wrapper and threw it into the pile of crumpled papers and ribbons.

"Oh, I know, but . . ." Dad was wearing a turtleneck and his Perry Como sweater and Hush Puppies, but he was acting like he did when he had a suit on.

He got Ben and me ice skates and records we'd asked for. Mom opened her gift. Inside was a pair of suede gloves with black rabbit fur around the wrists. "I don't know where I'd ever wear these." She put them on the floor. "I didn't get you anything."

Dad made a wide smile to show that big tough men don't need Christmas presents, and said, "Oh, that's okay."

Grandma said quickly, "I think Santa Claus didn't forget you, John. Crosby, get me that little present under the rocking-horse decoration, the one with the snowman wrapping paper."

I dug around for the one she was talking about. She took the present from me and turned around and removed the name tag and gave it to Dad.

Dad opened it and made a big fuss about how he'd always wanted an Avon Volkswagen soap-on-a-rope.

At dinner Mom brought out a bottle of wine she'd gotten as a gift from one of the men at work. She fished some juice glasses with oranges on the sides out of the cupboard. There were only four so Ben and I got ours in Welch's grape jelly glasses with clowns holding balloons.

The wine tasted like cranberries and cough syrup. I thought maybe the reason it was so bad was because we had the wrong kind. "My French teacher said you're not supposed to drink red wine with poultry," I said. "What does white wine taste like? Is it better?"

"No red wine with poetry?" Ben said, laughing to show he got the joke.

"No actually," Dad said, "Red wine is fine with . . ."

"Well, tell your French teacher if he doesn't approve to send us over a bottle of white wine next year," Mom said.

I had fun drinking the wine, even though it tasted terrible. Ben bolted his back like a cowboy with whiskey, and Grandpa held his emptied glass out like a little kid wanting more chocolate milk. Grandma took one sip and let her glass sit. Mom made a face and I almost thought she was going to be heading for the bathroom.

Later, Mom and Dad went out for a ride and came back in an odd frame of mind—Dad was in his suit mood, but tense, and Mom was in her half-giggly, half-cynical mood.

Grandma passed me the freshly replenished plate of divinity and nudged Grandpa, who was sleeping in front of the football game.

"Come on," Grandma said to me. "Let's go into the kitchen and play Monopoly." I guess she wanted Mom and Dad to be alone.

She and I found Ben in front of the kitchen cupboard, drinking something. He jumped when he saw us, and something clunked to the floor. I went over and picked it up. It was an empty bottle of vanilla extract.

He smiled a little crazily, and his breath smelled like vanilla. Once, because I'd been curious as to what vanilla tasted like, I'd stuck my tongue to the top of the bottle. It tasted so bitter I'd had to spit for about an hour. And here Ben had drunk the whole bottle.

"See ya later, weirdo," I said as he went to his bedroom. Grandma and I sat at the kitchen table to play. Spot came in and sat at my feet and I stuck my bare feet under her belly.

Mom and Dad came into the kitchen smiling. Remarriage was written all over their faces. Everything seemed okay now, even if Ben was screwed up and outside it was now drizzling and melting all of last night's snow.

"Should I tell them, hon?" Dad said.

Mom nodded and looked at the ceiling.

"Wait," Dad said, "We have to get Ben. Too bad Wendell's sleeping."

Dad went to Ben's room, and then in a minute we heard Dad yelling and we all got nervous, and then Dad shouted, "Vera—come in here quick, Vera."

After a minute, I followed Mom. Grandpa was shuffling in from the living room, and Spot was barking. "Call an ambulance," Mom yelled.

"No, we'll take him to the hospital," Dad said. "I don't think it's that much of an emergency."

"I can't believe it, I can't believe it," Mom said to Grandma, "Listerine."

Ben had drunk a bottle of Listerine and was groaning that his stomach burned. Grandma pulled a pint bottle of cherry brandy from his sheets. "Where did you get this?"

Ben mumbled that a man at the shopping center bought it for him.

"Why, I never," she said.

"Now, Etta," Grandpa said. "Boys will be boys."

"Father," Mom screamed. "Get back in bed. John, look what you've done. He'll get sick."

She hurried Grandpa back to the couch.

Grandma wanted to go with them to the hospital. As soon as they were gone, Grandpa went to the refrigerator and got one of the beers Dad had brought and turned on the TV. I went into Ben's room and picked up the Listerine bottle. I read the ingredients, and then I noticed that it said it contained alcohol. I went to the kitchen and fished the bottle of vanilla out. Thirty-five percent alcohol. Ben was drunk. An alcoholic, maybe, in addition to being crazy. But he was so crazy he couldn't even be a normal alcoholic.

Grandpa went to bed and I felt as if the world were a dry little box of frustration after disappointment after frustration. Just as I was about to go to bed myself, Mom and Dad and Ben returned. I could tell by their faces and the slump of their shoulders that there'd been a fight over whose fault Ben was and any wedding plans they'd been kicking around were off.

~~~

THIRTY-FIVE

D AD'S APARTMENT was ultra-modern. He had it decorated like his Christmas presents, with stripes and dots and plaids in matching or coordinating colors. The living room carpet was brown tweed, the wallpaper brown and gold and orange-striped, and the zigzags and circles on the couch upholstery picked up the orange and gold. There was a picture on the wall of a hunter and his dog and even it matched. Everything was so coordinated it almost made you dizzy.

There was plastic over the chairs, couch, and lampshades, and a strip of it for walking on the carpet. The only thing that hadn't been touched by a decorator was Dad's easy chair. I don't know why he left it that way. Maybe the lumps and faded fabric and stains reminded him of his family. The bedroom was done in the fabrics and colors that harmonized, as they said in magazine ads, with those in the living room. The bedspread was green and gold paisley with gold thread running through it. It looked thick and luxurious, until you touched it and found out it was stiff and cold and made of a plasticky fabric. Mom's spread was a faded blue chenille full of snags and stains and brown-ringed cigarette burns. But at least it was soft and you could scrunch it up just the right way when you lay on it to talk to her or watch her TV. Unless you were rich, it seemed you had to make your choices in life between things that looked good and things that felt good.

I got to sleep on the sofabed. It made crinkly noises all night. Ben slept on the bedroom floor in Dad's old Army sleeping bag. He ended up out in the living room with me because he was afraid there were hand grenades someone had forgotten about hidden among all those pockets and snaps.

Dad alternated between treating Ben like he was normal and giving up and letting him be as nutso as he wanted. One afternoon, after we'd been visiting for about a week, Dad came home from work early and changed clothes and came out of the bedroom with a baseball and bat. Ben and I were watching an old movie, *Curse of the Mummy,* on TV. Ben wasn't scared by things that were supposed to be scary, like monsters, but more by things that were supposed to be normal, everyday things.

Dad, still acting like he had his suit on, said, "What do you say, Benny boy? How about if we go hit a few?"

I tried to remember if Dad and Ben had ever played baseball before. I didn't think so; there'd just been a few stabs at football, and they hadn't been successful. Otherwise, Dad had always seemed too busy working or, on weekends, doing the lawn. I would have volunteered to play ball with Dad, but I figured the point was to get Ben out there, so I kept quiet.

"Nah," Ben said, moving a little closer to me.

"Oh, come on. Your problem is you don't get enough exercise. Boys have to play baseball."

"Maybe after this show."

"No, let's go right now," Dad said in his non-suit voice. "Do you want to grow up to be a sissy?"

"I don't care."

Dad swallowed about a gallon of anger that was building up, and it made his face red. Dad had thin cheeks, sort of sunken-in, and one of them twitched when he was making a successful attempt at controlling his rage. "Come on, let's go out and get our blood pumping."

Ben looked longingly at the mummy and made a loud sigh, "Oh, all right."

They went out for about half an hour, and then reappeared. I was reading. Ben flicked the TV back on. *"Mummy*'s over," I said. "It was good."

I could have really rubbed it in how he'd missed the best horror movie ever, but this seemed like the wrong time to torment him. He turned the dial until he found "Augie Doggie."

Dad went into the kitchen and slammed drawers around and came out and said, "I'm out of a few things. I'll go to the grocery store."

By the time he got back with the groceries, Dad was in a better mood. He turned on Frank. We put the groceries away as Dad and Frank sang, "I've got a woman crazy for me, she's funny that way."

Dad really was different since the divorce. Here he was, picking on Ben about sports, but then doing a complete turnaround by being unusually polite, like he was afraid we wouldn't like him anymore. He was nervous now, choosing his words carefully, half-treating us like grownups.

Just as the mood was starting to be able to float on its own, the phone rang. Dad lurched for it, catching it on the second ring. But this wasn't whatever call he was hoping for, because while he was talking he got all sweaty and tense. "Mmmmm. And when did it happen? Mmmm. How is she now?" And after a real long pause, he said, "Okay, I'll be there tomorrow."

When he hung up, he looked at the phone for a minute, his brow wrinkled into a thinking-hard position, his hands curled up tight like big, pink shells. Then he shook his head, looked up at us blankly, and said, "Kids, it's my—your—my mother. That was Francy, your Aunt Francine, my sister-in-law, who called. My—your grandmother, she's in the hospital, and I'm afraid it's serious."

I hadn't seen this grandmother since I was about six or seven. All I remembered of her was a shrill voice and a southern accent, from the few times she called and I answered. At Christmas she never sent any gifts, just a check for Dad to buy our gifts.

"Francine had to drive over to Carter's Corners."

"What's that?" Ben said.

"That's where your, uh, your grandmother lives." I have to fly down there tomorrow. You kids will have to go back to your mother's early."

I felt sorry for Dad. He made some Manhattans. I saw him crying as he scraped carrots for the cole slaw. Ben was watching TV, so I helped Dad out with dinner a little bit. "If you don't have time to take us to the airport, we can stay here alone until you get back," I said.

Dad looked into the living room at Ben. Thirteen years old and his eyes were big as saucers as he watched cartoons. Then Dad looked away from Ben, like someone averting his eyes after seeing a crippled person on the street, and said, "No, you should go back to your mother's."

He made the mayonnaise dressing and said in a low voice, "Crosby, don't tell your mother this, she'd just laugh, but I've been getting a little, uh, professional help. You know, someone to talk to about things. They have a fellow at work, an industrial psychologist. Not that I'm some lunatic or anything, just to help with the stress, you know."

I told Dad I knew, that we'd studied this a little bit in health education, and I'd done some reading at the library.

Dad listened carefully, then went on about the industrial-strength psychologist. "So the fellow says to me, he says Ben maybe ought to see a counselor, you know, nothing like a psychiatrist is necessary, or anything that would suggest he's crazy. But I told your mother. She said Ben's not nuts and he's not seeing anyone because if we sent him to a—uh, counselor, then he might start thinking he really is crazy. And he said maybe I could spend more time with you kids, especially Ben. What I mean is, you're always able to find a way to spend time with me and your mother, but Ben—he needs more attention."

I didn't know what to say. This was pretty embarrassing. So I just looked down at the nice, clean, plastic-covered carpet.

Dad went on. "I knew he liked baseball a lot, ever since Wendell took you two to a game in Detroit. That's why I got him out to the baseball field. It went so wrong. He doesn't hit very well, and some kids started ragging him, and the next thing I knew . . ." Dad paused and finished his second Manhat-

272   ≈   *Susan Sullivan Saiter*

tan in a quick, jerky movement. His voice shrank lower.
"Ben, he was doing cheerleader jumps like you. Can you
imagine? Oh Jesus, I feel so awful, so bad about everything.
And now this with my mother . . ."

Unfortunately, I could very well imagine Ben doing cheers.
And now I was getting depressed, and I hadn't even let the
fact that my grandmother was dying hit me yet. Even if I
didn't know her, I didn't like the idea of one of my relatives
dying, or anyone dying, for that matter.

"It makes sense to me that you'd want to play baseball with
Ben. But he's weird about things," I said. "It's like everything
is shrivelling up inside him."

He handed me some blue and brown plaid paper napkins
and I folded them into neat triangles, the way he did them.
"He can't go forward in life, only back," I went on. "That's
about the best explanation I can find for things he does. He
wants to go back and back and back. So he listens to the
games on the radio and watches them on TV, but he won't
play them, he won't do anything new." I set out the matching
plaid paper plates, making sure they were all the same distance from the edge of the table. "All I can say is that he
doesn't make sense. Nothing about him makes any sense
anymore."

Dad was quiet for a while, then said, "I shouldn't have left
you alone while you were visiting. Just because Ben has problems doesn't mean you should go ignored."

"It's all right. I got to watch TV, which I don't do so much
anymore."

"Too busy, huh?" he said, trying to sound cheerful.

"Yeah. I'm in some clubs, and I got placed in the hardest
English class. And I got third place at the school science fair
for a plaster model I did of the digestive system."

"No kidding?" He looked like he'd had a face lift. He tried
reaching Mom again, and again after dinner. But he couldn't
get hold of her all night, or the next morning.

"Well, kids," he said nervously. "I guess you'll have to go
with me to Carter's Corners."

~~~

THIRTY-SIX

A UNT FRANCY met us at the airport in Louisville.
Her real name was Francine Clancy Rawson. She was
married to Dad's brother, Uncle Mattie Jay, who was home
with a bad back watching my cousins.

Francy was the first middle-aged woman I'd ever seen with
long hair. It was curly and the color of orange Kool-Aid
except at the roots. The front was all pincurls, like they wore
it in the nineteen forties. She wore a lot of jangly bracelets
that seemed to make Dad even more nervous.

In the car on the way to my grandmother's house, she told
Dad that Grandma had passed out in the grocery store.

"She didn't never take care of herself, never. She's got
sugar, you knew that, didn't you? Sugar, and the cancer on
top of that, oh my God, I could just cry with pity for that poor
woman."

"It's definitely cancer, then?" Dad said.

"Cancer, but the sugar makes it what's so serious. Honey,
she could go any day now. Oh yes, sugar runs in your family,
in the Rawsons, but us Clancys got it too, oh I tell you. My
doctor, he says to me, he says, 'Francine, honey, I'm gon' tell
you somethin'—this is when I was pregnant with my last

one—he says, 'Francine, you got to come into the hospital for your last three months of confinement, because you got sugar, honey.' "

"Was that supposed to be a joke?" Ben whispered to me.

"What's that, hon?" Francy said to Ben.

"Did he ask if you had maple syrup, too?" Ben made his feeble, little-kid joke in such a shy, flirtatious way that I was knocked silent.

Francy looked at him with narrowed eyes, then slapped his knee and said, "Whoeee, that's what I like, a boy with a sense of humor."

Dad turned and smiled tensely with his teeth together.

Aunt Francy grabbed Ben's knee and wiggled it until he laughed. "Hey there, good-lookin'," and she turned back to Dad, "So what's your story, Lemmy Luke? You got sugar, too?"

I started to laugh at what she called him, but Dad's reddening ears stopped me. "No, Francine, I don't."

"Well now, you ought to be grateful for small favors, because I will tell you, havin' that baby was an ordeal like you would not believe. Especially at my age. And he was breech, the little shit come out"—and she turned to the back seat and pushed my knees—"excuse my French, honey, little feller come out ass backwards and head over heels, and I told Mattie Jay, I says, 'Honey, you keep that little pecker thing of yours to yourself,' " and she turned around again and gave us a sly smile. "An' you know what he says to me?"

"Is that right?" Dad said quickly to interrupt her. He had a new look on his face and a new tone in his voice, "I understand you're going to have a new governor."

"Yeah—Democrats, Republicans, don't make no mind to me, one's as bad as t'other."

"I hate the goddamn Democrats," Ben piped in.

Ben knew Dad wouldn't yell at us in front of her; he just turned and gave us a stiff smile. Francy leaned over the seat and playfully smacked his arm, "Hey, them's fightin' words with most people down here. What, your Dad's gone Republican?" She smacked Dad's shoulder. "He must be ri-i-ich, or tryin' to make like it. Puttin' on the dog a little bit, huh, Lemmy Luke?"

We drove through Carter's Corners listening to Aunt Francy and dodging her blows. The town was only two blocks long. The hospital was about three miles outside of town, Francy said. As we got closer, her voice lowered and she started talking about our grandmother, about how sick she'd been for so long, how no one knew because she hardly ever visited with her neighbors or relatives. "Honey, I was over to her house this morning, gettin' it ready for you-all, and I seen she had a phone bill opened, and there wasn't one single call on it. Not a one. And her bein' sick. And in the corner of her bedroom was a shoebox full of old yellowed newspaper articles." Francy opened her compact and swabbed her face with long, hard strokes of the puff. She turned and looked at Dad with her nose wrinkled up. "Articles about people bein' executed. They was goin' way back. Hell, they was clippings of them Rosenberg people, them two Jewish folks that it was found out later might not of really been spyin', and all kinds of others, lots of murderers—white and nigra—it about turned my stomach. She had one picture of a woman sittin' on the electric chair. I looked at some other things and—"

"She had an interest in current events," Dad said quickly and jerked the car around the corner so we all lost our balance. "I understand the new hospital is the best in the county."

"That's what they say."

The hospital stood alone in a field of weeds and concrete. Even though it was new, under the windows there were dark, leaky rain stains. "It looks like the windows are crying," Ben said.

Everybody looked.

"And up at the top those two windows look like Bugs Bunny's eyes."

"Don't make fun of the new hospital, Ben," Dad said, "It's all this town can afford."

"Well, I'll be damned," Aunt Francy said, "if they *don't* look like Bugs Bunny's eyes, Lemuel. Take a look."

Dad was staring at the hospital door, not the windows, like when he walked through it he was going to be the subject of the next newspaper clipping of an execution.

A half-dozen grownups were in the hospital room, slumped in chairs or perched on the windowsill. When we walked in, they jumped up.

My grandmother was so thin and small in the bed it reminded me of when you see mummy cases at the museum and can't believe people used to be that tiny. Her dark eyes were liquid with fear.

Her voice was so thick with a southern accent I almost couldn't understand her. By the way she talked to Dad, I could tell there was a lot I didn't know between the two of them.

Finally she said something clearly. "Lemuel, I'm goin' die, maybe."

The other relatives stepped back a bit.

"Nonsense," Dad said, his voice greasy. He cleared his throat. "You're going to pull out of this."

"You always was a little shitass of a liar." She lay with her eyes closed. The other relatives left the room on tiptoes. "I don't guess it harmed ya none, neither. Wearin' a necktie to work and all. Who finally taught you to wear a necktie, Lemmy? Remember that time when you was graduatin' high school, and you borrowed a necktie from Uncle Mike, and you didn't know how to tie the damn thing?"

"I remember."

"Who taught ya?" She opened her eyes and looked at him.

Dad grinned a tough-guy grin with his teeth together. "Guy that hired me. Guy that hired me for my first job out of school."

Ben couldn't stand it any more. "Dad, how come they call you that funny name?"

"That used to be my name," Dad said quickly, and he dug into his pockets and gave Ben some change and told him to go get a pop.

I didn't get the feeling that my grandmother cared much about Ben and me. Or about Dad, for that matter, but then maybe she acted the way she did because she was so sick or because she was so scared of dying. With all the tension in the air I felt nervous, so I went to look for Ben. He was sitting in the waiting room watching "That Was The Week That

Was" with the other people. When he saw me, he complained that all they had was Dr. Pepper and Mountain Dew.

Back at our grandmother's house that evening, I sat off in a kitchen corner trying not to let my misery at being there show too much. The kitchen looked like a comic strip room, with too many colors and patterns, scribbled quickly so that the floor buckled up and the ceiling dipping in. There was red oilcloth on the table, and dark blue linoleum with silver flowers on the floor. One wall was painted bright yellow, another bright blue, and two other walls had paper with metallic fish, paper most people would put in the bathroom. The curtains were lime green with black pompoms. Unlike at my other Grandma's, there were no knickknacks, just some Christmas lights tacked up around the window, framing a plastic Santa and reindeer that were covered with grime and dust and cobwebs.

Mom said she once thought she was getting a real prize in Dad. I could see now where Dad would have thought Mom was a prize, too, Mom with her nice, stable family—certainly not wealthy, but respectable.

Dad came into the kitchen and stood looking at Ben and me. Then Aunt Francy came in and said she'd cook dinner. Dad got a pinched look on his face and said not to bother, that he'd take us to Big Boy's.

"You know how kids are," he said. "They don't eat nothing but burgers." Then he immediately realized what he'd said, and looked embarrassed. I'd already noticed that when he talked to his family there was a hint of a southern accent, just enough of one, I suspected to keep them from razzing him about talking like a Yankee, of trying to put on airs and be something he wasn't. I just hoped he wouldn't forget his northern accent and go home talking like they did here, because Mom would really make fun of him when she heard that on the phone, divorced or not.

"Ah hell, they think they like hamburgs because they ain't had southern cookin'. She took a frying pan out of the cupboard and hurled a hunk of lard into it. It began to sizzle and the room smelled like pork chops and fish. " 'Sides, I already done the shopping. Tongue was on special. You kids like tongue?"

Ben and I looked at each other from across the dinette.

"Huh? You kids ever ate tongue?" She smiled and made a funny face and then stuck out her tongue.

"Are we eating your tongue?" Ben said.

Aunt Francy almost spilled the lard in the frying pan she was laughing so hard. "No, honey, we're eating yours. Hold it out, will ya, while I get that there butcher knife."

I was surprised, but Ben laughed. Then Francy opened the refrigerator and took out a package wrapped in bloody butcher paper. She opened it and waved at us a reddish brown piece of meat. It looked exactly like a great big tongue.

Ben said, "That's disgusting."

Francy laughed. "You just wait. You'll like it real good. I whipped up some of Aunt Francy's famous potato salad to go with it. You need something substantial after all them snacks you was eatin' at the hospital. You'll get the backdoor trots from all them Dr. Peppers."

"Crosby," Ben said under his breath, "does it hurt when you bite the tongue?"

"No, but it's going to hurt when I punch you," I said. I wanted to go home. Actually, I was beginning to wonder if Ben might not have gotten along better here with Aunt Francy, with people who didn't want to be cheerleaders or district managers or nurses, people who didn't care if they ever got to move to bigger split levels on streets with names like Knob Knoll Way. Ben could say all the stupid things he wanted, and no one would mind. They'd just laugh.

There was a rattling of the screen door, and a teenage girl came in. She said her name was Debbie and she was our third cousin. She must have weighed two hundred and fifty pounds.

"I live just across the road," she said. "Mama wanted to see could you come for supper, but it looks like youse is already fixin' to eat."

"You just pull you up a chair and visit a while," Francy said. "I'd join you, but I got blood runnin' outta my ass like you wouldn't believe, and it hurts like the dickens to sit."

Debbie went to the door and shouted out, "They ain't coming, Ma. Whyn't you and the others come on over?" She turned to me. "Do 'em good to get the stink blowed off'n 'em."

Debbie started to drag a chrome dinette chair over from a corner, but Dad shot up and helped her with it. It groaned loudly as she sat on it, but once she was settled, the chair sighed, like it was used to people like her.

"How's your Ma, Lemmy?" Debbie said.

"Not so w—" He started to say "well," but changed it to "good." And then his southern accent showed in the way the "good" slid a little bit, became fancy.

"Oh hell, I tell't her, I said, 'Honey, when you got sugar, you have to take care of yourself.' I tell't her that," Francy said. "Hell, Mattie Jay's had him a liver condition and sugar since he was twenty-five years old. I make him take care of hisself."

Ben said, "We've got sugar, too, in the cupboard. And my other Grandma, my real Grandma, keeps it in a jar next to the flour, and we're all okay."

I thought what a dumb thing for a thirteen-going-on-four-teen-year-old kid to say. But this caused the two women to break into uncontrollable laughter. It was refreshing the way people around here didn't give Ben that look like he was weird. They looked at him with respect, the way they did Dad and me. Or maybe with more respect—with Dad and me, they acted like we'd said something wrong half the time, like *we* were being snotty and superior-acting, which I guess in a way we were. Ben wouldn't know what snotty and superior was.

I couldn't eat the tongue, and neither could Ben, so Francy gave us some rock candy to chew on while she fried some fatback and cornmeal. I ate it, reluctantly, and I had to admit it was not all that bad.

"Tomorrow night we have fried chicken," Francy said. "You like fried chicken, kids?"

I said I loved it, and Ben said, "Are you going to make the whole chicken, or just the tongue?"

Francy laughed so hard I thought she'd burst her hemor-rhoids, then she said, "How 'bout some pee-e-e-each pie. I made it myself." She cut us some pie, and then turned to Dad, "Lemmy, you don't like sweets, I remember that. Like a high-ball, or don't you indulge these days?"

"No, yes, I mean you could twist my arm on that one," Dad said, looking relieved.

Debbie said, "I'll have me a short one, if it's all the same."

So the three of them mixed some whiskey and Seven-Up and sat around the kitchen table while Ben and I moved into the living room and watched TV and ate the pie. It was different from Grandma's, sweeter, more buttery, and it was almost as good if not better—it made Grandma's hard-topped, tart cherry and rhubarb pies seem aloof and northern. There weren't any doors inside the little house, just curtains, so I could hear everything going on in the kitchen. Something about those faded, dusty curtains made me feel really sad for Dad and even for his mother, who was lying in a hospital bed dying and no one was even talking about her, just drinking up her whiskey.

They started talking about people I didn't know, and voices got louder and louder. Dad used some southern expressions I'd never heard before. Seven-Up tops got popped off and whiskey got poured and pretty soon Debbie's mother, Aunt Aimee-Louise, came in, and then Uncle Willie, and some more grownups I didn't know, and then someone turned on the radio and violin music sawed the air, and the next thing I knew they were all coming into the living room.

I didn't want any part of this so I got up to go in a bedroom, though Ben looked like he was going to stay.

Uncle Willie held out a bottle of whiskey and said to me, "Want a nip, just a little bit?"

And Dad was there in an instant and he said we had to get to bed.

There was nothing to do in the bedroom except look through the stuff in the dressers. In one drawer were old-fashioned hairpins, boxes of loose powder, rouge that was so old it was cracked, cake mascara. In another were some old pictures. It was a shame that I didn't recognize anyone. There was one of a young woman wearing a big hat tied with a ribbon under her chin. She was smiling and she had a dimple. That could be my grandmother, now that I looked at it carefully. I'd have to ask Dad if his mother had a dimple. He'd never said.

I went through another drawer, and I found some more

yellowed newspaper clippings. UFO sightings, goats with two heads, babies weighing twenty pounds at birth. I dug deeper: mother eats baby alive, plane crash survivors become cannibals.

I slammed that drawer shut and went to lie on the bed. Ben, in the bedroom next door, said through the curtain, "Croz, is Dad drunk?"

"If anyone ought to know when someone's drunk, it's you, Listerine brain."

I wished to God I were at school, where everything was clean and plain and people acted like they were supposed to. I added, "I know one thing, though—if I were Dad right now, I'd get plastered."

My grandmother died that night. We had to stay in Carter's Corners for two more days while the arrangements were made for the funeral.

Ben and I mostly kept company with the broken-down wringer-washer and a set of bedsprings on the front porch, which was inches from the two-lane highway. We'd watch car licence plates as a game. Most were from Kentucky, but there were some from Ohio, people from Cincinnati who probably said, "Look at those kids. How *do* people live that way?" There were probably people driving by who grew up here like Dad did, who got mad at TV's Gomer Pyles and Beverly Hillbillies, and I didn't blame them, because some folks in this part of the world were a pretty savvy and decent lot, especially Aunt Francy was at all typical.

We went for walks through the hills. You could hear the water from streams way before you saw them. I tried to let myself feel sorry for my dead grandmother. I managed a little sadness, which was about as much as she was going to get from anyone other than Dad, I suspected.

At the funeral, Dad had a look on his face like he was cold and in pain. At one point, he put his face in his hands and I looked away. I didn't want to know if he was crying again. If you've never seen your father cry, you're lucky. I'd rather see him drunk, myself.

Neighbors brought over food—deviled eggs, macaroni salad, baked beans, cakes, fried chicken, Jello with carrots and lettuce, Jello with bananas, Jello with fruit cocktail, Jello with every imaginable addition the human mind could come up with. Aunt Francy sat with Ben and me, that perpetual smile on her face.

At one point, she said, "Your pa ever talk much about his pa?"

"He said his parents were divorced, that's all," I said. "He doesn't like us to bring it up."

"Well, I'll bring it up. Your grandad was something else. I think that's why you two kids, why your pa, have such piss and vinegar. Oh that man, Cody Jenkins Rawson, he was something else. A real man of the world until he died. Died young."

"A man of the world like Dad?" Ben said.

Francy screwed up her mouth like she was thinking. "Yes and no. He gave your Dad ambition, maybe. But your grandpa didn't have no sense of responsibility. He liked painting and high-class music and books more than he liked people, I guess. But he didn't have no sense of responsibility."

She scooped some cherry Jello with canned peach slices and Cool Whip onto my plate. "Eat this, honey, it's good for you." She gave Ben some. "This'll put hair on your chest. Oh yeah, he left your grandma when she was pregnant with your pa, the baby of the family. Oh your grandad, he used to go to Louisville to the concerts and art galleries, up to Cincinnati even. Pretty soon we heard he had a lady friend there, and that she was related to some of the monkey-monks, oh I forget all the details. Your grandad, he used to come back and tell us the things he saw—famous paintings, famous opera singers."

She looked at me directly, seriously, and she looked older. But when she smiled again, she looked younger. Her dyed red hair really helped. I wasn't sure whether it would be polite to tell her that her dyed hair made her look younger, but I hoped she knew that.

"And then he went away to Europe. He just up and left and went to Europe. You imagine that? Some hillbilly in Rome, Italy, and elsewheres, Paris, France, going into all them museums? Your grandma, she had to go to work at the cannery, then got laid off, and your grandad was off to London to visit the queen."

Dad interrupted. "Kids, I finally reached your mother. Come and talk to her if you want."

We ran to the phone, leaving Aunt Francy with the family gossip to lock back up. I was so damned happy to hear Mom's voice. It was like having been lost in outer space and finally catching sight of earth. She sounded so normal, so mainstream in comparison to these people, and she probably sounded it to herself. And again I thought of the big jump she and Dad made, the huge leap from poverty into the middle class. No wonder they hadn't landed on completely safe ground, no wonder they were hanging onto the edge by their fingernails, at times feeling like giving up or kicking the dirt on the side of the hill until they started a rock slide.

"Sorry you had to go down there," Mom said. "Has it been awful?"

"Yes," I said.

"I told your father I felt bad that I couldn't go to the funeral, even though I never got along with his mother. I was away."

"Where to?"

"Oh, here and there. Had a little fun." She said it without enthusiasm. I guessed she'd gone with the rosy-cheeked boyfriend.

Dad got back on the phone and sounded better than he had the whole time we'd been with him. He was laughing and joking, and he told us to say good-bye because he and Mom wanted to talk privately.

It was such a goddamn relief for all of us to get on our planes to go home. Dad said, "I'll see you kids real soon. Real soon." He seemed happy, considering the circumstances.

I didn't know what that meant until Mom met us at the airport. "Your Dad and I are getting back together," she said.

The world quickly reassembled itself.

"Crosby, Ben, I'm so tired," she said as we drove home. "Do you know how hard it is to make enough money for all of us to live on, even with the lousy child support? Do you know how hard it is to get credit? Boy oh boy, I set out to be tough, and I learned what tough is, I'll tell you, kids. Tough is learning to endure being married."

"I can't wait to see Spot," Ben said.

"Me too," I said. "She'll go nuts when she sees us."

"Well, you can forget that one," Mom said, checking her lipstick in the rearview mirror.

"Forget what?" Ben said.

"The dog. When you went away, she howled and cried so much I couldn't stand it. And she was piddling all over the furniture. I had to send her to the pound."

She turned and looked at us after a few minutes of silence. "Hey, kids, it's only a damn dog. You didn't have it very long." For a moment, she really looked surprised, then genuinely sorry, like she hadn't known how we'd feel. "Oh, come on, we have to start having nice things like everyone else." Then she shifted gears and chewed on her freshly lipsticked lip for a few seconds and frowned. "Don't you see? You have to be tough, kids, or you'll never make it in this world. Nope, not in this world."

When we got home and were sitting in the driveway and Ben and I were still silent, she said, "Oh, I don't know. I don't know anything anymore, right from wrong, up from down, here from there. I just don't know."

$\approx$

THIRTY-SEVEN

T HAT FALL MOM and Dad got married again. He had an
offer from Transcontinental Tires and we moved to Sea-
brook Vista, Nebraska, just outside of Lincoln.

I checked out what the coolest kids were wearing. Then I
did some heavy shoplifting, and by the time school started,
I was ready to go. I over-shoplifted, in fact; I had so many
clothes that I could afford to be generous. I gave snazzy
things to the football season kickoff clothing drive for Asian
kids—pink Capezio flats, a cranberry Jonathan Logan A-line
skirt, a Garland heather green cable-knit sweater, a yellow
Villager blouse with a Peter Pan collar. I also threw in some
things I'd had for a while—eight pairs of out-of-style swizzle
socks. My guess was they'd be fine in a country where your
life depended on picking enough rice for the day rather than
on shoplifting enough of the latest kind of clothing to get you
through the school day so teachers and kids wouldn't pick on
you.

I often wondered what it would have been like if I'd lived
in just one place, like Dick and Jane. I also wondered what
it would have been like if they'd made a sequel to the Dick
and Jane series and had them move all the time. Would Dick

have chugged Listerine and vanilla extract? Would Jane have become a liar and a shoplifter? Would their mother have sent Spot to the pound while they were at their grandmother's funeral?

Or did moving have nothing to do with it? Maybe you just became what you were to become, whether you were raised by wolves or by New York millionaires or by Dick and Jane's stiff, never-wrong parents.

I got a part-time job working in one of the better stores at the shopping center and it was a gold mine for my shoplifting. I was making money now and didn't have to rip things off, but it had gotten to be a habit. I didn't think I was doing anything immoral, though. To me, different people had to do different things in life to survive. I saw life as a game like Monopoly. Everyone received a set the day he was born. Some got a brand-spanking-new game, complete with a rule book and nice shiny new characters to play with. Others got a crummy broken set with pieces missing. Some got pieces but no rule book enclosed. A few people opened up the box, and there was nothing inside. Sometimes you had a nearly complete set, but you had to take a couple of things from the first guy's set when he got up to go to the bathroom.

I said all that when we had a civics class discussion about it. The teacher, Mr. McIntyre, laughed and admitted it was a pretty good analogy. Actually, my real economic philosophy was one I wouldn't tell even Mr. McIntyre. I did tell Ben about it one night, though, after we'd seen a filmstrip at school telling us that shoplifters cause department stores to raise their prices so that everyone suffers.

"Stealing from big stores is okay, in my opinion," I said.
"Yeah?"
"Yup. Because it's just rich stockholders losing money."
"And it's okay to steal from them?"
"Absolutely. Oh, they say they pass the shoplifting costs along to customers by raising prices, but that's unfair. It has nothing to do with anything. They should take the shoplifting losses out of their profits. It's not a customer's fault if the store can't stop other people from shoplifting, is it?"
"No," Ben said thoughtfully.
A few days later the principal called Mom and said Ben got

in trouble in social studies for saying it was okay to steal from department stores because the stock boys got blamed for it. He didn't get kicked out of school or anything, but he got an Unsatisfactory attitude rating in social studies that marking period. I aced all my classes and got Excellents in all my attitude ratings. I knew when to keep my mouth shut, and sometimes I thought that was the only difference between Ben and me and between an Unsatisfactory and an Excellent rating.

Ben didn't actually go out and steal anything until I gave it up.

I had been wanting to see *Playboy* magazine ever since our geography teacher went into a tirade because some boy was caught with one and expelled for the semester. After that, I just had to see one, but of course I couldn't let anyone know.

I pulled the car—our getaway car—right up to the door of Kruger's Drugs. I told Ben to go in and buy me a copy of the *Playboy* and I gave him the money, money I'd stolen from his bank because I was temporarily broke.

"Why do I have to get it?" he said, looking at me suspiciously.

"Because you're a boy. How would it look for a girl to go in there and ask for it? They'd think I was a queer, a pervert."

Ben got a nasty look on his face. Ben didn't have much interest in girls; I doubt if he even knew how to do "it." But he knew enough about the subject to know he was supposed to act mysterious and nasty about it. "Mom would get mad."

"Do you think I'm dumb enough to show her?"

I closed his hand around his money. "Go," I said. I waited in the car, and after about twenty minutes, when he didn't come out, I parked the car and went in to check up on him.

He was standing there in front of the cough syrups. "Ben, goddammit," I whispered. "Just get the frigging magazine."

"What one was it you wanted me to buy you, Crosby?" he said in a booming voice. *"Playboy?"* About five people turned around and looked at me.

I stomped out and he followed me. In the car, I said, "If you don't get me the damn magazine, I'll . . ." and then I thought what the hell, I'd go back in myself.

So I marched in, with Ben trailing behind me. To get up my nerve, I walked around the store, and Ben followed me. We stood in front of the sleeping-pill section. The pharmacist, Mr. Kruger, who lived down the street and whose wife Mom met at the Newcomers' Club, came by and said hello. I was afraid it might look as if we were contemplating suicide, so I moved on to toothpaste and stared at the boxes and checked out the instructions on the dental flosses and mouthwashes while I readied myself to make a move. Finally, I nonchalantly walked over to the counter that was in front of the dirty magazines in brown wrappers. The clerk wasn't there. As I stood waiting, it came to me that I should just take it, and then I wouldn't have to go through all the embarrassment of buying it.

I looked around and then dropped my purse over the counter, like it was an accident, and looked around again, and then went behind it and bent over and reached up and grabbed the *Playboy* and stuck it in my purse. I went back around and walked out of the store, not caring if Ben came or not.

The next thing I knew, someone had a hold of my arm and was saying, "Just a minute, young lady."

I can't say whether Ben ratted on me or the pharmacist saw me on his own, but I blamed it on Ben. He denied it.

The police let me go after giving me a good scare, but nevertheless the whole incident got everyone down. Mom and Dad were quiet for a few days, then finally Mom said to me, "Why did you have to pick a magazine like that? And you know Mr. Kruger lives two doors down, and every time he's out watering his lawn now I have to speed up or else turn around and go somewhere else until he's done. And I'll have to drop out of Newcomers' Club."

"Ben's been doing things like that all his life. I do one lousy thing and your whole, perfect lives are destroyed."

"Really, Crosby, a sex magazine. Aren't you concerned about your reputation?"

Now I got it. Craziness was one thing, you could pretend it away. But sex wasn't so easy to get away from.

"I should have known," Mom went on. "All that cheerleading stuff. It's just not healthy for a young girl to flash her ass at the world. Why you couldn't have been a member of the marching band is beyond me."

I told her that *Playboy* was semirespectable, but I knew I wasn't going to win this one. I almost felt sorry for her, sitting there knowing she'd missed the boat, realizing how confusing the world was now that it was 1966, thinking that if only we could have a Depression again, things would make more sense.

I heard her and Dad in the kitchen that night, talking about the goddamned magazine that wouldn't go away. The Chairman of the Board was crooning, "You and you alone bring out the gypsy in me."

"But Vera, the fellows at work say they all look at the magazine from time to time—for the interviews, of course. But they even take it home. It's socially acceptable now."

"I suppose it would be socially acceptable for me to whip out my tits at one of those corporate parties."

"Now, Vera."

"We shouldn't have moved here. I knew we shouldn't have moved here. Cleveland was so much more civilized."

Not long after that, we were sitting at dinner listening to Dad's new album and eating dinner. Frank belted out, "It's one town that won't let you down, it's my kind of town."

Dad took a bite of his goulash and then announced that he had been asked to head a new division in Camden.

"Where the hell is Camden?" Mom asked.

"It's in New Jersey. At least I think."

"Are you out of your mind?"

"I thought you didn't like Nebraska."

"I don't like anywhere, and I'm not moving to another place that I don't like."

"I think this might be a golden opportunity."

"Let me put it this way," Mom said calmly. "I'll divorce you if you accept."

"You've tried that. A couple of times, if memory serves me me correctly."

Something really amazing happened. Dad turned down the golden opportunity. Then a few months later, he quit his job. Or he got fired, I'm not sure. But he went out and started his own business, a tire dealership, and we didn't move.

There was something a little quieter about Dad these days. Something that made you think he was holding a big disappointment inside him somewhere.

Mom, on the other hand, went out and started nursing school. The summer before classes began, she wallpapered the kitchen in a wild psychedelic pattern, fuchsia swirls and yellow circles and chartreuse flowers. She liked it so much she did the whole house, though not in the same paper. We had wallpaper everywhere, iridescent flowers here, checks there, polka dots in another spot. She even did the closets and the laundry room.

Mom liked the Beatles. She'd sing "Eleanor Rigby" and "Yellow Submarine" as she danced around the house doing work. One time I said to her, "I feel like you're the rebellious hippie and I'm the straightlaced fuddy-duddy sometimes."

She jokingly gave me the bullshit sign with two fingers and went on singing. Mom had had a tough time in Middle America as something of a nonconformist. I think the sixties were helping her.

Funk and soul were what Ben liked. I couldn't stand most of it, but I did like the Temptations. One time he came home with one of their new hits, "Poppa Was a Rolling Stone." He and I sat in his room listening to it. Mom came in and sat on the bed and snapped her fingers to the rhythm. Dad passed by the room and ducked his head in.

"How's it going?" he asked in his new eager-to-please mode.

We all started giggling. Dad said, "Did I miss a good joke?"

"It's no joke," Mom said.

"Ben, the A's are on at eight. They're playing Cleveland." He said it loud to compete with the record.

Ben was lying there, all five-foot ten of him, his long white-yellow hair spread out on the pillow like a girl's. Dad said, "Maybe we can go to a game next weekend."

Ben sang out in a falsetto, "Wherever he laid his hat was his home."

Finally, Dad stopped and listened to the record. I could see his face get red and annoyed, and it looked like he might explode, but he didn't. He just said, "I'll see about those tickets," and he went out and when the record stopped, we heard the angry buzz of the lawn mower.

Ben didn't like going to the baseball games, he just liked the statistics, the faces of the players, the atmosphere. He kept score of every single game that he watched or listened to on the radio. He also tried to listen to out-of-town games. He had this old transistor radio, and he would be up late at night for the games Detroit and Chicago and Cincinnati played on the West Coast. You'd walk by his room, and you'd hear this scratchy sound coming out, and "weeooo, weeeoo," when the signal got distant, and then you'd hear the voice coming in faintly once again. If the voice faded out, he'd do his own commentary making it up until the voice came in again. Or he'd break for a commercial, singing perfect imitations in his rather good singing voice. "From the land of sky blue waters, Hamms the beer refreshing, Hamms the beer refreshing," or, "I'm from Milwaukee, and I ought to know, it's Blatz Blatz Blatz Blatz, wherever you go." You'd just pretend he was doing something every other kid in America was doing, and thank God none of your friends was over to see this, especially when he did his own pre- and postgame shows, interviewing players and giving their answers for them.

He'd be in there in the dark under his covers, half the time stoned or drunk, lately. Mom and Dad seemed to be giving up on him, to have decided that it was best to ignore him and try to live happily ever after.

The psychiatrist thing, I'd heard them say on various occasions, was (a) too expensive, (b) too embarrassing, (c) too unlikely to work, (d) too much an admission that something was wrong, and (e) too expensive.

Then he started talking about becoming a baseball player. "Hey, Croz, remember that time in Detroit, when I was on the field?"

"How could I forget?"

"I could tell by the way Al Kaline was looking at me that he wanted me to be the bat boy. I was all set to ask. Damn, I should have asked. I could just kill myself for not asking.

Oh well, I wrote to them about tryouts. I think I'm going to try out for first base."

"You're not going to bother with the minor leagues first, huh?"

"Not unless it's absolutely necessary."

Ben got busted that fall, the very first time he tried shoplifting.

He did it at the grocery store.

He decided to rip off some of his favorite foods, a few cans of hearts of palm and beef tamales. He waltzed into the Piggly Wiggly and stuck them and a few other things under this jacket and spun around and headed for the exit. Just before he got to the automatic door, a bottle of ginger ale fell out and hit the floor and exploded.

With boy shoplifters, they don't fool around. The manager had him at gunpoint, and the cops roughed him up a bit, because he had long hair and looked like a hippie. They even put handcuffs on him. When Mom and Dad brought him home, he had a welt on his shin from a kick his cellmate gave him.

Mom was so mad she went and filed a complaint with the police review board. Then some social worker came out to visit the house the following week. He gave Mom the name of a psychologist. Ben went that Saturday for a consultation. When he came home, Mom and Dad yelled at him about how expensive it was, and if he'd only straighten up then they could have a nice vacation and not have to waste their money on some fat jellyfish of a quack psychologist. The next Saturday, Ben left the house early so that when Mom went to get him for his appointment, he was gone. That was the end of the fat jellyfish psychologist.

The very next day, he went out to a hardware store and stole some stupid things he'd never use, like a handful of bolts and a can of floor wax and some light-switch covers.

He came into my room and threw them on the bed, like he'd just knocked off a jewelry store and I was his moll. He pulled a paper cup of coffee out of a White Castle bag and took off the lid and without even testing to see if it was hot, sucked up the coffee.

I put my history book down and said, "What, may I ask, are you planning to do with this junk?"

His face showed he hadn't even thought about that.

"Oh, Ben," I said, shaking my head. "Oh, Benny Benny Benny."

~~~

THIRTY-EIGHT

A s PRESIDENT of the senior class, I was to oversee our charity car-wash one Saturday morning.

I liked weekends at dawn. Mom and Dad slept in late. Ben was always in bed anyway, interviewing a shortstop or singing a commercial, but by early morning he was actually asleep.

I wandered down the hall, enjoying the smell of crisp autumn, looking forward to hearing the leaves rustle outside the window as I had a quick cup of coffee and some toast.

I scuffled into the living room toward Dad's big easy chair, that poor old gray thing with the swirly pattern, with Mom's cigarette burns here and there, with a tear in the hem where he'd kicked it once and his shoe caught, with the marks that Ben and I had put on it. I glanced at the chair, then I looked again, and I froze. The big kitchen butcher knife was stuck in the back, all the way in, with only the handle showing.

I stood numb, trying to understand, to put things in perspective. It would all make sense in a moment. But I got a low buzzing in my ears, and I half-expected the chair to twirl around, like in *Psycho,* with the unknown thing in it.

The unknown thing, though, would be Dad.

I stared and I stared, not daring to move, because the chair might turn around.

And then I told myself that when Dad sat in the chair, you could see the top of his head, and there was nothing at the top of the chair, so probably Dad wasn't in it.

Unless he was slumped down dead. I stood still some more, my feet still in the position I left them in, wanting myself to take a step, but stuck, like in cement.

The branches on the tree outside the window began bouncing and waving for me to hurry up. The outside world—my salvation, the outside world. It didn't care how fucked up my family was. I took a deep inhalation and summoned up my nerve and took a giant step around the chair to see if Dad, or anyone, was dead.

No Dad, dead or alive, no anyone. Dad must have been safely snoring away in bed. There was nothing but the blade of the knife—a good four or five inches of it sticking through.

Before I could even think, I pulled the knife out and put it back in the kitchen drawer.

I made my toast and opened the window to get fresh air, and sat down and looked out. I'd just sent out my college applications, and I couldn't wait. I'd be so fucking glad to get out of this place I'd do cartwheels all the way to Evanston, or Madison, or wherever I was going.

I didn't say anything to anyone, not even Ben, about it. I didn't say anything that afternoon, either, when Mom asked me if I knew anything about the big gash in the chair. If I'd told her, it would have just been one more Rawson family blowout. Even if Ben hadn't done it.

I guessed I'd never know for sure that he did it. I didn't want to know.

But I knew.

That year sped by, with Mom and Dad yelling at Ben now instead of each other. I joined every club at school I could get into, and I must have set a record for time spent away from home.

The day I was to leave for college, just about a year after

the knife-in-the-chair incident, I got up early to finish packing and pick out clothes for the farewell party my friends were throwing me that afternoon.

When I went into the bathroom, I found blood everywhere. Real blood. Blood in streams on the floor, the sink, the toilet, the mirror. It was splattered in the bathtub, and it was trickling down the drain. Some droplets had beaded on the melting, stuck bar of Ivory Soap.

Slowly, I let my eyes travel around the room. It was on the walls, maroon already, in swirls and speckles. And then, in a thick pool on the sink, I saw the razor blades, three of them. I felt light, no longer a human weighed down by a mortal body that could be harmed.

I followed a trail of blood into the living room. There was more red, then blue-red. But it wasn't all blood. Part of it was Mom's lipsticks, a good dozen of them, smeared everywhere. Some had been sliced off their tubes. Razor blades were stuck to a couple of them still, the blades perched oddly at angles in the lipsticks. The gold tubes looked like bullets. On the living room windows was some crazy writing in lipstick. The scribbling seemed, at closer examination, to be drawings of faces and some misspelled words I couldn't read, except for one: *ALONE.*

In the kitchen doorway, I saw Ben's bare feet, then the lower part of his legs lying on the floor. I yelled until the noise that came out was hoarse and I broke into coughing. It felt like an earthquake as Dad came running. He was in pajamas. He didn't have his slippers on and you could see his sawed-off toe stumps with blood all over them. Mom came out in her bra and pants. Dad's face seemed to fill up with muscles as he saw Ben on the floor and went into action. Mom's face was blank as she rubbed her hands up and down her bare arms to keep warm.

Dad got into the ambulance with his pajamas on. Mom and I got dressed and drove to the hospital.

After about an hour of tension, of not knowing how to talk to each other under these brand-new conditions, we found out Ben was going to be okay.

"Cut his cheeks, his fingers up pretty good," the doctor said. "Kid's old enough he shouldn't hurt himself on razor blades."

"We've had so much trouble with him. So much," Mom said, ready to sob. "Do you have any suggestions, recommendations as to what we should do?"

The doctor shrugged and said, "Get him an electric razor."

We all felt relief that the doctor didn't think it was a totally nutso act. That we had passed for an average family where these kinds of things didn't happen. How would the doctor know? Dad took the cue and acted like it was just an accident, and maybe it was. He shook his head with a relieved smile. The doctor patted him on the back. They let Ben rest for another hour, then he came out with his hands and face bandaged up, and we all went home. I was so glad I was leaving for Northwestern that I tried to show some sympathy.

"Why'd you do it?" I asked as we walked up to the house.

He didn't answer. I asked a few more times later that day, then annoyance returned. "I hope you know you cocked up my going-away party. You messed up my leaving for college. You've always tried to screw things up for me. Why the hell don't you just stab me? Or slice me up with razors and be done with it?"

He didn't say anything, so I went on. "I suppose you're going to stick me with that butcher knife next time. Stick me, not just the chair. I know you're the one who did it. Are you going to try to kill me sometime?"

After a few minutes, he said, "Can't."

"Can't, huh? You tried to stab Dad, in your own cowardly way. And you tried to slash up Mom, again with your own peculiar style. Or do you figure you've done it to me all my life, Ben? Ruined my life by always messing everything up for me, humiliating me in public, always acting crazy."

"Can't hurt you, Crosby. If someone stabbed you, you wouldn't bleed."

I opened my mouth to say something back, but I couldn't think of just the right thing. I went to my room and finished packing my sweaters.

Maybe there was a little truth to what Ben said. I'd developed a thick skin, that was for sure. But the more I thought about what Ben had said, the more I knew it wasn't true. And that was why I had to get out of there.

THIRTY-NINE

U NDERNEATH HIS FLATTOP HAIRCUT, Tyrone wore the look of little a kid whose mother has just slapped him in the face in front of everyone at the store. Poor guy, I thought, tough life, never had a chance.

"I ain't staying at this shelter tonight. But Randy tells me you been looking for me."

"I certainly have." I asked what his cabfare back downtown would be, and I thought, on the other hand, Ben never had much of a chance either. But wait, I didn't either. What was the difference? Was it that females are better survivors? Did it say anything at all about women, or was it just that I had the luck of the first-born, or the luck of a more sturdy set of genes?

"That cab would be forty-five."

"Where you goin'?" Jack yelled out. "Philadelphia?"

"Hey, you can suck my dick."

I handed him a fifty.

"Well now, ain't you sweet," he said, and tucked it into his shoe. The bracelets on his arm clanged as he dusted off his baggy jeans and adjusted the collar of the matching jacket. "Now what is it, baby, what can I do for you?"

I pulled up two folding chairs. "Please sit down," I said, intending to get my fifty-dollars' worth. Antonia came within earshot and folded linens as Tyrone talked to me about Ben.

He and Ben had been panhandling down around Eighty-sixth Street and Columbus Avenue when the thunderstorm began blowing off awnings, knocking over garbage cans.

"Ben, man, he don't care, he say he like the rain so he don't have to take a bath. He ripped his shirt off and damn near his pants." He made a whooping laugh. "Good thing I was there. I say I ain't standing in no rain shit, so we find us some steps under a porch. Then this white lady come and open the door and let herself in. She drop her keys and Ben pick them up and give them to her and when she open the door, he hold it. And he axe do she have a Coke or a beer he can drink or maybe some cigarettes. She say to just leave her alone, man, and hurry up the stairs. Ben still have the door open, so we go in and sit and watch the rain. Pretty soon we sleeping."

The next thing he knew, a big white guy in a suit was standing over them.

"He threaten to kick me and I show him my blade and back out the door. And then he start kickin' shit outta Ben, and Ben wake up and say okay he gonna split, and the white man drag Ben by the shirt out to the porch. And I can't do shit for Ben because my young ass is out on recog, I can't get into no kind of shit. Next the white man be knocking Ben's head against the wall and saying the bums this and winos that and we ain't nothing but cockroaches and ruining the value of his home. And then Ben's head bleeding on the side, and the white man knocked old Ben down them stairs. And I hear the po-lice and I gotta go, Ben or no Ben, and the last I see of Ben that night he's laying half in the street, half on the sidewalk."

I sat silent for a moment. Antonia's forehead was forked with wrinkles. Finally I said, "Why didn't you get him some help?"

Tyrone's big, upturned eyes narrowed. "Man, who gonna help some dude like Ben? You must be daydreamin' you think somebody goin' to help him. And me I can't help no-body, I got my own problems. Somebody should of helpt'ed Ben long time ago."

I opened my mouth to respond, but didn't. We stared into

each others' eyes, communicating better this way than with words.

"Do you remember the address of the building?" Antonia asked.

"No baby, I don't remember nothin' like that."

"Could you find it again?" I asked.

"Don't know, I ain't tried."

"Do you think Ben would be able to find it? I want that man arrested."

Tyrone looked at me with his mouth open, then broke into a squealing laugh. "Arrested? Shit, man, they pin a medal on that motherfucker."

Antonia and I exchanged looks. Then I asked, "Have you seen Ben since that night?"

"Seen him today, man."

"Today? He's okay?"

"He still got that mess on his head. But he's pretty okay."

"How bad is it."

"Ain't no doctor, how would I know? Anyhows, he won't go to no hospital because they got a warrant out for his arrest, and because he got some crazyass shit in his head about germs in hospitals. He sleep in garbage but he don't want no one to breathe near him. Ben don't hang out so much. He don't make friends easy, he keep to himself a lot. I tell him he be wise to don't make no waves with no po-lice, neither."

"The charges against him have been dropped."

His eyes narrowed as if he thought I were setting a trap, then he seemed to decide to believe me since I was after all Ben's sister. "Well man, I take you to Ben right now. He be layin' his ass low in a abandoned building over on Avenue B."

At least the stories were jibing and Tyrone apparently was telling the truth. But I couldn't face that neighborhood at night. "Not tonight. Can you find Ben and send him up here?"

"Ain't no messenger for you."

"I'll give you some more money," I said, and went to Antonia, who was fighting with Randy over who would make the hotdogs.

"Guests do not prepare food," she said.

"Hey man, I can cook a wiener without settin' the place on fire."

"Nevertheless."

I asked her if I could borrow twenty dollars.

"Of course," she said, getting her purse, not asking what for. She handed me three fives, two ones, and had to search the bottom of her purse for the rest.

I gave Tyrone the money. "Give Ben a dollar out of this for subway fare. Tell him I'll have more for him back at my hotel."

Tyrone's expression had changed. He was trying to figure me out now. "I don't guarantee nothin'." He looked down to count out the money, then stuffed the bills in his shoe. He paused to reexamine the fifty. "Maybe if I see Benjamin tonight, I give him your message."

"Or have him contact me at my hotel if I'm gone," I said, writing down the address and phone number of the Royale Payne. I also gave him my California phone number and address. "Please, Tyrone, it's very important to me. I have to see him before I leave New York tomorrow. If he can't be here tonight, he can come to my hotel room anytime tonight or early tomorrow morning."

"If this so important, why you leavin' town, baby?" he said, his eyes big in mock confusion as he stood up and put a baseball cap on.

"Emergency of another sort back home," I said, trying to sound sure of myself.

"Must be one motherfucker of a emergency," he said, heading out the door.

As the door closed, I told myself I should take the chance and go down there tonight. But I couldn't stop picturing bloody needles and vomit. I tried not to worry about Ben having AIDS. The combination of drug sellers running free and mental patients left uncared for was not a healthy one.

Antonia seemed unusually cheery tonight. I was almost glad to be at the shelter, glad to be busy to get my mind off this.

I was comfortable now here, comfortable around these people. Was it because I was looking for Ben, or was it also because I had passed a test?

All my life, the most important thing had been to become

a card-carrying member of the real world. I'd done it—gotten myself into a decent law school and a happy relationship with a man. I could relax now. Be September Crosby Rawson, average American girl. Maybe now I could relax around the Benjamin John Rawsons of the world, too.

I was so comfortable with the knowledge that I was okay that I could let myself be comfortable around these people. Maybe now I could be a little more kind and generous and all those things that I'd suppressed for so long. I had proven to myself that nuttiness doesn't rub off, or at least it doesn't work its way under your skin.

I went to help Antonia, who was still in a power struggle with Randy. I told her how I had left it with Tyrone.

"You've got to get Ben to a hospital," she said.

"Yes, but then what?" I said. "I hadn't really thought too far ahead about what would happen if I found him and he was unable to care for himself."

"Tell him to give me a call. He'll have to get back on the bottom of the waiting list here, but I'd be glad to help him with counseling and rehab services, and maybe I can pull strings to get him into something better than a city shelter while he waits for an opening here."

"Back here? No, I'm hoping he'll come to California. You said he had a job here. Maybe he can get one there. Or at least do something useful."

"Hmmm," she said. "Maybe I've presented too optimistic a picture for you, Crosby. It's not like he's going to be buying a house in Westchester next week and commuting to a swell Wall Street job."

"I know that. I just want to help him. I want to be part of his life. I miss him."

"Let's see what kind of condition he's in."

I knew Antonia and I were not on the same wave-length, but I confided anyway, "My only worry about Ben coming back to California is the man I'm seeing. I don't know if he can take Ben."

"He doesn't know about Ben?"

"Well, actually, no."

"Tell him."

"I don't know if he could take it."

She looked at me the way mothers look at their daughters, the way mine never did. "He can."

Randy made another crack about Antonia and some illegal Irish immigrant who had used the shelter and whom he thought she was sleeping with. I still didn't believe it. She needed these people, but not for sex. And any other ideas planted in my mind by Randy's innuendos about her and Ben completely disappeared as I watched Antonia in action that night.

After the two appointed men returned from the nightly donut-run, Antonia sang out, "Hotdogs. I brought them myself from home. We're having a picnic tonight." She smiled with her whole face, not just her mouth, and the entire shelter seemed cheerier.

Tonight there was the usual assortment of guests. As I became more comfortable at the shelter and got to know the men, I came to see that they fell into a few broad categories. There were the old guys, some of them pretty far gone. You just did what you could for them. But the majority were young and you tried to think how to save them, but you didn't know how. Some were lazy, some were stupid, some were bad, some innocent and helpless, some crazy. A lot of them were crazy.

I noticed Antonia smiling at a new, good-looking guest. His name was Sean and he was from California. At first I wondered what he was doing here, but then I saw that his eyes had a look, almost a glow, that I'd seen in certain groups of people—crazy people, religious fanatics, and geniuses. Ben, for one, had it.

I sat down between Randy and Jack. There was a new volunteer tonight named Heather. She was quiet and sweet, but jumpy.

"Who wants mustard?" Antonia called out cheerfully from under the harsh light of the kitchen.

The men just stared at the pot, listless and hungry.

She called again. "Mustard or ketchup?"

No one answered again. They just clutched their forks, waiting.

"All right," she said in a crabby voice. "See if I try to have fun again." She stormed around the kitchen. "I'll just throw the damn mustard out, if that's how much anyone cares."

Sean said, "I'll have some of both." And then Randy said, "Oh Jesus Christ, so will I. Just bring the damn food over here, will ya?" He added, in a low voice to Jack, "She can put horseshit on it for all I care."

As we ate, Sean talked softly of his years of surfing and reading on the beach, then of wanting to see the rest of the world. And somehow, here he was.

"More beans?" Antonia said. I got the feeling that she was angry with me, and then I saw that it was because of Sean. He was her homeless person—hers. I had my own.

While we washed dishes, she said to me, "I seldom bring food. It doesn't seem as cozy, somehow. I like feeling the excitement of barely getting by, like being a pioneer and having five potatoes to last until spring." She paused. "Why, last Thanksgiving I thought of bringing in a turkey dinner. But it wouldn't be as Spartan, I decided, this wouldn't be a shelter, and the whole thing wouldn't seem right." She gave a little laugh. "Do you know what I mean?"

"I'm afraid not," I admitted.

"Oh, you wouldn't."

Heather came over and said to her, "I brought a lemon coconut cake. Should I put it out now?"

"Let them eat cake, huh, that's your attitude?"

Heather gave her a bewildered look.

Later, Heather and Sean were laughing together. Antonia slammed the pantry door so hard it fell off. She strained to overhear their conversation, about some religious group he'd encountered in Utah. "They buried you alive. That was about the weirdest religion I ever ran into."

"I guess," Heather said, and noticing Antonia's look, she got up and began to throw out the paper plates. As she was about to throw away the plastic forks, Antonia stomped over and grabbed her hand. "Don't throw those away."

The volunteer hurled the forks into the sink, grabbed her purse, and left.

Antonia's widow's peak seemed to deepen. "A lot she cares about the homeless." She looked at me, scanned my face, and burst out, "Oh, this work gets on your nerves. Believe me, it gets on your nerves."

I stuck around for the rest of the night because I was hoping to see Ben and because I felt sorry for Antonia. She seemed, despite it all, harmless.

But Ben didn't show and I hugged Antonia good-bye and took a cab back to my hotel.

All this and I will probably leave town without seeing him, I thought, tired, sad. But not completely depressed. After all, I had tried, harder than I remembered ever having tried before.

~~~
FORTY

B EN STOOD in the dim light of my hotel lobby, his hands hanging apart from his body. He looked confused, like he was wondering what to expect from me.

He was very thin, taller than I remembered. But then maybe he'd grown—he was so young when I last had seen him.

I went to him and patted his arm—we didn't hug or kiss or even touch each other if we could help it in the Rawson family.

His hairline had receded. A series of little lines ran across his forehead. The bandage on the side over his ear could have belonged to a mummy.

"How you doin', Crosby," he said offhandedly, as if we'd spoken only yesterday.

"I've been looking for you."

"Yeah."

Neither of us seemed to know what to say. Finally he said, "Got any beer on ya?"

"No, I don't."

"You can give me some change and I'll go out to a deli and get some."

"How about a Coke? There's a machine upstairs."

"That'd be okay. Got some money?"

Under the elevator's strong light, I could see that his face was much different. Of course his features were still good—strong jaw and cheekbones, perfect nose. But he was no longer handsome.

As we talked, I felt I could have been anyone to him. There was no emotion, no joy or sorrow or anger or anything at seeing me after so long.

I bought him a Coke. He sucked it down like a bear I'd once seen at a carnival. "Got any more quarters?"

I had enough change for two more Cokes and a pack of cigarettes. He emptied the two cans before we got to the room.

"Go ahead and sit down on the bed," I said. "Let me look at your head. And tell me what happened to you. Tyrone says you were beaten up."

Ben's few details pretty much corroborated Tyrone's story.

"How did you get help, the bandage?" I asked.

"Oh, I woke up and it was dark, still raining. So I went to a subway station to sleep. Next morning, my ear was bleeding, the same ear as when I fell down the stairs at Mom's, remember? My head hurt a lot. It hurt so much I couldn't see. Next thing I knew, some other guys who live in the subway were walking me all the way down to the Village to St. Vincent's Hospital, and they bandaged it."

"Did they say what it was, give you any medication?"

"They wouldn't give me pain pills. Told me to take Tylenol. They gave me antibiotics, but I lost them."

I started to take the bandage off, but thought I should ask him about AIDS first. It may have been a tacky or insulting question, but look at where he'd been.

"AIDS," he said. "That's their way of trying to exterminate the street people. They want you to catch it, so I'm real careful."

"Who are *they?*"

"The power structure. Rich people, even average people like Mom and Dad."

"Mom and Dad said hello. They'll send you some money," I said.

"Good. I need some. Some guy stole my dough the minute I cashed my last SSI check."

"That's awful, Ben. Maybe you need to hide your money better."

"Yeah? Where?"

I didn't know where to suggest.

Ben started smiling. I smiled back, until I realized he wasn't smiling at me. And then I saw that it wasn't even a real smile. It was a grimace, or maybe an involuntary smile.

"Got any potato chips or jalapeño Fritos or maybe some canned artichoke hearts?"

"I have some snacks, but none of those things. Tell you what, I'll take you out to eat in a minute. Let me look at that wound."

He looked around the room as I dug out the rubber gloves from my suitcase. "Nice place you got here."

The wound looked pretty awful to me, and it was full of pus. He needed to see a doctor immediately.

"Does it hurt?" I said.

"Sometimes. Hey, Croz, can we watch TV? The 'Honey-mooners' might be on. Or 'Joe Franklin.' Have you seen him? He's like something out of the nineteen fifties. He's like Arthur Godfrey except his voice isn't all sleepy. Oh wow," he said, sinking back on the bed, "Remember when Arthur Godfrey died of lung cancer?"

I stopped to think. "Yeah, sort of. Ben, I think this is getting infected. I'd better take you to the hospital."

"I can't go. I'll get arrested. Besides, they probably have some of his germs in the air there."

"What germs?"

"The ones he breathed."

"Who?"

"Arthur Godfrey."

I looked to see if this might be—please God—a joke. His eyes were narrow and serious.

"That was about thirty years ago. Those germs are all gone. And Ben, the police dropped the charges against you."

"That's what they tell you, but they're waiting for me. I can't even go back to the shelter. Antonia's in on it. I'm on the most-wanted list, Tyrone said."

"That's not true."

"Oh, dang, there they are again." He looked around the room.

"What?"

"People whispering."

I listened. No one was talking in the next room that I could hear. "That's just noise from the streets."

"No, they're whispering about us, Croz. I'm glad you're here."

I listened some more. Nothing. "What whispering? Who's whispering?"

"Wilma Flintstone and Elroy Jetson. They get loud sometimes. I tell them to shut up. I yell at them but the cops always tell me to stop."

"Can you put on your Walkman? Where is your Walkman?"

He dug through the bag of snacks next to my bed. He pulled out the Oriental party mix. "Can I have some, Croz? They talk on my Walkman, too."

"Who?"

"Mrs. Horner from fourth grade when she's not helping Bob Prince announce Pittsburgh Pirates games. I had to get rid of my Walkman because they kept interrupting the game. I threw it away today. Brand new Walkman and Mrs. Horner ruined it."

"Who else did you hear?"

He thought for a minute. "Mostly old ladies cackling and laughing. I hear that when I try to sleep. They try to make me think that the buildings are going to fall over on their side and onto my head." He looked up at me, the old Ben for a moment, big eyes asking for help. "Sometimes I'm scared when I hear the cackling so I have to go outside where there's people, even if it's the middle of the night."

I sat and looked at the maroon carpet for a while. Then I asked, "Are you in a lot of pain? Have you been for long?"

"Just my teeth. I need to see a dentist, too, but the only one that will help me is at a clinic where they don't wash off the drills and instruments. And they recycle the spit in the mouthwash thing and make you swish it around in your mouth. So I've got rotten teeth."

He opened his mouth. Behind what was left of his incisors

and canines, there wasn't a single tooth in his head.

"Where are your teeth?"

"Some of them got pulled."

"Which ones hurt?"

"Right now the one in back on the top left."

"But you don't have any teeth in back."

He felt with his tongue, "Hey you're right." He looked behind his shoulder, then up, shaking his head in disgust. "There's that sound again."

"What?"

"Someone crunching apples to the speed of sound. That makes my teeth hurt."

"I'll take you to a dentist tomorrow. A good one who sterilizes his equipment."

"Let's go get some beer, Croz, and watch TV."

"I've got some wine." I switched on the TV.

We watched a talk show and sipped wine, then we turned on a black-and-white movie and sipped tea. It really didn't seem to matter what he was drinking—beer, Coke, wine—as long as something was going down his gullet.

"You've got to go back to Bellevue," I said. "You've got to get back on your medication. Doesn't it help?"

"You can't drink alcohol when you're on medication. Besides, the medication makes me not want to do anything. I swear I'm still feeling the Thorazine."

"What's that like?"

"It makes things quiet so I don't hear the cowboys shooting me and I don't hear the baseball games or the Flintstones, but I feel like a zombie."

I dozed off during an all-night phone-in-auction program. I woke up at six. He was sitting next to me, stiff, a smile on his face as he watched an exercise show. I felt like shit from the wine and insufficient sleep. I got a drink of water in the bathroom and ran the faucet and stared down the drain while I thought for a few minutes.

"Mind if I turn the TV off for a while?" I said, coming back.

"Okay, Crosby."

I turned it off. The city lights from outside were reflected on the blank screen. We both looked at them for a minute or two. I thought of our childhood impression of New York, the New York of "My Little Margie" and Arthur Godfrey and Arlene Francis and John C. Daley and Eva Gabor and Jean Harlow and Dick Van Dyke. New York. This wasn't their New York, but look at it this way, I said to myself, it's the only city that would take Ben in, give him a corner to beg on, let him be as crazy as he is.

"I want to take you to the hospital now," I said, trying to look authoritative.

"Do you know what they do in hospitals? They make you wear gowns that cadavers wore. They make you sleep in beds where dead people were. You lay in a bed where someone died. And you're not supposed to think about it. You're not supposed to think that an old lady with cancer was puking and bleeding in that bed."

"No, they're clean. Hospitals have to be very sanitary."

"There are dead people's skin cells in the mattress you sleep on. And they give you meatloafs that the cook's hair fell into. Eggs that a nurse touched after she went to the bathroom. They throw amputated arms and appendixes into the incinerator and expect you to breathe them."

"But you're going to get sick from that wound if it's not treated. It's infected."

"Cops are waiting for me. In jail you have to use soap that someone else used. The guards play those boom boxes all night until your head feels like someone's been hitting it all night with a wooden spoon."

"I'm friends with a cop. You won't go to jail, I promise. You'll go to the hospital with me to see Henrietta and she'll get you your own special bed. I'll go out and buy you new sheets and blankets that no one has touched."

"Henrietta used to buy me jars of instant coffee. You got any coffee around here, Croz?"

"Let's go get some. Later you can come to California and I'll help out. I'm going to law school and . . ." I paused. Who was I kidding? I went on anyway. "When I get out I can afford to help you. I can pay for a private hospital."

Law school. The sun was rising outside my hotel window. If I were going to catch my plane to make the meeting with the Harboils and the Loebroes, I'd have to change into a suit and get packed immediately.

"Ben, look at me," I said.

Ben looked at me but he didn't really see me. His eyes didn't focus on me. They focused on something far away, something long ago.

I couldn't leave him like this. I stood by the window and watched the city come to life. Well, Crosby, it looks like it's going to be the Theodore Grundy School of Law for you. I felt very, very sorry for myself.

"Come on," I said. "Let's get some breakfast first."

On the way out of the hotel, I told the manager I'd be there a few more days.

I took Ben's limp hand and walked down the street with him. Cabs were already stampeding. People in flapping business clothes and crisp haircuts, their skin tight and shiny with soap, strode by, taking long strides to avoid Ben.

I thought of the things I had to do for Ben. One of the things I had to do was tell him I loved him. I didn't know that anyone had ever told him that in his life. In fact I was just about positive no one ever had.

But at the same time, I understood Mom and Dad. They'd never known what to do, and their apparent lack of concern now was probably a coverup, an attempt to distance themselves from a problem that could eat you alive if you let it.

I knew, too, that when you had a family like I had, you often had to settle for something less than you wanted. That admission hurt, but it wasn't going to stop me from trying to go for it all, anyway.

I wondered what Dean was going to say when he heard all this. The guy was wildly in love with me, so my guess, my hope, was he wouldn't take it *too* hard. But then you never knew about things like that.

Ben inhaled deeply and smiled, smiled as much as he ever had. With the golden light shining on him, I could almost see the handsomeness of the little boy who had not yet totally succumbed to the illness that had tried to destroy all of us. "This is like it used to be, Croz."

I patted his big, limp hand. "Yeah."

The Theodore Grundy School of Law. Oh well, I guessed I could always study like crazy and take the LSAT again. If by some miracle I did well on it again, and if the real estate market picked up, I could try to transfer to USC next year.